COLLINS COBUILD STUDENT'S GRAMMAR

SELF-STUDY EDITION
WITH ANSWERS

Practice Material by Dave Willis

THE UNIVERSITY
OF BIRMINGHAM

COLLINS
COBUILD

HarperCollins*Publishers*

first edition 1991

© HarperCollins Publishers 1991

latest reprint 2000

HarperCollins Publishers
Westerhill Road, Bishopbriggs, Glasgow G64 2QT

ISBN 0-00-370563-3

Collins®, COBUILD®, and Bank of English® are registered trademarks of
HarperCollins Publishers Limited

www.cobuild.collins.co.uk

Acknowledgements

The author and publishers are grateful to the following for permission to reproduce
material on the pages indicated:

The late Roald Dahl and Jonathan Cape Ltd and Penguin Ltd for the extract from
The Hitch-Hiker from *The Marvellous Story of Henry Sugar and Six Others*, 94;

Fleetway Publications for the extract from *The Eagle*, 95;

William Boyd and Hamish Hamilton Ltd for the extract from *On the Yankee Station*, 215.

Every effort has been made to contact owners of copyright material. If there are any
omissions, the publishers will be glad to rectify these, when the title is reprinted.

Note

Entered words that we have reason to believe constitute trademarks have been
designated as such. However, neither the presence nor absence of such designation
should be regarded as affecting the legal status of any trademark.

A catalogue record for this book is available from the British Library.

Computer Typeset by Promenade Graphics, Cheltenham.

Printed and Bound in Great Britain by Omnia Books Limited, Glasgow.

Editorial Team

Editor-in-Chief	John Sinclair
Managing Editor	Gwyneth Fox
Senior Editor	Ramesh Krishnamurthy
Editor	Jenny Watson
Assistant Editors	Christina Rammell Keith Stuart
Computational Assistance	Tim Lane Zoe James Stephen Bullon
Secretarial Staff	Sue Smith Sue Crawley

HarperCollins Publishers
Annette Capel, Lorna Heaslip, Douglas Williamson

Illustrators
John Batten, Gillian Martin, David Parkins, Clyde Pearson, Peter Schrank

We would like to thank Dave Willis additionally for his valuable contributions to the grammar pages; Sylvia Chalker and Sue Inkster for their detailed comments and suggestions on the text; Annette Capel for writing the Key to the Exercises; Richard Fay and Paschalena Groutka for their part in the original drafting of the units; Kirsty Haynes for secretarial assistance during the earlier stages of the project; Sue Inkster, Anthony Harvey, John Curtin, John Dyson, Tom Stableford, Bob Walker, David Evans, and Angus Oliver for their comments on the initial list of Units.

We would also like to thank all the people who contributed to the Collins COBUILD English Grammar, whose original work provided the impetus for this book.

Contents

Note: numbers in **bold** are unit numbers.

Grammar units

Bank of further exercises 204

See next page for full details

Index 233

Bank of further exercises - contents

Numbers in **bold** are exercise numbers. At the Bank, each exercise has a cross-reference back to the relevant Unit and paragraph.

Introduction

The COBUILD approach to grammar is simple and direct. We study a large collection of English texts, and find out how people are actually using the language. We pick the most important points and we show how the words and phrases are used by quoting actual examples from our text collection. As a student of English, you can be sure that you are presented with real English, as it is actually used.

In this book we give explanations of the most important, frequent, and typical points of English grammar along with a lot of practice material so that you can put the knowledge to use immediately. This makes the book suitable both as a classroom text, and also for private study. This is a grammar of meanings as well as structures. The exercises help you to link the meanings and structures, not just to practise the structures. There are two editions available: with or without a key to the exercises.

The grammar is often very direct and easy to understand. Sometimes English speakers and writers prefer a simple structure and only very advanced students need to know more than that. At other times we give more details, because they are necessary for clear understanding and accurate usage.

This book has developed from the same database which was used in the Collins Cobuild English Grammar. Our first grammar book has been well received, and we are continuing full scale research on grammar in order to be ever more accurate and relevant to the needs of the teacher and student.

I would be very glad to have your comments on this book, especially on how useful you find it. It is designed for use by anyone who has enough English to understand the explanations, which we expect to be intermediate and above.

John Sinclair
Editor in Chief
Cobuild
Professor of Modern English Language
University of Birmingham

How to use the Grammar

This book is designed so that you can find the answers to particular problems of English grammar. You are not expected to start at Unit 1 and study the Units one by one, or to study a whole Unit at a time. Different people have different problems, so they need to look at different points in different Units.

Finding what you want

Contents

There is a complete list of contents on pages iv to v. This gives the numbers and titles of all the Units. The Units are grouped under various headings to help you, for example 'Nouns', 'Prepositions', and 'Modals'.

Index

There is an Index at the back of the book on pages 233 to 240. The Index is an alphabetical list of grammar points covered in this book. For each point, the Index gives the Unit number and paragraph number where the point is explained. Grammar terms such as 'adjectives', 'nouns', and 'verbs' are in bold letters. The ideas that you can express, such as 'ability' and 'certainty', are also in bold letters. The actual words and forms explained in the grammar, such as 'able' and 'this', are in italic letters. So you can find the point you want by looking in the index.

Glossary

There is a Glossary on pages x to xiv. The Glossary explains the meaning of the grammar terms used in this book, with examples. The terms are listed in alphabetical order. If you are not sure what a term means, you can look at the Glossary.

Using the grammar units

Each Unit has two parts. The left-hand page contains the explanation of the grammar rules and patterns. The right-hand page contains practice material.

Left-hand pages

Main points
The left-hand page has two columns. At the top of the first column you will find a section headed 'Main points'. This is a summary of the important information given in the Unit. Each Main point is introduced by a large bold dot. You will find more detailed information about the point in the numbered paragraphs on the same page.

Numbered paragraphs

The rest of the left hand-page is divided into numbered paragraphs. These give more detailed information about the topic covered in the Unit.

Example sentences

Each point is illustrated with example sentences printed in italic letters. When particular words in the example sentences show the point that is being explained, the words are underlined.

Lists

With many rules and patterns, a number of words are used in the same way. When this is the case, a list of words is given. For some points, a complete list of the words would be very long, so only the commonest words are included.

Warnings

Some points of English grammar frequently cause learners to make mistakes. Sometimes they are exceptions to a rule. Sometimes the rules are different in other languages. We have used the label 'WARNING' before such points.

Cross-references

Sometimes, more information about a rule or pattern is contained in another Unit. When this is the case, we tell you which Unit to refer to.

Right-hand pages

The right-hand page contains practice material for you to do. There are many different types of exercise, so you should read the instructions carefully. A bold triangle at the bottom of the page followed by the word 'Bank' indicates that you will find more practice material on the same topic in the 'Bank of further exercises' at the back of the book.

Model answers

For each exercise, the first answer has been supplied. You can use this as a model for the rest of the exercise.

Bank of further exercises

The Bank of further exercises is at the back of the book. Some of the exercises relate to a particular Unit, and the Unit or paragraph number is given. Other exercises have been designed to give you more general grammar practice.

Key to exercises

In the Self-study edition, a Key to all the exercises is given at the back of the book.

Glossary of grammar terms

Note: entries in **bold** are terms used in this grammar.

abstract noun a noun used to refer to a quality, idea, feeling, or experience, rather than a physical object; EG *size, reason, joy.*

active voice verb groups such as 'gives', 'took', 'has made', which are used when the subject of the verb is the person or thing doing the action or responsible for it. Compare with **passive voice.**

adjective a word used to tell you more about a person or thing, such as their appearance, colour, size, or other qualities; EG *...a pretty blue dress.*

adjunct another name for **adverbial.**

adverb a word that gives more information about when, how, where, or in what circumstances something happens; EG *quickly, now.*

adverbial an adverb, or an adverb phrase, prepositional phrase, or noun group which does the same job as an adverb, giving more information about when, how, where, or in what circumstances something happens; EG *then, very quickly, in the street, the next day.*

adverbial of degree an adverbial which indicates the amount or extent of a feeling or quality; EG *She felt extremely tired.*

adverbial of duration an adverbial which indicates how long something continues or lasts; EG *He lived in London for six years.*

adverbial of frequency an adverbial which indicates how often something happens; EG *She sometimes goes to the cinema.*

adverbial of manner an adverbial which indicates the way in which something happens or is done; EG *She watched carefully.*

adverbial of place an adverbial which gives more information about position or direction; EG *They are upstairs... Move closer.*

adverbial of probability an adverbial which gives more information about how sure you are about something; EG *I've probably lost it.*

adverbial of time an adverbial which gives more information about when something happens; EG *I saw her yesterday.*

adverb phrase two adverbs used together; EG *She spoke very quietly... He did not play well enough to win.*

affirmative a clause or sentence in the affirmative has the subject followed by the verb.

apostrophe s an ending ('s) added to a noun to indicate possession; EG *...Harriet's daughter... the professor's husband... the Managing Director's secretary.*

article see **definite article, indefinite article.**

auxiliary another name for **auxiliary verb.**

auxiliary verb one of the verbs 'be', 'have', and 'do' when they are used with a main verb to form tenses, negatives, and questions. Some grammars include modals in the group of auxiliary verbs.

base form the form of a verb without any endings added to it, which is used in the 'to'-infinitive and for the imperative; EG *walk, go, have, be.* The base form is the form you look up in a dictionary.

cardinal number a number used in counting; EG *one, seven, nineteen.*

clause a group of words containing a verb. See also **main clause** and **subordinate clause.**

collective noun a noun that refers to a group of people or things, which can be used with a singular or plural verb; EG *committee, team, family.*

comparative an adjective or adverb with '-er' on the end or 'more' in front of it; EG *slower, more important, more carefully.*

complement a noun group or adjective, which comes after a link verb such as 'be', and gives more information about the subject of the clause; EG *She is a teacher... She is tired.*

complex sentence a sentence consisting of a main clause and a subordinate clause; EG *She wasn't thinking very quickly because she was tired.*

compound sentence a sentence consisting of two or more main clauses linked by 'and', 'or' or 'but'; EG *They picked her up and took her into the house.*

contrast clause a subordinate clause, usually introduced by 'although' or 'in spite of the fact that', which contrasts with a main clause; EG *Although I like her, I find her hard to talk to.*

conditional clause a subordinate clause, usually starting with 'if' or 'unless', which is used to talk about possible situations and their results; EG *They would be rich if they had taken my advice... We'll go to the park, unless it rains.*

conjunction a word such as 'and', 'because', or 'nor', that links two clauses, groups, or words.

continuous tense a tense which contains a form of the verb 'be' and a present participle; EG *She was laughing... They had been playing badminton.*

coordinating conjunction a conjunction such as 'and', 'but', or 'or', which links two main clauses.

count noun a noun which has both singular and plural forms; EG *dog/dogs, lemon/lemons, foot/feet.*

countable noun another name for **count noun.**

declarative another name for **affirmative.**

defining relative clause a relative clause which identifies the person or thing that is being talked about. EG *...the lady **who lives next door***... *I wrote down everything **that she said**.*

definite article the determiner 'the'.

delexical verb a common verb such as 'give', 'have', 'make', or 'take', which has very little meaning in itself and is used with a noun as object that describes the action; EG *She **gave** a small cry... I've just **had** a bath.*

demonstrative one of the words 'this', 'that', 'these', and 'those'; EG *...**this** woman... ...**that** tree... **That** looks interesting... **This** is fun.*

descriptive adjective an adjective which describes a person or thing, for example indicating their size, age, shape, or colour, rather than expressing your opinion of that person or thing. Compare with **opinion adjective.**

determiner one of a group of words including 'the', 'a', 'some', and 'my', which are used at the beginning of a noun group.

direct object a noun group referring to the person or thing affected by an action, in a clause with a verb in the active voice; EG *She wrote **her name**... I shut **the windows**.*

direct speech the actual words spoken by someone.

ditransitive verb another name for a verb with two objects, such as 'give', 'take', or 'sell'; EG *She **gave** me a kiss.*

double-transitive verb another name for a verb with two objects.

'-ed' adjective an adjective which has the same form as the '-ed' form of a regular verb, or the past participle of an irregular verb. EG *...**boiled** potatoes... ...a **broken** wing.*

'-ed' form the form of a regular verb used for the past simple and for the past participle.

ellipsis the leaving out of words when they are obvious from the context.

emphasizing adverb an adverb such as 'absolutely' or 'utterly', which modifies adjectives that express extreme qualities, such as 'astonishing' and 'wonderful'; EG *You were **absolutely** wonderful.*

ergative verb a verb which is both transitive and intransitive in the same meaning. The object of the transitive use is the subject of the intransitive use; EG *He **boiled** a kettle... The kettle **boiled**.*

first person see **person.**

gerund another name for the '-ing' form when it is used as a noun.

'if'-clause see **conditional clause.**

imperative the form of a verb used when giving orders and commands, which is the same as its base form; EG ***Come** here... **Take** two tablets every four hours... **Enjoy** yourself.*

impersonal 'it' 'it' used as an impersonal subject to introduce new information. EG *It's raining... It's ten o'clock.*

indefinite article the determiners 'a' and 'an'.

indefinite adverb a small group of adverbs including 'anywhere' and 'somewhere' which are used to indicate place in a general way.

indefinite pronoun a small group of pronouns including 'someone' and 'anything' which are used to refer to people or things without saying exactly who or what they are.

indirect object an object used with verbs that take two objects. For example, in 'I gave him the pen' and 'I gave the pen to him', 'him' is the indirect object and 'pen' is the direct object. Compare **direct object.**

indirect question a question used to ask for information or help; EG *Do you know **where Jane is**?... I wonder **which hotel it was.***

indirect speech the words you use to report what someone has said, rather than using their actual words. Also called reported speech.

infinitive the base form of a verb; EG *I wanted to go... She helped me **dig** the garden.*

'-ing' adjective an adjective which has the same form as the present participle of a verb; EG *...a **smiling** face... ...a **winning** streak.*

'-ing' form a verb form ending in '-ing' which is used to form verb tenses, and as an adjective or a noun. Also called the present participle.

interrogative pronoun one of the pronouns 'who', 'whose', 'whom', 'what', and 'which', when they are used to ask questions.

interrogative sentence a sentence in the form of a question.

intransitive verb a verb which does not take an object; EG *She arrived... I was yawning.*

irregular a word or form which does not follow the normal rules.

irregular verb a verb that has three forms or five forms, or whose forms do not follow the normal rules.

link verb a verb which takes a complement rather than an object; EG *be, become, seem, appear.*

main clause a clause which does not depend on another clause, and is not part of another clause.

main verb all verbs which are not auxiliaries or modals.

manner clause a subordinate clause which describes the way in which something is done, usually introduced with 'as' or 'like'; EG *She talks like her mother used to.*

modal a verb such as 'can', 'might', or 'will', which is always the first word in a verb group and is followed by the base form of a verb. Modals are used to express requests, offers, suggestions, wishes, intentions, politeness, possibility, probability, certainty, obligation, and so on.

mood the mood of a clause is the way in which the verb forms are used to show whether the clause is a statement, command, or question.

negative a negative clause, question, sentence, or statement is one which has a negative word such as 'not', and indicates the absence or opposite of something, or is used to say that something is not the case; EG *I don't know you... I'll never forget.* Compare with **positive**.

negative word a word such as 'never', 'no', 'not', 'nothing', or 'nowhere', which makes a clause, question, sentence, or statement negative.

non-defining relative clause a relative clause which gives more information about someone or something, but which is not needed to identify them because we already know who or what they are; EG *That's Mary, who was at university with me.* Compare with **defining relative clause**.

non-finite clause a 'to'-infinitive clause, '-ed' clause, or '-ing' clause.

noun a word which refers to people, things, ideas, feelings, or qualities EG *woman, Harry, guilt.*

noun group a group of words which acts as the subject, complement, or object of a verb, or as the object of a preposition.

object a noun group which refers to a person or thing that is affected by the action described by a verb. Compare with **subject**. Prepositions also have noun groups as objects.

object pronoun one of a set of pronouns including 'me', 'him', and 'them', which are used as the object of a verb or preposition. Object pronouns are also used as complements after 'be'; EG *I hit him... It's me.*

opinion adjective an adjective which you use to express your opinion of a person or thing, rather than just describing them. Compare with **descriptive adjective**.

ordinal number a number used to indicate where something comes in an order or sequence; EG *first, fifth, tenth, hundredth.*

participle a verb form used for making different tenses. Verbs have two participles, a present participle and a past participle.

particle an adverb or preposition which combines with verbs to form phrasal verbs.

passive voice verb groups such as 'was given', 'were taken', 'had been made', which are used when the subject of the verb is the person or thing that is affected by the action. Compare with **active voice**.

past form the form of a verb, often ending in '-ed', which is used for the past simple tense.

past participle a verb form which is used to form perfect tenses and passives. Some past participles are also used as adjectives. EG *watched, broken, swum.*

past tense see **tense**.

perfect tense see **tense**.

person one of the three classes of people who can be involved in something that is said. The person who is speaking or writing is called the first person. The people who are listening or reading are called the second person. The people or things that are being talked about are called the third person.

personal pronoun one of the group of words including 'I', 'you', and 'me', which are used to refer back to yourself, the people you are talking to, or the people or things you are talking about. See also **object pronoun and subject pronoun**.

phrasal verb a combination of a verb and a particle, which together have a different meaning to the verb on its own; EG *back down, hand over, look forward to.*

plural the form of a count noun or verb, which is used to refer to or talk about more than one person or thing; EG *Dogs have ears... The women were outside.*

plural noun a noun which is normally used only in the plural form; EG *trousers, scissors.*

positive a positive clause, question, sentence, or statement is one which does not contain a negative word such as 'not'.

possessive one of the determiners 'my', 'your', 'his', 'her', 'its', 'our', or 'their', which is used to show that one person or thing belongs to another; EG *your car.*

possessive adjective another name for **possessive**.

possessive pronoun one of the pronouns 'mine', 'yours', 'hers', 'his', 'ours', or 'theirs'.

preposition a word such as 'by', 'with' or 'from', which is always followed by a noun group.

prepositional phrase a structure consisting of a preposition followed by a noun group as its object; EG *on the table, by the sea.*

present participle see '-ing' form.

present tense see **tense**.

pronoun a word which you use instead of a noun, when you do not need or want to name someone or something directly; EG *it, you, none.*

progressive tense another name for **continuous tense**.

proper noun a noun which is the name of a particular person, place, organization, or building. Proper nouns are always written with a capital letter; EG *Nigel, Edinburgh, the United Nations, Christmas.*

purpose clause a subordinate clause which is used to talk about the intention that someone has when they do something; EG *I came here in order to ask you out to dinner.*

qualifier a word or group of words, such as an adjective, prepositional phrase, or relative clause, which comes after a noun and gives more information about it; EG *...the person involved... ...a book with a blue cover... ...the shop that I went into.*

question a sentence which normally has the verb in front of the subject, and which is used to ask someone about something; EG *Have you any money?*

question tag an auxiliary or modal with a pronoun, which is used to turn a statement into a question. EG *He's very friendly, isn't he?... I can come, can't I?*

reason clause a subordinate clause, usually introduced by 'because', 'since', or 'as', which is used to explain why something happens or is done; EG *Since you're here, we'll start.*

reciprocal verb a verb which describes an action which involves two people doing the same thing to each other; EG *I met you at the dance... We've met one another before... They met in the street.*

reflexive pronoun a pronoun ending in '-self' or '-selves', such as 'myself' or 'themselves', which you use as the object of a verb when you want to say that the object is the same person or thing as the subject of the verb in the same clause. EG *He hurt himself.*

reflexive verb a verb which is normally used with a reflexive pronoun as object; EG *He contented himself with the thought that he had the only set of keys.*

regular verb a verb that has four forms, and follows the normal rules.

relative clause a subordinate clause which gives more information about someone or something mentioned in the main clause. See also **defining relative clause** and **non-defining relative clause**.

relative pronoun 'that' or a 'wh'-word such as 'who' or 'which', when it is used to introduce a relative clause; EG *...the girl who was carrying the bag.*

reported clause the clause in a report structure which indicates what someone has said; EG *She said that I couldn't see her.*

reported question a question which is reported using a report structure rather than the exact words used by the speaker. See also **indirect question**.

reported speech the words you use to report what someone has said, rather than using their actual words. Also called indirect speech.

reporting clause the clause in a report structure which contains the reporting verb.

reporting verb a verb which describes what people say or think; EG *suggest, say, wonder.*

report structure a structure which is used to report

what someone says or thinks, rather than repeating their exact words; EG *She told me she'd be late.*

result clause a subordinate clause introduced by 'so', 'so...that', or 'such...(that)', which indicates the result of an action or situation; EG *I don't think there's any more news, so I'll finish.*

second person see **person**.

semi-modal a term used by some grammars to refer to the verbs 'dare', 'need', and 'used to', which behave like modals in some structures.

sentence a group of words which express a statement, question, or command. A sentence usually has a verb and a subject, and may be a simple sentence with one clause, or a compound or complex sentence with two or more clauses. In writing, a sentence has a capital letter at the beginning and a full-stop, question mark, or exclamation mark at the end.

short form a form in which one or more letters are omitted and two words are joined together, for example an auxiliary or modal and 'not', or a subject pronoun and an auxiliary or modal; EG *aren't, couldn't, he'd, I'm, it's, she's.*

simple tense a present or past tense formed without using an auxiliary verb; EG *I wait... she sang.*

singular the form of a count noun or verb which is used to refer to or talk about one person or thing; EG *A dog was in the back of the car... That woman is my mother.*

singular noun a noun which is normally used only in the singular form; EG *the sun, a bath.*

strong verb another name for **irregular verb**.

subject the noun group in a clause that refers to the person or thing who does the action expressed by the verb; EG *We were going shopping.*

subject pronoun one of the set of pronouns including 'I', 'she', and 'they', which are used as the subject of a verb.

subordinate clause a clause which must be used with a main clause and is not usually used alone, for example a time clause, conditional clause, relative clause, or result clause, and which begins with a subordinating conjunction such as 'because' or 'while'.

subordinating conjunction a conjunction such as 'although', 'as if', 'because' or 'while', which you use to begin a subordinate clause.

superlative an adjective or adverb with '-est' on the end or 'most' in front of it; EG *thinnest, quickest, most beautiful.*

tag question a statement to which a question tag has been added; EG *She's quiet, isn't she?*

tense the form of a verb which shows whether you are referring to the past, present, or future.

    future 'will' or 'shall' with the base form of the verb, used to refer to future events; EG *She **will come** tomorrow.*

future continuous 'will' or 'shall' with 'be' and a present participle, used to refer to future events; EG *She **will be going** soon.*

future perfect 'will' or 'shall' with 'have' and a past participle, used to refer to future events; EG *I **shall have finished** by tomorrow.*

future perfect continuous 'will' or 'shall' with 'have been' and a present participle, used to refer to future events; EG *I **will have been walking** for three hours by then.*

past simple the past form of a verb, used to refer to past events; EG *They **waited**.*

past continuous 'was' or 'were' with a present participle, usually used to refer to past events. EG *They **were worrying** about it yesterday.*

past perfect 'had' with a past participle, used to refer to past events; EG *She **had finished**.*

past perfect continuous 'had been' with a present participle, used to refer to past events; EG *He **had been waiting** for hours.*

present simple the base form and the third person singular form of a verb, usually used to refer to present events; EG *I **like** bananas… My sister **hates** them.*

present continuous the present simple of 'be' with a present participle, usually used to refer to present events; EG *Things **are improving**.*

present perfect 'have' or 'has' with a past participle, used to refer to past events which exist in the present; EG *She **has loved** him for ten years.*

present perfect continuous 'have been' or 'has been' with a present participle, used to refer to past events which continue in the present; EG *We **have been sitting** here for hours.*

'that'-clause a clause starting with 'that', used mainly when reporting what someone has said; EG *She said **that she'd wash up for me**.*

third person see **person.**

time clause a subordinate clause which indicates the time of an event; EG *I'll phone you **when I get back**.*

time expression a noun group used as an adverbial of time; EG *last night, the day after tomorrow, the next time.*

'to'-infinitive the base form of a verb preceded by 'to'; EG *to go, to have, to jump.*

transitive verb a verb which takes an object; EG *She's **wasting** her money.*

uncount noun a noun which has only one form, takes a singular verb, and is not used with 'a' or numbers. Uncount nouns often refer to substances, qualities, feelings, activities, and abstract ideas. EG *coal, courage, anger, help, fun.*

verb a word which is used with a subject to say what someone or something does, or what happens to them; EG *sing, spill, die.*

verb group a main verb, or a main verb with one or more auxiliaries, a modal, or a modal and an auxiliary, which is used with a subject to say what someone does, or what happens to them; EG *I'll **show** them… She's **been** sick.*

'wh'-question a question which expects the answer to give more information than just 'yes' or 'no'. EG *What happened?… Where did he go?* Compare with **'yes/no'-question.**

'wh'-word one of a group of words starting with 'wh-', such as 'what', 'when' or 'who', which are used in 'wh'-questions. 'How' is also called a 'wh'-word because it behaves like the other 'wh'-words.

'yes/no'-question a question which can be answered by just 'yes' or 'no', without giving any more information; EG *Would you like some more tea?* Compare with **'wh'-question.**

Corpus Acknowledgements

We wish to thank the following, who have kindly given permission for the use of copyright material in the Birmingham Collection of English Texts.

Associated Business Programmes Ltd for: *The Next 200 Years* by Herman Kahn with William Brown and Leon Martel first published in Great Britain by Associated Business Programmes Ltd 1977 © Hudson Institute 1976. David Attenborough and William Collins Sons & Co Ltd for: *Life on Earth* by David Attenborough first published by William Collins Sons & Co Ltd 1979 © David Attenborough Productions Ltd 1979. James Baldwin for: *The Fire Next Time* by James Baldwin published in Great Britain by Michael Joseph Ltd 1963 © James Baldwin 1963. B T Batsford Ltd for: *Witchcraft in England* by Christina Hole first published by B T Batsford Ltd 1945 © Christina Hole 1945. Michael Billington for: 'Lust at First Sight' by Michael Billington in the *Illustrated London News* July 1981 and 'Truffaut's Tolerance' by Michael Billington in the *Illustrated London News* August 1981. Birmingham International Council For Overseas Students' Aid for: BICOSA Information Leaflets 1981. Basil Blackwell Publishers Ltd for: *Breaking the Mould? The Birth and Prospects of the Social Democratic Party* by Ian Bradley first published by Martin Robertson & Co Ltd 1981 © Ian Bradley 1981. *Seeing Green (The Politics of Ecology Explained)* by Jonathon Porritt first published by Basil Blackwell Publisher Ltd 1984 © Jonathon Porritt 1984. Blond & Briggs Ltd for: *Small is Beautiful* by E F Schumacher first published in Great Britain by Blond & Briggs Ltd 1973 © E F Schumacher 1973. The Bodley Head Ltd for: *The Americans (Letters from America 1969-1979)* by Alistair Cooke first published by Bodley Head Ltd 1979 © Alistair Cooke 1979. *Baby and Child Care* by Dr Benjamin Spock published in Great Britain by The Bodley Head Ltd 1955 © Benjamin Spock MD 1945, 1946, 1957, 1968, 1976, 1979. *What's Wrong With The Modern World?* by Michael Shanks first published by The Bodley Head Ltd 1978 © Michael Shanks 1978. *Future Shock* by Alvin Toffler first published in Great Britain by The Bodley Head Ltd 1970 © Alvin Toffler 1970. *Zen and the Art of Motorcycle Maintenance* by Robert M Pirsig first published in Great Britain by The Bodley Head Ltd 1974 © Robert M Pirsig 1974. *Marnie* by Winston Graham first published by The Bodley Head Ltd 1961 © Winston Graham 1961. *You Can Get There From Here* by Shirley MacLaine first published in Great Britain by The Bodley Head Ltd 1975 © Shirley MacLaine 1975. *It's An Odd Thing, But ...* by Paul Jennings first published by Max Reinhardt Ltd 1971 © Paul Jennings 1971. *King of the Castle (Choice and Responsibility in the Modern World)* by Gai Eaton first published by the Bodley Head Ltd 1977 © Gai Eaton 1977. *Revolutionaries in Modern Britain* by Peter Shipley first published by The Bodley Head Ltd 1976 © Peter Shipley 1976. *The Prerogative of the Harlot (Press Barons and Power)* by Hugh Cudlipp first published by The Bodley Head Ltd 1980 © Hugh Cudlipp 1980. *But What About The Children (A Working Parents' Guide to Child Care)* by Judith Hann first published by The Bodley Head Ltd 1976 © Judith Hann 1976. *Learning to Read* by Margaret Meek first published by The Bodley Head Ltd 1982 © Margaret Meek 1982. Bolt & Watson for: *Two is Lonely* by Lynne Reid Banks first published by Chatto & Windus 1974 © Lynne Reid Banks 1974. The British and Foreign Bible Society with William Collins Sons & Co Ltd for: *Good News Bible (with Deuterocanonical Books/Apocrypha)* first published by The British and Foreign Bible Society with William Collins Sons & Co Ltd 1979 © American Bible Society: Old Testament 1976, Deuterocanonical Books/Apocrypha 1979, New Testament 1966, 1971, 1976 © Maps, British and Foreign Bible Society 1976, 1979. The British Council for: *How to Live in Britain (The British Council's Guide for Overseas Students and Visitors)* first published by The British Council 1952 © The British Council 1984. Mrs R Bronowski for: *The Ascent of Man* by J Bronowski published by Book Club Associates by arrangement with The British Broadcasting Corporation 1977 © J Bronowski 1973. Alison Busby for: *The Death of Trees* by Nigel Dudley first published by Pluto Press Ltd 1985 © Nigel Dudley 1985. Tony Buzan for: *Make The Most of your Mind* by Tony Buzan first published by Colt Books Ltd 1977 © Tony Buzan 1977. Campbell Thomson & McLaughlin Ltd for: *Ring of Bright Water* by Gavin Maxwell first published by Longmans Green & Co 1960, published in Penguin Books Ltd 1976 © The Estate of Gavin Maxwell 1960. Jonathan Cape Ltd for: *Manwatching (A Field Guide to Human Behaviour)* by Desmond Morris first published in Great Britain by Jonathan Cape Ltd 1977 © Text, Desmond Morris 1977 © Compilation, Elsevier Publishing Projects SA, Lausanne, and Jonathan Cape Ltd, London 1977. *Tracks* by Robyn Davidson first published by Jonathan Cape Ltd 1980 © Robyn Davidson 1980. *In the Name of Love* by Jill Tweedie first published by Jonathan Cape Ltd 1979 © Jill Tweedie 1979. *The Use of Lateral Thinking* by Edward de Bono first published by Jonathan Cape 1967 © Edward de Bono 1967. *Trout Fishing in America* by Richard Brautigan first published in Great Britain by Jonathan Cape Ltd 1970 © Richard Brautigan 1967. *The Pendulum Years: Britain and the Sixties* by Bernard Levin first published by Jonathan Cape Ltd 1970 © Bernard Levin 1970. *The Summer Before The Dark* by Doris Lessing first published in Great Britain by Jonathan Cape Ltd 1973 © Doris Lessing 1973. *The Boston Strangler* by Gerold Frank first published in Great Britain by Jonathan Cape Ltd 1967 © Gerold Frank 1966. *I'm OK - You're OK* by Thomas A Harris MD first published in Great Britain as The Book of Choice by Jonathan Cape Ltd 1970 © Thomas A Harris MD, 1967, 1968, 1969. *The Vivisector* by Patrick White first published by Jonathan Cape Ltd 1970 © Patrick White 1970. *The Future of Socialism* by Anthony Crosland first published by Jonathan Cape Ltd 1956 © C A R Crosland 1963.

Funeral in Berlin by Len Deighton first published by Jonathan Cape Ltd 1964 © Len Deighton 1964. Chatto & Windus Ltd for: *A Postillion Struck by Lightning* by Dirk Bogarde first published by Chatto & Windus Ltd 1977 © Dirk Bogarde 1977. *Nuns and Soldiers* by Iris Murdoch published by Chatto & Windus Ltd 1980 © Iris Murdoch 1980. *Wounded Knee (An Indian History of the American West)* by Dee Brown published by Chatto & Windus Ltd 1978 © Dee Brown 1970. *The Virgin in the Garden* by A S Byatt first published by Chatto & Windus Ltd 1978 © A S Byatt 1978. *A Story Like The Wind* by Laurens van der Post published by Clarke Irwin & Co Ltd in association with The Hogarth Press Ltd 1972 © Laurens van der Post 1972. *Brave New World* by Aldous Huxley published by Chatto & Windus Ltd 1932 © Aldous Huxley and Mrs Laura Huxley 1932, 1960. *The Reivers* By William Faulkner first published by Chatto & Windus Ltd 1962 © William Faulkner 1962. *Cider With Rosie* by Laurie Lee published by The Hogarth Press 1959 © Laurie Lee 1959 *The Tenants* by Bernard Malamud first published in Great Britain by Chatto & Windus Ltd 1972 © Bernard Malamud 1971. *Kinflicks* by Lisa Alther first published in Great Britain by Chatto & Windus Ltd 1976 © Lisa Alther 1975. William Collins Sons & Co Ltd for: *The Companion Guide to London* by David Piper published by William Collins Sons & Co Ltd 1964 © David Piper 1964. *The Bedside Guardian 29* edited by W L Webb published by William Collins & Sons Ltd 1980 © Guardian Newspapers Ltd 1980. *Bear Island* by Alistair MacLean first published by William Collins Sons & Co Ltd 1971 © Alistair MacLean 1971. *Inequality in Britain: Freedom, Welfare and the State* by Frank Field first published by Fontana Paperbacks 1981 © Frank Field 1981. *Social Mobility* by Anthony Heath first published by Fontana Paperbacks 1981 © Anthony Heath 1981. *Yours Faithfully* by Gerald Priestland first published by Fount Paperbacks 1979 © British Broadcasting Corporation 1977, 1978. *Power Without Responsibility: The Press and Broadcasting in Britain* by James Curran and Jean Seaton first published by Fontana Paperbacks 1981 © James Curran and Jean Seaton 1981. *The Times Cookery Book* by Katie Stewart first published by William Collins Sons & Co Ltd 1972 © Times Newspapers Ltd 1972. *Friends from the Forest* by Joy Adamson by Collins and Harvill Press 1981 © Elsa Limited 1981. *The Media Mob* by Barry Fantoni and George Melly first published by William Collins Sons & Co Ltd 1980 © Text, George Melly 1980 © Illustrations, Barry Fantoni 1980. *Shalom (a collection of Australian and Jewish Stories)* compiled by Nancy Keesing first published by William Collins Publishers Pty Ltd 1978 © William Collins Sons &Co Ltd 1978. *The Bedside Guardian 31* edited by W L Webb first published by William Collins Sons & Co Ltd 1982 © Guardian Newspapers Ltd 1982. *The Bedside Guardian 32* edited by W L Webb first published by William Collins Sons & Co Ltd 1983 © Guardian Newspapers Ltd 1983. *Design for the Real World* by Victor Papanek first published in Great Britain by Thames & Hudson Ltd 1972 © Victor Papanek 1971. *Food For Free* by Richard Mabey first published by William Collins Sons & Co Ltd 1972 © Richard Mabey 1972. *Unended Quest* by Karl Popper (first published as Autobiography of Karl Popper in The Philosophy of Karl Popper in The Library of Philosophers edited by Paul Arthur Schlipp by the Open Court Publishing Co 1974) published by Fontana Paperbacks 1976 © The Library of Living Philosophers Inc 1974 © Karl R Popper 1976. *My Mother My Self* by Nancy Friday first published in Great Britain by Fontana Paperbacks 1979 © Nancy Friday 1977. *The Captain's Diary* by Bob Willis first published by Willow Books/William Collins Sons & Co Ltd 1984 © Bob Willis and Alan Lee 1984 © New Zealand Scorecards, Bill Frindall 1984. *The Bodywork Book* by Esme Newton-Dunn first published in Great Britain by Willow Books/William Collins Sons & Co Ltd 1982 © TVS Ltd/Esme Newton-Dunn 1982. *Collins' Encyclopaedia of Fishing in The British Isles* edited by Michael Prichard first published by William Collins Sons & Co Ltd 1976 © William Collins Sons & Co Ltd 1976. *The AAA Runner's Guide* edited by Heather Thomas first published by William Collins Sons & Co Ltd 1983 © Sackville Design Group Ltd 1983. *Heroes and Contemporaries* by David Gower with Derek Hodgson first published by William Collins Sons & Co Ltd 1983 © David Gower Promotions Ltd 1983. *The Berlin Memorandum* by Adam Hall first published by William Collins Sons & Co Ltd 1965 © Jonquil Trevor 1965. *Arlott on Cricket: His Writings on the Game* edited by David Rayvern Allen first published by William Collins (Willow Books) 1984 © John Arlott 1984. *A Woman in Custody* by Audrey Peckham first published by Fontana Paperbacks 1985 © Audrey Peckham 1985. *Play Golf with Peter Alliss* by Peter Alliss published by the British Broadcasting Corporation 1977 © Peter Alliss and Renton Laidlaw 1977. Curtis Brown Ltd for: *The Pearl* by John Steinbeck first published by William Heinemann Ltd 1948 © John Steinbeck 1948. *An Unfinished History of the World* by Hugh Thomas first published in Great Britain by Hamish Hamilton Ltd 1979 © Hugh Thomas 1979, 1981. *The Winter of our Discontent* by John Steinbeck first published in Great Britain by William Heinemann Ltd 1961 © John Steinbeck 1961. *Burr* by Gore Vidal first published in Great Britain by William Heinemann Ltd 1974 © Gore Vidal 1974. *Doctor on the Job* by Richard Gordon first published by William Heinemann Ltd 1976 © Richard Gordon Ltd 1976. Andre Deutsch Ltd for: *How to be an Alien* by George Mikes first published by Andre Deutsch Ltd 1946 © George Mikes and Nicholas Bentley 1946. *Jaws* by Peter Benchley first published in Great Britain by Andre Deutsch Ltd 1974 © Peter Benchley 1974. *A Bend in the River* by V S Naipaul first published by

August 1981, 26 August 1981 and 9 September 1981) © published by Punch Publications Ltd 1981. Radala and associates for: *The Naked Civil Servant* by Quentin Crisp first published by Jonathan Cape Ltd 1968 © Quentin Crisp 1968. The Rainbird Publishing Group Ltd for: *The Making of Mankind* by Richard E Leakey first published in Great Britain by Michael Joseph Ltd 1981 © Sherma BV 1981. Robson Books Ltd for: *The Punch Book of Short Stories 3* selected by Alan Coren first published in Great Britain by Robson Books Ltd in association with Punch Publications Ltd 1981 © Robson Books Ltd 1981.*The Best of Robert Morley* by Robert Morley first published in Great Britain by Robson Books Ltd 1981 © Robert Morley 1981. Deborah Rogers Ltd for: 'Picasso's Late Works' by Edward Lucie-Smith in the *Illustrated London News* July 1981, 'David Jones at the Tate' by Edward Lucie-Smith in the *Illustrated London News* August 1981 and 'Further Light on Spanish Painting' by Edward Lucie-Smith in the *Illustrated London News* September 1981. *The Godfather* by Mario Puzo first published in Great Britain by William Heinemann Ltd 1969 © Mario Puzo 1969. Routledge & Kegan Paul Ltd for: *How To Pass Examinations* by John Erasmus first published by Oriel Press Ltd 1967 © Oriel Press Ltd 1980. *Daisy, Daisy* by Christian Miller first published by Routledge & Kegan Paul Ltd 1980 © Christian Miller 1980. *The National Front* by Nigel Fielding first published by Routledge & Kegan Paul Ltd 1981 © Nigel Fielding 1981. *The Myth of Home Ownership* by Jim Kemeny first published by Routledge & Kegan Paul Ltd 1981 © J Kemeny 1981. *Absent With Cause (Lessons of Truancy)* by Roger White first published by Routledge & Kegan Paul Ltd 1980 © Roger White 1980. *The Powers of Evil (in Western Religion, Magic and Folk Belief)* by Richard Cavendish first published by Routledge & Kegan Paul Ltd 1975 © Richard Cavendish 1975. *Crime and Personality* by H J Eysenck first published by Routledge & Kegan Paul Ltd 1964 © H J Eysenck 1964, 1977. Martin Secker & Warburg Ltd for: *Changing Places* by David Lodge first published in England by Martin Secker & Warburg Ltd 1975 © David Lodge 1975. *The History Man* by Malcolm Bradbury first published by Martin Secker & Warburg 1975 © Malcolm Bradbury 1975. *Humboldt's Gift* by Saul Bellow first published in England by the Alison Press/Martin Secker & Warburg Ltd 1975 © Saul Bellow 1973, 1974, 1975. *Wilt* by Tom Sharpe first published in England by Martin Secker & Warburg Ltd 1976 © Tom Sharpe 1976. *The Last Days of America* by Paul E Erdman first published in England by Martin Secker & Warburg Ltd 1981 © Paul E Erdman 1981. *Autumn Manoeuvres* by Melvyn Bragg first published in England by Martin Secker & Warburg Ltd 1978 © Melvyn Bragg 1978. *The Act of Being* by Charles Marowitz first published in England by Martin Secker & Warburg Ltd 1978 © Charles Marowitz 1978. *As If By Magic* by Angus Wilson first published in England by Martin Secker & Warburg Ltd 1973 © Angus Wilson 1973. *All the President's Men* by Carl Bernstein and Bob Woodward first published in England by Martin Secker & Warburg Ltd 1974 © Carl Bernstein and Bob Woodward 1974. *The Myth of the Nation and the Vision of Revolution* by J L Talmon first published by Martin Secker & Warburg Ltd 1981 © J L Talmon 1980. *Animal Farm* by George Orwell first published by Martin Secker & Warburg 1945 © Eric Blair 1945. Anthony Sheil Associates Ltd for: *Daniel Martin* by John Fowles first published in Great Britain by Jonathan Cape Ltd 1977 © J R Fowles Ltd 1977. *Love Story* by Erich Segal published by Hodder & Stoughton Ltd 1970 © Erich Segal 1970. Sidgwick & Jackson Ltd for: *The Third World War* by General Sir John Hackett and others first published in Great Britain by Sidgwick & Jackson Ltd 1978 © General Sir John Hackett 1978. *Superwoman* by Shirley Conran first published by Sidgwick & Jackson Ltd 1975 © Shirley Conran 1975, 1977. *An Actor and His Time* by John Gielgud first published in Great Britain by Sidgwick & Jackson Ltd 1979 © John Gielgud, John Miller and John Powell 1979 © Biographical Notes, John Miller 1979. Simon & Schuster for: *Our Bodies Ourselves (A Health Book by and for Women)* by the Boston Women's Health Book Collective (British Edition by Angela Phillips and Jill Rakusen) published in Allen Lane and Penguin Books Ltd 1978 © The Boston Women's Health Collective Inc 1971, 1973, 1976 © Material for British Edition, Angela Phillips and Jill Rakusen 1978. Souvenir Press Ltd for: *The Bermuda Triangle* by Charles Berlitz (An Incredible Saga of Unexplained Disappearances) first published in Great Britain by Souvenir Press Ltd 1975 © Charles Berlitz 1974. Souvenir Press Ltd and Michael Joseph Ltd for: *Airport* by Arthur Hailey first published in Great Britain by Michael Joseph Ltd in association with Souvenir Press Ltd 1968 © Arthur Hailey Ltd 1968. Sunmed Holidays Ltd for: 'Go Greek' (Summer 1983) holiday brochure. Maurice Temple Smith Ltd for: *Friends of the Earth Pollution Guide* by Brian Price published by Maurice Temple Smith Ltd 1983 © Brian Price 1983. Maurice Temple Smith and Gower Publishing Co Ltd for: *Working the Land (A New Plan for a Healthy Agriculture)* by Charlie Pye-Smith and Richard North first published by Maurice Temple Smith Ltd 1984 © Charlie Pye-Smith and Richard North 1984. Times Newspapers Ltd for: *The Sunday Times Magazine* (13 January 1980, 20 January 1980 and 11 May 1980) © published by Times Newspapers Ltd 1981. *The Times* (7 September 1981) © published by Times Newspapers Ltd 1981. Twenty's Holidays for: 'The Best 18-33 Holidays' (Winter 1982/83) holiday brochure. University of Birmingham for: *Living in Birmingham* (1984) © published by The University of Birmingham 1984. Birmingham University Overseas Student Guide © The University of Birmingham. *Working with Industry and Commerce* © published by The University of Birmingham 1984. University of Birmingham Prospectus (June 1985) © published by The University of Birmingham 1985. University of Birmingham Library Guide © published by The University of Birmingham. University of Birmingham Institute of Research and Development (1984) © published by the University of Birmingham 1984. Biological Sciences at The University of Birmingham (1985) © published by The University of Birmingham 1985. History at the University of Birmingham (1985) © published by the University of Birmingham 1985. Faculty of Arts Handbook (1984-85) © published by The University of Birmingham 1984. Virago Press Ltd for: *Benefits* by Zoe Fairbairns published by Virago Press Ltd 1979 © Zoe Fairbairns 1979. *Simple Steps to Public Life* by Pamela Anderson, Mary Stott and Fay Weldon published in Great Britain by Virago Press Ltd 1980 © Action Opportunities 1980. *Tell Me A Riddle* published by Virago Press Ltd 1980 © this edition Tillie Olsen 1980. A P Watt (& Sons) Ltd for: *The Glittering Prizes* by Frederic Raphael first published in Great Britain by Penguin Books Ltd 1976 © Volatic Ltd 1976. *Then and Now* by W Somerset Maugham first published by William Heinemann Ltd 1946 © W Somerset Maugham 1946. *The Language of Clothes* by Alison Lurie published by William Heinemann Ltd 1981 © Alison Lurie 1981. 'Herschel Commemorative' by Patrick Moore in the *Illustrated London News* July 1981. 'The Outermost Giant' by Patrick Moore in the *Illustrated London News* August 1981. 'Cosmic Bombardment' by Patrick Moore in the *Illustrated London News* September 1981. Weidenfeld & Nicolson Ltd for: 'The Miraculous Toy' by Susan Briggs in the *Illustrated London News* August 1981. *The Needle's Eye* by Margaret Drabble first published by Weidenfeld & Nicolson Ltd 1972 © Margaret Drabble 1972. *Success Without Tears: A Woman's Guide to the Top* by Rachel Nelson first published in Great Britain by Weidenfeld & Nicolson Ltd 1979 © Rachel Nelson 1979. *Education in the Modern World* by John Vaizey published by Weidenfeld & Nicolson Ltd 1967 © John Vaizey 1967. *Rich Man, Poor Man* by Irwin Shaw first published in Great Britain by Weidenfeld & Nicolson Ltd 1970 © Irwin Shaw 1969, 1970. *Lolita* by Vladimir Nabokov first published in Great Britain by Weidenfeld & Nicolson Ltd 1959 © Vladimir Nabokov 1955, 1959, 1968, © G P Putnam's Sons 1963 © McGraw-Hill International Inc 1971. *The Third World* by Peter Worsley first published by Weidenfeld & Nicolson Ltd 1964 © Peter Worsley 1964, 1967. *Portrait of a Marriage* by Nigel Nicolson published by Weidenfeld & Nicolson Ltd 1973 © Nigel Nicolson 1973. *The Dogs Bark: Public People and Private Places* by Truman Capote first published in Great Britain by Weidenfeld & Nicolson Ltd 1974 © Truman Capote 1974. *Great Planning Disasters* by Peter Hall first published in Great Britain by George Weidenfeld & Nicolson Ltd 1980 © Peter Hall 1980. The Writers and Readers Publishing Co-operative Ltd for: *Working with Words, Literacy Beyond School* by Jane Mace published by The Writers and Readers Publishing Co-operative Ltd 1979 © Jane Mace 1979. *The Alienated: Growing Old Today* by Gladys Elder OAP published by The Writers and Readers Publishing Co-operative Ltd 1977 © Text, The Estate of Gladys Elder 1977 © Photographs, Mike Abrahams 1977. *Beyond the Crisis in Art* by Peter Fuller published by The Writers and Readers Publishing Cooperative Ltd 1980 © Peter Fuller 1980. *The War and Peace Book* by Dave Noble published by The Writers and Readers Publishing Co-operative Ltd 1977 © Dave Noble 1977. *Tony Benn: A Political Biography* by Robert Jenkins first published by The Writers and Readers Publishing Co-operative Ltd 1980 © Robert Jenkins 1980. *Nuclear Power for Beginners* by Stephen Croall and Kaianders Sempler first published by The Writers and Readers Publishing Co-operative Ltd 1978 © Text, Stephen Croall 1978, 1980 © Illustrations Kaianders Sempler 1978, 1980. Yale University Press for: *Life in the English Country House: A Social and Architectural History* by Mark Girouard published by Yale University Press Ltd, London 1978 © Yale University 1978. The British Broadcasting Corporation for transcripts of radio transmissions of 'Kaleidoscope', 'Any Questions', 'Money Box' and 'Arts and Africa' 1981 and 1982. The British Broadcasting Corporation and Mrs Shirley Williams for transcripts of television interviews with Mrs Shirley Williams 1979. Dr B L Smith, School of Mathematics and Physical Sciences, University of Sussex for programmes on Current Affairs, Science and The Arts originally broadcast on Radio Sussex 1979 and 1980 © B L Smith. The following people in the University of Birmingham: Professor J McH Sinclair, Department of English, for his tapes of informal conversation (personal collection). Mr R Wallace, formerly Department of Accounting and Finance, and Ms D Houghton, Department of English, for transcripts of his accountancy lectures. Dr B K Gazey, Department of Electrical Engineering and Dr M Montgomery, University of Strathclyde, Department of English, for a transcript of Dr Gazey's lecture. Dr L W Poel, Department of Plant Biology, and Dr M Montgomery, University of Strathclyde, Department of English, for a transcript of Dr Poel's lecture. Professor J G Hawkes, formerly Department of Plant Biology, for recordings of his lectures. Dr M S Snaith, Department of Transportation for recordings of his lectures. Dr M P Hoey, Department of English, and Dr M Cooper, The British Council, for a recording of their discussion on discourse analysis. Ms A Renouf, Department of English, for recordings of job and academic interviews 1977. Mr R H Hubbard, formerly a B Phil (Ed) student, Faculty of Education, for his research recordings of expressions of uncertainty 1978-79. Mr A E Hare, formerly a B Phil (Ed) student, Faculty of Education, for his transcripts of telephone conversations 1978. Dr A Tsui, formerly Department of English, for her recordings of informal conversation. Mr J Couperthwaite, formerly Department of English, for a recording of informal conversation 1981. Ms C Emmott, M Litt student, Department of English, for a recording of informal conversation 1981. Mrs B T Atkins for the transcript of an account of a dream 1981. The British Council for 'Authentic Materials Numbers 1-28' 1981. Professor M Hammerton and Mr K Coghill, Department of Psychology, University of Newcastle-upon-Tyne, for tape recordings of their lectures 1981. Mr G P Graveson, formerly research student, University of Newcastle, for his recordings of teacher discussion 1977. Mr W R Jones, formerly research student, University of Southampton, for his recordings of classroom talk. Mr Ian Fisher, formerly BA student, Newcastle Polytechnic, for his transcripts of interviews on local history 1981. Dr N Coupland, formerly PhD student, Department of English, UWIST, for his transcripts of travel agency talk 1981. Professor D B Bromley, Department of Psychology, University of Liverpool, for his transcript of a research recording. Mr Brian Lawrence, of Saffron Walden County High School, for a tape of his talk on 'The British Education System' 1979.

Thanks are also due to Times Newspapers Ltd for providing machine-readable copies of The Times and The Sunday Times for linguistic analysis.

Every effort has been made to trace the copyright holders, but if any have been inadvertently overlooked the publishers will be pleased to make the necessary acknowledgments at the first opportunity.

Unit 1 Clause and sentence structure

Main points

- Simple sentences have one clause.
- Clauses usually consist of a noun group as the subject, and a verb group.
- Clauses can also have another noun group as the object or complement.
- Clauses can have an adverbial, also called an adjunct.
- Changing the order of the words in a clause can change its meaning.
- Compound sentences consist of two or more main clauses. Complex sentences always include a subordinate clause, as well as one or more main clauses.

1 A simple sentence has one clause, beginning with a noun group called the subject. The subject is the person or thing that the sentence is about. This is followed by a verb group, which tells you what the subject is doing, or describes the subject's situation.

I waited.
The girl screamed.

2 The verb group may be followed by another noun group, which is called the object. The object is the person or thing affected by the action or situation.

He opened the car door.
She married a young engineer.

After link verbs like 'be', 'become', 'feel', and 'seem', the verb group may be followed by a noun group or an adjective, called a complement. The complement tells you more about the subject.

She was a doctor.
He was angry.

3 The verb group, the object, or the complement can be followed by an adverb or a prepositional phrase, called an adverbial. The adverbial tells you more about the action or situation, for example how, when, or where it happens. Adverbials are also called adjuncts.

They shouted loudly.
She won the competition last week.
He was a policeman in Birmingham.

4 The word order of a clause is different when the clause is a statement, a question, or a command.

He speaks English very well. (statement)
Did she win at the Olympics? (question)
Stop her. (command)

Note that the subject is omitted in commands, so the verb comes first.

5 A compound sentence has two or more main clauses: that is, clauses which are equally important. You join them with 'and', 'but', or 'or'.

He met Jane at the station and went shopping.
I wanted to go but I felt too ill.
You can come now or you can meet us there later.

Note that the order of the two clauses can change the meaning of the sentence.

He went shopping and met Jane at the station.

If the subject of both clauses is the same, you usually omit the subject in the second clause.

I wanted to go but felt too ill.

6 A complex sentence contains a subordinate clause and at least one main clause. A subordinate clause gives information about a main clause, and is introduced by a conjunction such as 'because', 'if', 'that', or a 'wh'-word. Subordinate clauses can come before, after, or inside the main clause.

When he stopped, no one said anything.
If you want, I'll teach you.

They were going by car because it was more comfortable.
I told him that nothing was going to happen to me.

The car that I drove was a Ford.
The man who came into the room was small.

Unit 1 Practice

A Change the meaning of these sentences by changing the subject and the object.

1 John loves Mary. / ...*Mary loves John.*.......................

2 Charlie Brown kicked the horse. / ....

3 A big fish ate Jonah. / ....

4 Mrs Jackson taught my father. / ....

5 The giant killed Jack. / ....

B Put these words and phrases in the right order to make sentences. The letters in brackets show the structure of your sentences. S stands for Subject, V for Verb, O for Object, and A for Adverbial.

1 a bone / the dog / ate. / (S + V + O) ...*The dog ate a bone.*..........

2 everybody / hard / worked. / (S + V + A) ....

3 the cat / the mouse / caught. / (S + V + O) ....

4 children / kittens / love. / (S + V + O) ....

5 the answer / nobody / knows. / (S + V + O) ....

6 a new dress / Mary / bought / yesterday. / (S + V + O + A) ....

7 the film / all of us / last night / enjoyed. / (S + V + O + A) ....

8 John Black / to the supermarket / went. / (S + V + A) ....

9 her car / Janet Black / to the airport / drove. / (S + V + O + A) ......

10 a cup of coffee / Mike / after lunch / drank. / (S + V + O + A) ......

C Read the following sentences and write down their structure using the letters S (for Subject), V (for Verb), O (for Object), and A (for Adverbial).

1 The dog bit Peter very badly. / ...*S + V + O + A*...............

2 Bill ran fast. / ....

3 I ate some fish and chips for supper. / ....

4 We all went home. / ....

5 Most of my friends enjoyed the game last week. / ....

6 John saw Fred yesterday. / ....

D Change these sentences from negative statements to negative questions.

1 They don't live near here. / ...*Don't they live near here?*..........

2 You didn't see Jill last Friday. / ....

3 They haven't arrived yet. / ....

4 Peter won't help you. / ....

5 Henry can't speak French. / ....

6 He doesn't smoke any more. / ....

7 They didn't understand him. / ....

8 John hasn't met Mary yet. / ....

Unit 2 The noun group

Main points

- Noun groups can be the subject, object, or complement of a verb, or the object of a preposition.
- Noun groups can be nouns on their own, but often include other words such as determiners, numbers, and adjectives.
- Noun groups can also be pronouns.
- Singular noun groups take singular verbs, plural noun groups take plural verbs.

1 Noun groups are used to say which people or things you are talking about. They can be the subject or object of a verb.

Strawberries are very expensive now.
Keith likes strawberries.

A noun group can also be the complement of a link verb such as 'be', 'become', 'feel', or 'seem'.

She became champion in 1964.
He seemed a nice man.

A noun group can be used after a preposition, and is often called the object of the preposition.

I saw him in town.
She was very ill for six months.

2 A noun group can be a noun on its own, but it often includes other words. A noun group can have a determiner such as 'the' or 'a'. You put determiners at the beginning of the noun group.

The girls were not in the house.
He was eating an apple.

3 A noun group can include an adjective. You usually put the adjective in front of the noun.

He was using blue ink.
I like living in a big city.

Sometimes you can use another noun in front of the noun.

I like chocolate cake.
She wanted a job in the oil industry.

A noun with 's (apostrophe s) is used in front of another noun to show who or what something belongs to or is connected with.

I held Sheila's hand very tightly.
He pressed a button on the ship's radio.

4 A noun group can also have an adverbial, a relative clause, or a 'to'-infinitive clause after it, which makes it more precise.

I spoke to a girl in a dark grey dress.
She wrote to the man who employed me.
I was trying to think of a way to stop him.

A common adverbial used after a noun is a prepositional phrase beginning with 'of'.

He tied the rope to a large block of stone.
The front door of the house was wide open.
I hated the idea of leaving him alone.

Participles and some adjectives can also be used after a noun. See Units 19 and 29.

She pointed to the three cards lying on the table.
He is the only man available.

5 Numbers come after determiners and before adjectives.

I had to pay a thousand dollars.
Three tall men came out of the shed.

6 A noun group can also be a pronoun. You often use a pronoun when you are referring back to a person or thing that you have already mentioned.

I've got two boys, and they both enjoy playing football.

You also use a pronoun when you do not know who the person or thing is, or do not want to be precise.

Someone is coming to mend it tomorrow.

7 A noun group can refer to one or more people or things. Many nouns have a singular form referring to one person or thing, and a plural form referring to more than one person or thing. See Unit 4.

My dog never bites people.
She likes dogs.

Similarly, different pronouns are used in the singular and in the plural.

I am going home now.
We want more money.

When a singular noun group is the subject, it takes a singular verb. When a plural noun group is the subject, it takes a plural verb.

His son plays football for the school.
Her letters are always very short.

Unit 2 Practice

A Expand the noun group in these sentences by adding the words given.

1 There's a man.
    There's an old man. (old)
    There's an old man standing by the bus stop. (standing by the bus stop)
    There's an old man with an umbrella standing by the bus stop. (with an umbrella)

2 There's a dog.
    .... (big)
    .... (running out of the shop)
    .... (carrying a bone)

3 There's a man.
    .... (fat)
    .... (with a knife in his hand)
    .... (running after the dog)

4 There's a woman.
    .... (young)
    .... (with long hair)
    .... (standing outside the shop)

B Complete the following by adding these 'to'-infinitives.

to carry	to catch	to do	to drive through	to wear	to meet
to post	to play	to read	to visit	to eat	

1 I'm hungry. I haven't had anything ...*to eat.*............................

2 He's very busy. He has a lot of work ....

3 It's a wonderful place for children ....

4 I mustn't be late. I have some important people ....

5 Can you call at the post office? There are a few letters ....

6 When I am travelling I always take a good book ....

7 If I'm going to the party I must buy a new dress ....

8 I'll have to take a taxi. I've got too much luggage ....

9 I'll have to leave now. I have a train ....

10 Oxford is a wonderful place .... , but it's a dreadful place
    ....

5

Unit 3 The verb group

Main points

- In a clause, the verb group usually comes after the subject and always has a main verb.
- The main verb has several different forms.
- Verb groups can also include one or two auxiliaries, or a modal, or a modal and one or two auxiliaries.
- The verb group changes in negative clauses and questions.
- Some verb groups are followed by an adverbial, a complement, an object, or two objects.

1 The verb group in a clause is used to say what is happening in an action or situation. You usually put the verb group immediately after the subject. The verb group always includes a main verb.

I waited.
They killed the elephants.

2 Regular verbs have four forms: the base form, the third person singular form of the present simple, the '-ing' form or present participle, and the '-ed' form used for the past simple and for the past participle.

ask	⇨ asks	⇨ asking	⇨ asked
try	⇨ tries	⇨ trying	⇨ tried
reach	⇨ reaches	⇨ reaching	⇨ reached
dance	⇨ dances	⇨ dancing	⇨ danced
dip	⇨ dips	⇨ dipping	⇨ dipped

Irregular verbs may have three forms, four forms, or five forms. Note that 'be' has eight forms.

cost	⇨ costs	⇨ costing		
think	⇨ thinks	⇨ thinking	⇨ thought	
swim	⇨ swims	⇨ swimming	⇨ swam	⇨ swum
be	⇨ am / is / are	⇨ being	⇨ was / were	⇨ been

See the Appendix for details of verb forms.

3 The main verb can have one or two auxiliaries in front of it.

I had met him in Zermatt.
The car was being repaired.

The main verb can have a modal in front of it.

You can go now.
I would like to ask you a question.

The main verb can have a modal and one or two auxiliaries in front of it.

I could have spent the whole year on it.
She would have been delighted to see you.

4 In negative clauses, you have to use a modal or auxiliary and put 'not' after the first word of the verb group.

He does not speak English very well.
I was not smiling.
It could not have been wrong.

Note that you often use short forms rather than 'not'.

I didn't know that.
He couldn't see it.

5 In 'yes/no' questions, you have to put an auxiliary or modal first, then the subject, then the rest of the verb group.

Did you meet George?
Couldn't you have been a bit quieter?

In 'wh'-questions, you put the 'wh'-word first. If the 'wh'-word is the subject, you put the verb group next.

Which came first?
Who could have done it?

If the 'wh'-word is the object or an adverbial, you must use an auxiliary or modal next, then the subject, then the rest of the verb group.

What did you do?
Where could she be going?

6 Some verb groups have an object or two objects after them. See Units 72 and 73.

He closed the door.
She sends you her love.

Verb groups involving link verbs, such as 'be', have a complement after them. See Unit 80.

They were sailors.
She felt happy.

Some verb groups have an adverbial after them.

We walked through the park.
She put the letter on the table.

Unit 3 Practice

A Underline the main verbs in these sentences. The number in brackets tells you how many main verbs there are.

1 Jack will <u>kill</u> the giant. (1)
2 We can come round tomorrow.(1)
3 I haven't heard from her since she went on holiday. (2)
4 I would have told her, if she had asked. (2)
5 Did you walk to school, or did you go on your bike? (2)
6 You could have stayed with us, if we had known you were coming. (3)
7 He said he didn't know who was coming. (3)
8 They woke up when they heard the noise. (2)
9 You must do what the boss tells you. (2)
10 Do you always do what the boss tells you? (2)

B Underline the auxiliaries.

1 I <u>don't</u> speak English very well. (1)
2 We haven't seen them. They weren't at home when we called. (1)
3 We were playing tennis when the storm started. (1)
4 They are coming as soon as they have finished work. (2)
5 John had seen Mary just twice before. (1)
6 Do you live here or are you just visiting? (2)
7 Do you know each other or haven't you met before? (2)
8 Will you be coming early or are you arriving later? (2)
9 This cup has been broken. (2)
10 They will have been found by now. (2)

C Underline the modals.

1 You <u>will</u> get a good seat if you get there early. (1)
2 I'll ask Fred if he can help. (2)
3 Ken will certainly come if he can find the time. (2)
4 Could you keep quiet while we are trying to listen to the music? (1)
5 I would help you if I could. (2)
6 I suppose you should tell her as soon as you can. (2)
7 They might agree but on the other hand they might not. (2)
8 I think they may come if they can find the time. (2)
9 You should have known that Jack would try to make trouble. (2)
10 They would probably have done it if they could have found the money. (2)

Unit 4 Count nouns

Main points

- Count nouns have two forms, singular and plural.
- They can be used with numbers.
- Singular count nouns always take a determiner.
- Plural count nouns do not need a determiner.
- Singular count nouns take a singular verb and plural count nouns take a plural verb.

In English, some things are thought of as individual items that can be counted directly. The nouns which refer to these countable things are called count nouns. Most nouns in English are count nouns. See Unit 6 for information on uncount nouns.

1 Count nouns have two forms. The singular form refers to one thing or person.

...a _book_... ...the _teacher_.

The plural form refers to more than one thing or person.

..._books_... ...some _teachers_.

2 You add '-s' to form the plural of most nouns.

book ⇨ books	school ⇨ schools

You add '-es' to nouns ending in '-ss', '-ch', '-s', '-sh', or '-x'.

class ⇨ classes	watch ⇨ watches
gas ⇨ gases	dish ⇨ dishes
fox ⇨ foxes	

Some nouns ending in '-o' add '-s', and some add '-es'.

photo ⇨ photos	piano ⇨ pianos
hero ⇨ heroes	potato ⇨ potatoes

Nouns ending in a consonant and '-y' change to '-ies'.

country ⇨ countries	lady ⇨ ladies
party ⇨ parties	victory ⇨ victories

Nouns ending in a vowel and '-y' add an '-s'.

boy ⇨ boys	day ⇨ days
key ⇨ keys	valley ⇨ valleys

Some common nouns have irregular plurals.

child ⇨ children	foot ⇨ feet
man ⇨ men	mouse ⇨ mice
tooth ⇨ teeth	woman ⇨ women

WARNING: Some nouns that end in '-s' are uncount nouns, for example 'athletics' and 'physics'. See Unit 6.

3 Count nouns can be used with numbers.

..._one table_... ..._two cats_... ..._three hundred pounds_.

4 Singular count nouns cannot be used alone, but always take a determiner such as 'a', 'another', 'every', or 'the'.

We've killed a pig.
He was eating another apple.
She had read every book on the subject.
I parked the car over there.

5 Plural count nouns can be used with or without a determiner. They do not take a determiner when they refer to things or people in general.

Does the hotel have large rooms?
The film is not suitable for children.

Plural count nouns do take a determiner when they refer precisely to particular things or people.

Our computers are very expensive.
These cakes are delicious.

See Unit 11 for more information on determiners.

6 When a count noun is the subject of a verb, a singular count noun takes a singular verb.

My son likes playing football.
The address on the letter was wrong.

A plural count noun takes a plural verb.

Bigger cars cost more.
I thought more people were coming.

See also Unit 5 on collective nouns.

Unit 4 Practice

A Give the plurals of the following nouns.

cow	_cows_	child	....	tooth	....
glass	....	wish	....	lorry	....
story	....	friend	....	bus	....
tomato	....	parent	....	monkey	....
box	....	piano	....	house	....
mouse	....	key	....	way	....

B Rewrite these sentences in the plural.

1 A train is much quicker than a bus. / ...*Trains are much quicker than buses.*..........

2 A lion is a dangerous animal. / ....

3 A lawyer generally earns more than a teacher. / ....

4 A computer is an expensive piece of equipment. / ....

5 A student has to work hard. / ....

6 A policeman only does what he is told. / ....

7 A cat is supposed to have nine lives. / ....

8 A bus is the best way of getting into town. / ....

9 A woman tends to live longer than a man. / ....

10 A good book helps to pass the time. / ....

C Complete these sentences with a singular or plural count noun.

1 The ...*bus*............ stops right outside our house. (bus / buses)

2 The .... were waiting for me. (child / children)

3 The .... are in the cupboard. (dish / dishes)

4 The .... have gone bad. (tomato / tomatoes)

5 The .... is full. (box / boxes)

6 Do you know the .... that lives next door? (man / men)

7 The .... who were here have gone home. (person / people)

8 The dentist pulled out the .... that was hurting. (tooth / teeth)

9 Have you washed the .... that were in the kitchen? (dish / dishes)

10 Do you know the .... that delivers the newspapers? (boy / boys)

D Complete these sentences with a singular or a plural verb.

1 The children ...*are getting*............ ready for school. (is getting / are getting)

2 My brother .... in the army. (is / are)

3 The cake .... delicious. (smell / smells)

4 The mice .... the cheese. (has eaten / have eaten)

5 The books we bought .... very expensive. (was / were)

6 Did you notice the picture that .... on the wall? (was hanging / were hanging)

7 The young man you met .... to college with my sister. (go / goes)

8 The letters you posted .... wrongly addressed. (was / were)

9 The woman they were meeting .... telephoned to say she can't come. (has / have)

10 Mary and Peter, the couple I met last week, ... invited us to dinner. (has / have)

Unit 5 Singular, plural, and collective nouns

Main points

- Singular nouns are used only in the singular, always with a determiner.
- Plural nouns are used only in the plural, some with a determiner.
- Collective nouns can be used with singular or plural verbs.

1 Some nouns are used in particular meanings in the singular with a determiner, like count nouns, but are not used in the plural with that meaning. They are often called 'singular nouns'.

Some of these nouns are normally used with 'the' because they refer to things that are unique.

air	daytime	moon	sky
country	end	past	sun
countryside	future	sea	wind
dark	ground	seaside	world

The sun was shining.
I am scared of the dark.

Other singular nouns are normally used with 'a' because they refer to things that we usually talk about one at a time.

bath	go	ride	snooze
chance	jog	run	start
drink	move	shower	walk
fight	rest	smoke	wash

I went upstairs and had a wash.
Why don't we go outside for a smoke?

2 Some nouns are used in particular meanings in the plural with or without determiners, like count nouns, but are not used in the singular with that meaning. They are often called 'plural nouns'.

His clothes looked terribly dirty.
Troops are being sent in today.

Some of these nouns are always used with determiners.

activities	feelings	pictures	travels
authorities	likes	sights	

I went to the pictures with Tina.
You hurt his feelings.

Some are usually used without determiners.

airs	goods	riches
expenses	refreshments	

Refreshments are available inside.
They have agreed to pay for travel and expenses.

WARNING: 'Police' is a plural noun, but does not end in '-s'.

The police were informed immediately.

3 A small group of plural nouns refer to single items that have two linked parts. They refer to things that people wear or tools that people use.

glasses	pyjamas	~	scales
jeans	shorts	binoculars	scissors
knickers	tights	pincers	shears
pants	trousers	pliers	tweezers

She was wearing brown trousers.
These scissors are sharp.

You can use 'a pair of' to make it clear you are talking about one item, or a number with 'pairs of' when you are talking about several items.

I was sent out to buy a pair of scissors.
Liza had given me three pairs of jeans.

Note that you also use 'a pair of' with words such as 'gloves', 'shoes', and 'socks' that you often talk about in twos.

4 With some nouns that refer to a group of people or things, the same form can be used with singular or plural verbs, because you can think of the group as a unit or as individuals. Similarly, you can use singular or plural pronouns to refer back to them. These nouns are often called 'collective nouns'.

army	enemy	group	staff
audience	family	herd	team
committee	flock	navy	~
company	gang	press	data
crew	government	public	media

Our little group is complete again.
The largest group are the boys.
Our family isn't poor any more.
My family are perfectly normal.

The names of many organizations and sports teams are also collective nouns, but are normally used with plural verbs in spoken English.

The BBC is showing the programme on Saturday.
The BBC are planning to use the new satellite.
Liverpool is leading 1-0.
Liverpool are attacking again.

Unit 5 Practice

A Use the singular nouns below to complete the sentences which follow.

| a bath | a go | a drink | a fight | a jog | a rest |
| a shower | a move | a walk | a wash | a ride |

1 I need some fresh air. I think I'll go out for …*a walk*……… .
2 I'm going to lie down and have ………………… .
3 I haven't time for ………………… . I'll just have ………………… instead.
4 The children are covered in dirt. They need a ………………… .
5 Can I have ………………… on your bike?
6 He keeps fit by going for ………………… every evening.
7 This is thirsty work. Let's stop for ………………… .
8 Bill's in trouble. He started ………………… and got himself arrested.
9 You can't succeed if you don't have ………………… .
10 It's time to go. Let's make ………………… .

B Use these plural nouns to complete the sentences that follow.

| belongings | clothes | expenses | feelings | goods |
| holidays | papers | pictures | refreshments | sights |

1 If I spend a lot of money, can I claim …*expenses*…………?
2 Britain needs to export more ………………… .
3 There was a short break for ………………… .
4 My ………………… are soaking wet. I need to change.
5 He's very unhappy. You must have hurt his ………………… .
6 The kids aren't at home. They're on their ………………… .
7 What's on at the cinema? I haven't been to the ………………… for ages.
8 You're famous. I saw your picture in the ………………… .
9 He carries all his ………………… with him in an old suitcase.
10 We took some time off to walk round the town and see the ………………… .

C Use these collective nouns to complete the sentences that follow.

| audience | crew | enemy | family | gang | government | media | public | staff | team |

1 Take cover. The …*enemy*………… are attacking.
2 Do you think Liverpool are the best ………………… in Europe?
3 Dad is out but the rest of the ………………… are at home.
4 The ………………… has decided to increase taxes.
5 The ship sank but the ………………… are safe.
6 The office is closed. The ………………… are on strike.
7 The house was surrounded and the ………………… were arrested.
8 The ………………… is much bigger than at last night's performance.
9 The railways should provide a better service for the travelling ………………… .
10 Some sports stars are very badly treated by the newspapers and other ………………… .

▶ **Bank**

Unit 6 Uncount nouns

Main points

- Uncount nouns have only one form, and take a singular verb.
- They are not used with 'a', or with numbers.
- Some nouns can be both uncount nouns and count nouns.

1 English speakers think that some things cannot be counted directly. The nouns which refer to these uncountable things are called uncount nouns. Uncount nouns often refer to:

> **substances:** coal food ice iron rice steel water
> **human qualities:** courage cruelty honesty patience
> **feelings:** anger happiness joy pride relief respect
> **activities:** aid help sleep travel work
> **abstract ideas:** beauty death freedom fun life luck

The donkey needed food and water.
Soon, they lost patience and sent me to Durban.
I was greeted with shouts of joy.
All prices include travel to and from London.
We talked for hours about freedom.

See Unit 4 for information on count nouns.

2 Uncount nouns have only one form. They do not have a plural form.

I needed help with my homework.
The children had great fun playing with the puppets.

WARNING: Some nouns which are uncount nouns in English have plurals in other languages.

> advice   homework   machinery
> baggage   information   money
> equipment   knowledge   news
> furniture   luggage   traffic

We want to spend more money on roads.
Soldiers carried so much equipment that they were barely able to move.

3 Some uncount nouns end in '-s' and therefore look like plural count nouns. They usually refer to:

> **subjects of study:** mathematics physics
> **activities:** athletics gymnastics
> **games:** cards darts
> **illnesses:** measles mumps

Mathematics is too difficult for me.
Measles is in most cases a harmless illness.

4 When an uncount noun is the subject of a verb, it takes a singular verb.

Electricity is dangerous.
Intelligence develops very slowly in these children.
Food was very expensive in those days.

5 Uncount nouns are not used with 'a'.

They resent having to pay money to people like me.
My father started work when he was ten.

Uncount nouns are used with 'the' when they refer to something that is specified or known.

I am interested in the education of young children.
She buried the money that Hilary had given her.
I liked the music, but the words were boring.

6 Uncount nouns are not used with numbers. However, you can often refer to a quantity of something which is expressed by an uncount noun by using a word like 'some'. See Unit 11.

Please buy some bread when you go to town.
Let me give you some advice.

Some uncount nouns that refer to food or drink can be count nouns when they refer to quantities of the food or drink.

Do you like coffee? (uncount)
We asked for two coffees. (count)

Uncount nouns are often used with expressions such as 'a loaf of', 'packets of', or 'a piece of', to talk about a quantity or an item. 'A bit of' is common in spoken English.

I bought two loaves of bread yesterday.
He gave me a very good piece of advice.
They own a bit of land near Cambridge.

7 Some nouns are uncount nouns when they refer to something in general and count nouns when they refer to a particular instance of something.

Victory was now assured. (uncount)
In 1960, the party won a convincing victory. (count)

Unit 6 Practice

A Use these uncount nouns to complete the sentences below.

advice	electricity	equipment	happiness	help
information	knowledge	luggage	money	traffic

1 We've got a lot of ...*luggage*...................... but it's not too heavy.

2 At that time my .... of German was minimal.

3 I'd like some .... about trains, please.

4 They exported a million dollars' worth of stereo ....

5 Do you have any .... on you?

6 If you want my .... , I think you ought to start all over again.

7 There's always a lot of .... in the rush hour.

8 Do you cook by gas or ....?

9 You can always telephone, if you need any ....

10 Money doesn't always bring ....

B Look at the following pairs of sentences. In one the noun in bold is used as a count noun and in the other as an uncount noun. Mark the sentences C for count or U for uncount.

1 Shakespeare's **language** is magnificent. *U*.
  It's easier to work with someone who speaks your own **language**. *C*.

2 She's had nine months' **experience** as a secretary. ....
  The funeral was a painful **experience**. ....

3 People spend their **lives** worrying about money. ....
  How's **life?** ....

4 Are you in San Francisco for **business** or pleasure? ....
  He set up a small travel **business**. ....

5 She never completely gave up **hope**. ....
  Ken has high **hopes** of a promotion before the end of the year. ....

6 There was general **agreement** on the problem. ....
  We hope to come to a general **agreement** on future action. ....

C Use these phrases with **the** and an uncount noun to complete the sentences which follow.

the news about Bill	the furniture in the sitting room	the traffic in London
the advice you gave me	the information you need	the strength to go on

1 I liked ...*the furniture in the sitting room*........... I thought it looked very smart.

2 I'd like to thank you for ....

3 I'm tired out. I haven't got ....

4 You can find .... in any good grammar book.

5 .... is dreadful — particularly in the rush hour.

6 Have you heard ....?

Unit 7 Personal pronouns

Main points

- You use personal pronouns to refer back to something or someone that has already been mentioned.
- You also use personal pronouns to refer to people and things directly.
- There are two sets of personal pronouns: subject pronouns and object pronouns.
- You can use 'you' and 'they' to refer to people in general.

1 When something or someone has already been mentioned, you refer to them again by using a pronoun.

John took the book and opened it.
He rang Mary and invited her to dinner.
'Have you been to London ?'—'Yes, it was very crowded.'
My father is fat — he weighs over fifteen stone.

In English, 'he' and 'she' normally refer to people, occasionally to animals, but very rarely to things.

2 You use a pronoun to refer directly to people or things that are present or are involved in the situation you are in.

Where shall we meet, Sally?
I do the washing; he does the cooking; we share the washing-up.
Send us a card so we 'll know where you are.

3 There are two sets of personal pronouns, subject pronouns and object pronouns. You use subject pronouns as the subject of a verb.

| I | you | he | she | it | we | they |

Note that 'you' is used for the singular and plural form.

We are going there later.
I don't know what to do.

4 You use object pronouns as the direct or indirect object of a verb.

| me | you | him | her | it | us | them |

Note that 'you' is used for the singular and plural form.

The nurse washed me with cold water.
The ball hit her in the face.
John showed him the book.
Can you give me some more cake?

Note that, in modern English, you use object pronouns rather than subject pronouns after the verb 'be'.

'Who is it?' — 'It's me.'
There was only John, Baz, and me in the room.

You also use object pronouns as the object of a preposition.

We were all sitting in a cafe with him.
Did you give it to them?

5 You can use 'you' and 'they' to talk about people in general.

You have to drive on the other side of the road on the continent.
They say she's very clever.

6 You can use 'it' as an impersonal subject in general statements which refer to the time, the date, or the weather. See Unit 86.

'What time is it?' — 'It's half past three.'
It is January 19th.
It is rainy and cold.

You can also use 'it' as the subject or object in general statements about a situation.

It is too far to walk.
I like it here. Can we stay a bit longer?

7 A singular pronoun usually refers back to a singular noun group, and a plural pronoun to a plural noun group. However, you can use plural pronouns to refer back to:

- indefinite pronouns, even though they are always followed by a singular verb

If anybody comes, tell them I'm not in.

- collective nouns, even when you have used a singular verb

His family was waiting in the next room, but they had not yet been informed.

14

Unit 7 Practice

A Complete these sentences by adding the names given.

| Mr Brown   Mr and Mrs Jackson   Mary   Tom and Jane |

1 I spoke to ..... *Mr Brown* .... yesterday. He said he'd call me back.
2 .... says she'll see you tomorrow.
3 .... said we should meet them at their house.
4 Good morning sir. Good morning madam. You must be .... You have
   a reservation, haven't you?

B Now do the same with these.

| Mr Brown   Mr and Mrs Jackson   Mary   Tom and Jane |

1 ..... *Mary* .... 's feeling much better. I spoke to her in the hospital this
   morning.
2 If you see ...., give them my love.
3 .... ? This way please. The room is ready for you.
4 Is .... in ? I have a message for him.

C Look at the picture and add personal pronouns to complete the story.
The other day when I was shopping a woman stopped ..... *me* .... and asked .... the way to
the post office. .... gave her directions and .... thanked .... politely, then
ran off quickly in the opposite direction. .... put my hand in my pocket and found that my
wallet was missing. .... must have taken it while .... were talking. ....
shouted and ran after .... but .... was no good. .... had disappeared in
the crowd.

Unit 8 This, that, these, those, one, ones

Main points

- You use the demonstrative pronouns 'this', 'that', 'these', and 'those' when you are pointing to physical objects or identifying people.
- You use 'one' or 'ones' instead of a noun that has been mentioned or is known.

1 You use the demonstrative pronouns 'this', 'that', 'these', and 'those' when you are pointing to physical objects. 'This' and 'these' refer to things near you, 'that' and 'those' refer to things farther away.

This is a list of rules.
'I brought you these'. Adam held out a bag of grapes.
That looks interesting.
Those are mine.

You can also use 'this', 'that', 'these', and 'those' as determiners in front of nouns. See Unit 11.

This book was a present from my mother.
When did you buy that hat?

2 You use 'this', 'that', 'these', and 'those' when you are identifying or introducing people, or asking who they are.

Who's this?
These are my children, Susan and Paul.
Was that Patrick on the phone?

3 You use 'this', 'that', 'these', and 'those' to refer back to things that have already been mentioned.

That was an interesting word you used just now.
More money is being pumped into the education system, and we assume this will continue.
'Let's go to the cinema.' — 'That's a good idea'.
These are not easy questions to answer.

You also use 'this' and 'these' to refer forward to things you are going to mention.

This is what I want to say: it wasn't my idea.
These are the topics we will be looking at next week: how the accident happened, whether it could have been avoided, and who was to blame.

This is the important point: you must never see her again.

4 You use 'one' or 'ones' instead of a noun that has already been mentioned or is known in the situation, usually when you are adding information or contrasting two things of the same kind.

My car is the blue one.
Don't you have one with buttons instead of a zip?
Are the new curtains longer than the old ones?

You can use 'which one' or 'which ones' in questions.

Which one do you prefer?
Which ones were damaged?

You can say 'this one', 'that one', 'these ones', and 'those ones'.

I like this one better.
We'll have those ones, thank you.

You can use 'each one' or 'one each', but note that there is a difference in meaning. In the following examples, 'each one' means 'each brother' but 'one each' means 'one for each child'.

I've got three brothers and each one lives in a different country.
I bought the children one each.

5 In formal English, people sometimes use 'one' to refer to people in general.

One has to think of the practical side of things.
One never knows what to say in such situations.

6 There are several other types of pronoun, which are dealt with in other units.
See Unit 27 for information on possessive pronouns.
See Unit 51 for information on 'who', 'whom', 'whose', 'which', and 'what' as interrogative pronouns.
See Units 97 and 98 for information on 'that', 'which', 'who', 'whom', and 'whose' as relative pronouns.
Most determiners, except 'the', 'a', 'an', 'every', 'no', and the possessives, are also pronouns. See Units 15 to 18.

Unit 8 Practice

A Each of the pronouns in bold below refers back to a clause. Underline the clause in each case.

1 <u>I'm tired out.</u> **That**'s why I'm going home early.

2 He's always complaining and **this** is why nobody likes him.

3 **That**'s why George was so pleased with himself. He had just got a new job.

4 I've mended the radiator. I hope **this** will solve the problem.

5 Finally, Mary told him she was tired of him. I think **that**'s what really annoyed him.

6 George likes Mary, but she doesn't like him. **That**'s what annoys him.

7 The engine's all right but the brakes are useless. **That**'s why it needs to go into the garage.

8 Even when they go to bed late the children sometimes stay awake all night. **That**'s why they get so tired.

9 The traffic was dreadful even though we left home early. **That**'s why we're late.

10 The engine starts and after a few seconds the light goes on. **That**'s when you press the button.

B Look at the picture and complete the answers to these questions using **one** or **ones**.

1 How many cars are there?

 Five. Three big ....*ones*......... and two small ....*ones*............ .

2 What colour are they?

 There are three white .... and two black ....

3 How many small cars are there?

 Two. A black .... and a white..................... .

4 How many big cars are there?

 Three. Two white .... and one black ....

5 Where is the small white car?

 Between the small black .... and the big black ....

C Here is a puzzle.

There are some books on a shelf. There are three big ones and two small ones. One of the big ones is red. There is a small green book. There are two green ones altogether and two blue ones. Only one of the small books is green.

1 How many books are there altogether? ....

2 What colour are the big books? ....

3 What colour are the small ones? ....

Unit 9 Reflexive pronouns

Main points

- Reflexive pronouns can be direct or indirect objects.
- Most transitive verbs can take a reflexive pronoun as object.
- Reflexive pronouns can be the object of a preposition.
- Reflexive pronouns can emphasize a noun or pronoun.

1 The reflexive pronouns are:

singular: myself yourself himself herself itself **plural:** ourselves yourselves themselves

Note that, unlike 'you' and 'your', there are two forms for the second person: 'yourself' in the singular and 'yourselves' in the plural.

2 You use reflexive pronouns as the direct or indirect object of the verb when you want to say that the object is the same person or thing as the subject of the verb in the same clause.
For example, 'John taught himself' means that John did the teaching and was also the person who was taught, and 'Ann poured herself a drink' means that Ann did the pouring and was also the person that the drink was poured for.

She stretched herself out on the sofa.
The men formed themselves into a line.
He should give himself more time.

Note that although the subject 'you' is omitted in imperatives, you can still use 'yourself' or 'yourselves'.

Here's the money, go and buy yourself an ice cream.

3 Most transitive verbs can take a reflexive pronoun.

I blame myself for not paying attention.
He introduced himself to me.

WARNING: Verbs which describe actions that people normally do to themselves do not take reflexive pronouns in English, although they do in some other languages.

I usually shave before breakfast.
She washed very quickly and rushed downstairs.

See Unit 74 for more information.

4 You use a reflexive pronoun as the object of a preposition when the object of the preposition refers to the same person or thing as the subject of the verb in the same clause.

I was thoroughly ashamed of myself.
They are making fools of themselves.
Tell me about yourself.

Note that you use personal pronouns, not reflexive pronouns, when referring to places and after 'with' meaning 'accompanied by'.

You should have your notes in front of you.
He would have to bring Judy with him.

5 You use reflexive pronouns after nouns or pronouns to emphasize the person or thing that you are referring to.

The town itself was so small that it didn't have a bank.
I myself have never read the book.

6 You use a reflexive pronoun at the end of a clause to emphasize that someone did something without any help from anyone else.

She had printed the card herself.
I'll take it down to the police station myself.
Did you make these yourself?

7 You use reflexive pronouns with 'by' to say:

- that someone does something without any help from other people

...when babies start eating their meals by themselves.
She was certain she could manage by herself.

- that someone is alone

He went off to sit by himself.
I was there for about six months by myself.

You can also use 'on my own', 'on your own', and so on, to say that someone is alone or does something without any help.

We were in the park on our own.
They managed to reach the village on their own.

You can use 'all' for emphasis.

Did you put those shelves up all by yourself?
We can't solve this problem all on our own.

WARNING: 'One another' and 'each other' are not reflexive pronouns.

See Unit 75 for more information on 'one another' and 'each other'.

Unit 9 Practice

A Choose a personal pronoun or a reflexive pronoun to complete these sentences correctly.

1 He was tired out but he forced ....*himself*................ to go on.
2 I could hear someone walking along behind ...*me*...................... .
3 She had cut .... so badly she had to be rushed to hospital.
4 She realised that the car in front of .... had stopped suddenly.
5 They built .... a garage behind the house.
6 He boiled .... a couple of eggs for breakfast.
7 Put it down in front of ....
8 If you've got a sleeping bag bring it with ....
9 They had promised .... a summer holiday abroad.
10 On Sunday mornings the children were left to take care of ....

B Change the phrases **on my own** etc to **by myself** etc.

1 It looked extremely heavy. I knew I couldn't lift it **on my own.** / ...*by myself*................... .
2 She hated being in the house **on her own.** / ....
3 If the rest of you can't help we'll have to do it **on our own.** / ....
4 You can't expect them to do everything **on their own.** / ....
5 Mothers had to go out to work and leave children in the house **on their own.** / ....
   ....
6 If there are three of you, you should be able to manage **on your own.** / ....
7 I hate living **on my own.** / ....
8 It's a horror film so children aren't allowed to see it **on their own.** / ....
9 John had to walk home **on his own.** / ....
10 It's too difficult for me. I can't do it all **on my own.** / ....

C Use the correct reflexive pronouns to complete the following sentences.

1 The chairman announced the news ...*himself*...................... .
2 Helen will be very upset. I'll have to tell her the news ....
3 We built most of the house ....
4 The president .... appeared on television. She spoke for about ten minutes.
5 The children .... did most of the work for the school play.

D Rewrite the following sentences to start with the words given.

1 It was the BBC correspondent himself who told me. / I was told ...*by the BBC correspondent*....
   himself................................
2 The Chief of Police himself made the arrest. / It was ....
3 This picture can't have been painted by Rembrandt himself. / It can't have been ....
   ....
4 There can be no doubt that Shakespeare himself wrote this play. / There can be no doubt that this
   play ....
5 The captain himself scored the winning goal. / It was ....

▶ **Bank**   19

Unit 10 Indefinite pronouns

Main points

- Indefinite pronouns refer to people or things without saying exactly who or what they are.
- When an indefinite pronoun is the subject, it always takes a singular verb.
- You often use a plural pronoun to refer back to an indefinite pronoun.

1 The indefinite pronouns are:

anybody	everybody	nobody	somebody
anyone	everyone	no one	someone
anything	everything	nothing	something

Note that 'no one' is written as two words, or sometimes with a hyphen: 'no-one'.

2 You use indefinite pronouns when you want to refer to people or things without saying exactly who or what they are. The pronouns ending in '-body' and '-one' refer to people, and those ending in '-thing' refer to things.

I was there for over an hour before <u>anybody</u> came.
It had to be <u>someone</u> with a car.
Jane said <u>nothing</u> for a moment.

3 When an indefinite pronoun is the subject, it always takes a singular verb, even when it refers to more than one person or thing.

<u>Everyone knows</u> that.
<u>Everything was</u> fine.
<u>Is anybody</u> there?

When you refer back to indefinite pronouns, you use plural pronouns or possessives, and a plural verb.

Ask <u>anyone</u>. <u>They</u> 'll tell you.
Has <u>everyone</u> eaten as much as <u>they</u> want?
You can't tell <u>somebody</u> why <u>they</u>'ve failed.

WARNING: Some speakers prefer to use singular pronouns. They prefer to say 'You can't tell somebody why he or she has failed'.

4 You can add apostrophe s ('s) to indefinite pronouns that refer to people.
She was given a room in <u>someone's</u> studio.
That was <u>nobody's</u> business but mine.

WARNING: You do not usually add apostrophe s ('s) to indefinite pronouns that refer to things. You do not say 'something's value', you say 'the value of something'.

5 You use indefinite pronouns beginning with 'some-' in:

- affirmative clauses

<u>Somebody</u> shouted.
I want to introduce you to <u>someone</u>.

- questions expecting the answer 'yes'

Would you like <u>something</u> to drink?
Can you get <u>someone</u> to do it?

6 You use indefinite pronouns beginning with 'any-':

- as the subject or object in statements

<u>Anyone</u> knows that you need a licence.
You still haven't told me <u>anything</u>.
I haven't given <u>anyone</u> their presents yet.

You do not use them as the subject of a negative statement. You do not say 'Anybody can't come in'.

- in both affirmative and negative questions

Does <u>anybody</u> agree with me?
Won't <u>anyone</u> help me?

7 If you use an indefinite pronoun beginning with 'no-', you must not use another negative word in the same clause. You do not say 'There wasn't nothing'.

There was <u>nothing</u> you could do.
<u>Nobody</u> left, <u>nobody</u> went away.

8 You use the indefinite adverbs 'anywhere', 'everywhere', 'nowhere', and 'somewhere' to talk about places in a general way. 'Nowhere' makes a clause negative.

I thought I'd seen you <u>somewhere</u>.
No-one can find Howard or Barbara <u>anywhere</u>.
There was <u>nowhere</u> to hide.

9 You can use 'else' after indefinite pronouns and adverbs to refer to people, things, or places other than those that have been mentioned.

Everyone <u>else</u> is downstairs.
I don't like it here. Let's go <u>somewhere else</u>.

Unit 10 Practice

A Complete each of the sentences below by choosing one of the indefinite pronouns in brackets.

1 .....*Everybody*........... arrived in good time and the meeting started promptly at 3.30. (Anybody / / Everybody / Nobody)

2 .... in the village went to the party but .... enjoyed it very much. (Everyone / No one / Someone) (anybody / somebody / nobody)

3 When the show finished there was complete silence. .... clapped. (Everyone / No one / Someone)

4 Mohammed Ali is .... I have always admired. (everybody / nobody / somebody)

5 .... heard anything. (Everyone / Nobody / Somebody)

6 'Who shall I give this one to?' — 'You can give it to .... It doesn't matter.' (anybody / nobody / somebody)

7 That's a very easy job. .... can do it. (Anybody / Nobody / Somebody)

B Complete these sentences using the correct form of the verb in brackets.

1 I don't know why everybody ....*hates*........... me. (hate)

2 Let me know as soon as anyone .... (arrive)

3 Nobody .... being poor. (like)

4 It's no good if everyone .... to get their own way. (want)

5 The house is deserted. Nobody .... there now. (live)

6 If anybody .... , you can tell them I'll be back soon. (ask)

C Complete the following sentences with **they, them,** or **their.**

1 Has everybody collected ....*their*........... luggage?

2 Tell everyone I'll wait for .... here.

3 If somebody had called, ... would have left a message.

4 Nobody offered to help. .... probably didn't have the time.

5 If anybody wants to know, tell .... to phone this number.

D Complete these sentences using **something, nothing, everything,** or **anything.**

1 Excuse me, you've dropped ....*something*........... . Yes, look, it's your passport.

2 I agree with most of what he said, but I don't agree with ....

3 It's all finished. I'm afraid there's .... left.

4 Did you turn the oven off? I think I can smell .... burning.

5 'Can I have whatever I want?' 'Yes, ... you like.'

E Complete the following sentences by using one of the indefinite pronouns given in brackets.

1 The box was completely empty. There was ....*nothing*............... in it. (nothing / anything)

2 I heard a noise, but I didn't see .... (anyone / no one)

3 I'm sorry, but there's .... at home. (anybody / nobody)

4 It's too late. We can't do .... to help. (anything / nothing)

5 No, I don't want ...., thanks. I'm not hungry. (nothing / anything)

6 It was very disappointing. Absolutely .... happened. (anything / nothing)

7 I didn't meet .... new. (anybody / nobody)

8 He claimed to be an expert, but he knew almost .... about it. (anything / nothing)

9 .... knew what to do next. (Anybody / Nobody)

▶ **Bank**

21

Unit 11 Determiners

Main points

- Determiners are used at the beginning of noun groups.
- You use specific determiners when people know exactly which things or people you are talking about.
- You use general determiners to talk about people or things without saying exactly who or what they are.

a	both	few	more	other
all	each	fewer	most	several
an	either	less	much	some
another	enough	little	neither	
any	every	many	no	

1 When you use a determiner, you put it at the beginning of a noun group, in front of numbers or adjectives.

I met the two Swedish girls in London.
Our main bedroom is through that door.
Have you got another red card?
Several young boys were waiting outside.

2 When the people or things that you are talking about have already been mentioned, or the people you are talking to know exactly which ones you mean, you use a specific determiner.

The man began to run towards the boy.
Young people don't like these operas.
Her face was very red.

The specific determiners are:

the definite article: the
demonstratives: this that these those
possessives: my your his her its our their

Note that 'your' is used both for the singular and plural possessive.
See Unit 8 for 'this', 'that', 'these', and 'those' as pronouns.

3 When you are mentioning people or things for the first time, or talking about them generally without saying exactly which ones you mean, you use a general determiner.

There was a man in the lift.
We went to an art exhibition.
You can stop at any time you like.
There were several reasons for this.

The general determiners are:

4 Each general determiner is used with particular types of noun. You use some general determiners with:

- singular count nouns

a	another	each	every	no
an	any	either	neither	

I got a postcard from Susan.
Any big tin container will do.
He opened another shop last month.

- plural count nouns

all	enough	many	no	some
any	few	more	other	
both	fewer	most	several	

There were few doctors available.
He spoke many different languages.
Several projects had to be postponed.

- uncount nouns

all	enough	little	most	no
any	less	more	much	some

There was little applause.
We need more information
He did not speak much English.

WARNING: The following general determiners can never be used with uncount nouns.

a	both	every	neither
an	each	few	several
another	either	many	

5 Most of the determiners are also pronouns, except 'the', 'a', 'an', 'every', 'no' and the possessives.

I saw several in the woods last night.
Have you got any that I could borrow?
There is enough for all of us.

You use 'one' as a pronoun instead of 'a' or 'an', 'none' instead of 'no', and 'each' instead of 'every'.

Have you got one?
There are none left.
Each has a separate box and number.

Unit 11 Practice

A Underline the determiners in the following sentences. The numbers in brackets tell you how many determiners there are.

1 <u>My</u> friend Alec works in <u>a</u> hotel on <u>the</u> corner of <u>this</u> street. (4)

2 There weren't many people at the match. But it was very exciting and our team scored twice in each half. (4)

3 Would you like another piece of this cake, or would you prefer a chocolate biscuit? (3)

4 Most young people like this sort of music. (2)

5 Every child at the party was given a present to take home. (3)

6 Thank you for your letter and the lovely flowers. (2)

7 We live in a small village in the country. It's a quiet, comfortable place with several useful shops. (4)

8 I hope to spend another month in your country sometime this summer. (3)

9 There was little information at the airport. Few people seemed to have any idea what time the flight was likely to leave. (5)

10 Can you give me another call at the office? I don't have much time to spare right now. (3)

B Now do these. Remember that a determiner comes at the front of a noun phrase.

1 <u>These</u> oranges cost ten pence each. (1)

2 Each orange costs ten pence. (1)

3 A: Is this your coat? (1)

   B: No, I'm fairly sure it belongs to that man over there in the corner. I left my coat in the cloakroom. (4)

4 Most students read both books, but they didn't find either very useful. (2)

5 There were several people at the meeting earlier, but most of them left early so there aren't many left now. (2)

6 This is what I always have for my breakfast. (1)

7 If I haven't any books, I can't do my homework. (2)

8 There's another bottle of milk in the fridge. Help yourself to a glass if you'd like some. (3)

9 Have you finished that glass of milk? There's plenty more in the fridge if you'd like another. (2)

10 Most people enjoyed the show, but I was definitely the one who enjoyed it most. (3)

Unit 12 Main uses of 'the'

Main points

- You can use 'the' in front of any noun.
- You use 'the' when the person you are talking to knows which person or thing you mean.
- You use 'the' when you are referring back to someone or something.
- You use 'the' when you are specifying which person or thing you are talking about.
- You use 'the' when you are referring to something that is unique.
- You use 'the' when you want to use one thing as an example to say something about all things of the same type.

1 'The' is called the definite article, and is the commonest determiner. You use 'the' when the person you are talking to knows which person or thing you mean. You can use 'the' in front of any noun, whether it is a singular count noun, an uncount noun, or a plural count noun.

She dropped the can.
I remembered the fun I had with them.
The girls were not at home.

2 You use 'the' with a noun when you are referring back to someone or something that has already been mentioned.

I called for a waiter... ...The waiter with a moustache came.
I have bought a house in Wales... ...The house is in an agricultural area.

3 You use 'the' with a noun and a qualifier, such as a prepositional phrase or a relative clause, when you are specifying which person or thing you are talking about.

I've no idea about the geography of Scotland.
The book that I recommended now costs over three pounds.

4 You use 'the' with a noun when you are referring to something of which there is only one in the world.

They all sat in the sun.
We have landed men on the moon.
The sky was a brilliant blue.

You also use 'the' when you are referring to something of which there is only one in a particular place.

Mrs Robertson heard that the church had been bombed.
He decided to put some words on the blackboard.

5 You can use 'the' with a singular count noun when you want to make a general statement about all things of that type. For example, if you say 'The whale is the largest mammal in the world', you mean all whales, not one particular whale.

The computer allows us to deal with a lot of data very quickly.
My father's favourite flower is the rose.

6 You can use 'the' with a singular count noun when you are referring to a system or service. For example, you can use 'the phone' to refer to a telephone system and 'the bus' to refer to a bus service.

I don't like using the phone.
How long does it take on the train?

7 You can use 'the' with the name of a musical instrument when you are talking about someone's ability to play the instrument.

'You play the guitar, I see,' said Simon.
Geoff plays the piano very well.

Unit 12 Practice

A Read this passage.

Three learned Christian monks were travelling through Turkey hoping to meet (1) **the** wisest **man** in (2) **the** whole **country**. (3) **The monks** explained that they wanted to meet him because they each had a question to ask him. (4) **The sultan** sent for Nasreddin Hodja who came to (5) **the palace** at once. (6) **The** first **monk** stepped up and asked his question.

'Where is (7) **the centre** of (8) **the earth?'** 'At this moment the centre of the earth is exactly below (9) **the** front right **foot** of my donkey.'

'How can you possibly know that?' asked (10) **the monk**.

'If you measure the earth carefully you will find that I am correct,' replied Hodja.

(11) **The** second **monk** stepped up and asked his question.

'How many stars are there in (12) **the sky?'**

'As many as there are hairs on my donkey,' replied Hodja. 'As you will see if you count them.'

(13) **The** third **monk** came forward. 'How many hairs are there in my beard?' he asked.

'That is easy,' said Hodja. 'As many as there are hairs in (14) **the** donkey's **tail**. If you do not believe me step forward and we can pull out (15) **the hairs** from your beard and (16) **the hairs** from (17) **the** donkey's **tail** one by one and count them.'

The third monk was not very keen on this idea so he had to admit he was beaten, so everyone could see that Hodja was (18) **the** wisest **man** of all.

Look at the 18 phrases with **the** above. How do you know in each case which person or thing the writer is talking about?

Now answer these questions:
1 Which man? ....*The wisest man.*...
2 Which country? ....
3 Which monks? ....
4 Which sultan? ....
5 Which palace? ....
6 Which monk? ....
7 Which centre? ....
9 Which foot? ....
10 Which monk? ....
11 Which monk? ....
13 Which monk? ....
14 Which donkey? ....
15 Which hairs? ....
16 Which hairs? ....
17 Which tail? ....

What about (8), (12), and (18)? How do you know which one the writer means in each case?
8 ....
12 ....
18 ....

▶ **Bank**

Unit 13 Other uses of 'the'

Main points

- You do not normally use 'the' with proper nouns referring to people. You do use 'the' with many proper nouns referring to geographical places.
- You use 'the' with some adjectives to talk about groups of people.

1 You do not normally use 'the' with proper nouns that are people's names. However, if you are talking about a family, you can say 'the Browns'.
You use 'the' with some titles, such as 'the Queen of England', and with the names of some organizations, buildings, newspapers, and works of art.

… _the_ United Nations… … _the_ Taj Mahal…
… _the_ Times… … _the_ Mona Lisa.

2 You do use 'the' with some proper nouns referring to geographical places.

… _the_ Bay of Biscay… … _the_ Suez Canal.
… _the_ Arabian Gulf… … _the_ Pacific Ocean.

You use 'the' with countries whose names include words such as 'kingdom', 'republic', 'states', or 'union'.

… _the_ United Kingdom… … _the_ Soviet Union.

You use 'the' with countries that have plural nouns as their names.

… _the_ Netherlands… … _the_ Philippines.

Note that you do not use 'the' with countries that have singular nouns as their names, such as 'China', 'Italy', or 'Turkey'.
You use 'the' with names of mountain ranges and groups of islands.

… _the_ Alps… … _the_ Himalayas.
… _the_ Bahamas… … _the_ Canaries.

Note that you do not use 'the' with the names of individual mountains such as 'Everest' or 'Etna', or the names of individual islands such as 'Sicily', 'Minorca', or 'Bali'.
You use 'the' with regions of the world, or regions of a country that include 'north', 'south', 'east', or 'west'.

… _the_ Middle East… … _the_ Far East.
… _the_ north of England… … _the_ west of Ireland.

Note that there are some exceptions.

… North America… … South-East Asia… … East Anglia.

You do not use 'the' with 'northern', 'southern', 'eastern', or 'western' and a singular name.

… _northern_ England… … _western_ Africa.

You use 'the' with the names of areas of water such as seas, oceans, rivers, canals, gulfs, and straits.

… _the_ Mediterranean Sea… … _the_ Atlantic Ocean.
… _the_ river Ganges… … _the_ Panama Canal.
… _the_ Gulf of Mexico… … _the_ straits of Gibraltar.

Note that you do not use 'the' with lakes.

… _Lake Geneva… … Lake Superior._

Note that you do not use 'the' with continents, cities, streets, or addresses.

… _Asia… … Tokyo… … Oxford Street… … 15 Park Street._

3 You use 'the' with adjectives such as 'rich', 'poor', 'young', 'old', and 'unemployed' to talk about a general group of people. You do not need a noun.

Only the rich could afford his firm's products.
They were discussing the problem of the unemployed.

When you use 'the' with an adjective as the subject of a verb, you use a plural verb.

In the cities the poor are as badly off as they were in the villages.

4 You use 'the' with some nationality adjectives to talk about the people who live in a country.

They will be increasingly dependent on the support of the French.
The Spanish claimed that the money had not been paid.

With other nationalities, you use a plural noun.

… _Germans… … the Americans._

When you use 'the' with a nationality adjective as the subject of a verb, you use a plural verb.

The British are worried.

5 You use 'the' with superlatives.

He was the cleverest man I ever knew.
He was the youngest.
His shoulders hurt the worst.
It was the most exciting summer of their lives.

Unit 13 Practice

A In each of the following sentences the word **the** has been left out at least once. Read the sentences and mark where **the** should be. The number in brackets tells you how many times **the** occurs. In 1, for example, you need to put **the** in twice.

1 I have been to ⌃*the* United Kingdom, Germany, and ⌃*the* Soviet Union, but never to Poland. (2)

2 Amazon in Brazil is the longest river in South America. (1)

3 Japan and United States are separated by Pacific Ocean. (2)

4 Liverpool is in north of England, fairly close to Wales. (1)

5 I would love to go to Jamaica, Bahamas or somewhere else in Caribbean. (2)

6 Suez Canal flows through north of Egypt from Port Said to Suez, joining Mediterranean to Gulf of Suez and Red Sea. (5)

7 Lake Windermere in north-west of England is one of the largest lakes in British Isles. (2)

8 Iran has borders with Iraq, Turkey, USSR, Afghanistan and West Pakistan. (1)

9 Mount Everest is in Himalayas on the border between Nepal and Tibet, which is part of People's Republic of China. (2)

10 Biarritz stands on the mouth of Adour river which flows into Gulf of Gascony in Bay of Biscay. (3)

B Now do the same with these sentences.

1 While we were in London we stayed at ⌃*the* Royal Hotel in Albert Street near Trafalgar Square. (1)

2 On the first morning we went to British Museum and had lunch at MacDonald's in Church Street. (1)

3 In the evening we went to a pub just off Leicester Square, then we went to a play at National Theatre. (1)

4 Next day we went to Houses of Parliament and Westminster Abbey and had lunch at Peking Restaurant. (2)

5 We looked in Evening Standard newspaper and found there was a good film at Odeon cinema near Piccadilly Circus. (2)

C Complete the sentences below using **the** with these adjectives.

blind dead disabled poor rich unemployed

1 It is said that we should never speak ill of ...*the dead*....................... .

2 Buildings should be specially designed so they can be used by ....

3 It is only fair that .... should pay higher taxes than ....
....

4 In St John's Park there is a special garden for .... with strongly scented flowers.

5 Life is bound to be difficult for ....

Unit 14 'A' and 'an'

Main points

- You only use 'a' or 'an' with singular count nouns.
- You use 'a' or 'an' to talk about a person or thing for the first time.

1 You only use 'a' or 'an' with singular count nouns. 'A' and 'an' are called the indefinite article.

I got a postcard from Susan.
He was eating an apple.

Remember that you use 'a' in front of a word that begins with a consonant sound even if the first letter is a vowel, for example 'a piece, a university, a European language'. You use 'an' in front of a word that begins with a vowel sound even if the first letter is a consonant, for example 'an exercise, an idea, an honest man'.

2 You use 'a' or 'an' when you are talking about a person or thing for the first time.

She picked up a book.
After weeks of looking, we eventually bought a house.
A colleague and I got some money to do research on rats.

Note that the second time you refer to the same person or thing, you use 'the'.

She picked up a book... ... The book was lying on the table.
After weeks of looking, we eventually bought a house... ... The house was in a small village.

3 After the verb 'be' or another link verb, you can use 'a' or 'an' with an adjective and a noun to give more information about someone or something.

His brother was a sensitive child.
He seemed a worried man.
It was a really beautiful house.

You can also use 'a' or 'an' with a noun followed by a qualifier, such as a prepositional phrase or a relative clause, when you want to give more information about someone or something.

The information was contained in an article on biology.
I chose a picture that reminded me of my own country.

4 You use 'a' or 'an' after the verb 'be' or another link verb when you are saying what someone is or what job they have

He became a school teacher.
She is a model and an artist.

5 You use 'a' or 'an' to mean 'one' with some numbers. You can use 'a' or 'an' with nouns that refer to whole numbers, fractions, money, weights, or measures.

a hundred	a quarter	a pound	a kilo
a thousand	a half	a dollar	a litre

6 You do not use 'a' or 'an' with uncount nouns or plural count nouns. You do not need to use a determiner at all with plural count nouns, but you can use the determiners 'any' 'a few', 'many', 'several', or 'some'.

I love dogs.
Do you have any dogs?
Many adults don't listen to children.
I have some children like that in my class.

Note that if you do not use a determiner with a plural count noun, you are often making a general statement about people or things of that type. For example, if you say 'I love dogs', you mean all dogs. However, if you say 'There are eggs in the kitchen', you mean there are some eggs. If you do use a determiner, you mean a number of people or things but not all of them, without saying exactly how many.

I have some friends coming for dinner.
He has bought some plants for the house.
I have some important things to tell them.

Unit 14 Practice

A Rewrite the sentences using singular nouns with **a** or **an** instead of the plural nouns in bold.

1 **Dogs** make good **pets.** / ...*A dog makes a good pet.*...

2 **Lawyers** usually earn more than **policemen.** / ....

3 I love reading good **books.** / ....

4 You don't often see good **programmes** on TV nowadays. / ....

5 **Sons** are always a lot more trouble than **daughters.** / ....

6 I often have **eggs** for breakfast. / ....

7 Nowadays you can buy computer-controlled **washing machines.** / ....

8 I hate to hear **babies** crying or **dogs** barking. / ....

B Where you find a noun phrase with a singular count noun but no determiner, put in **a** or **an**.

1 In English *a* noun phrase with *a* singular count noun can hardly ever stand on its own.

2 We have just bought new house with large garden.

3 My brother is teacher and I have cousin who works with young children as well.

4 Would you like biscuit or piece of cake?

5 I spoke to official and he gave me very good advice.

C Look at the following pairs of sentences. For each pair fill one blank with **a** or **an,** and the other with **the**.

1 I wrote ...*a*.......... long letter to Jenny this morning.
Did I show you ....*the*....... letter I got from Peter this morning?

2 My uncle used to be .... dentist before he retired.
Arthur Brown is .... dentist who lives next door to my parents.

3 Is there .... bookshop on the High Street?
I bought this at .... bookshop in the High Street.

4 Has anyone seen .... newspaper I left in the sitting room?
I usually buy .... newspaper on my way to work.

5 London is easily .... biggest city in Britain.
Manchester is .... big city in the north of England.

6 It's not easy to learn .... foreign language which is very different from your own language.
Japanese is certainly .... most difficult language I have tried to learn.

7 Agatha Christie was .... well known writer of detective stories.
Agatha Christie was .... writer who invented Hercule Poirot.

8 The police are looking for .... young man aged about 23.
.... young man the police are looking for is about 23.

9 Last night I saw .... interesting TV programme about Eastern Europe.
I really enjoyed .... programme about Eastern Europe last night.

10 I learned to drive .... car when I was eighteen.
Dad, can I borrow ....car tonight?

▶ **Bank**

Unit 15 All, most, no, none

Main points

- You use 'all' with plural count nouns and uncount nouns. You use 'all' to talk about every person or thing in the world, or in the group you are talking about.
- You use 'most' with plural count nouns and uncount nouns. You use 'most' to talk about nearly all of a number of people or things, or nearly all of a quantity of something.
- You use 'no' with singular and plural count nouns and uncount nouns. You use 'no' to say that something does not exist or is not present.

1 You use 'all' with plural count nouns and uncount nouns to talk about every person or thing in the world or in the group that you are talking about.

All children should complete the primary course.
All important decisions were taken by the government.
He soon lost all hope of becoming a rock star.
All luggage will be searched.

2 You use 'most' with plural count nouns and uncount nouns to talk about nearly all of a number of people or things, or nearly all of a quantity of something.

The method was suitable for most purposes.
Most good drivers stop at zebra crossings.
Most milk is still delivered to people's houses.
He ignored most advice, and did what he thought best.

3 You use 'no' with singular count nouns, plural count nouns, and uncount nouns to say that something does not exist or is not present.

There was no chair for me to sit on.
They had no immediate plans to change house.
No money was available for the operation.

Note that if there is another word in the clause that makes it negative, you use 'any', not 'no'.

It hasn't made any difference.
He will never do any work for me again.

4 'All' and 'most' are also pronouns, so you can say 'all of' and 'most of'. 'No' is not a pronoun, so you must say 'none of'.

He spent all of the money on a new car.
Most of my friends live in London.
None of those farmers had ever driven a tractor.

Note that you use 'all of', 'most of', and 'none of' with an object pronoun.

All of us were sleeping.
I had seen most of them before.
None of them came to the party.

Note that if the clause is already negative, you use 'any of', not 'none of'.

I hadn't eaten any of the biscuits.

When 'none of' is followed by a plural noun or pronoun, the verb is usually plural, but can be singular.

None of us are the same.

None of them has lasted very long.

5 You can use 'all the' with a plural count noun or an uncount noun. There is no difference in meaning between 'all the' and 'all of the'.

All the girls think it's great.
All the best jokes came at the end of the programme.
Thank you for all the help you gave me.

WARNING: You cannot say 'most the' or 'none the'. You must say 'most of the' or 'none of the'.

6 You can use 'all' after a noun or pronoun to emphasize that the noun or pronoun refers to everyone or everything that has been mentioned or is involved. Note that you can use 'all' to emphasize the subject or the object.

The band all live together in the same house.
I enjoyed it all.

Unit 15 Practice

A Use the phrases below to complete the sentences which follow.

> all alcoholic drinks   all banks   all cars   all children   all doctors   all old people

1 .....*All children*..................... must go to school until the age of 16.
2 .... must be licensed.
3 .... receive a pension from the state.
4 There is a tax on ....
5 .... are closed on Sunday.
6 .... must have at least five years' training.

All these sentences are true for Britain. How many are true for your country?

B Choose phrases from the list to say where you might see the notices given below.

> at an airport   in a bank   in a hotel   at a railway station
> in a department store in a library in a park   in a restaurant

1 All dogs must be kept on a lead. ....*In a park.*....................................
2 All books must be returned within three weeks. ....
3 All customers should wait to be seated. ....
4 All goods must be taken to the cash desk. ....
5 All luggage must be checked at the security desk. ....
6 All traveller's cheques must be signed and dated. ....
7 All passengers must have a valid ticket. ....
8 All bills must be paid before guests check out. ....

C Rewrite the following sentences using **all of** or **most of.**
1 The children were all fast asleep. / ...*All of the children were fast asleep.*.............
2 The children were nearly all fast asleep. / ....
3 Nearly all the students passed the exam. / ....
4 All my friends came to the party. / ....
5 The clothes were all very expensive. / ....
6 Nearly all the seats were booked. / ....
7 The ice cream was nearly all finished. / ....
8 The garden was nearly all full of weeds. / ....

D Rewrite these sentences using **no.**
1 I haven't any free time this week. / ...*I have no free time this week.*.................
2 John didn't have any money left. / ....
3 He hasn't any friends. / ....
4 There isn't any milk in the fridge. / ....
5 We didn't get any letters today. / ....
6 There weren't any girls in the class. / ....

▶ **Bank**

Unit 16 Both, either, neither

Main points

- You use 'both', 'either', and 'neither' to talk about two people or things that have been mentioned or are known to the hearer.
- You use 'both' with plural nouns, and 'either' and 'neither' with singular nouns.
- You use 'both of', 'either of', and 'neither of' with plural nouns or pronouns.

1 You use 'both', 'either', and 'neither' when you are saying something about two people or things that have been mentioned, or are known to the person you are talking to.

There were excellent performances from both actresses.
Denis held his cocoa in both hands.
No argument could move either man from this decision.
Neither report mentioned the Americans.

2 You use 'both' when you think of the two people or things as a group. You use 'both' with a plural noun.

Both children were happy with their presents.
Both policies make good sense.

3 You use 'either' when you think of the two people or things as individuals. You use 'either' with a singular noun.

Either way is acceptable.
She could not see either man.

4 You use 'neither' when you are thinking of the two people or things as individuals and you are making a negative statement about them. You use 'neither' with a singular noun.

In reality, neither party was enthusiastic.
Neither man knew what he was doing.

5 You can use 'both' with a specific determiner such as 'the', 'these', or 'my'.

Both the young men agreed to come.
Both these books have been recommended to us.
Both her parents were dead.

WARNING: You cannot use 'either' or 'neither' with a specific determiner.

6 You can use 'both of', 'either of', or 'neither of' with a plural noun or pronoun. Note that when 'both of', 'either of', and 'neither of' are followed by a noun rather than a pronoun, you must use a specific determiner such as 'the', 'these', or 'her' before the noun.

Both of these restaurants are excellent.
Either of them could have done the job.
Neither of our boys was involved.

Note that 'neither of' is normally used with a singular verb but it can be used with a plural verb.

Neither of us was having any luck.
Neither of the children were there.

7 Remember that you can also use 'both', 'either', and 'neither' as conjunctions. You use 'both...and' to give two alternatives and say that each of them is possible or true.

I am looking for opportunities both in this country and abroad.
Both I and my wife were surprised to see you there.

You use 'either...or' to give two alternatives and say that only one of them is possible or true.

You can have either fruit or ice cream.
I was expecting you either today or tomorrow.
You either love him or hate him.

You also use 'neither...nor' to give two alternatives and say that each of them is not possible or is not true.

Neither Margaret nor John was there.
He did it neither quickly nor well.

Unit 16 Practice

A Choose the correct form of the verb in brackets to complete these sentences.

1 Both my brothers ......*live*............ in London. (lives / live)

2 Neither of his parents .... alive. (is / are)

3 Neither John nor Mary .... at home. (was / were)

4 We both .... football but neither of us .... tennis. (likes / like)

5 Both Peter and Michael .... here quite often but neither of them .... us much help. (comes / come) (gives / give)

6 Both of us .... been to Paris but neither of us .... been to Rome. (has / have)

B Which of the cities below do the following sentences refer to?

| London   Milan   New York   Rome   Washington |

1 Neither is a capital city. ...*Milan and New York.*...

2 Both of them are in America. ....

3 None of them is in America. ....

4 All of them are capital cities. ....

5 They are both in Italy. ....

6 They are all in Europe. ....

C Complete the sentences about the cities, choosing suitable phrases from the table below.

All Neither Both None	of them	is are

1 Birmingham and Manchester.
   ...*Both of them are*................ in Britain. / ...*Neither of them is*................ in Asia.

2 Valencia and Hiroshima.
   .... a capital city.

3 Hong Kong, Singapore, and Peking.
   .... in Asia. / .... in Europe.

4 San Francisco, Bangkok, and Canberra.
   .... in Europe.

5 Bangkok, Tokyo, and Athens.
   .... capital cities. / .... in America.

6 Marseilles and Lyons.
   .... in France. / .... the capital of France.

▶ **Bank**

Unit 17 Much, little, many, few, more, less, fewer

Main points

- You use 'much' and 'little' with uncount nouns to talk about a quantity of something.
- You use 'many' and 'few' with plural nouns to talk about a number of people or things.
- You use 'much' in negative sentences and questions, and 'a lot of' or 'plenty of' rather than 'much' in affirmative sentences.
- You use 'more' and 'less' with uncount nouns, and 'more' and 'fewer' with plural count nouns.

1 You use 'much' to talk about a large quantity of something, and 'little' to talk about a small quantity of something. You only use 'much' and 'little' with uncount nouns.

I haven't got much time.
We've made little progress.

2 You use 'many' to talk about a large number of people or things, and 'few' to talk about a small number of people or things. You can only use 'many' and 'few' with plural count nouns.

He wrote many novels.
There were few visitors to our house.

3 You normally use 'much' in negative sentences and questions.

He did not speak much English.
Why haven't I given much attention to this problem?

In affirmative sentences you do not use 'much', you use 'a lot of', 'lots of', or 'plenty of' instead. You can use them with both uncount nouns and plural nouns.

He demanded a lot of attention.
I make a lot of mistakes.
They spent lots of time on the project.
He remembered a large room with lots of windows.
I've got plenty of money.
There are always plenty of jobs to be done.

Note that you can use 'so much' and 'too much' in affirmative sentences.

She spends so much time here.
There is too much chance of error.

4 You use 'so much' to emphasize that a large quantity of something is involved.

I have so much work to do.
They have so much money and we have so little.

You use 'too much' and 'too many' to say that the quantity of something, or the number of people or things, is larger than is reasonable or necessary.

He has too much work.
Too many people still smoke.

You use 'very many' to emphasize that a large number of people or things are involved.

Very many old people live alone.

Note that 'very much' is used with nouns and verbs.

There isn't very much time.
I liked it very much.

5 You use 'few' and 'little' to emphasize that only a small quantity of something or a small number of people or things are involved. They can be used with 'very' for greater emphasis.

The town has few monuments.
I have little time for anything but work.
Very few cars had reversing lights.
I had very little money left.

Note that 'a few' and 'a little' just indicate that a quantity or number is small.

He spread a little honey on a slice of bread.
I usually do a few jobs for him in the house.

6 You use 'more' with uncount nouns and plural count nouns to refer to a quantity of something or a number of people or things that is greater than another quantity or number.

His visit might do more harm than good.
He does more hours than I do.

You use 'less' with uncount nouns to refer to an amount of something that is smaller than another amount.

The poor have less access to education.
This machinery uses less energy.

You use 'fewer', or 'less' in informal English, with plural nouns to refer to a number of people or things that is smaller than another number.

There are fewer trees here.
They have sold less computers this year.

Unit 17 Practice

A Complete these sentences using the determiners given in brackets.

1 She speaks ....*a lot of*........ English but she doesn't speak ...*much*........... French. (a lot of / much)

2 He didn't sell very .... books. That's why he never made .... money. (many / much)

3 There weren't .... trains to Birmingham, but there were .... buses. (plenty of / many)

4 Very .... people could manage to live on so .... money. (few / little)

5 There's .... work to do, so we haven't .... time to spare. (a lot of / much)

6 If you can spare me .... time, I'd like to make .... suggestions. (a few / a little)

7 He spends so .... time playing football that he has .... time for anything else. (little / much)

8 There are .... cars in the city centre at rush hour, but very .... late at night. (few / lots of)

B Complete these sentences using **little** or **few.**

1 He is very successful even though he has very ...*little*........... education.

2 .... people really understood what the lecture was about.

3 Diana tried hard but she was very .... help.

4 He made so .... mistakes that he came top in the exam.

5 I can't do much I'm afraid. I have so .... time.

C Complete these using **a little** or **a few.**

1 Would you like ...*a little*.............. cake?

2 Would you like .... apples?

3 I have to see .... people this afternoon.

4 Could you give me .... help?

5 I don't know the answer, but I've got .... ideas.

D Complete these sentences using **very few, a few, very little** or **a little.**

1 There are lots of boys in our class, but ...*very few*............... girls.

2 He's an expert on languages, but he knows .... about mathematics.

3 There are lots of cinemas in town as well as .... good theatres.

4 I took plenty of sugar and .... milk.

5 When I'm busy, I always do .... work before breakfast.

6 I come home so tired that I can do .... work in the evenings.

7 Jack is very helpful. He's sure to have .... good ideas.

8 Jack is usually very helpful but he had .... advice for us this time.

9 .... unskilled jobs are well paid, but not very many.

10 I was tired and hungry, but fortunately I had .... money left.

Unit 18 Some, any, another, other, each, every

Main points

- You use 'some' to talk about a quantity or number without being precise.
- You use 'any' to talk about a quantity or number that may or may not exist.
- You use 'another', or 'another' and a number, to talk about additional people or things.
- You use 'each' and 'every' to talk about all the members of a group of people or things.

1 You use 'some' with uncount nouns and plural nouns to talk about a quantity of something or a number of people or things without being precise.

I have left some food for you in the fridge.
Some trains are running late.

You normally use 'some' in affirmative sentences.

There's some chocolate cake over there.
I had some good ideas.

You use 'some' in questions when you expect the answer to be 'yes', for example in offers or requests.

Would you like some coffee?
Could you give me some examples?

You can use 'some' with a singular noun when you do not know which person or thing is involved, or you think it does not matter.

Some man phoned, but didn't leave his number.
Is there some problem?

2 You use 'any' in front of plural and uncount nouns to talk about a quantity of something that may or may not exist. You normally use 'any' in questions and negative sentences.

Are there any jobs men can do but women can't?
It hasn't made any difference.

You use 'any' with a singular noun to emphasize that it does not matter which person or thing is involved.

Any container will do.

You can use 'no' with an affirmative verb instead of 'not any'.

There weren't any tomatoes left.
There were no tomatoes left.

You can also use 'not' and 'any', or 'no', with a comparative.

Her house wasn't any better than ours.
Her house was no better than ours.

3 You use 'another' with singular nouns to talk about an additional person or thing.

Could I have another cup of coffee?
He opened another shop last month.

You can also use 'another' with a number and a plural noun to talk about more people or things.

Another four years passed before we met again.
I've got another three books to read.

You use 'other' with plural nouns and 'the other' with singular or plural nouns.

I've got other things to think about.
The other man has gone.
The other European countries have beaten us.

4 You use 'each' or 'every' with a singular noun to talk about all the members of a group of people or things. You use 'each' when you are thinking about the members as individuals, and 'every' when you are making a general statement about all of them.

Each county is subdivided into several districts.
Each applicant has five choices.
Every child would have milk every day.
She spoke to every person at that party.

You can modify 'every' but not 'each'.

He spoke to them nearly every day.
We went out almost every evening.

5 You can use 'some of', 'any of', or 'each of', and a noun group to talk about a number of people or things in a group of people or things.

Some of the information has already been analysed.
It was more expensive than any of the other magazines.
He gave each of us advice about our present goals.

You can use 'each of' and a plural noun group but 'every' must be followed by 'one of'.

Each of the drawings is different.
Every one of them is given a financial target.

Note that you can also use 'each' with 'one of'.

This view of poverty influences each one of us.

Unit 18 Practice

A Complete these sentences by using **some** or **any**.

1 I've met ..._some_.... people, but I don't have ..._any_...... real friends yet.

2 I'd like to make .... friends, but I haven't met .... young people yet.

3 A: Is there .... petrol in the tank?

   B: Well, I filled it yesterday. There must be .... left.

4 There are .... biscuits left, but there isn't .... cake.

5 I know you speak .... French, but do you speak .... German?

6 A: Have you got .... matches?

   B: Yes, I think I've got .... in my pocket.

7 I thought I had met .... of the people here but I don't know .... of them.

8 Have you .... idea what time it is?

B Rewrite these sentences using **some** or **any.**

1 **All** children can learn to read and write. / ..._Any child can learn to write and write._.........

2 **Not all** of the children understood. / ....

3 I will be free **every** day next week. / ....

4 **All** the buses will take you to the city centre. / ....

5 **A few** people said that they would be late. / ....

6 You can buy it at **all** good bookshops. / ....

7 I'd like to give you **a bit of** advice. / ....

8 **One** of the guides will show you the way. / ....

9 **A few** of the children missed the bus. / ....

10 I like **all** fruit except bananas. / ....

C Choose which determiner in brackets best completes each sentence.

1 There are ..._plenty_.......... of chocolate biscuits. Would you like another one? (some / a few / plenty)

2 I have .... books with me. I've read most of them, but I haven't read ....

   one. (a few / any / plenty) (another / any / every)

3 He gave .... of the children a small gift. (any / each / every)

4 You can ask the doctor if you want .... advice. (any / every / another)

5 I wanted .... pound of meat but there wasn't .... left. (another / other / each) (any / other / some)

6 We hadn't .... oil left, but .... people lent us some. (any / some) (another / other)

7 I'd like to ask you for .... advice. (another / any / some)

8 I see Jack at work almost .... day. (any / each / every)

9 There was a prize for .... one of the competitors. (any / every / some)

10 Jenny was older than .... of the other girls. (any / every)

37

Unit 19 Position of adjectives

Main points

- There are two main positions for adjectives: in front of a noun, or as the complement of a link verb.
- Most adjectives can be used in either of these positions, but some adjectives can only be used in one.

1 Most adjectives can be used in a noun group, after determiners and numbers if there are any, in front of the noun.

He had a beautiful smile.
She bought a loaf of white bread.
There was no clear evidence.

2 Most adjectives can also be used after a link verb such as 'be', 'become', or 'feel'.

I'm cold.
I felt angry.
Nobody seemed amused.

3 Some adjectives are normally used only after a link verb.

afraid	asleep	due	ready	unable
alive	aware	glad	sorry	well
alone	content	ill	sure	

For example, you can say 'She was glad', but you do not talk about 'a glad woman'.

I wanted to be alone.
We were getting ready for bed.
I'm not quite sure.
He didn't know whether to feel glad or sorry.

4 Some adjectives are normally used only in front of a noun.

eastern	~	existing	neighbouring
northern	atomic	indoor	occasional
southern	countless	introductory	outdoor
western	digital	maximum	

For example, you talk about 'an atomic bomb', but you do not say 'The bomb was atomic'.

He sent countless letters to the newspapers.
This book includes a good introductory chapter on forests.

5 When you use an adjective to emphasize a strong feeling or opinion, it always comes in front of a noun.

absolute	outright	pure	true
complete	perfect	real	utter
entire	positive	total	

Some of it was absolute rubbish.
He made me feel like a complete idiot.

6 Some adjectives that describe size or age can come after a noun group consisting of a number or determiner and a noun that indicates the unit of measurement.

deep	long	tall	wide
high	old	thick	

He was about six feet tall.
The water was several metres deep.
The baby is nine months old.

Note that you do not say 'two pounds heavy', you say 'two pounds in weight'.

7 A few adjectives are used alone after a noun.

designate	elect	galore	incarnate

She was now the president elect.
There are empty houses galore.

8 A few adjectives have a different meaning depending on whether they come in front of or after a noun.

concerned	involved	present	proper	responsible

For example, 'the concerned mother' means a mother who is worried, but 'the mother concerned' means the mother who has been mentioned.

It's one of those incredibly involved stories.
The people involved are all doctors.

I'm worried about the present situation.
Of the 18 people present, I knew only one.

Her parents were trying to act in a responsible manner.
We do not know the person responsible for his death.

Unit 19 Practice

A Rewrite the phrases by putting one of these adjectives in front of the appropriate noun.

atomic	countless	digital	eastern	indoor	introductory
maximum	neighbouring	northern	outdoor		

1 ... the region in the east of the country. / *the eastern region.* ....

2 ... power produced by nuclear fission. / ....

3 ... a watch which uses figures to show the time. / ....

4 ... the first paragraph in a piece of writing. / ....

5 ... the largest number possible. / ....

6 ... the border to the north of the country. / ....

7 ... countries on the borders. / ....

8 ... a party held in the open air. / ....

9 ... plants which can be kept in the house. / ....

10 ... a huge number of people. / ....

B Complete the definitions using the adjectives below.

afraid	asleep	aware	content	due	glad	ready	sorry	sure	unable

1 If you are ..... *afraid* .... to do something, you feel fear because you think it will hurt you in some way.

2 If you are .... about something, you are pleased and happy about it.

3 If you are .... to do something, it is impossible for you to do it.

4 If something is .... at a particular time, it is expected to happen or arrive at that time.

5 If you feel .... about something, you are sad or disappointed about it.

6 If you say that someone is .... of himself or herself, you mean that they are very confident.

7 If you are .... of something, you know that it exists or that it is important.

8 If you are half .... , you are not listening or paying attention because you are very tired.

9 If you are .... to do something, you are willing to do it.

10 If you are .... , you are fairly happy.

C Match the phrases and definitions below. The first has been done for you.

1 Someone who is very stupid is ...
2 Someone who is very troublesome is ...
3 Something which is extremely unfortunate is ...
4 Something which is quite ridiculous is ...
5 Someone who wins a sports competition is ...
6 Something which will cause a lot of difficulties is ...
7 Someone who is always loyal is ...
8 Something that does not work at all is ...
9 Something which is extremely dangerous is ...

a ... an utter disaster.
b ... a real problem.
c ... a positive menace.
d ... a champion.
e ... a true friend.
f ... a total failure.
g ... a perfect nuisance.
h ... a complete fool.
i ... absolute nonsense.

▶ **Bank**

Unit 20 Order of adjectives

Main points

- You put opinion adjectives in front of descriptive adjectives.
- You put general opinion adjectives in front of specific opinion adjectives.
- You can sometimes vary the order of adjectives.
- If you use two or more descriptive adjectives, you put them in a particular order.
- If you use a noun in front of another noun, you put any adjectives in front of the first noun.

1 You often want to add more information to a noun than you can with one adjective, so you need to use two or more adjectives. In theory, you can use the adjectives in any order, depending on the quality you want to emphasize. In practice, however, there is a normal order.
When you use two or more adjectives in front of a noun, you usually put an adjective that expresses your opinion in front of an adjective that just describes something.

You live in a nice big house.
He is a naughty little boy.
She was wearing a beautiful pink suit.

2 When you use more than one adjective to express your opinion, an adjective with a more general meaning such as 'good', 'bad', 'nice', or 'lovely' usually comes before an adjective with a more specific meaning such as 'comfortable', 'clean', or 'dirty'.

I sat in a lovely comfortable armchair in the corner.
He put on a nice clean shirt.
It was a horrible dirty room.

3 You can use adjectives to describe various qualities of people or things. For example, you might want to indicate their size, their shape, or the country they come from.
Descriptive adjectives belong to six main types, but you are unlikely ever to use all six types in the same noun group. If you did, you would normally put them in the following order:

size	shape	age	colour	nationality	material

This means that if you want to use an 'age' adjective and a 'nationality' adjective, you put the 'age' adjective first.

We met some young Chinese girls.

Similarly, a 'shape' adjective normally comes before a 'colour' adjective.

He had round black eyes.

Other combinations of adjectives follow the same order. Note that 'material' means any substance, not only cloth.

There was a large round wooden table in the room.
The man was carrying a small black plastic bag.

4 You usually put comparative and superlative adjectives in front of other adjectives.

Some of the better English actors have gone to live in Hollywood.
These are the highest monthly figures on record.

5 When you use a noun in front of another noun, you never put adjectives between them. You put any adjectives in front of the first noun.

He works in the French film industry.
He receives a large weekly cash payment.

6 When you use two adjectives as the complement of a link verb, you use a conjunction such as 'and' to link them. With three or more adjectives, you link the last two with a conjunction, and put commas after the others.

The day was hot and dusty.
The room was large but square.
The house was old, damp and smelly.
We felt hot, tired and thirsty.

Unit 20 Practice

A Take adjectives from the phrases below and put them into the columns given. The first phrase has been done for you.

Opinion adjectives		Descriptive adjectives					
1	2	3	4	5	6	7	8
general	specific	size	shape	age	colour	nationality	material
1 *lovely*	*comfortable*						*leather*

1 ... a lovely comfortable leather armchair.
2 ... a large round wooden table.
3 ... a nice intelligent young man.
4 ... a nasty ugly blue china vase.
5 ... an old Spanish song.
6 ... a big square metal box.
7 ... a horrible stinking fish.
8 ... a small brown paper bag.
9 ... a valuable ancient Egyptian manuscript.
10 ... a huge red American automobile.

You should finish with four adjectives in column 1; five in column 2; four in 3; two in 4; three in 5; three in 6; three in 7; and five in 8.

B Are the adjectives in these phrases in the normal order? Answer 'Yes' or 'No'.

1 ... a long hot day. ...*No.*......
2 ... a large black dog. ....
3 ... a tall handsome young man. ....
4 ... short fat legs. ....
5 ... a new red dress. ....
6 ... a big juicy steak. ....
7 ... a slim graceful woman. ....
8 ... a grey woollen pullover. ....
9 ... a large comfortable armchair. ....
10 ... a long difficult journey. ....

C Are the adjectives and nouns in front of the final noun in the normal order? Answer 'Yes' or 'No'.

1 ... a weekly cash payment. ...*Yes.*......
2 ... the French film industry. ....
3 ... the highest monthly figures. ....
4 ... a serious political force. ....
5 ... the long bitter struggle. ....
6 ... a clever optical illusion. ....
7 ... a great personal triumph. ....
8 ... the worst British air disaster. ....
9 ... finite energy resources. ....
10 ... a violent armed robbery. ....

Unit 21 Adjectives with prepositions

Main points

- Some adjectives used after link verbs can be used alone or followed by a prepositional phrase.
- Some adjectives must be followed by particular prepositions.
- Some adjectives can be followed by different prepositions to introduce different types of information.

1 When you use an adjective after a link verb, you can often use the adjective on its own or followed by a prepositional phrase. See Unit 22 for other patterns.

He was afraid.
He was afraid of his enemies.

2 Some adjectives cannot be used alone after a link verb. If they are followed by a prepositional phrase, it must have a particular preposition:

aware of	unaware of	fond of
accustomed to	unaccustomed to	used to

I've always been terribly fond of you.
He is unaccustomed to the heat.

3 Some adjectives can be used alone, or followed by a particular preposition:
- used alone, or with 'of' to specify the cause of a feeling

afraid	critical	jealous	suspicious
ashamed	envious	proud	terrified
convinced	frightened	scared	tired

They may feel jealous of your success.
I was terrified of her.

- used alone, or with 'of' to specify the person who has a quality

brave	good	polite	thoughtful
careless	intelligent	sensible	unkind
clever	kind	silly	unreasonable
generous	nice	stupid	wrong

That was clever of you!
I turned the job down, which was stupid of me.

- used alone or with 'to', usually referring to:

similarity:	close equal identical related similar
marriage:	married engaged
loyalty:	dedicated devoted loyal
rank:	junior senior

My problems are very similar to yours.
He was dedicated to his job.

- used alone, or followed by 'with' to specify the cause of a feeling

bored	displeased	impatient	pleased
content	dissatisfied	impressed	satisfied

I could never be bored with football.
He was pleased with her.

- used alone or with 'at', usually referring to:

strong reactions:	amazed astonished shocked surprised
ability:	bad excellent good hopeless useless

He was shocked at the hatred they had shown.
She had always been good at languages.

- used alone, or with 'for' to specify the person or thing that quality relates to

common	essential	possible	unusual
difficult	important	unnecessary	usual
easy	necessary		

It's difficult for young people on their own.
It was unusual for them to go away at the weekend.

4 Some adjectives can be used alone, or used with different prepositions.
- used alone, with an impersonal subject and 'of' and the subject of the action, or with a personal subject and 'to' and the object of the action

cruel	good	nasty	rude
friendly	kind	nice	unfriendly
generous	mean	polite	unkind

It was rude of him to leave so suddenly.
She was rude to him for no reason.

- used alone, with 'about' to specify a thing or 'with' to specify a person

angry	delighted	fed up	happy
annoyed	disappointed	furious	upset

She was still angry about the result.
They're getting pretty fed up with him.

Unit 21 Practice

A Complete these definitions by adding the adjective with the right meaning. Use a different adjective in each sentence. See the lists on the opposite page for adjectives to use.

1 If something makes you very frightened you are ..... *terrified* ..... of it.

2 If you continue to support someone who is in trouble you are .... to them.

3 If two things are almost the same one is .... to the other.

4 If two things are exactly the same one is .... to the other.

5 If you buy someone an expensive present they might say 'That's very .... of you.'

6 Someone who is a fine athlete is .... at games.

B Use the adjectives below to complete the sentences that follow.

> bored delighted different fond proud responsible senior stupid surprised used

1 My brother did well. I was ... *proud* .... of him.

2 He made a silly mistake. It was very .... of him.

3 I can't stand the heat. I'm not .... to it.

4 Things have changed. Life is very .... from what it used to be.

5 I'm .... at you. I can't understand the way you behaved.

6 I'm .... with the result. It's exactly what I wanted.

7 Who is .... for this mess? Who left all these things lying around?

8 Jack is .... with school. He wants to leave as soon as possible.

9 Mary is an old friend of mine. I'm very .... of her.

10 In the army, a sergeant is .... to a corporal.

C Complete the definitions using one of the adjectives below with the correct preposition.

> engaged furious jealous kind responsible sensible suspicious upset

1 If something makes you very worried and unhappy, you are very ... *upset about* .... it.

2 If someone makes you very angry, you are .... them.

3 If you make a wise decision, someone might say 'That's very .... you'.

4 If you feel that you do not trust someone, you are .... them.

5 If someone else has something and you wish you had it, you are .... them.

6 If you treat someone very well, you are being .... them.

7 If you have agreed to marry someone, you are .... them.

8 If you think someone is to blame for something, you think they are .... it.

D Rewrite the sentences below using an adjective, the appropriate preposition, and **way.**

1 He drives dangerously. It makes me terrified. / I'm ... *terrified of the way he drives.* .....

2 She played very well. I was proud of her. / I was ....

3 He behaved badly. Everyone was very critical. / ....

4 They looked lovely. I was delighted. / ....

5 They treated us very well. We were very happy. / ....

Unit 22 Adjectives with 'to'-infinitive or 'that'-clauses

Main points

- Adjectives used after link verbs are often followed by 'to'-infinitive clauses or 'that'-clauses.
- Some adjectives are always followed by 'to'-infinitive clauses.
- You often use 'to'-infinitive clauses or 'that'-clauses after adjectives to express feelings or opinions.
- You often use 'to'-infinitive clauses after adjectives when the subject is impersonal 'it'.

1 After link verbs, you often use adjectives that describe how someone feels about an action or situation. With some adjectives, you can add a 'to'-infinitive clause or a 'that'-clause to say what the action or situation is.

afraid	disappointed	happy	sad
anxious	frightened	pleased	surprised
ashamed	glad	proud	unhappy

If the subject is the same in both clauses, you usually use a 'to'-infinitive clause. If the subject is different, you must use a 'that'-clause.

I was _happy to see_ them again.
He was _happy that_ they were coming to the party.

You often use a 'to'-infinitive clause when talking about future time in relation to the main clause.

I am _afraid to go_ home.
He was _anxious to leave_ before it got dark.

You often use a 'that'-clause when talking about present or past time in relation to the main clause.

He was _anxious that_ the passport was missing.
They were _afraid that_ I might have talked to the police.

2 You often use 'sorry' with a 'that'-clause. Note that 'that' is often omitted.

I'm very _sorry that_ I can't join you.
I'm _sorry_ I'm so late.

3 Some adjectives are not usually used alone, but have a 'to'-infinitive clause after them to say what action or situation the adjective relates to.

able	due	likely	unlikely
apt	inclined	prepared	unwilling
bound	liable	ready	willing

They were _unable to help_ her.
They were _not likely to forget_ it.
I am _willing to try._
I'm _prepared to say_ I was wrong.

4 When you want to express an opinion about someone or something, you often use an adjective followed by a 'to'-infinitive clause.

difficult	easy	impossible	possible	right	wrong

She had been _easy to deceive._
The windows will be almost _impossible to open._
Am I _wrong to stay_ here?

Note that in the first two examples, the subject of the main clause is the object of the 'to'-infinitive clause. In the third example, the subject is the same in both clauses.

5 With some adjectives, you use a 'that'-clause to express an opinion about someone or something.

awful	extraordinary	important	sad
bad	funny	interesting	true
essential	good	obvious	

I was _sad that_ people had reacted in this way.
It is _extraordinary that_ we should ever have met!

6 You can also use adjectives with 'to'-infinitive clauses after 'it' as the impersonal subject. You use the preposition 'of' or 'for' to indicate the person or thing that the adjective relates to.

It was _easy to find_ the path.
It was _good of John to help_ me.
It was _difficult for her to find_ a job.

See Unit 86 for 'it' as impersonal subject.
See Unit 21 for more information about adjectives followed by 'of' or 'for'.

Unit 22 Practice

A Rewrite each pair of sentences, using a 'to'-infinitive clause in one and a 'that'-clause in the other.

1 a I didn't go home. I was afraid. / ...*I was afraid to go home.*................

  b We might be late. I was worried. / ...*I was worried that we might be late.*.........

2 a I met George again. I was happy. / ....

  b George was waiting to meet me. I was pleased. / ....

3 a Mary was ill. I was sorry. / ....

  b Mary heard the news. She was unhappy. / ....

4 a We saw them. We were surprised. / ....

  b Everyone enjoyed the picnic. We were delighted. / ....

5 a Peter missed the match. He was disappointed. / ....

  b Anne missed the match. Peter was disappointed. / ....

6 a She didn't tell the children. She was ashamed. / ....

  b The children didn't tell her. She was ashamed. / ....

B Use these adjectives to complete the sentences below.

bound   due   important   impossible   likely   unlikely   willing   wrong

1 He will probably win. / He is ...*likely*............. to win.

2 You must arrive on time. / It is .... to arrive on time.

3 They probably won't come. / They are .... to come.

4 I am certain he will agree. / He is .... to agree.

5 Michael has offered to lend you the money. / Michael is .... to lend you the money.

6 The plane is expected at 7.30. / The plane is .... to land at 7.30.

7 Nobody can read his writing. / His writing is .... to read.

8 You ought not to have done that. / You were .... to do that.

C Rewrite these sentences to begin with **it** as the impersonal subject.

1 You shouldn't have lost the money. That was stupid. / ...*It was stupid of you to lose the money.*..

2 They stopped the thief. That was brave. / ....

3 You forgot to lock the door. That was very careless. / ....

4 She looked after the children. That was kind. / ....

5 Mary paid the bill. That was very generous. / ....

6 You solved the problem. That was clever. / ....

7 Joe sent us the flowers. That was kind. / ....

8 He kept everything for himself. That was mean. / ....

D Rewrite these sentences to begin with **it** as the impersonal subject.

1 We can help you. It will be easy. ...*It will be easy for us to help you.*...............

2 They must succeed. It's very important. / ....

3 I don't think I can do it. It will be very difficult. / ....

4 They often complain. It's very common. / ....

5 I'll give you a lift. It's very easy. / ....

6 You don't need to come early. It's unnecessary. / ....

Unit 23 Adjectives ending in '-ing' or '-ed'

Main points

- Many adjectives ending in '-ing' describe the effect that something has on someone's feelings.
- Some adjectives ending in '-ing' describe a process or state that continues over a period of time.
- Many adjectives ending in '-ed' describe people's feelings.

1 You use many '-ing' adjectives to describe the effect that something has on your feelings, or on the feelings of people in general. For example, if you talk about 'a surprising number', you mean that the number surprises you.

alarming	charming	embarrassing	surprising
amazing	confusing	exciting	terrifying
annoying	convincing	frightening	tiring
astonishing	depressing	interesting	welcoming
boring	disappointing	shocking	worrying

He lives in a charming house just outside the town.
She always has a warm welcoming smile.

Most '-ing' adjectives have a related transitive verb. See Unit 72 for information on transitive verbs.

2 You use some '-ing' adjectives to describe something that continues over a period of time.

ageing	decreasing	existing	living
booming	dying	increasing	remaining

Britain is an ageing society.
Increasing prices are making food very expensive.

These adjectives have related intransitive verbs. See Unit 72 for information on intransitive verbs.

3 Many '-ed' adjectives describe people's feelings. They have the same form as the past participle of a transitive verb and have a passive meaning. For example, 'a frightened person' is a person who has been frightened by something.

alarmed	delighted	frightened	surprised
amused	depressed	interested	tired
astonished	disappointed	satisfied	troubled
bored	excited	shocked	worried

She looks alarmed about something.
A bored student complained to his teacher.
She had big blue frightened eyes.

Note that the past participles of irregular verbs do not end in '-ed', but can be used as adjectives. See the Appendix for a list of irregular past participles.

The bird had a broken wing.
His coat was dirty and torn.

4 Like other adjectives, '-ing' and '-ed' adjectives can be:
- used in front of a noun

They still show amazing loyalty to their parents.
This is the most terrifying tale ever written.
I was thanked by the satisfied customer.
The worried authorities cancelled the match.

- used after link verbs

It's amazing what they can do.
The present situation is terrifying.
He felt satisfied with all the work he had done.
My husband was worried.

- modified by adverbials such as 'quite', 'really', and 'very'

The film was quite boring.
There is nothing very surprising in this.
She was quite astonished at his behaviour.
He was a very disappointed young man.

- used in the comparative and superlative

His argument was more convincing than mine.
He became even more depressed after she died.
This is one of the most boring books I've ever read.
She was the most interested in going to the cinema.

5 A small number of '-ed' adjectives are normally only used after link verbs such as 'be', 'become', or 'feel'. They are related to transitive verbs, and are often followed by a prepositional phrase, a 'to'-infinitive clause, or a 'that'-clause.

convinced	interested	prepared	tired
delighted	involved	scared	touched
finished	pleased	thrilled	

The Brazilians are pleased with the results.
He was always prepared to account for his actions.
She was scared that they would find her.

Unit 23 Practice

A Use the '-ing' adjectives below to complete the sentences which follow.

> ageing existing growing increasing living rising

1 The main problem is ...*rising*.................. prices. Things are getting much too expensive.
2 Factories in Japan are becoming even more automated, making .... use of robots.
3 Things will have to change. The .... system simply doesn't work.
4 Mohammed Ali, the former heavyweight champion of the world, has been described as a .... legend.
5 The young folk have all gone. There is no one left in the village apart from a few .... people.
6 Unemployment is on the increase. A .... number of young people, in particular, are finding themselves out of work.

B Use the '-ed' adjectives below to complete the definitions which follow.

> alarmed amused astonished bored depressed satisfied

1 When you find something funny, you are ...*amused*................. by it.
2 If something makes you sad and unhappy, you feel ....
3 If you are .... , you feel very surprised.
4 If something makes you very worried, you are .... by it.
5 If you are reasonably content with something, you feel ....
6 When you are .... , you feel tired and impatient because you have nothing to do.

C Complete the following pairs of sentences using the correct form of the verb in brackets. You must use the '-ed' form for one sentence in each pair and the '-ing' form for the other.

1 a I had nothing to do. I was ...*bored*.................. and lonely. (bore)
   b I had only one book with me but I didn't read it. It was so ...*boring*.................. .
2 a I enjoyed Dr Brown's visit. He is a very .... speaker. (interest)
   b We invited them to join us, but they weren't really ....
3 a The bad news was very .... (depress)
   b It was a bad day. We were all thoroughly ....
4 a I enjoyed the film. The monster was absolutely .... (terrify)
   b We were told there was a bomb in the building. Everyone was absolutely ....
5 a We were rather .... with the results. (disappoint)
   b The results were very ....
6 a We were dreadfully late. It was very .... (embarrass)
   b George made a perfect fool of himself. He was awfully ....
7 a Jack looked even more .... than he felt. (amaze)
   b She is a brilliant woman. She has the most .... ideas.
8 a Have you heard what's happened? Isn't it .... ? (excite)
   b Mary looked calm, but inside she felt really ....

▶ **Bank**

Unit 24 Comparatives and superlatives: forms

Main points

- You add '-er' for the comparative and '-est' for the superlative of one-syllable adjectives and adverbs.
- You use '-er' and '-est' with some two-syllable adjectives.
- You use 'more' for the comparative and 'most' for the superlative of most two-syllable adjectives, all longer adjectives, and adverbs ending in '-ly'.
- Some common adjectives and adverbs have irregular forms.

1 You add '-er' for the comparative form and '-est' for the superlative form of one-syllable adjectives and adverbs. If they end in '-e', you add '-r' and '-st'.

cheap ⇨ cheaper ⇨ cheapest		
safe ⇨ safer ⇨ safest		

cold	light	rough	young	large
fast	poor	small	~	nice
hard	quick	weak	close	wide

They worked harder.
I've found a nicer hotel.

If they end in a single vowel and consonant (except '-w'), you double the consonant.

big ⇨ bigger ⇨ biggest

fat	hot	sad	thin	wet

The day grew hotter.
Henry was the biggest of them.

2 With two-syllable adjectives ending in a consonant followed by '-y', you change the '-y' to '-i' and add '-er' and '-est'.

happy ⇨ happier ⇨ happiest

angry	dirty	friendly	heavy	silly
busy	easy	funny	lucky	tiny

It couldn't be easier.
That is the funniest bit of the film.

3 You use 'more' for the comparative and 'most' for the superlative of most two-syllable adjectives, all longer adjectives, and adverbs ending in '-ly'.

careful	⇨ more careful	⇨ most careful
beautiful	⇨ more beautiful	⇨ most beautiful
seriously	⇨ more seriously	⇨ most seriously

Be more careful next time.
They are the most beautiful gardens in the world.
It affected Clive most seriously.

Note that for 'early' as an adjective or adverb, you use 'earlier' and 'earliest', not 'more' and 'most'.

4 With some common two-syllable adjectives and adverbs, you can either add '-er' and '-est', or use 'more' and 'most'.

common	gentle	likely	pleasant	simple
cruel	handsome	narrow	polite	stupid

Note that 'clever' and 'quiet' only add '-er' and '-est'.

It was quieter outside.
He was the cleverest man I ever met.

5 You normally use 'the' with superlative adjectives in front of nouns, but you can omit 'the' after a link verb.

It was the happiest day of my life.
It was one of the most important discoveries.
I was happiest when I was on my own.

WARNING: When 'most' is used without 'the' in front of adjectives and adverbs, it often means almost the same as 'very'.

This book was most interesting.
I object most strongly.

6 A few common adjectives and adverbs have irregular comparative and superlative forms.

good/well ⇨ better		⇨ best
bad/badly ⇨ worse		⇨ worst
far	⇨ farther/further	⇨ farthest/furthest
old	⇨ older/elder	⇨ oldest/eldest

She would ask him when she knew him better.
She sat near the furthest window.

Note that you use 'elder' or 'eldest' to say which brother, sister, or child in a family you mean.

Our eldest daughter couldn't come.

Unit 24 Practice

A Put the adjectives below into two columns.

| black | careful | certain | difficult | expensive | fashionable | great | |
| intelligent | long | old | short | slow | small | useful | warm |

One syllable adjectives with comparative in '-er' and superlative in '-est':
black ....

Adjectives of two or more syllables using 'more' and 'most':
careful ....

....

....

Write down the comparative and superlative forms of three adjectives from each column.
blacker, blackest ....

more careful, most careful ....

....

....

....

....

B Look at these adjectives and underline those ending in '-y'. All of these form the comparative and superlative with '-ier' and '-iest'.

| crafty | disappointed | funny | helpful | important | interesting |
| pretty | silly | unhappy | unlucky | unusual | valuable |

Look at the remaining adjectives. Do they all have two or more syllables? How do they form the comparative and superlative? Write the comparative and superlative of these adjectives.

unhappy ... _unhappier, unhappiest_ ....

valuable ....

important ....

funny ....

C Write the comparative and superlative of the following adjectives.

bad ... _worse, worst_ ....

good ....

fine ....

hot ....

big ....

white ....

fit ....

slim ....

D Review exercises A to C above and write down the comparative and superlative form of these adjectives.

tiny ... _tinier, tiniest_ ....

simple ....

angry ....

convenient ....

cold ....

wide ....

fat ....

thin ....

slender ....

generous ....

friendly ....

gentle ....

Unit 25 Comparatives and superlatives: uses

Main points

- Comparative adjectives are used to compare people or things.
- Superlative adjectives are used to say that one person or thing has more of a quality than others in a group or others of that kind.
- Comparative adverbs are used in the same way as adjectives.

1 You use comparative adjectives to compare one person or thing with another, or with the same person or thing at another time. After a comparative adjective, you often use 'than'.

She was much <u>older than</u> me.
I am <u>happier than</u> I have ever been.

2 You use a superlative to say that one person or thing has more of a quality than others in a group or others of that kind.

Tokyo is Japan's <u>largest city.</u>
He was <u>the tallest person</u> there.

3 You can use comparative and superlative adjectives in front of a noun.

I was <u>a better writer than</u> he was.
He had <u>more important things</u> to do.
It was <u>the quickest route</u> from Rome to Naples.

You can also use comparative and superlative adjectives after link verbs.

My brother is <u>younger</u> than me.
He feels <u>more content</u> now.
The sergeant was <u>the tallest.</u>
This book was <u>the most interesting</u>.

4 You can use adverbs of degree in front of comparative adjectives.

a bit	a great/good deal	a lot	rather
far	a little	much	slightly

This car's <u>a bit more expensive.</u>
Now I feel <u>a great deal more confident.</u>
It's <u>a rather more complicated</u> story than that.

You can also use adverbs of degree such as 'by far', 'easily', 'much', or 'quite' in front of 'the' and superlative adjectives.

It was <u>by far the worst hospital</u> I had ever seen.
She was <u>easily the most intelligent person</u> in the class.

Note that you can put 'very' between 'the' and a superlative adjective ending in '-est'.

It was of <u>the very highest quality.</u>

5 When you want to say that one situation depends on another, you can use 'the' and a comparative followed by 'the' and another comparative.

<u>The smaller</u> it is, <u>the cheaper</u> it is to post.
<u>The larger</u> the organisation is, <u>the greater</u> the problem of administration becomes.

When you want to say that something increases or decreases, you can use two comparatives linked by 'and'.

It's getting <u>harder and harder</u> to find a job.
Cars are becoming <u>more and more expensive.</u>

6 After a superlative adjective, you can use a prepositional phrase to specify the group you are talking about.

Henry was <u>the biggest of them.</u>
These cakes are probably <u>the best in the world.</u>
He was <u>the most dangerous man in the country.</u>

7 You use the same structures in comparisons using adverbs as those given for adjectives:

- 'than' after comparative adverbs

Prices have been rising <u>faster than</u> incomes.

- 'the' and a comparative adverb followed by 'the' and another comparative adverb

<u>The quicker</u> we finish, <u>the sooner</u> we will go home.

- two comparative adverbs linked by 'and'

He sounded <u>worse and worse.</u>
He drove <u>faster and faster</u> till we told him to stop.

Unit 25 Practice

A Make sentences with a comparative adjective and **than,** using the words given.
1 Tokyo - big - New York. / ...*Tokyo is bigger than New York.*.......
2 My sister - old - me. / ....
3 Our new house - big - the one we used to live in. / ....
....
4 Travelling by train - comfortable - travelling by bus. / ....
....
5 Shopping at a supermarket - cheap - going to the local shops. / ....
....

B Complete these sentences using the comparative of the adjectives in brackets and **than.**
1 You certainly look much ...*happier than*.................. you did yesterday. (happy)
2 He is obviously .... in sport .... I am. (interested)
3 The game will certainly be much .... it was last year. (exciting)
4 Children nowadays seem to be much .... they used to be. (noisy)
5 She's actually a good deal .... she looks. (old)

C Form the comparative of the adjectives in these phrases and use the phrases in the sentences below.

a good idea   a big house   a healthy climate   a young man   a good job

1 California certainly has ...*a healthier climate*....... than New York.
2 I'm getting too old. This is a job for ....
3 When the children get a bit older we'll really need ....
4 I'm sure it won't work. Can't you come up with ....?
5 Perhaps we could afford it if I could get ....

D Complete these sentences using a superlative adjective in each one.
1 I've never heard a more ridiculous story.
   That's...*the most ridiculous story*...... I've ever heard.
2 We had never stayed in a more expensive hotel.
   It was .... we had ever stayed in.
3 I had never had such a tiring journey before.
   It was .... I had ever had.
4 I've never had nearly such a tasty meal before.
   That was .... I have ever had.
5 It's years since I saw a game as good as that.
   That's .... I've seen for years.

▶ **Bank**

Unit 26 Other ways of comparing things

Words like: as ... as, the same (as), like

Main points

- You use 'as...as...' to compare people or things.
- You can also compare people or things by using 'the same (as)'.
- You can also compare people or things by using a link verb and a phrase beginning with 'like'.

1 You use 'as...as...' to compare people or things that are similar in some way. You use 'as' and an adjective or adverb, followed by 'as' and a noun group, an adverbial, or a clause.

You're as bad as your sister.
The airport was as crowded as ever.
I am as good as she is.
Let us examine it as carefully as we can.

2 You can make a negative comparison using 'not as...as...' or 'not so...as...'.

The food wasn't as good as yesterday.
They are not as clever as they appear to be.
He is not so old as I thought.

3 You can use the adverbs 'almost', 'just', 'nearly', or 'quite' in front of 'as...as...'.

He was almost as fast as his brother.
Mary was just as pale as before.
She was nearly as tall as he was.

In a negative comparison, you can use 'not nearly' or 'not quite' before 'as...as...'.

This is not nearly as complicated as it sounds.
The hotel was not quite as good as they expected.

4 When you want to say that one thing is very similar to something else, you can use 'the same as' followed by a noun group, an adverbial, or a clause.

Your bag is the same as mine.
I said the same as always.
She looked the same as she did yesterday.

If people or things are very similar or identical, you can also say that they are 'the same'.

Teenage fashions are the same all over the world.
The initial stage of learning English is the same for many students.

You can use some adverbs in front of 'the same as' or 'the same'.

almost	just		much	roughly
exactly	more or less		nearly	virtually

He did exactly the same as John did.
You two look almost the same.

You can use 'the same' in front of a noun group, with or without 'as' after the noun group.

They reached almost the same height.
It was painted the same colour as the wall.

5 You can also compare people or things by using a link verb such as 'be', 'feel', 'look', or 'seem' and a phrase beginning with 'like'.

It was like a dream.
He still feels like a child.
He looked like an actor.
The houses seemed like mansions.

You can use some adverbs in front of 'like'.

a bit	exactly	least	more	quite	somewhat
a little	just	less	most	rather	very

He looks just like a baby.
Of all his children, she was the one most like me.

6 If the noun group after 'as' or 'like' in any of these structures is a pronoun, you use an object pronoun or possessive pronoun.

Jane was as clever as him.
His car is the same as mine.

7 You can also use 'less' and 'least' to make comparisons with the opposite meaning to 'more' and 'most'.

They were less fortunate than us.
He was the least skilled of the workers.
We see him less frequently than we used to.

Unit 26 Practice

A Rewrite these sentences using **as** .... **as** .... .
1 John's father is handsome and so is John. / ...*John is as handsome as his father.*...............
2 Jean's mother is generous and so is Jean. / ....
3 Neil's brother is mischievous and so is Neil. / ....
4 Mary drives fast and so does Helen. / ....
5 Our home is comfortable and so is yours. / ....
6 Last summer was very hot and so is this summer. / ....
7 Jenny works hard and so does Becky. / ....
8 Jack can run fast and so can Jill. / ....

B Use these adjectives and adverbs to complete the sentences that follow.

cheap   clever   cold   hard   long   much   quick   well

1 I'm getting old. I can't work as ....*hard*............ as I used to.
2 Prices have gone up. Things aren't as .... as they used to be.
3 Have you been ill? You're not looking as .... as you usually do.
4 Jack's doing well at school. He's nearly as .... as his sister.
5 It's freezing. It must be nearly as .... as last winter.
6 Joe still plays tennis. He says he enjoys it as .... as ever.
7 The bus wasn't as .... as the train. It took over two hours.
8 Cats don't usually live as .... as dogs.

C Write sentences using **the same.** Here are some nouns to help you.

age   length   size   height   weight

1 Mary and Jan are both 17. / ...*They're the same age.*...
2 John is six feet tall and so is Henry. / ....
3 I weigh seventy-five kilos and so does Jack. / ....
4 This box is exactly as big as that one. / ....
5 This piece of string is just as long as that one. / ....

D Match these sentences. The first has been done for you.
1 It was an enormous house.
2 The dog gave a dreadful growl.
3 The city centre is dreadfully crowded.
4 This cheese is awful.
5 I recognised Eleanor easily.
6 This is lovely soft cotton.

a It sounded like a tiger.
b It smells like bad eggs.
c It feels like silk.
d She looks just like her sister.
e It looked like a castle.
f It's just like London.

Unit 27 Possession

Main points

- Possessives and possessive pronouns are used to say that one person or thing belongs to another or is connected with another.
- You use apostrophe s ('s) to say who something belongs to.
- You use phrases with 'of' to say that one person or thing belongs to another or is connected with another.

1 You use possessives to say that a person or thing belongs to another person or thing or is connected with them. The possessives are sometimes called 'possessive adjectives'.

| my | your | his | her | its | our | their |

Note that 'your' is both singular and plural.

I'd been waiting a long time to park my car.
They took off their shoes.

WARNING: The possessive 'its' is not spelled with an apostrophe. The form 'it's' with an apostrophe is the short form for 'it is' or 'it has'.

2 You put numbers and adjectives after the possessive and in front of the noun.

Their two small children were playing outside.
She got a bicycle on her sixth birthday.

3 You use a possessive pronoun when you want to refer to a person or thing and to say who that person or thing belongs to or is connected with. The possessive pronouns are:

| mine | yours | his | hers | ours | theirs |

Note that 'yours' is both singular and plural.

Is that coffee yours or mine?
It was his fault, not theirs.

WARNING: There is no possessive pronoun 'its'.

4 You can also say who or what something belongs to or is connected with by using a noun with apostrophe s ('s). For example, if John owns a motorbike, you can refer to it as 'John's motorbike'.

Sylvia put her hand on John's arm.
I like the car's design.

You add apostrophe s ('s) to singular nouns and irregular plural nouns, usually referring to people rather than things.

I wore a pair of my sister's boots.
Children's birthday parties can be boring.

With plural nouns ending in '-s' you only add the apostrophe (').

It is not his parents' problem.

You add apostrophe s ('s) to people's names, even when they end in '-s'.

Could you give me Charles's address?

Note that when you use two or more names linked by 'and', you put the apostrophe s ('s) after the last name.

They have bought Sue and Tim's car.

5 When you want to refer to someone's home, or to some common shops and places of work, you can use apostrophe s ('s) after a name or noun on its own.

He's round at David's.
I bought it at the chemist's.
She must go to the doctor's.

6 You can also use apostrophe s ('s) with some expressions of time to identify something, or to say how much time is involved.

Did you see the cartoon in yesterday's newspaper?
They have four weeks' holiday per year.

7 You can use a prepositional phrase beginning with 'of' to say that one person or thing belongs to or is connected with another.

She is the mother of the boy who lives next door.
Ellen aimlessly turned the pages of her magazine.

After 'of' you can use a possessive pronoun, or a noun or name with apostrophe s ('s).

He was an old friend of mine.
That word was a favourite of your father's.
She's a friend of Stephen's.

8 You can add 'own' after a possessive, or a noun or name with apostrophe s ('s), for emphasis.

My own view is that there are no serious problems.
The professor's own answer may be unacceptable.

Unit 27 Practice

A Complete these sentences by adding a possessive.

1 I left ....*my*........ car in the garage.

2 Mary hung .... coat on the peg.

3 Jack had .... hair cut.

4 Neil and David ate .... supper.

5 I hope you enjoy .... holiday.

6 We'll invite you round to .... house sometime.

And complete these by adding a possessive with **own**.

7 You must make up ....*your own*............. mind.

8 The children had to cook .... supper.

9 Bill borrowed Jenny's car. .... car was being repaired.

10 I'll bring .... sheets and towels.

11 Every dog had .... special basket to sleep in.

12 You should do .... washing up.

B Complete the sentences by adding apostrophe or apostrophe s ('s) to the noun group in brackets.

1 They're having a ...*children's*.................... party on Saturday. (children)

2 This is my .... house. (parents)

3 You know John? He's .... father. (David and Neil)

4 I borrowed .... bike. (James)

5 I'll be staying in my .... flat. (friends)

6 That looks like .... car. (John and Jean)

7 This is .... coat, isn't it? (Sylvia)

8 We're going away for .... holiday. (a week)

9 You need .... rest. (a couple of days)

10 We usually have .... holiday in summer. (two weeks)

C Rewrite the replies to these questions.

1 A: Is this Becky's coat?
   B: No, it belongs to Jenny. / ...*No, it's Jenny's.*...

2 A: Whose keys are these?
   B: They belong to me. / ....

3 A: Is this your money?
   B: No, I think it belongs to you. / ....

4 A: Is this John's pen?
   B: Yes, I think it belongs to him. / ....

5 A: Is this Jane's book?
   B: Yes, I'm sure it belongs to her. / ....

6 A: Is that Neil and David's car?
   B: Yes, it belongs to them. / ....

▶ **Bank**

Unit 28 Nouns with prepositions

Main points

- 'Of' can be used to add many different types of information, 'with' is used to specify a quality or possession.
- Some nouns are always followed by particular prepositions.

1 You can give more information about a noun by adding a prepositional phrase after it.

Four men on holiday were in the car.
A sound behind him made him turn.

2 You often use the preposition 'of' after a noun to add various kinds of information. For example, you can use 'of' to indicate:

- what something is made of or consists of

...a wall of stone.
A feeling of panic was rising in him.

- what the subject matter of speech, writing, or a picture is

She gave a brief account of her interview.
There was a picture of them both in the paper.

- what a person or thing belongs to or is connected with

She was the daughter of the village priest.
The boys sat on the floor of the living room.

- what qualities a person or thing has

She was a woman of energy and ambition.
They faced problems of great complexity.

3 After nouns referring to actions, you use 'of' to indicate the subject or object of the action.

...the arrival of the police.
...the destruction of their city.

After nouns referring to people who perform an action, you use 'of' to say what the action involves or is aimed at.

...supporters of the hunger strike.
...a student of English.

Note that you often use two nouns, rather than a noun and a prepositional phrase. For example, you say 'bank robbers', not 'robbers of the bank'.

4 After nouns referring to measurement, you use 'of' to give the exact figure.

...an average annual temperature of 20 degrees.
...a speed of 25 kilometres an hour.

You can use 'of' after a noun to give someone's age.

Jonathan was a child of seven when it happened.

5 You use 'with' after a noun to say that a person or thing has a particular quality, feature, or possession.

...a girl with red hair.
...the man with the gun.

Note that you use 'in' after a noun to say what someone is wearing.

...a grey-haired man in a raincoat.
...the man in dark glasses.

6 Some nouns are usually followed by a particular preposition. Here are some examples of:

- nouns followed by 'to'

alternative	attitude	invitation	relevance
answer	devotion	reaction	resistance
approach	introduction	reference	return

This was my first real introduction to Africa.

- nouns followed by 'for'

admiration	need	responsibility	taste
desire	reason	search	thirst
dislike	respect	substitute	

Their need for money is growing fast.

- nouns followed by 'on'

agreement	attack	comment	effect	tax

She had a dreadful effect on me.

- nouns followed by 'with' or 'between'

connection	contact	link	relationship

His illness had some connection with his diet.

- nouns followed by 'in'

decrease	difficulty	fall	increase	rise

They demanded a large increase in wages.

Unit 28 Practice

A Use the nouns below to complete the sentences which follow.

> contribution   cure   damage   demand   invitation   recipe   reply   room   solution   sympathy

1 In the last storm there was a lot of ..... *damage* .... to the roof.
2 They asked me for a .... to the church so I gave them £25.
3 What did you say in your .... to David's letter?
4 They were kind enough to send me an .... to the wedding.
5 I'm afraid I can't offer any .... to the problem.
6 Do you think they will ever find a .... for the common cold?
7 Sit here. We can make .... for another one.
8 I have no .... for people who get into trouble through dangerous driving.
9 Can I have the .... for that lovely cake?
10 There's not much .... for firewood nowadays.

B Now do these in the same way.

> advantage   cause   comment   contact   decision   difference   difficulty   relationship   increase   tax

1 The government is going to increase the ..... *tax* .... on cigarettes.
2 I'd like to make just one .... on your answer.
3 She has always had a very close .... with her father.
4 I haven't heard from Angela for ages. I've almost lost .... with her.
5 There is always a big .... in sales just before Christmas.
6 Heart disease is the commonest .... of death in industrialised societies.
7 The main .... of air travel is that it's so quick.
8 I always have great .... in getting up early in the morning.
9 Have you reached a .... on whether or not to sell your house?
10 What's the .... between a house and a bungalow?

C Complete these sentences using the correct prepositions.
1 Some people have a very strange attitude ..... *to* .... animals.
2 The Sunday Times made a fierce attack .... the Prime Minister.
3 There was a sharp rise .... prices last month.
4 People used to believe that air pollution was the cause .... malaria.
5 You should try to have more sympathy .... other people.
6 Surely we can come to some agreement .... the price.
7 In the long run there is no alternative .... hard work.
8 We should have respect .... other people's beliefs.
9 The main disadvantage .... air travel is the high cost.
10 Our school has close links .... several schools overseas.

▶ **Bank**

Unit 29 Nouns with '-ing', '-ed', or 'to'-infinitive clauses

Main points

- Nouns are followed by '-ing' clauses that say what a person or thing is doing.
- Nouns are followed by '-ed' clauses that show that a person or thing has been affected or caused by an action.
- Nouns are followed by 'to'-infinitive clauses that indicate the aim, purpose, or necessity of something, or that give extra information.

1 You can often give more information about a noun, or an indefinite pronoun such as 'someone' or 'something', by adding a clause beginning with an '-ing' form, an '-ed' form, or a 'to'-infinitive.

He gestured towards the box lying on the table.
I think the idea suggested by Tim is the best one.
She wanted someone to talk to.

2 You use an '-ing' clause after a noun to say what someone or something is doing or was doing at a particular time.

The young girl sitting opposite him was his daughter.
Most of the people strolling in the park were teenagers.

3 You can also use an '-ing' clause after a noun to say what a person or thing does generally, rather than at a particular time.

Problems facing parents should be discussed.
The men working there were not very friendly.

4 You often use an '-ing' clause after a noun which is the object of a verb of perception, such as 'see', 'hear', or 'feel'. See also Unit 84.

Suddenly we saw Amy walking down the path.
He heard a distant voice shouting.

5 You use an '-ed' clause after a noun to show that someone or something has been affected or caused by an action.

He was the new minister appointed by the President.
The man injured in the accident was taken to hospital.

Remember that not all verbs have regular '-ed' forms.

A story written by a young girl won the competition.
She was wearing a dress bought in Paris.

6 You use a 'to'-infinitive clause after a noun to indicate the aim of an action or the purpose of physical object.

We arranged a meeting to discuss the new rules.
He had nothing to write with.

You also use a 'to'-infinitive clause after a noun to say that something needs to be done.

I gave him several things to mend.
'What's this?'—'A list of things to remember.'

7 You use a 'to'-infinitive clause after a noun group that includes an ordinal number, a superlative, or a word like 'next', 'last', or 'only'.

She was the first woman to be elected to the council.
Mr Holmes was the oldest person to be chosen.
The only person to speak was James.

8 You use a 'to'-infinitive clause after abstract nouns to give more specific information about them.

All it takes is a willingness to learn.
He'd lost the ability to communicate with people.

The following abstract nouns are often followed by a 'to'-infinitive clause:

ability	desire	need	willingness
attempt	failure	opportunity	
chance	inability	unwillingness	

Note that the verbs or adjectives which are related to these nouns can also be followed by a 'to'-infinitive clause. For example, you can say 'I attempted to find them', and 'He was willing to learn'.
See Unit 30 for information on nouns that are related to reporting verbs and can be followed by a 'to'-infinitive clause.

Unit 29 Practice

A Complete the following sentences using the correct part of the verb in brackets. One sentence in each pair should have an '-ing' form and the other an '-ed' form.

1 a There was a table ...*covered*............. by a clean white cloth. (cover)

   b There was a clean white cloth ...*covering*............. the table.

2 a The man .... by the dog was seriously injured. (attack)

   b The dog .... my friend was pulled off by its owner.

3 a Everyone went home early .... a dreadful mess behind. (leave)

   b We cleared up the things .... behind after the party.

4 a I saw a man .... a heavy wooden box. (carry)

   b We lost most of the luggage .... in the plane.

5 a The problems .... by the government are growing more serious every day. (face)

   b There are a lot of problems .... us at the moment.

6 a I heard someone .... French. (speak)

   b Tagalog is one of the languages .... in the Philippines.

B Use these '-ing' forms to complete the sentences below.

> burning   climbing   crying   drowning   lying   screaming   standing

1 If I saw someone ...*climbing*............... in my neighbour's window, I would call the police.

2 If I smelled something .... , I would check in the kitchen.

3 If I saw a disabled man .... in a train, I would offer him my seat.

4 If I saw a child .... , I would ask what was the matter.

5 If you saw someone .... , would you try to rescue them?

6 If you found a lot of money .... in the street, would you take it to the police station?

7 If you heard someone .... , what would you do?

C Use the following words to complete the sentences below.

> box   key   matches   meeting   money   party   pen   room

1 We held a ...*party*................... to celebrate Vera's birthday.

2 Do you have enough .... to pay for all the tickets?

3 I have a master .... to open all the doors.

4 There's a big .... to pack the clothes in.

5 Have you got a .... to sign these papers with?

6 Is there a .... to hang our coats in?

7 There will be a .... tomorrow to elect a new chairman.

8 Do you have any .... to light the fire?

▶ **Bank**

Unit 30 Other ways of adding to a noun group

Main points

- Some adjectives can be used after nouns.
- You can use relative clauses after nouns.
- Adverbials of place and time can come after nouns.
- A noun can be followed by another noun group.
- You can use 'that'-clauses after some nouns.

1 You can use some adjectives after a noun to give more information about it, but the adjectives are usually followed by a prepositional phrase, a 'to'-infinitive clause, or an adverbial.

This is a warning to people eager for a quick profit.
These are the weapons likely to be used.
For a list of the facilities available here, ask the secretary.
You must talk to the people concerned.

See Unit 19 for more information on adjectives used after nouns.

2 When you want to give more precise information about the person or thing you are talking about, you can use a defining relative clause after the noun.

The man who had done it was arrested.
There are a lot of things that are wrong.
Nearly all the people I used to know have gone.

Note that you can also use defining relative clauses after indefinite pronouns such as 'someone' or 'something'.

I'm talking about somebody who is really ill.

See Unit 97 for more information on defining relative clauses.

3 You can use an adverbial of place or time after a noun.

People everywhere are becoming more selfish.
This is a reflection of life today.

4 You can add a second noun group after a noun. The second noun group gives you more precise information about the first noun.

Her mother, a Canadian, died when she was six.

Note that the second noun group is separated by commas from the rest of the clause.

5 Nouns such as 'advice', 'hope', and 'wish', which refer to what someone says or thinks, can be followed by a 'that'-clause. Here are some examples:

advice	claim	feeling	threat
agreement	conclusion	hope	warning
belief	decision	promise	wish

It is my firm belief that more women should stand for Parliament.
I had a feeling that no-one thought I was good enough.

Note that all these nouns are related to reporting verbs, which also take a 'that'-clause. For example, 'information' is related to 'inform', and 'decision' is related to 'decide'.
Some of these nouns can also be followed by a 'to'-infinitive clause.

agreement	hope	promise	warning
decision	order	threat	wish

The decision to go had not been an easy one.
I reminded Barnaby of his promise to buy his son a horse.

6 A few other nouns can be followed by a 'that'-clause.

advantage	effect	idea	opinion
confidence	evidence	impression	possibility
danger	fact	news	view

He didn't want her to get the idea that he was rich.
I had no evidence that Jed was the killer.
He couldn't believe the news that his house had just burned down.

Note that when a noun group is the object of a verb, it may be followed by different structures. See Units 81 to 84 for more information.

Unit 30 Practice

A Complete these sentences by adding one of the names below.

Abraham Lincoln   Amazon   Canada   Kyoto   Marilyn Monroe   Yuri Gagarin

1 *Abraham Lincoln* .... , the sixteenth US president, was assassinated in 1865.

2 .... , the Russian cosmonaut, was born in 1934.

3 The woman who was born Norma Jean Mortenson later became
.... , the glamorous film star.

4 .... , the second largest country in the world, has a population
of less than 25 million.

5 .... , a city in central Japan, was the nation's capital until
1868.

6 The .... , the longest river in the world, flows from the Peruvian
Andes to the Atlantic Ocean.

B Write six true sentences from the table below.

People Life	in the twentieth century in most parts of the world in the 1990's in Britain today	are much better off than they used to be. is much easier than it used to be. was often difficult. has changed very rapidly. have lived through difficult times. is changing very rapidly.

....

....

....

....

....

....

C Complete these sentences using **that** or **to.**

1 The decision ...*to*............... raise prices was bound to be unpopular.

2 Nobody accepted his claim .... he was the clear winner of the contest.

3 I have a feeling .... things will get worse before they get better.

4 The army attacked the plane in spite of the terrorists' threat .... kill the hostages.

5 There is a distinct possibility .... we will be late for the meeting.

6 They gave us a promise .... provide whatever help we needed.

7 There was a danger .... the building might catch fire.

Unit 31 Adverbials

Main points

- Adverbials are usually adverbs, adverb phrases, or prepositional phrases.
- Adverbials of manner, place, and time are used to say how, where, or when something happens.
- Adverbials usually come after the verb, or after the object if there is one.
- The usual order of adverbials is manner, then place, then time.

1 An adverbial is often one word, an adverb.

Sit there quietly, and listen to this music.

However, an adverbial can also be a group of words:
- an adverb phrase

He did not play well enough to win.

- a prepositional phrase

The children were playing in the park.

- a noun group, usually a time expression

Come and see me next week.

2 You use an adverbial of manner to describe the way in which something happens or is done.

They looked anxiously at each other.
She listened with great patience as he told his story.

You use an adverbial of place to say where something happens.

A plane flew overhead.
No birds or animals came near the body.

You use an adverbial of time to say when something happens.

She will be here soon.
He was born on 3 April 1925.

3 You normally put adverbials of manner, place, and time after the main verb.

She sang beautifully.
The book was lying on the table.
The car broke down yesterday.

If the verb has an object, you put the adverbial after the object.

I did learn to play a few tunes very badly.
Thomas made his decision immediately.
He took the glasses to the kitchen.

If you are using more than one of these adverbials in a clause, the usual order is manner, then place, then time.

They were sitting quite happily in the car. (manner, place)
She spoke very well at the village hall last night. (manner, place, time)

4 You usually put adverbials of frequency, probability, and duration in front of the main verb.

She occasionally comes to my house.
You have very probably heard the news by now.
They had already given me the money.

A few adverbs of degree also usually come in front of the main verb.

She really enjoyed the party.

5 When you want to focus on an adverbial, you can do this by putting it in a different place in the clause:

- you can put an adverbial at the beginning of a clause, usually for emphasis

Slowly, he opened his eyes.
In September I travelled to California.
Next to the coffee machine stood a pile of cups.

Note that after adverbials of place, as in the last example, the verb can come in front of the subject.

- you can sometimes put adverbs and adverb phrases in front of the main verb for emphasis, but not prepositional phrases or noun groups

He deliberately chose it because it was cheap.
I very much wanted to go with them.

- you can change the order of adverbials of manner, place, and time when you want to change the emphasis

They were sitting in the car quite happily. (place, manner)
At the meeting last night, she spoke very well. (place, time, manner)

Unit 31 Practice

A You are given the parts of a sentence in brackets below. Write the sentences in the normal order, without any special emphasis.

1 (the children / happily / in the garden / were playing)

The children ...*were playing happily in the garden.*...................

2 (last night / the concert / we enjoyed / very much)

We enjoyed ....

3 (Mary / yesterday / in the supermarket / I met)

I met ....

4 (in Greece / last year / we had / a holiday)

Last year ....

5 (in London / most people / about nine o'clock / start work)

In London ....

6 (very late / this morning / to work / I got)

This morning ....

7 (a new school / they are building / next year / in our town)

Next year ....

8 (most things / cheaply / you can buy / in the supermarket)

You can buy ....

9 (Andreas / five languages / fluently / speaks)

....

10 (at the meeting / yesterday / Jack / very angrily / spoke)

....

11 (very heavily / it rained / last night / in London)

....

12 (neatly / his name / at the bottom of the page / he wrote)

....

B Make the adverbials in these sentences emphatic by putting them at the front of the sentence.

1 They visit their grandparents every weekend. / ...*Every weekend they visit their*...............
grandparents....

2 He opened the door quietly. / ....

3 I have tried to call you several times. / ....

4 We waited for him for over an hour. / ....

5 He posted the wrong letter by mistake. / ....

6 She drove to town as quickly as possible. / ....

7 He folded the paper carefully. / ....

8 I spoke to him about it only yesterday. / ....

9 There are some wonderful paintings in the National Gallery. / ....

....

10 He walked out of the room angrily. / ....

▶ **Bank**

63

Unit 32 Adverbials of manner

Main points

- Most adverbs of manner are formed by adding '-ly' to an adjective, but sometimes other spelling changes are needed.
- You cannot form adverbs from adjectives that end in '-ly'.
- Some adverbs have the same form as adjectives.
- You do not use adverbs after link verbs, you use adjectives.
- Adverbials of manner are sometimes prepositional phrases or noun groups.

1 Adverbs of manner are often formed by adding '-ly' to an adjective.

Adjectives	Adverbs
bad	⇨ badly
beautiful	⇨ beautifully
careful	⇨ carefully
quick	⇨ quickly
quiet	⇨ quietly
soft	⇨ softly

2 Adverbs formed in this way usually have a similar meaning to the adjective.

She is as clever as she is beautiful.
He talked so politely and danced so beautifully.

'We must not talk. We must be quiet,' said Sita.
She wanted to sit quietly, to relax.

3 There are sometimes changes in spelling when an adverb is formed from an adjective.

	Adjectives	Adverbs
'-le' changes to '-ly':	gentle	⇨ gently
'-y' changes to '-ily':	easy	⇨ easily
'-ic' changes to '-ically':	automatic	⇨ automatically
'-ue' changes to '-uly':	true	⇨ truly
'-ll' changes to '-lly':	full	⇨ fully

Note that 'public' changes to 'publicly', not 'publically'.

WARNING: You cannot form adverbs from adjectives that already end in '-ly'. For example, you cannot say 'He smiled at me friendlily'. You can

sometimes use a prepositional phrase instead: 'He smiled at me in a friendly way'.

4 Some adverbs of manner have the same form as adjectives and have similar meanings, for example 'fast', 'hard', and 'late'.

I've always been interested in fast cars. (adjective)
The driver was driving too fast. (adverb)

Note that 'hardly' and 'lately' are not adverbs of manner and have different meanings from the adjectives 'hard' and 'late'.

It was a hard decision to make.
I hardly had any time to talk to her.

The train was late as usual.
Have you seen John lately?

5 The adverb of manner related to the adjective 'good' is 'well'.

He is a good dancer.
He dances well.

Note that 'well' can sometimes be an adjective when it refers to someone's health.

'How are you?'—'I am very well, thank you.'

6 You do not use adverbs after link verbs such as 'be', 'become', 'feel', 'get', 'look', and 'seem'. You use an adjective after these verbs. For example, you do not say 'Sue felt happily'. You say 'Sue felt happy'. See Unit 80 for more information on link verbs.

7 You do not often use prepositional phrases or noun groups as adverbials of manner. However, you occasionally need to use them, for example when there is no adverb form available. The prepositional phrases and noun groups usually include a noun such as 'way', 'fashion', or 'manner', or a noun that refers to someone's voice.

She asked me in such a nice manner that I couldn't refuse.
He did it the right way.
They spoke in angry tones.

Prepositional phrases with 'like' are also used as adverbials of manner.

I slept like a baby.
He drove like a madman.

Unit 32 Practice

A Use the adjective or adverb in brackets to complete each of the following pairs of sentences correctly.

1 It's an ...*easy*........................... question.
   You should be able to answer it quite ...*easily*........................... (easy / easily)

2 I can type a bit but I'm very .... I'm afraid I can only type very
   .... (slow / slowly)

3 Mr Robbins shouted .... at the children. The children made Mr Robbins very
   .... (angry / angrily)

4 Use this chair if you want to sit .... Use this chair. It's very
   .... (comfortable / comfortably)

5 Mary sang .... at the concert last night. Mary sang a
   .... song at the concert last night. (beautiful / beautifully)

6 There's no need to feel .... Peter answered the questions
   .... (nervous / nervously)

7 What was wrong with Bill? He looked very .... Bill shook his head
   .... (sad / sadly)

8 The children played together very .... (happy / happily)
   The children looked very .... as they played together.

9 I'm afraid you have done this piece of work .... (careless / carelessly)
   I'm afraid your work has been very ....

10 The letter I received this morning was quite .... (unexpected /
   unexpectedly)
   I received a letter this morning quite ....

B Fill each of the gaps below with one of the following adverbs. You will need to use some more than once.

anxiously badly carefully fast hard late lately quietly slowly suddenly well

1 We had to work very ...*hard*.................. to finish in time.

2 I play the piano, but I don't play it very ....

3 You should drive very .... in wet weather. It's dangerous to drive ....
   ....

4 He drove very .... to Liverpool, but he still arrived too .... for
   the meeting.

5 It'll take us hours to get there. Chris always drives so ....

6 Could you speak .... please. The baby is sleeping.

7 He didn't work very .... That's why he did so .... in the
   exam.

8 The exams were over and everyone was waiting ....

9 Do you know how David is? I haven't heard anything ....

10 We got a dreadful shock. We were just sitting here .... and ....
   .... there was a loud knock at the door.

65

Unit 33 Adverbials of time

Main points

- Adverbials of time can be time expressions such as 'last night'.
- Adverbials of time can be prepositional phrases with 'at', 'in', or 'on'.
- 'For' refers to a period of time in the past, present, or future.
- 'Since' refers to a point in past time.

1 You use adverbials of time to say when something happens. You often use noun groups called time expressions as adverbials of time.

yesterday	last year	the day after tomorrow
today	next Saturday	last night
tomorrow	next week	the other day

Note that you do not use the prepositions 'at', 'in', or 'on' with time expressions.

One of my children wrote to me today.
So, you're coming back next week?

You often use time expressions with verbs in the present tense to talk about the future.

The plane leaves tomorrow morning.
They're coming next week.

2 You can use prepositional phrases as adverbials of time:

- 'at' is used with:

clock times: at eight o'clock, at three fifteen
religious festivals: at Christmas, at Easter
mealtimes: at breakfast, at lunchtimes
specific periods: at night, at the weekend, at weekends, at half-term

- 'in' is used with:

seasons: in autumn, in the spring
years and centuries: in 1985, in the year 2000, in the nineteenth century
months: in July, in December
parts of the day: in the morning, in the evenings

Note that you also use 'in' to say that something will happen during or after a period of time in the future.

I think we'll find out in the next few days.

- 'on' is used with:

days: on Monday, on Tuesday morning, on Sunday evenings
special days: on Christmas Day, on my birthday, on his wedding anniversary
dates: on the twentieth of July, on June 21st

3 You use 'for' with verbs in any tense to say how long something continues to happen.

He is in Italy for a month.
I remained silent for a long time.
I will be in London for three months.

WARNING: You do not use 'during' to say how long something continues to happen. You cannot say 'I went there during three weeks'.

4 You use 'since' with a verb in the present perfect or past perfect tense to say when something started to happen.

Marilyn has lived in Paris since 1984.
I had eaten nothing since breakfast.

5 You can use many other prepositional phrases as adverbials of time. You use:

- 'during' and 'over' for a period of time in which something happens

I saw him twice during the summer holidays.
Will you stay in Edinburgh over Christmas?

- 'from...to/till/until' and 'between...and' for the beginning and end of a period of time

The building is closed from April to May.
She worked from four o'clock till ten o'clock.
Can you take the test between now and June?

- 'by' when you mean 'not later than'

By eleven o'clock, Brody was back in his office.
Can we get this finished by tomorrow?

- 'before' and 'after'

I saw him before the match.
She left the house after ten o'clock.

'Since', 'till', 'until', 'after', and 'before' can also be conjunctions with time clauses. See Unit 90.

I've been wearing glasses since I was three.

You use the adverb 'ago' with the past simple to say how long before the time of speaking something happened. You always put 'ago' after the period of time.

We saw him about a month ago.
John's wife died five years ago.

WARNING: You do not use 'ago' with the present perfect tense. You cannot say 'We have gone to Spain two years ago'.

Unit 33 Practice

A Complete these sentences using **at, in, on,** or nothing at all.

1 I'll come round ....*at*......... six o'clock.
2 The Second World War began .... September 1939 and ended .... 1945.
3 It's my birthday .... Friday.
4 The meeting is .... half past two .... the afternoon .... next Monday.
5 This house gets dreadfully cold .... winter, especially .... night. We nearly froze to death .... last Christmas.
6 It's our twenty fifth anniversary next month. We were married .... 1966, ... the 17th of September.
7 Come round .... lunchtime and have something to eat. We normally start lunch .... about one o'clock .... the weekend.
8 The programme is .... six o'clock .... Saturday evening.
9 In Europe we have our weekend break .... Saturday and Sunday, but .... the Middle East the weekend is .... Thursday and Friday.
10 In Scotland the main winter celebration is not .... Christmas but .... New Year, or Hogmanay as the Scots call it. There are lots of parties .... New Year's Eve and .... midnight everyone joins hands to sing Auld Lang Syne.

B Complete the following sentences using **ago, for,** or **since.**

1 Columbus discovered America about six hundred years ....*ago*............. .
2 Ghana has been an independent country .... 1957.
3 Russia has been a republic .... over seventy years.
4 Oxford has been a centre of learning .... more than a thousand years.
5 Most British universities were founded less than fifty years ....
6 There has been a university in Birmingham .... about 1900.
7 William Shakespeare was born about four hundred years ....
8 It is nearly four hundred years .... Shakespeare's birth.
9 Two thousand years .... Britain was part of the Roman Empire.
10 England and Scotland have been united .... 1707.

C Use the prepositions and adverbs in brackets to complete the following sentences.

1 I had to work ...*during*.......... the summer holidays, ... the beginning of July .... the end of August. (during / from / until)
2 We got married .... 1970 so we have been married .... more than twenty years now. (for / in)
3 I should have handed in my homework a week .... My teacher isn't very pleased. She says I must finish it .... six o'clock .... Monday at the latest. (ago / by / on)
4 The last time we went to England was .... 1983, that's nearly ten years .... We haven't been back .... then even though our friends have often invited us. (ago / in / since)
5 My parents lived in Liverpool .... 1960 .... 1975. .... 1978, when I was born, they had moved to Birmingham. (by / from / until)

▶ **Bank**

Unit 34 Adverbials of frequency and probability

Words like: always, ever, never, perhaps, possibly, probably

Main points

- Adverbials of frequency are used to say how often something happens.
- Adverbials of probability are used to say how sure you are about something.
- These adverbials usually come before the main verb, but they come after 'be' as a main verb.

1 You use adverbials of frequency to say how often something happens.

a lot	frequently	normally	rarely
always	hardly ever	occasionally	sometimes
ever	never	often	usually

We *often* swam in the sea.
She *never* comes to my parties.

2 You use adverbials of probability to say how sure you are about something.

certainly	maybe	perhaps	probably
definitely	obviously	possibly	really

I *definitely* saw her yesterday.
The driver *probably* knows the quickest route.

3 You usually put adverbials of frequency and probability before the main verb and after an auxiliary or a modal.

He *sometimes works* downstairs in the kitchen.
You *are definitely wasting* your time.
I *have never had* such a horrible meal!
I *shall never forget* this day.

Note that you usually put them after 'be' as a main verb.

He *is always* careful with his money.
You *are probably* right.

'Perhaps' usually comes at the beginning of the sentence.

Perhaps the beaches are cleaner in the north.
Perhaps you need a membership card to get in.

'A lot' always comes after the main verb.

I go swimming *a lot* in the summer.

4 'Never' is a negative adverb.

She *never* goes abroad.
I've *never* been to Europe.

You normally use 'ever' in questions, negative sentences, and 'if'-clauses.

Have you *ever* been to a football match?
Don't *ever* do that again!
If you *ever* need anything, just call me.

Note that you can sometimes use 'ever' in affirmative sentences, for example after a superlative.

She is the *best* dancer I have *ever* seen.

You use 'hardly ever' in affirmative sentences to mean almost never.

We *hardly ever* meet.

The bus is always late.

Perhaps it has broken down.

It's probably stuck in traffic.

Unit 34 Practice

A Choose one of the following adverbials to add to each of these sentences so that they are true for you.

never	hardly ever	rarely	occasionally	sometimes
often	usually	always	nearly always	

1 I ...*sometimes*... watch TV in the evening.
2 I .... take a holiday in the summer.
3 I .... go shopping at the weekend.
4 I .... do the cooking at home.
5 I .... do the washing up.
6 I .... go out somewhere at the weekend.
7 I .... go to bed before eleven.

B Give true replies to the following questions using one of these adverbials for each answer.

definitely	certainly	probably	possibly	probably not	definitely not

1 Will you enjoy your next English lesson? ...*Definitely.*...
2 Will you do your next piece of homework on time? ....
3 Do you think you will visit England within the next year? ....
4 Will you ever be very rich? ....
5 Will you be moving to a new house within the next year? ....
6 Do you think you will learn to speak English really fluently? ....
7 Do you think the best way of learning a language is by living in a country where that language is spoken? ....
8 Do you think that reading a lot in English is a good way to improve your English? ....

C Rewrite the sentences below to include the adverbials in brackets.

1 I go swimming. / ...*I usually go swimming at the weekend.*........... (usually / at the weekend)
2 My brother goes swimming. / .... (normally / twice a week)
3 Peter went to visit his grandparents. / .... (on Sundays / often)
4 The British are talking about the weather. / .... (always)
5 I'll be back. / .... (in a couple of minutes / probably)
6 He will be at home. / .... (probably / at lunchtime)
7 He should have telephoned. / .... (by now / certainly)
8 I locked the door. / .... (last night / definitely)
9 He phoned home. / .... (usually / every day)
10 They didn't get there. / .... (in time / perhaps)
11 We go to the theatre. / .... (hardly ever / nowadays)
12 John will call round. / .... (tomorrow / probably)

Unit 35 Adverbials of duration - already, still, yet

Main points

- 'Already' is used to say that something has happened earlier than expected.
- 'Still' is used to say that something continues to happen until a particular time.
- 'Yet' is used to say that something has not happened before a particular time.
- 'Any longer', 'any more', 'no longer', and 'no more' are used to say that something has stopped happening.

1 You use adverbials of duration to say that an event or situation is continuing, stopping, or is not happening at the moment.

She still lives in London.
I couldn't stand it any more.
It isn't dark yet.

2 You use 'already' to say that something has happened sooner than it was expected to happen. You put 'already' in front of the main verb.

He had already bought the cups and saucers.
I've already seen them.
The guests were already coming in.

You put 'already' after 'be' as a main verb.

Julie was already in bed.

You can also use 'already' to emphasize that something is the case, for example when someone else does not know or is not sure.

I am already aware of that problem.

You do not normally use 'already' in negative statements, but you can use it in negative 'if'-clauses.

Show it to him if he hasn't already seen it.

You can put 'already' at the beginning or end of a clause for emphasis.

Already he was calculating the profit he could make.
I've done it already.

3 You use 'still' to say that a situation continues to exist up to a particular time in the past, present, or future. You put 'still' in front of the main verb.

We were still waiting for the election results.
My family still live in India.
You will still get tickets, if you hurry.

You put 'still' after 'be' as a main verb.

Martin's mother died, but his father is still alive.

You can use 'still' after the subject and before the verb group in negative sentences to express surprise or impatience.

You still haven't given us the keys.
He still didn't say a word.
It was after midnight, and he still wouldn't leave.

Remember that you can use 'still' at the beginning of a clause with a similar meaning to 'after all' or 'nevertheless'.

Still, he is my brother, so I'll have to help him.
Still, it's not too bad. We didn't lose all the money.

4 You use 'yet' at the end of negative sentences and questions to say that something has not happened or had not happened up to a particular time, but is or was expected to happen later.

We haven't got the tickets yet.
Have you joined the swimming club yet?
They hadn't seen the baby yet.

Remember that 'yet' can also be used at the beginning of a clause with a similar meaning to 'but'.

I don't miss her, yet I do often wonder where she went.
They know they won't win. Yet they keep on trying.

5 You use 'any longer' and 'any more' at the end of negative clauses to say that a past situation has ended and does not exist now or will not exist in the future.

I wanted the job, but I couldn't wait any longer.
He's not going to play any more.

In formal English, you can use an affirmative clause with 'no longer' and 'no more'. You can put them at the end of the clause, or in front of the main verb.

He could stand the pain no more.
He no longer wanted to buy it.

Unit 35 Practice

A Fill the blanks with **yet** or **any longer / any more.**

1 I've started learning French but I haven't learned very much ...*yet*............................ .

2 Time is running out. We can't wait ....

3 We aren't ready to start .... Let's wait a little longer.

4 Mary posted the letter last week but I haven't got it ....

5 You mustn't leave .... The party is only just beginning.

6 If you stand there talking .... we'll miss our train.

B Fill the blanks with **still** or **already.**

1 You needn't tell Harry. He ...*already*............... knows.

2 I didn't know you were .... working at Brown's. You've been there for ages.

3 Joe .... lives in Manchester, where he was born.

4 I'm .... trying to finish my homework. I've .... been at it for three hours.

5 The children are grown up now but they .... like to come home for the holidays.

6 I've .... seen that film and I don't want to see it again.

C Complete these sentences using **still, yet, already, any longer,** or **any more.**

1 John doesn't live in London ...*any more*............... . He's moved to Bristol.

2 The children haven't gone to bed .... They're .... watching television.

3 A: Is Anne .... here? B: No, she has .... left.

4 Becky hasn't gone to university .... She's .... at school.

5 Have you started your new job .... or are you .... working in London?

6 Tom had eaten well but he was .... hungry.

7 Since her accident, Susan .... plays golf but she doesn't play tennis ....

8 I offered to help Joe with the car but he had .... mended it.

9 Thanks for your help. I won't trouble you ....

10 A: Have you finished your homework ...., or are you .... working on it? B: I've .... finished it.

Unit 36 Adverbials of degree

Main points

- Adverbs of degree usually modify verbs.
- Some adverbs of degree can modify adjectives, other adverbs, or clauses.

1 You use adverbs of degree to modify verbs. They make the verb stronger or weaker.

I totally disagree.
I can nearly swim.

2 Some adverbs can come in front of a main verb, after a main verb, or after the object if there is one.

badly	greatly	strongly
completely	seriously	totally

Mr Brooke strongly criticized the Bank of England.
I disagree completely with John Taylor.
That argument doesn't convince me totally.

Some adverbs are mostly used in front of the verb.

almost	largely	nearly	really	quite

He almost crashed into a lorry.

Note that 'really' is used at the beginning of a clause to express surprise, and at the end of a clause as an adverb of manner.

Really, I didn't know that!
He wanted it really, but he was too shy to ask.

'A lot' and 'very much' come after the main verb if there is no object, or after the object.

She helped a lot.
We liked him very much.

'Very much' can come after the subject and in front of verbs like 'want', 'prefer', and 'enjoy'.

I very much wanted to take it with me.

3 Some adverbs of degree go in front of adjectives or other adverbs and modify them.

awfully	fairly	quite	really
extremely	pretty	rather	very

...a fairly large office, with filing space.

Note that you can use 'rather' before or after 'a' or 'an' followed by an adjective and a noun.

Seaford is rather a pleasant town.
He told me a rather long and complicated story.

When 'quite' means 'fairly', you put it in front of 'a' or 'an' followed by an adjective and a noun.

My father gave me quite a large sum of money.

However, when 'quite' means 'extremely', you can put it after 'a'. You can say 'a quite enormous sum'.

4 You use some adverbs of degree to modify clauses and prepositional phrases.

entirely	just	largely	mainly	partly	simply

Are you saying that simply because I am here?
I don't think it's worth going just for a day.

5 You use 'so' and 'such' to emphasize a quality that someone or something has. 'So' can be followed by an adjective, an adverb, or a noun group beginning with 'many', 'much', 'few', or 'little'.

John is so interesting to talk to.
Science is changing so rapidly.
I want to do so many different things.

'Such' is followed by a singular noun group with 'a', or a plural noun group.

There was such a noise we couldn't hear.
They said such nasty things about you.

WARNING: 'So' is never followed by a singular noun group with 'a' or a plural noun group.

6 You use 'too' when you mean 'more than is necessary' or 'more than is good'. You can use 'too' before adjectives and adverbs, and before 'many', 'much', 'few', or 'little'.

The prices in that shop are too high.
I've been paying too much tax.

You use 'enough' after adjectives and adverbs.

I waited until my daughter was old enough to read.
He didn't work quickly enough.

Note that 'enough' is also a determiner.

We've got enough money to buy that car now.

7 You use emphasizing adverbs to modify adjectives such as 'astonishing', 'furious', and 'wonderful', which express extreme qualities.

absolutely	entirely	purely	really	totally
completely	perfectly	quite	simply	utterly

I think he's absolutely wonderful.

Unit 36 Practice

A Look at the pairs of sentences below. Each sentence has an adverb of degree that is modifying a verb. In each case, say whether the adverb of degree is in the right place or not.

1 I **really** enjoyed our visit to the art gallery. ...*Right*....

   I enjoyed **really** our visit to the art gallery. ...*Wrong*..

2 I have finished **nearly** . I'll be with you in a minute. ....

   I have **nearly** finished. I'll be with you in a minute. ....

3 He wanted to find a new job **very badly.** ....

   Very badly he wanted to find a new job. ....

4 Jack **completely** forgot to sign the cheque. ....

   Jack forgot to sign the cheque **completely.** ....

5 Maria understood what he was talking about **only half.** ....

   Maria **only half** understood what he was talking about. ....

6 It was a dreadful accident but fortunately nobody was **seriously** injured. ....

   It was a dreadful accident but fortunately nobody **seriously** was injured. ....

B The adverbs of degree given can modify phrases or clauses. Put them in the right place in each sentence.

1 It was   *mainly*   because of Henry that we were invited. (mainly)

2 His success was the result of hard work. (largely)

3 They finally came to an agreement because they were tired of arguing. (simply)

4 You can often get what you want by asking. (simply)

5 He usually disagreed with the majority to make things difficult. (just)

6 I missed my flight to Cairo owing to a traffic hold-up. (partly)

7 He finally got what he wanted, but it was by good luck. (mainly)

8 He used to play the fool to annoy his father. (just)

C Rewrite these sentences with **rather a/an** or **quite a/an.**

1 The book was rather interesting. / It was ...*rather an interesting book.*...........................

2 The house we lived in was quite big. / We lived in ....

3 The film was quite exciting. / It was ....

4 My childhood was rather sad. / I had ....

5 The car was rather expensive. / It was ....

6 The school is quite good. / It is ....

7 I met a man who was quite interesting. / I met ....

8 When she was a child she was rather naughty. / She was ....

9 The problem was rather difficult. / It was ....

10 The letter she wrote him was quite rude. / She wrote him ....

Now rewrite sentences 1, 4, 5, and 9 with **a rather.**

1 *It was a rather interesting book.* ....

4 ....

5 ....

9 ....

▶ **Bank**

Unit 37 Prepositions of place and direction

Words like: above, below, down, from, to, towards, up

Main points

- You normally use prepositional phrases to say where a person or thing is, or the direction they are moving in.
- You can also use adverbs and adverb phrases for place and direction.
- Many words are both prepositions and adverbs.

1 You use prepositions to talk about the place where someone or something is. Prepositions are always followed by a noun group, which is called the object of the preposition.

above	below	in	opposite	through
among	beneath	inside	outside	under
at	beside	near	over	underneath
behind	between	on	round	

He stood _near_ the door.
Two minutes later we were safely _inside_ the taxi.

Note that some prepositions consist of more than one word.

in between	in front of	next to	on top of

There was a man standing _in front of_ me.
The books were piled _on top of_ each other.

2 You can also use prepositions to talk about the direction that someone or something is moving in, or the place that someone or something is moving towards.

across	into	past	to
along	onto	round	towards
back to	out of	through	up
down			

They dived _into_ the water.
She turned and rushed _out of_ the room.

3 Many prepositions can be used both for place and direction.

The bank is just _across_ the High Street. (place)
I walked _across_ the room. (direction)

We live in the house _over_ the road. (place)
I stole his keys and escaped _over_ the wall. (direction)

4 You can also use adverbs and adverb phrases for place and direction.

abroad	here	underground	everywhere
away	indoors	upstairs	nowhere
downstairs	outdoors	~	somewhere
downwards	there	anywhere	

Sheila was _here_ a moment ago.
Can't you go _upstairs_ and turn the bedroom light off?

Note that a few noun groups can also be used as adverbials of place or direction.

Steve lives _next door_ at number 23.
I thought we went _the other way_ last time.

5 Many words can be used as prepositions and as adverbs, with no difference in meaning. Remember that prepositions have noun groups as objects, but adverbs do not.

Did he fall _down the stairs_?
Please do sit _down_.
I looked _underneath the bed_, but the box had gone!
Always put a sheet of paper _underneath_.

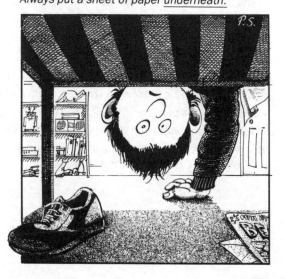

74

Unit 37 Practice

A Look at the picture carefully, then look at the following pairs of sentences. In each case one sentence is true and the other is not true. Write 'True' or 'Not true' for each.

1 The cinema is next to the bank. .....*True.*..........

The cinema is between the bank and the hotel. ....

2 There's a dog running across the road. ....

There's a dog running along the pavement. ....

3 There's a girl standing by the telephone box. ....

There's a girl standing in front of the cinema. ....

4 The dog is running towards the girl. ....

The dog is running away from the girl. ....

5 There's an old man walking across the road. ....

There's an old man walking down the street. ....

6 There's a car waiting at the traffic lights. ....

There's a bus waiting at the traffic lights. ....

7 There's a woman waiting outside the cinema. ....

There's a woman waiting inside the cinema. ....

8 There's a man walking towards her. ....

There's a man walking away from her. ....

9 The telephone box is just outside the bank. ....

The telephone box is just outside the hotel. ....

10 The boy is standing in front of his mother. ....

The boy is standing behind his mother. ....

B Complete the following sentences by putting the prepositions in brackets in the right place.

1 I work at Woolworth's, just ....*across*..........the road from the cinema and ....*next to*.......... the bank. (across / next to)

2 He ran .... the corner, ... the road to the other side and .... the street. (across / down / round)

3 They said it was .... the railway station so it must be somewhere .... here. (opposite / round)

4 We sat .... the front of the cinema but not right .... the front row. (at / in)

5 Jill sat in the front .... the driver and I sat .... her. (behind / next to)

6 My office is .... town, ... the post office. (close to / in the middle of)

to / in the middle of)

Unit 38 Prepositions of place - at, in, on

Main points

- You use 'at' to talk about a place as a point.
- You use 'in' to talk about a place as an area.
- You use 'on' to talk about a place as a surface.

1 You use 'at' when you are thinking of a place as a point in space.

She waited at the bus stop for over twenty minutes.
'Where were you last night?' - 'At Mick's house.'

2 You also use 'at' with words such as 'back', 'bottom', 'end', 'front', and 'top' to talk about the different parts of a place.

Mrs Castle was waiting at the bottom of the stairs.
They escaped by a window at the back of the house.
I saw a taxi at the end of the street.

You use 'at' with public places and institutions. Note that you also say 'at home' and 'at work'.

I have to be at the station by ten o'clock.
We landed at a small airport.
A friend of mine is at Training College.
She wanted to stay at home.

You say 'at the corner' or 'on the corner' when you are talking about streets.

The car was parked at the corner of the street.
There's a telephone box on the corner.

You say 'in the corner' when you are talking about a room.

She put the chair in the corner of the room.

3 You use 'in' when you are talking about a place as an area. You use 'in' with:

- a country or geographical region

When I was in Spain, it was terribly cold.
A thousand homes in the east of Scotland suffered power cuts.

- a city, town, or village

I've been teaching at a college in London.

- a building when you are talking about people or things inside it

They were sitting having dinner in the restaurant.

You also use 'in' with containers of any kind when talking about things inside them.

She kept the cards in a little box.

4 Compare the use of 'at' and 'in' in these examples.

I had a hard day at the office. ('at' emphasizes the office as a public place or institution)

I left my coat behind in the office. ('in' emphasizes the office as a building)

There's a good film at the cinema. ('at' emphasizes the cinema as a public place)

It was very cold in the cinema. ('in' emphasizes the cinema as a building.)

5 When talking about addresses, you use 'at' when you give the house number, and 'in' when you just give the name of the street.

They used to live at 5, Weston Road.
She got a job in Oxford Street.

Note that American English uses 'on': 'He lived on Penn Street.'
You use 'at' when you are talking about someone's house.

I'll see you at Fred's house.

6 You use 'on' when you are talking about a place as a surface. You can also use 'on top of'.

I sat down on the sofa.
She put her keys on top of the television.

You also use 'on' when you are thinking of a place as a point on a line, such as a road, a railway line, a river, or a coastline.

Scrabster is on the north coast.
Oxford is on the A34 between Birmingham and London.

See Unit 33 for information on 'at', 'in', and 'on' in adverbials of time.

Unit 38 Practice

A Use these words to complete the sentences below.

back	bottom	bus	car		corner	door	flat
front row	Park Street	left	phone box	picture	table	floor

1 There's someone at the ....*door*............

2 There's a .... on the wall above the TV set in a .... of the
room.

3 I waited at the .... of the queue.

4 I wanted to use the phone on the .... of the street but there was an old lady in the
....

5 I had a seat on the .... in the ....

6 Jack lives in a .... in .... on the third ....

7 There was a note on the .... It was from Elsie. She had signed her name at the
....

8 Jenny went to work in the .... and I went home on the ....

B Complete the following sentences using **at**, **in**, or **on**.

1 They live ....*in*.......... Coronation Street ....*at*......... number 32.

2 Jack works .... Oxford .... the University.

3 I've left my briefcase .... the office. I think I left it .... the chair .... the
corner.

4 Meet me .... the bus-stop .... the end of Bristol Road.

5 They live .... Seal, a small village .... the road to Folkestone.

6 When we were .... the south we stayed .... a small hotel .... the coast.

7 My diary is .... the table .... the sitting room.

8 Sign your name .... the dotted line .... the bottom of the page.

9 Meet me .... the entrance to the Supermarket .... the High Street.

10 I've applied for a job .... the United Nations .... Geneva.

11 Hello. This is Gina. I'm .... Athens .... the Acropolis Hotel.

▶ **Bank**

Unit 39 Prepositions with forms of transport

Phrases like: by bus, in a car, on the plane, off the train

Main points

- You can use 'by' with most forms of transport.
- You use 'in', 'into', and 'out of' with cars.
- You normally use 'on', 'onto', and 'off' with other forms of transport.

1 When you talk about the type of vehicle or transport you use to travel somewhere, you use 'by'.

by bus	by car	by plane	by train
by bicycle	by coach		

She had come by car with her husband and her four children.
I left Walsall in the afternoon and went by bus and train to Nottingham.

WARNING: If you want to say you walk somewhere, you say you go 'on foot'. You do not say 'by foot'.

Marie decided to continue on foot.

2 You use 'in', 'into', and 'out of' when you are talking about cars, vans, lorries, taxis, and ambulances.

I followed them in my car.
The carpets had to be collected in a van.
Mr Ward happened to be getting into his lorry.
She was carried out of the ambulance and up the steps.

3 You use 'on', 'onto', and 'off' when you are talking about other forms of transport, such as buses, coaches, trains, ships, and planes.

Why don't you come on the train with me to New York?
Peter Hurd was already on the plane from California.
The last thing he wanted was to spend ten days on a boat with Hooper.
He jumped back onto the old bus, now nearly empty.
Mr Bixby stepped off the train and walked quickly to the exit.

You can use 'in', 'into', and 'out of' with these other forms of transport, usually when you are focusing on the physical position or movement of the person, rather than stating what form of transport they are using.

The passengers in the plane were beginning to panic.
He got back into the train quickly, before Batt could stop him.
We jumped out of the bus and ran into the nearest shop.

Unit 39 Practice

A Look at the pictures and use these phrases to complete the sentences below.

by bullet train	on a bullet train
by luxury liner	on a luxury liner
by Concorde	on a jumbo jet
by bus	on a double-decker bus
by coach	in an air-conditioned coach
by car ferry	on a car ferry

1 a The fastest way of getting from Kyoto to Tokyo is ..... *by bullet train* ....

   b I've been on an express train, but I've never been ....

2 a The most comfortable way of travelling is ....

   b I'd love to spend a holiday ....

3 a Concorde is very fast, but you are more comfortable ....

   b You could take a jumbo jet, but it's quicker ....

4 a You can get about sixty passengers ....

   b For short journeys it's convenient to travel ....

5 a We drove to the airport ....

   b We were taken to the airport ....

6 a If you are taking the family, it's cheaper to go ....

   b You can relax and take it easy ....

B Complete the following sentences using **by, in, off, on,** or **out of.**

1 I usually go back home .... *by* .... bus. It's much cheaper than going .... train.

2 It gets so crowded in the rush hour that it's quicker to go .... foot than .... car.

3 We can take five people .... the car and the others will have to go .... the train.

4 It takes about half an hour to get home .... my bike and about twenty minutes ....
   the bus.

5 I have often travelled .... plane but I've never been .... a jumbo jet.

6 Since I broke my leg I have to travel .... bus because I can't get .... the car.

7 I have to get .... the train at the next stop.

8 Let me help you get your things .... the car.

9 The journey is uphill all the way so it's very tiring .... bike. I prefer to go .... foot.

10 We went for a trip up the Nile .... a big boat called a felucca.

Unit 40 Auxiliary verbs - be, have, do

Main points

- The auxiliaries 'be', 'have', and 'do' are used in forming tenses, negatives, and questions.
- The auxiliary 'be' is used in forming the continuous tenses and the passive.
- The auxiliary 'have' is used in forming the perfect tenses.
- The auxiliary 'do' is used in making negative and question forms from sentences that have a verb in a simple tense.

1 The auxiliary verbs are 'be', 'have', and 'do'. They are used with a main verb to form tenses, negatives, and questions.

He is planning to get married soon.
I haven't seen Peter since last night.
Which doctor do you want to see?

2 'Be' as an auxiliary is used:

- with the '-ing' form of the main verb to form continuous tenses

He is living in Germany.
They were going to phone you.

- with the past participle of the main verb to form the passive

These cars are made in Japan.
The walls of her flat were covered with posters.

3 You use 'have' as an auxiliary with the past participle to form the perfect tenses.

I have changed my mind.
I wish you had met Guy.

The present perfect continuous, the past perfect continuous, and the perfect tenses in the passive, are formed using both 'have' and 'be'.

He has been working very hard recently.
She did not know how long she had been lying there.
The guest-room window has been mended.
They had been taught by a young teacher.

4 'Be' and 'have' are also used as auxiliaries in negative sentences and questions in continuous and perfect tenses, and in the passive.

He isn't going.
Hasn't she seen it yet?
Was it written in English?

You use 'do' as an auxiliary to make negative and question forms from sentences that have a verb in the present simple or past simple.

He doesn't think he can come to the party.
Do you like her new haircut?
She didn't buy the house.
Didn't he get the job?

Note that you can use 'do' as a main verb with the auxiliary 'do'.

He didn't do his homework.
Do they do the work themselves?

You can also use the auxiliary 'do' with 'have' as a main verb.

He doesn't have any money.
Does anyone have a question?

You only use 'do' in affirmative sentences for emphasis or contrast.

I do feel sorry for Roger.

WARNING: You never use the auxiliary 'do' with 'be' except in the imperative.

Don't be stupid!
Do be a good boy and sit still.

5 Some grammars include modals among the auxiliary verbs. When there is a modal in the verb group, it is always the first word in the verb group, and comes before the auxiliaries 'be' and 'have'.

She might be going to Switzerland for Christmas.
I would have liked to have seen her.

Note that you never use the auxiliary 'do' with a modal. See Units 59–71 for more information on modals.

Unit 40 Practice

A Use these forms of the auxiliary **do** to complete the sentences below.

do don't does doesn't did didn't

1 I ....*didn't*........... enjoy the film very much. It was far too long.
2 Where .... you want to go for dinner this evening?
3 .... be silly!
4 How long .... it take you to drive to London last night?
5 How long .... it usually take?
6 .... anyone know the answer?

B Use these auxiliaries to complete the sentences that follow.

do don't had has hasn't have have been is will would have

1 John ....*has*............ left home. He ....*is*............... living in Italy now.
2 .... you still work in the shop, or .... you got another job now?
3 I .... want to be late, so I .... have to take a taxi.
4 We .... waiting for hours, but he still .... phoned.
5 You .... met her, if you .... come earlier.

And now do the same with these.

are didn't does don't had have haven't is was were will

6 I .... going to write to you, but I .... have time.
7 I wish I .... seen John and Mary while they .... staying here.
8 .... shout! You .... wake the baby.
9 We .... still working. We .... finished yet.
10 .... anyone know what time the meeting .... going to start?

C Here are some very common question forms in English. First complete the questions by adding **do, does, has,** or **have,** then match the questions and answers.

1 ...*Do*........ you know what time it is?
2 .... you finished yet?
3 .... anyone know where Angelo is?
4 .... anybody seen Maria?
5 .... you think we'll be late?
6 .... you ever been abroad?
7 .... anybody know the date?
8 .... you like living in England?
9 .... you ever read any Shakespeare?
10 .... anyone here got change for a pound?
11 .... you know what time the next train leaves?
12 .... anybody know where the key to this cupboard is?

a No. I'll be another ten minutes.
b No, I'm afraid my English isn't good enough.
c Sorry, I haven't got a watch.
d The seventeenth, isn't it?
e Not me. I haven't seen it for ages.
f In about ten minutes, I think.
g Yes, I've got two fifty-pence pieces.
h No. I don't think she's here this morning.
i Not yet. But I'm going to America next year.
j Yes, but I don't like the weather much.
k He was in the library a minute ago.
l Not if we hurry.

Unit 41 The present tenses

Main points

- There are four present tenses - present simple, present continuous, present perfect, and present perfect continuous.
- All the present tenses are used to refer to a time which includes the present.
- Present tenses can also be used for predictions made in the present about future events.

1 There are four tenses which begin with a verb in the present tense. They are the present simple, the present continuous, the present perfect, and the present perfect continuous. These are the present tenses.

2 The present simple and the present continuous are used with reference to present time. If you are talking about the general present, or about a regular or habitual action, you use the present simple.

George lives in Birmingham.
They often phone my mother in London.

If you are talking about something in the present situation, you use the present continuous.

He's playing tennis at the University.
I'm cooking the dinner.

The present continuous is often used to refer to a temporary situation.

She's living in a flat at present.

3 You use the present perfect or the present perfect continuous when you are concerned with the present effects of something which happened at a time in the past, or which started in the past but is still continuing.

Have you seen the film at the Odeon?
We've been waiting here since before two o'clock.

4 If you are talking about something which is scheduled or timetabled to happen in the future, you can use the present simple tense.

The next train leaves at two fifteen in the morning.
It's Tuesday tomorrow.

5 If you are talking about something which has been arranged for the future, you can use the present continuous. When you use the present continuous like this, there is nearly always a time adverbial like 'tomorrow', 'next week', or 'later' in the clause.

We're going on holiday with my parents this year.
The Browns are having a party next week.

6 It is only in main clauses that the choice of tense can be related to a particular time. In subordinate clauses, for example in 'if'-clauses, time clauses, and defining relative clauses, present tenses often refer to a future time in relation to the time in the main clause.

You can go at five if you have finished.
Let's have a drink before we start.
We'll save some food for anyone who arrives late.

7 The present simple tense normally has no auxiliary verb, but questions and negative sentences are formed with the auxiliary 'do'.

Do you live round here?
Does your husband do most of the cooking?
They don't often phone during the week.
She doesn't like being late if she can help it.

Unit 41 Practice

A In the sentences below, decide if the verb underlined refers to the present (P), the future (F), or to something habitual (H).

1 Joe wants to be a pilot when he <u>grows up</u>. ......*F*........
2 We always <u>go</u> abroad for our holidays. ....
3 I'm sorry, but I <u>feel</u> tired. ....
4 I just <u>want</u> to go to sleep. ....
5 Washington <u>is</u> the capital of the USA. ....
6 When <u>do you start</u> at the university next year? ....
7 Oh dear, this milk <u>tastes</u> awful. ....
8 You <u>look</u> really funny in that hat. ....
9 Give my love to Norman if you <u>see</u> him. ....
10 Do your children <u>help</u> about the house? ....
11 It's amazing how many people <u>eat</u> far too much. ....

B Complete these sentences using the correct form of the verb in brackets.

1 We enjoy the theatre but we ....*don't go*.. very often. (not go)
2 What time ....? (the train / leave)
3 My brother .... at home any more. (not live)
4 Where .... nowadays? (you / work)
5 I...Jill .... me very much. (not think) (like)
6 What time .... after work? (Ken / get home)
7 Penny .... Calgary in Canada. (come from)
8 How many languages ....? (you / speak)
9 How much .... for a return ticket? (it / cost)
10 Anne .... coffee, but she .... tea. (not drink) (like)

C Look carefully at the verbs in bold. Underline those which refer to the future.

1 A: **Are** you **doing** anything tomorrow?
   B: Not really. We**'re** just **staying** at home.
2 A: **Is** Peter **living** at home now?
   B: No, he **is** still at university in Sheffield.
3 A: How about your exams? **Have** you **passed?**
   B: I **don't know.** I'll let you know as soon as I**'ve heard** the results.
4 A: Is Jack the boy who **is coming** to stay next weekend?
   B: No. Jack **lives** just near us. It's Dan who**'s coming** to stay.
5 A: **Have** you **seen** Jenny recently?
   B: No, but we'll probably see her when we **go** to Leeds.
6 A: Will you come home after you**'ve finished** work?
   B: No. I**'m meeting** Joe in town and we**'re going** to the theatre.

Unit 42 The past tenses

Main points

- There are four past tenses - past simple, past continuous, past perfect, and past perfect continuous.
- All the past tenses are used to refer to past time.
- The past tenses are often used as polite forms.
- The past tenses have special meanings in conditional clauses and when referring to imaginary situations.

1 There are four tenses which begin with a verb in the past tense. They are the past simple, the past continuous, the past perfect, and the past perfect continuous. These are the past tenses. They are used to refer to past time, and also to refer to imaginary situations, and to express politeness.

2 The past simple and the past continuous are used with reference to past time. You use the past simple for events which happened in the past.

I woke up early and got out of bed.

If you are talking about the general past, or about regular or habitual actions in the past, you also use the past simple.

She lived just outside London.
We often saw his dog sitting outside his house.

If you are talking about something which continued to happen before and after a particular time in the past, you use the past continuous.

They were sitting in the kitchen, when they heard the explosion.
Jack arrived while the children were having their bath.

The past continuous is often used to refer to a temporary situation.

He was working at home at the time.
Bill was using my office until I came back from America.

3 You use the past perfect and past perfect continuous tenses when you are talking about the past and you are concerned with something which happened at an earlier time, or which had started at an earlier time but was still continuing.

I had heard it was a good film so we decided to go and see it.
It was getting late. I had been waiting there since two o'clock.

4 You sometimes use a past tense rather than a present tense when you want to be more polite. For example, in the following pairs of sentences, the second one is more polite.

Do you want to see me now?
Did you want to see me now?

I wonder if you can help me.
I was wondering if you could help me.

I wonder if you can help me.

5 The past tenses have special meanings in conditional clauses and when referring to hypothetical and imaginary situations, for example after 'I wish' or 'What if ...?'. You use the past simple and past continuous for something that you think is unlikely to happen.

If they saw the mess, they would be very angry.
We would tell you if we were selling the house.

You use the past perfect and past perfect continuous when you are talking about something which could have happened in the past, but which did not actually happen.

If I had known that you were coming, I would have told Jim.
They wouldn't have gone to bed if they had been expecting you to arrive.

Unit 42 Practice

A Make past tense questions and answers using the words given.

1 Who / you see / at the meeting? / *Who did you see at the meeting?* ....

2 I see / Jack / not Amy. / *I saw Jack, but I didn't see Amy.* ....

3 Where / you go / in England? / ....

4 We go / London / not Oxford. / ....

5 What plays / they see / at Stratford? / ....

6 They see / Hamlet / not Julius Caesar. / ....

7 Angelo / buy some records / in London? / ....

8 He buy / some clothes / not any records. / ....

9 You enjoy / your holiday? / ....

10 I enjoy / the holiday / not the food. / ....

B In the sentences below, decide if the modals and past simple verbs, which are underlined, are being used for narrative (N), a hypothetical situation (H), or for politeness (P).

1 Kathy was looking very well last time I <u>saw</u> her. ...*N*..........

2 Excuse me. I just <u>wanted</u> to know if you <u>were</u> free at the moment. ....

3 If I <u>wanted</u> to know, I <u>would</u> ask. ....

4 Frank <u>telephoned</u> yesterday and <u>left</u> a message. ....

5 I wish it <u>was</u> time for lunch. ....

6 I first <u>went</u> abroad when I <u>was</u> seventeen. ....

7 I am writing because I <u>wondered</u> if I <u>could</u> offer a useful suggestion. ....

8 Jenny <u>wished</u> she hadn't been so careless. ....

9 We <u>looked</u> everywhere for the money, but we <u>couldn't</u> find it. ....

10 You must take a map with you. Suppose you <u>got</u> lost, then what <u>would</u> you do? ....

11 Do you think I <u>could</u> borrow your bike tomorrow? ....

12 We were expecting a call from John, when Jill <u>phoned</u>. ....

C Complete these sentences, putting the verbs in the past simple or the past continuous.

1 I ...*was working*... upstairs when the accident ...*happened*..... (work) (happen)

2 He .... the book and .... to read. (open) (start)

3 We .... the film, when suddenly the electricity .... off. (enjoy) (go)

4 When she .... the news, she .... to cry. (hear) (begin)

5 Everyone .... quietly. Suddenly the door .... open. (talk) (burst)

6 When I .... the doorbell, I .... downstairs. (hear) (run)

▶ **Bank**

Unit 43 The continuous tenses

Main points

- Continuous tenses describe actions which continue to happen before and after a particular time.
- Continuous tenses can also indicate duration and change.

1 You use a continuous tense to indicate that an action continues to happen before and after a particular time, without stopping. You use the present continuous for actions which continue to happen before and after the moment of speaking.

I'm looking at the photographs my brother sent me.
They're having a meeting.

2 When you are talking about two actions in the present tense, you use the present continuous for an action that continues to happen before and after another action that interrupts it. You use the present simple for the other action.

The phone always rings when I'm having a bath.
Friends always talk to me when I'm trying to study.

3 When you are talking about the past, you use the past continuous for actions that continued to happen before and after another action, or before and after a particular time. This is often called the 'interrupted past'. You use the past simple for the other action.

He was watching television when the doorbell rang.
It was 6 o'clock. The train was nearing London.

WARNING: If two things happened one after another, you use two verbs in the past simple tense.

As soon as he saw me, he waved.

4 You can use continuous forms with modals in all their usual meanings. See Units 59 to 71 for more information on modals.

What could he be thinking of?
They might be telling lies.

5 You use continuous tenses to express duration, when you want to emphasize how long something has been happening or will happen for.

We had been living in Athens for five years.
They'll be staying with us for a couple of weeks.
He has been building up the business all his life.
By 1992, he will have been working for ten years.

Note that you do not have to use continuous tenses for duration.

We had lived in Africa for five years.
He worked for us for ten years.

6 You use continuous tenses to describe a state or situation that is temporary.

I'm living in London at the moment.
He'll be working nights next week.
She's spending the summer in Europe.

7 You use continuous tenses to show that something is changing, developing, or progressing.

Her English was improving.
The children are growing up quickly.
The video industry has been developing rapidly.

8 As a general rule, verbs which refer to actions that require a deliberate effort can be used in continuous tenses, verbs which refer to actions that do not require a deliberate effort are not used in continuous tenses.

I think it's going to rain. ('think' = 'believe'. Believing does not require deliberate effort)
Please be quiet. I'm thinking . ('think' = 'try to solve a problem'. Trying to solve a problem does require deliberate effort)

However, many verbs are not normally used in the continuous tenses. These include verbs that refer to thinking, liking and disliking, appearance, possession, and perception.
See Unit 45 for lists of these verbs.

Unit 43 Practice

A Put the verbs in brackets into the past simple or the past continuous tense to complete the sentences below.

1 He ...*was driving*.......... at over 100 kilometres an hour when the accident ...*happened*.......... .
(drive) (happen)

2 The thieves .... while we .... (break in) (sleep)

3 Someone .... with my clothes while I .... (run off) (swim)

4 I .... in the supermarket when I .... my purse. (shop) (lose)

5 He .... tennis and he .... his leg. (play) (break)

6 I first .... my wife when we .... in London. (meet) (work)

B Put the verbs in brackets into the present simple or the present continuous.

1 The baby always ...*wakes up*............... when we ...*are trying*............... to go to sleep. (wake up) (try)

2 It always .... raining when we .... tennis. (start) (play)

3 I .... a book at the moment so I .... very busy. (write) (be)

4 Sally always .... as if she .... herself. (look) (enjoy)

5 John .... with us when he .... London. (stay) (visit)

6 Mary .... to go on holiday so she .... as little money as possible. (save up) (spend)

C Complete the following sentences using the present perfect continuous tense of the verbs below.

> live   play   study   wait   walk   watch   work

1 We ...*have been living*............... in England for nearly two years now.

2 Why are you so late? I .... here for hours.

3 I .... German for three years, but I still don't speak it very well.

4 The boys must be tired. They .... football in the garden all afternoon.

5 It's time to do your homework. You .... television all night.

6 John .... in his father's business since he left school.

7 We must be nearly there by now. We .... for over an hour.

D Complete this dialogue by putting the verbs in brackets into the present continuous.

A: What ...*are you doing*.... Angela, now you have left school? (you do)

B: I .... in a restaurant. I .... to earn some money before I go to university. (work) (try)

A: .... at home? (you live)

B: No, I .... in a little village. I .... a cottage with some friends. (live) (share)

▶ **Bank**

Unit 44 The perfect tenses

Main points

- You use the present perfect to relate the past to the present.
- You use the past perfect to talk about a situation that occurred before a particular time in the past.

1 You use the present perfect tense when you are concerned with the present effects of something which happened at an indefinite time in the past.

I'm afraid I've forgotten my book.
Have you heard from Jill recently?

Sometimes, the present effects are important because the events are very recent.

Karen has just passed her exams.

You also use the present perfect when you are thinking of a time which started in the past and is still continuing.

Have you really lived here for ten years?
He has worked here since 1987.

You also use the present perfect in time clauses, when you are talking about something which will be done at some time in the future.

Tell me when you have finished.
I'll write to you as soon as I have heard from Jenny.

2 When you want to emphasize the fact that a recent event continued to happen for some time, you use the present perfect continuous.

She's been crying.
I've been working hard all day.

3 You use the past perfect tense when you are looking back from a point in past time, and you are concerned with the effects of something which happened at an earlier time in the past.

I apologized because I had forgotten my book.
He felt much happier once he had found a new job.
They would have come if we had invited them.

You also use the past perfect when you are thinking of a time which had started earlier in the past but was still continuing.

I was about twenty. I had been studying French for a couple of years.
He hated games and had always managed to avoid children's parties.

4 You use the future perfect tense when you are looking back from a point in the future and you are talking about something which will have happened at a time between now and that future point.

In another two years, you will have left school.
Take these tablets, and in twenty-four hours the pain will have gone.

You also use the future perfect when you are looking back from the present and guessing that an action will be finished.

I'm sure they will have arrived home by now.
It's too late to ring Don. He will have left the house by now.

5 You can also use other modals with 'have', when you are looking back from a point in time at something which you think may have happened at an earlier time.

I might have finished work by then.
He should have arrived in Paris by the time we phone.

For more information on modals with 'have', see Units 59 to 71.

88

Unit 44 Practice

A Look at these sentences and match questions and answers.

1 Where's Teresa?   a No, I've seen it before.
2 Are you going to the film tonight?   b After I've finished the washing up.
3 Do you know Michael?   c Yes, I've lived here for years.
4 Can we go out?   d She's gone shopping.
5 May I borrow your book?   e No, I've never met him before.
6 Do you know London well?   f I'm afraid I've left it at home.
7 How do you feel?   g Awful. I think I've caught a cold.
8 Why isn't John at work today?   h No, we've just moved to Oxford.
9 Do you still work at Smith's?   i I don't know. Perhaps he's had an accident.
10 Do you live near here?   j Yes, I've worked there ever since 1980.

B Use the information from the sentences above to complete these sentences.

1 He told me Teresa *had gone shopping.*
2 I didn't go to the film because ....
3 I didn't know Michael. In fact ....
4 We couldn't go out until ....
5 I couldn't lend Sally my book because ....
6 I knew London well ....
7 I felt so bad, I was sure that ....
8 John couldn't go to work because ....
9 We didn't live in Sevenoaks any more. We ....

C Use the following future perfect verb groups to complete the sentences below.

> will have driven   will have used up   will have learned   will have run   will have forgotten

1 You may be in love with her now, but in a couple of weeks you *will have forgotten* all about her.
2 By the time we get to Birmingham we .... over two hundred miles.
3 If they start school at four, most children .... to read and write by the age of six.
4 By the end of this century, we .... most of the world's oil supplies.
5 After two hours, the leading competitors .... about thirty kilometres.

D What do you think will have happened by the end of this century? Here are some ideas to help you.

1 Scientists / discover / a cure for cancer. / *Scientists will have discovered a cure for cancer.*
2 Scientists / learn / to control the weather. / ....
3 Third world war / break out. / ....
4 Man / destroy / the planet. / ....
5 World population / grow / to three billion. / ....
6 Atomic energy / replace / oil and coal. / ....
7 The rhinoceros / become / extinct. / ....
8 Scientists / build / factories in space. / ....

Unit 45 Talking about the present

Main points

- For the general present, general truths, and habitual actions, you use the present simple.
- For something which is happening now, or for temporary situations, you use the present continuous.

1 If you are talking about the present in general, you normally use the present simple tense. You use the present simple for talking about the general present including the present moment.

My dad works in Saudi Arabia.
He lives in the French Alps near the Swiss border.

2 If you are talking about general truths, you use the present simple.

Water boils at 100 degrees centigrade.
Love makes the world go round.
The bus takes longer than the train.

3 If you are talking about regular or habitual actions, you use the present simple.

Do you eat meat?
I get up early and eat my breakfast in bed.
I pay the milkman on Fridays.

4 If you are talking about something which is regarded as temporary, you use the present continuous.

Do you know if she's still playing tennis these days?
I'm working as a British Council officer.

5 If you are talking about something which is happening now, you normally use the present continuous tense.

We're having a meeting. Come and join in.
Wait a moment. I'm listening to the news.

6 There are a number of verbs which are used in the present simple tense even when you are talking about the present moment. These verbs are not normally used in the present continuous or the other continuous tenses. These verbs usually refer to:

> **thinking:** believe forget imagine know realize recognize suppose think understand want wish
> **liking and disliking:** admire dislike hate like love prefer
> **appearance:** appear look like resemble seem
> **possession:** belong to contain have include own possess
> **perception:** hear see smell taste
> **being:** be consist of exist

I believe he was not to blame.
She hates going to parties.
Our neighbours have two cars.

Note that you normally use verbs of perception with the modal 'can', rather than using the present simple tense.

I can smell gas.

Some other common verbs are not normally used in the present continuous or the other continuous tenses.

> concern   fit   involve mean   surprise
> deserve   interest   matter   satisfy

What do you mean?

WARNING: Some of the verbs listed above can be used in continuous tenses in other meanings. For example, 'have' referring to possession is not used in continuous tenses. You do not say 'I am having a car'. But note the following examples.

We're having a party tomorrow.
He's having problems with his car.
She's having a shower.

Unit 45 Practice

A Decide whether these sentences are talking about the present in general or about the present moment. Complete the sentences by putting the verbs in brackets into the present simple or the present continuous.

1 My wife normally ....*works*................ at home, but she ...*is spending*.......... this month in Nottingham. She ...*is teaching*.......... in a summer school there. (work) (spend) (teach)

2 A: Look, it .... again. B: Yes, it .... most days at this time of year. (rain) (rain)

3 Goodnight. I .... to bed. I always .... to bed early during the week. (go) (go)

4 Most days, John .... to work, but since it .... today he .... his car to work. So Mary .... her shopping at the local shop instead of the supermarket where she usually .... (cycle) (rain) (take) (do) (go)

5 A: Where are the children? B: They .... in the garden. They .... home from school at about four and usually .... straight out to play with their friends. (play) (get) (go)

6 A: What work .... ? B: He .... French and German, and this term he .... English as well. (your husband do) (teach) (teach)

7 We usually .... the news on TV at seven o'clock, but tonight we .... that new soap opera. (watch) (watch)

B Choose the form of the verb in brackets which best completes the following sentences.

1 My daughter ...*is working*........................... in a restaurant for the summer, but she ...*doesn't*.... *like*....................... it very much. (works / is working) (doesn't like / isn't liking)

2 This cheese .... awful. (smells / is smelling)

3 I often try to read the newspapers in English but I .... very much. (am not understanding / don't understand)

4 The children .... very quickly. They .... very like their mother now. (grow up / are growing up) (look / are looking)

5 Sara .... to be very upset. I .... she was worried about something. (seemed / was seeming) (think / am thinking)

6 .... to you? (Does this coat belong / Is this coat belonging)

7 No, my coat .... there behind the door. (hangs / is hanging)

8 I .... something downstairs. It .... as if someone .... to open a window. (can hear / am hearing) (sounds / is sounding) (tries / is trying)

Unit 46 Talking about the past

Main points

- For actions, situations, or regular events in the past, you use the past simple. For regular events in the past, you can also use 'would' or 'used to'.
- For events that happened before and after a time in the past, and for temporary situations, you use the past continuous.
- For present effects of past situations, you use the present perfect, and for past effects of earlier events you use the past perfect.
- For future in the past, you use 'would', 'was / were going to', or the past continuous.

1 When you want to talk about an event that occurred at a particular time in the past, you use the past simple.

The Prime Minister flew into New York yesterday.
The new term started last week.

You also use the past simple to talk about a situation that existed over a period of time in the past.

We spent most of our time at home last winter.
They earned their money quickly that year.

2 When you want to talk about something which took place regularly in the past, you use the past simple.

They went for picnics most weekends.
We usually spent the winter at Aunt Meg's house.

WARNING: The past simple always refers to a time in the past. A time reference is necessary to say what time in the past you are referring to. The time reference can be established in an earlier sentence or by another speaker, but it must be established.

When you want to talk about something which occurred regularly in the past, you can use 'would' or 'used to' instead of the past simple.

We would normally spend the winter in Miami.
People used to believe that the world was flat.

WARNING: You do not normally use 'would' with this meaning with verbs which are not used in the continuous tenses. For a list of these verbs, see Unit 45.

3 When you want to talk about something which continued to happen before and after a given time in the past, you use the past continuous.

I hurt myself when I was mending my bike.
It was midnight. She was driving home.

You also use the past continuous to talk about a temporary state of affairs in the past.

Our team were losing 2-1 at the time.
We were staying with friends in Italy.

For more information on continuous tenses, see Unit 43.

4 When you are concerned with the present effects or future effects of something which happened at an indefinite time in the past, you use the present perfect.

I'm afraid I've forgotten my book, so I don't know.
He's broken his leg, so he won't be able to come.

You also use the present perfect when you are thinking of a time which started in the past and still continues.

Have you ever stolen anything? (= at any time up to the present)
He has been here since six o'clock. (= and he is still here)

5 When you are looking back from a point in past time, and you are concerned with the effects of something which happened at an earlier time in the past, you use the past perfect.

I apologized because I had left my wallet at home.
They would have come if we had invited them.

6 When you want to talk about the future from a point of view in past time, you can use 'would', 'was / were going to', or the past continuous.

He thought to himself how wonderful it would taste.
Her daughter was going to do the cooking.
Mike was taking his test the week after.

Unit 46 Practice

A Complete the following sentences with one verb in the past simple and the other in the past continuous.

1 I ...*was reading*......... the newspaper, when suddenly I ...*heard*................ a loud knock on the door. (read) (hear)

2 I .... George an hour ago. He .... his homework. (phone) (do)

3 I first .... Mary a couple of years ago. She .... at the Royal Hospital at the time. (meet) (work)

4 We............................... Peter to come with us, but he .... the football on TV. (ask) (watch)

5 While I .... to work this morning, I almost .... a serious accident. (drive) (have)

6 When we .... the shopping last week, we .... a nice place to have coffee. (do) (find)

B Complete the following sentences, putting one verb in the present perfect and one in the past simple.

1 We ...*lived*................... in Manchester from 1985 to 1990, but we ...*have moved*...........to Liverpool now. (live) (move)

2 A: There's a great film at the Odeon this week. .... it? (you see)

   B: Not this week. I .... it in London last year. (see)

3 When we were kids, we .... to Blackpool for our holidays, but I .... back there for years. (go) (not be)

4 A: This is Mary. I don't think you .... (meet)

   B: Oh yes. We know each other well. We .... at school together. (be)

5 A: I .... to phone John, but he's not at home. (try)

   B: He should be. He .... work an hour ago. (leave)

C Complete these sentences with one verb in the past simple and the other in the past perfect.

1 I ...*was*................... late. The meeting ...*had started*...........an hour ago. (be) (start)

2 They .... , even though we .... them a special invitation. (not come) (send)

3 It .... a good story, but I .... it before. (be) (hear)

4 We .... our way. We .... what to do. (lose) (not know)

5 As soon as we .... work, we .... home. (finish) (go)

D Rewrite the sentences below using **going to**.

1 I didn't go to the cinema. I didn't have any money. / ...*I was going to the cinema, but I didn't have any money.*......................

2 He didn't play football. He forgot his boots. / ....

3 We didn't go swimming. It was too cold. / ....

4 They didn't visit Oxford. They didn't have time. / ....

5 He didn't see the play. There were no seats left. / ....

6 I couldn't do my homework. I had forgotten my books. / ....

▶ **Bank**

Unit 47 Reporting the past

Main points

- A report structure is used to report what people say or think.
- You use the present tense of the reporting verb when you are reporting something that someone says or thinks at the time you are speaking.
- You often use past tenses in report structures because a reported clause usually reports something that was said or believed in the past.

1 You use a report structure to report what people say or think. A report structure consists of two parts. One part is the reporting clause, which contains the reporting verb.

I told him nothing was going to happen to me.
I agreed that he should do it.

The other part is the reported clause.

He felt that he had to do something.
Henry said he wanted to go home.

See Units 88 and 89 for more information on report structures.

2 For the verb in the reporting clause, you choose a tense that is appropriate at the time you are speaking.
Because reports are usually about something that was said or believed in the past, both the reporting verb and the verb in the reported clause are often in a past tense.

Mrs Kaur announced that the lecture had begun.
At the time, we thought that he was mad.

3 Although you normally use past tenses in reports about the past, you can use a present tense in the reported clause if what you are saying is important in the present, for example:

- because you want to emphasize that it is still true

Did you tell him that this young woman is looking for a job?

- because you want to give advice or a warning, or make a suggestion for the present or future

I told you they have this class on Friday afternoon, so you should have come a bit earlier.

4 You use a present tense for the reporting verb when you are reporting:

- what someone says or thinks at the time you are speaking

She says she wants to see you this afternoon.
I think there's something wrong.

Note that, as in the last example, it may be your own thoughts that you are reporting.

- what someone often says

He says that no one understands him.

- what someone has said in the past, if what they said is still true

My doctor says it's nothing to worry about.

5 If you are predicting what people will say or think, you use a future tense for the reporting verb.

No doubt he will claim that his car broke down.
They will think we are making a fuss.

6 You very rarely try to report the exact words of a statement. You usually give a summary of what was said. For example, John might say:

'I tried to phone you about six times yesterday. I let the phone ring for ages but there was no answer. I couldn't get through at all so I finally gave up.'

You would probably report this as:

John said he tried to phone several times yesterday, but he couldn't get through.

7 When you are telling a story of your own, or one that you have heard from someone else, direct speech simply becomes part of the narrative.
In this extract a taxi driver picks up a passenger:

'What part of London are you headed for?' I asked him. 'I'm going to Epsom for the races. It's Derby day today.' 'So it is,' I said. 'I wish I were going with you. I love betting on horses.'

You might report this as part of the narrative without reporting verbs:

My passenger was going to Epsom to see the Derby, and I wanted to go with him.

Unit 47 Practice

A The following passage appeared in a children's comic called 'The Eagle' in 1958. It is about a teenager who wanted to be an atomic engineer. Rewrite the passage, putting the verbs in bold into the past tense.

'Andrew **is** intelligent and go-ahead. He **thinks** there **is** a great future for engineers in this atomic age. As a trainee, Andrew **works** 44 hours in a five day week and **earns** about £3 per week with an allowance of £1.70. His pay **rises** to £8.16 at 21. Hostel accommodation **is** available. Books and instruments **can** be borrowed and there **are** opportunities for sport.'

Andrew was intelligent and go-ahead. ....

....

....

....

....

B Now read out the same passage, using the past tense, and starting with the words: 'In 1958, the Eagle published an article about Andrew, who wanted to be an atomic engineer. It said that …'.

Why are the verbs in the past tense? Is it because of the tense of **said** or is it because you are talking about the past?

C Here are some sayings by well-known people. Look at the sayings, then complete the reports by putting the verbs in brackets in the right tense.

1   When I grow up I want to be a little boy. (Joseph Heller)
    When someone asked Joseph Heller what he ...*wanted*......................... to be when he
    ...*grew up*........................ he ...*said*........................ he ...*wanted*........................ to
    be a little boy. (want) (grow up) (say) (want)

2   I don't like baths. I do not enjoy them in the slightest and if I could I would prefer to go round dirty.
    (J.B. Priestley)
    J.B. Priestley .... baths. He .... that if he
    .... the choice he would prefer to stay dirty. (hate) (say) (have)

3   I am happy to say someone has stolen my wife's credit card. He will probably spend a lot less than she
    does. (Anon.)
    A man .... he .... delighted that someone ....
    .... his wife's credit card. He .... sure the thief ....
    .... less money than his wife. (say) (be) (steal) (be) (spend)

4   His ears are so big, he looks like a taxicab with both doors open. (Howard Hughes about Clark Gable)
    After meeting the film star, Clark Gable, Howard Hughes .... Gable ....
    .... such big ears he .... like a taxi with both doors open.
    (say) (have) (look)

5   I know only two tunes. One is Yankee Doodle and the other isn't. (Ulysses S. Grant)
    President Ulysses S. Grant .... that he only ....
    two tunes. One of them .... Yankee Doodle and the other ....
    .... (say) (know) (be) (not be)

▶ **Bank**

Unit 48 Talking about the future using 'will' and 'going to'

Main points

- When you are making predictions about the future or talking about future intentions, you can use either 'will' or 'going to'.
- For promises and offers relating to the future, you use 'will'.
- For future events based on arrangements, you use the future continuous.
- For events that will happen before a time in the future, you use the future perfect.

1 You cannot talk about the future with as much certainty as you can about the present or the past. You are usually talking about what you think might happen or what you intend to happen. This is why you often use modals. Although most modals can be used with future reference, you most often use the modal 'will' to talk about the future.

Nancy will arrange it.
When will I see them?

2 When you are making predictions about the future that are based on general beliefs, opinions, or attitudes, you use 'will'.

The weather tomorrow will be warm and sunny.
I'm sure you will enjoy your visit to the zoo.

This use of 'will' is common in sentences with conditional clauses.

You'll be late, if you don't hurry.

When you are using facts or events in the present situation as evidence for a prediction, you can use 'going to'.

It's going to rain. (I can see black clouds)
I'm going to be late. (I have missed my train)

3 When you are talking about your own intentions, you use 'will' or 'going to'.

I'll ring you tonight.
I'm going to stay at home today.

When you are saying what someone else has decided to do, you use 'going to'.

They're going to have a party.

WARNING: You do not normally use 'going to' with the verb 'go'. You usually just say 'I'm going' rather than 'I'm going to go'.

'What are you going to do this weekend?' - 'I'm going to the cinema.'

When you are announcing a decision you have just made or are about to make, you use 'will'.

I'm tired. I think I'll go to bed.

4 In promises and offers relating to the future, you often use 'will' with the meaning 'be willing to'.

I'll do what I can.
I'll help with the washing-up.

Note that you can use 'will' with this meaning in an 'if'-clause.

I'll put you through, if you'll hang on for a minute. (= if you are willing to hang on for a minute)

WARNING: Remember that you do not normally use 'will' in 'if'-clauses. See Unit 91 for more information on 'if'-clauses.

If you do that, you will be wasting your time.
The children will call out if they think he is wrong.

5 When you want to say that something will happen because arrangements have been made, you use the future continuous tense.

I'll be seeing them when I've finished with you.
I'll be waiting for you outside.
She'll be appearing at the Royal Festival Hall.

6 When you want to talk about something that has not happened yet but will happen before a particular time in the future, you use the future perfect tense.

By the time we phone he'll already have started.
By 1992, he will have worked for twelve years.

Unit 48 Practice

A Match these sentences, which supply present evidence, with the predictions below.

1 They are playing really well.   a He's going to blow his whistle.

2 I feel awful.   b It's going to be wet and windy tomorrow.

3 They've invited a lot of people.   c I think they're going to win.

4 We have a lot to do.   d They're going to fall asleep.

5 I listened to the weather forecast tonight.   e They are going to win again.

6 I can't hang on.   f I'm going to fall.

7 The kids are tired out.   g It's going to be a hard day.

8 The referee is looking at his watch.   h I think I'm going to faint.

9 Liverpool are three goals ahead.   i It's going to be very crowded.

B Now match these sentences with the predictions below, which are based on general beliefs.

1 John starts his new school tomorrow.   a The shops will probably be crowded.

2 It's Saturday morning.   b They'll probably fall asleep.

3 Liverpool have a very good side.   c He'll tell everybody.

4 The children get tired very easily.   d She'll be delighted.

5 It's a very difficult climb.   e I'm sure he'll enjoy it.

6 They're having a big party next week.   f If you're not careful you'll fall.

7 Fred can't keep a secret.   g I think they'll win easily.

8 Have you told Kate about your new job?   h It'll probably be very crowded.

C Complete the dialogues below using the verb in brackets with **will** or **going to.**

1 A: Have you decided how to spend the prize money?

   B: Well I think we ....*will buy*............................ a new car, but we haven't really decided yet.

   (buy)

2 A: Have you decided how to spend the prize money?

   B: Yes. We .... a new car. (buy)

3 A: Did you know Sue is in hospital? Do you think you could send her a get-well card?

   B: I didn't know that. Of course I .... her a card. (send)

4 A: I heard yesterday that Sue is in hospital.

   B: Yes I know. We .... some money at work to send her some flowers.

   (collect)

5 A: Have you got tickets for the concert?

   B: Yes. We .... on Saturday. (go)

6 A: Have you got tickets for the concert?

   B: Not yet. But I think we .... on Saturday if we can. (go)

Unit 49 Talking about the future using present tenses

Main points

- When you are talking about the future in relation to official timetables or the calendar, you use the present simple.
- When talking about people's plans and arrangements for the future, you use the present continuous.
- In 'if'-clauses, time clauses, and defining relative clauses, you can use the present simple to refer to the future.

1 When you are talking about something in the future which is based on an official timetable or calendar, you use the present simple tense. You usually put a time adverbial in these sentences.

My last train leaves Euston at 11.30.
The UN General Assembly opens in New York this month.
Our next lesson is on Thursday.
We set off early tomorrow morning in Ken's car.

2 In statements about fixed dates, you normally use the present simple.

Tomorrow is Tuesday.
It's my birthday next month.
Monday is the seventeenth of July.

3 When you want to talk about people's plans or arrangements for the future, you use the present continuous tense.

I'm meeting Bill next week.
They're getting married in June.

4 You often talk about the future using the present tense of verbs such as 'hope', 'expect', 'intend', and 'want' with a 'to'-infinitive clause, especially when you want to indicate your uncertainty about what will actually happen.

We hope to see you soon.
Bill expects to be back at work tomorrow.

After the verb 'hope', you often use the present simple to refer to the future.

I hope you enjoy your holiday.

5 In subordinate clauses, the relationship between tense and time are different. In 'if'-clauses and time clauses, you normally use the present simple for future reference.

If he comes, I'll let you know.
Please start when you are ready.
We won't start until everyone arrives.
Lock the door after you finally leave.

6 In defining relative clauses, you normally use the present simple, not 'will', to refer to the future.

Any decision that you make will need her approval.
Give my love to any friends you meet.
There is a silver cup for the runner who finishes first.

7 If you want to show that a condition has to be the case before an action can be carried out, you use the present perfect for future events.

We won't start until everyone has arrived.
I'll let you know when I have arranged everything.

Unit 49 Practice

A Write out these sentences. If they are based on an official timetable or the calendar, put the verb in the present simple. If they are about plans or arrangements that people have made for the future, put the verb in the present continuous.

1 .... just before midnight. (Simon's plane / arrive)
2 .... a barbecue tomorrow if it's fine. (We / have)
3 .... at half past two. (The meeting / start)
4 .... this evening. (A few friends / come round)
5 What time .... ? (the last bus / leave)
6 .... at nine so I'll be home by ten. (The match / finish)
7 .... Janet for lunch at about one thirty today. (I / meet)
8 .... school in September. (Becky / finish)
9 .... to the match tomorrow. (Everybody / go)
10 .... trains at Manchester. (We / change)

B Complete the following sentences, putting one of the verbs in brackets into the future with **will,** and the other into the present simple.

1 I ..._will come_.......... round tomorrow, if I ..._have_............... time. (come) (have)
2 I .... Jack the message if I .... him. (give) (see)
3 I .... you a call from the first phone box I .... (give) (see)
4 There .... presents for all the children who .... to the party.
   (be) (come)
5 We .... the party indoors if it .... (have) (rain)
6 There .... lots of games. I hope you .... yourselves. (be)
   (enjoy)
7 I .... to the cinema, unless you .... too. (not go) (go)
8 Keep a diary, then you .... all the places you ....
   (remember) (visit)
9 I think I .... here, until it .... raining. (stay) (stop)

C Complete the following sentences by putting one verb in the future with **will,** and putting the other verb in the present perfect.

1 I ..._will write_.......... to you as soon as I ..._have heard_..........from Helen. (write) (hear)
2 I .... you when I .... (tell) (finish)
3 We .... for a walk when I .... watching the film on television.
   (go) (finish)
4 I .... you with your homework when I .... the washing up.
   (help) (do)
5 John says he .... us as soon as he .... the results of his
   exams. (call) (get)

D Rewrite the following sentences, using the verbs in brackets with a 'to'-infinitive.
1 We will come and see you soon. / (hope) ..._We hope to come and see you soon._...................
2 We are going to spend our next holiday in Scotland. / (intend) ....
3 I am sure I will be back at work before long. / (expect) ....
4 We are going to drive to Glasgow. / (plan) ....

Unit 50 Questions

Main points

- In most questions the first verb comes before the subject.
- 'Yes/no'-questions begin with an auxiliary or a modal.
- 'Wh'-questions begin with a 'wh'-word.

1 Questions which can be answered 'yes' or 'no' are called 'yes/no'-questions.

'Are you ready?' - *'Yes.'*
'Have you read this magazine?' - *'No.'*

If the verb group has more than one word, the first word comes at the beginning of the sentence, before the subject. The rest of the verb group comes after the subject.

Is he coming?
Can John swim?
Will you have finished by lunchtime?
Couldn't you have been a bit quieter?
Has he been working?

2 If the verb group consists of only a main verb, you use the auxiliary 'do', 'does', or 'did' at the beginning of the sentence, before the subject. After the subject you use the base form of the verb.

Do the British take sport seriously?
Does that sound like anyone you know?
Did he go to the fair?

Note that when the main verb is 'do', you still have to add 'do', 'does', or 'did' before the subject.

Do they do the work themselves?
Did you do an 'O' Level in German?

3 If the main verb is 'have', you usually put 'do', 'does', or 'did' before the subject.

Does anyone have a question?
Did you have a good flight?

When 'have' means 'own' or 'possess', you can put it before the subject, without using 'do', 'does', or 'did', but this is less common.

Has he any idea what it's like?

4 If the main verb is the present simple or past simple of 'be', you put the verb at the beginning of the sentence, before the subject.

Are you ready?
Was it lonely without us?

5 When you want someone to give you more information than just 'yes' or 'no', you ask a 'wh'-question, which begins with a 'wh'-word:

what	where	who	whose	~
when	which	whom	why	how

Note that 'whom' is only used in formal English.

6 When a 'wh'-word is the subject of a question, the 'wh'-word comes first, then the verb group. You do not add 'do', 'does', or 'did' as an auxiliary.

What happened?
Which is the best restaurant?
Who could have done it?

7 When a 'wh'-word is the object of a verb or preposition, the 'wh'-word comes first, then you follow the rules for 'yes/no'-questions, adding 'do', 'does', or 'did' where necessary.

How many are there?
Which do you like best?

If there is a preposition, it comes at the end. However, you always put the preposition before 'whom'.

What's this for?
With whom were you talking?

Note that you follow the same rules as for 'wh'-words as objects when the question begins with 'when', 'where', 'why', or 'how'.

When would you be coming down?
Why did you do it?
Where did you get that from?

8 You can also use 'what', 'which', 'whose', 'how many', and 'how much' with a noun.

Whose idea was it?
How much money have we got in the bank?

You can use 'which', 'how many', and 'how much' with 'of' and a noun group.

Which of the suggested answers was the correct one?
How many of them bothered to come?

See Unit 51 for more information on 'wh'-words.

Unit 50 Practice

A Expand the 'What about…?' phrases to make 'yes/no'-questions.

1 John can swim. What about Henry? / ...*Can Henry swim?*...

2 I've read the newspaper. What about you? / ....

3 I often go for a walk in the park. What about you? / ....

4 Helen lives near here. What about Becky? / ....

5 My kids have gone back to school. What about your children? / ....

6 I'll be home for lunch. What about Sally and Peter? / ....

7 I could have eaten a bit more. What about you? / ....

8 John will have arrived by noon. What about Sandra? / ....

9 I never learned German at school. What about you? / ....

10 I do most of the cooking at home. What about you? / ....

11 Peter's here. What about Joe? / ....

12 John and Jean are here. What about Alan and Tina? / ....

B Rearrange the parts of the sentences to make questions with 'wh'-words as subject.

1 How many people / to the party / next week / will be coming? / ...*How many people will be*...
coming to the party next week?..

2 Which team / first prize / won / at the weekend? / ....

3 What / when you were late / happened / this morning / for work? / ....

4 Who / the answer / told you / to the exam question? / ....

5 Who / next door / lives / to you? / ....

6 What / to this question / the right answer / is? / ....

7 Whose car / that red one / over there / is? / ....

8 How many students / to your English class / come? / ....

C Expand the 'What about…?' phrases to make questions with 'wh'-words as object.

1 I've written twenty letters. What about you? / How many ...*letters have you written?*...

2 I like soft chocolates best. What about you? / Which ....

3 Jack came on his bike. What about you? / How ....

4 Karen can swim over ten kilometres. What about Jim? / How far ....

5 We got hundreds of cards. What about you? / How many ....

6 We'll be there at about six o'clock. What about Mary and Bill? / What time ....

7 John arrived at about eight. What about Kathy? / When ....

8 I will have finished work by five. What about you? / ....

D Now do these questions starting and finishing with the words given.

1 My wife works in the maths department. What about you? / Which ...*department do you work*... in?

2 I'm going to the dance with Sandy. What about you? / Who .... with?

3 My letter is from Fred. What about yours? / Who .... from?

4 My sister goes to Birmingham University. What about your brother? / Which university ....
.... to?

5 This morning's lecture is about Shakespeare. What about the afternoon lecture? / What ....
.... about?

▶ **Bank**

Unit 51 'Wh'-words

Main points

- You use 'who', 'whom', and 'whose' to ask about people, and 'which' to ask about people or things.
- You use 'what' to ask about things, and 'what for' to ask about reasons and purposes.
- You use 'how' to ask about the way something happens.
- You use 'when' to ask about times, 'why' to ask about reasons, and 'where' to ask about places and directions.

1 You use 'who', 'whom', or 'whose' in questions about people. 'Who' is used to ask questions about the subject or object of the verb, or about the object of a preposition.

Who discovered this?
Who did he marry?
Who did you dance with?

In formal English, 'whom' is used as the object of a verb or preposition. The preposition always comes in front of 'whom'.

Whom did you see?
For whom were they supposed to do it?

You use 'whose' to ask which person something belongs to or is related to. 'Whose' can be the subject or the object.

Whose is nearer?
Whose did you prefer, hers or mine?

2 You use 'which' to ask about one person or thing, out of a number of people or things. 'Which' can be the subject or object.

Which is your son?
Which does she want?

3 You use 'what' to ask about things, for example about actions and events. 'What' can be the subject or object.

What has happened to him?
What is he selling?
What will you talk about?

You use 'what...for' to ask about the reason for an action, or the purpose of an object.

What are you going there for?
What are those lights for?

4 You use 'how' to ask about the way in which something happens or is done.

How did you know we were coming?
How are you going to get home?

You also use 'how' to ask about the way a person or thing feels or looks.

'How are you?' - 'Well, how do I look?'

5 'How' is also used:

- with adjectives to ask about the degree of a quality that someone or something has

How good are you at Maths?
How hot shall I make the curry?

- with adjectives such as 'big', 'old', and 'far' to ask about size, age, and distance

How old are your children?
How far is it to Montreal from here?

Note that you do not normally use 'How small', 'How young', or 'How near'.

- with adverbs such as 'long' and 'often' to ask about time, or 'well' to ask about abilities

How long have you lived here?
How well can you read?

- with 'many' and 'much' to ask about the number or amount of something

How many were there?
How much did he tell you?

6 You use 'when' to ask about points in time or periods of time, 'why' to ask about the reason for an action, and 'where' to ask about place and direction.

When are you coming home?
When were you in London?
Why are you here?
Where is the station?
Where are you going?

You can also ask about direction using 'which direction...in' or 'which way'.

Which direction did he go in?
Which way did he go?

Unit 51 Practice

A Use the 'wh'-words below to complete the questions which follow. Look at Unit 50 as well as Unit 51.

| what   when   where   which   who   whose   why   how |

1 ....*What*........... time do you finish work?

2 .... is it who lives in that big house?

3 .... of these coats belong to you?

4 .... advice would you give to someone about to leave school?

5 .... old is your daughter now?

6 .... exactly did you buy that lovely dress? In London?

7 I haven't seen George for ages. .... did you last come across him?

8 .... bag is this? It's not yours, is it?

9 About .... long does it take to get to Birmingham?

10 .... do you get to the post office from here?

11 .... did you live before you came to London?

12 But .... can't you come? Are you busy?

13 .... day does Dad get home?

14 I don't know. .... do you ask?

B Make questions from these sentences by using **who** or **what** instead of the words in bold.

1 **George** bought her that necklace. / Who ....*bought her that necklace?*......

2 George bought her **a necklace**. / What ....*did George buy her?*......

3 They have invited **Mary** and **Philip**. / Who ....

4 I've lent that book to **Bill**. / Who ....

5 They gave **the keys** to Peter. / What ....

6 **My daughter** answered the telephone. / Who ....

7 The manager said **no**. / What ....

8 I asked **Andrew** to help. / Who ....

9 We can send **a bunch of flowers**. / What ....

10 **The children** will be at home. / Who ....

C Make questions from these words. The replies to the questions are given.

1 Where / your young brother / playing? He had been playing outside. / ....*Where had your young*....
   brother been playing?..

2 How long / your young brother / playing outside? All morning. / ....

3 What / he / ask for? He asked for something to eat. / ....

4 What / you / give him? Bread and peanut butter. / ....

5 How / he / hold the bread? He held it in both hands. / ....

6 Why / he / look so puzzled? Because he couldn't open the door. / ....

7 Why / he / not open the door? He couldn't open the door because his hands were full. / ....

8 What / he / do with the bread? He stuck it on the wall. / ....

9 Where / he / go then? Out into the garden to play. / ....

▶ **Bank**

Unit 52 Question tags: forms

Main points:

- You add a question tag to a statement to turn it into a question.
- A question tag consists of a verb and a pronoun. The verb in a question tag is always an auxiliary, a modal, or a form of the main verb 'be'.
- With a positive statement, you usually use a negative question tag containing a short form ending in '-n't'.
- With a negative statement, you always use a positive question tag.

1 A question tag is a short phrase that is added to the end of a statement to turn it into a 'yes/no'-question. You use question tags when you want to ask someone to confirm or disagree with what you are saying, or when you want to sound more polite. Question tags are rarely used in formal written English.

He's very friendly, isn't he?
You haven't seen it before, have you?

2 You form a question tag by using an auxiliary, a modal, or a form of the main verb 'be', followed by a pronoun. The pronoun refers to the subject of the statement.

David's school is quite nice, isn't it?
She made a remarkable recovery, didn't she?

3 If the statement contains an auxiliary or modal, the same auxiliary or modal is used in the question tag.

Jill's coming tomorrow, isn't she?
You didn't know I was an artist, did you?
You've never been to Benidorm, have you?
You will stay in touch, won't you?

4 If the statement does not contain an auxiliary, a modal, or 'be' as a main verb, you use 'do', 'does', or 'did' in the question tag.

You like it here, don't you?
Sally still works there, doesn't she?
He played for Ireland, didn't he?

5 If the statement contains the present simple or past simple of 'be' as a main verb, the same form of the verb 'be' is used in the question tag.

It is quite warm, isn't it?
They were really rude, weren't they?

6 If the statement contains the simple present or simple past of 'have' as a main verb, you usually use 'do', 'does', or 'did' in the question tag.

He has a problem, doesn't he?

You can also use the same form of 'have' in the question tag, but this is not very common.

She has a large house, hasn't she?

7 With a positive statement you normally use a negative question tag, formed by adding '-n't' to the verb.

You like Ralph a lot, don't you?
They are beautiful, aren't they?

Note that the negative question tag with 'I' is 'aren't'.

I'm a fool, aren't I?

8 With a negative statement you always use a positive question tag.

It doesn't work, does it?
You won't tell anyone else, will you?

Unit 52 Practice

A Here are some of the things people say at parties. Match the statements with the question tags. Look at Unit 53 as well as Unit 52.

1 It's a bit noisy, ...
2 We haven't met before, ...
3 You're Henry's brother, ...
4 Pass this plate round, ...
5 Don't drop it, ...
6 You live next door, ...
7 You're not leaving, ...
8 You can stay a bit later, ...
9 You'll come again, ...
10 That was fun, ...

a ...will you?
b ...don't you?
c ...isn't it?
d ...aren't you?
e ...will you?
f ...have we?
g ...wasn't it?
h ...won't you?
i ...can't you?
j ...are you?

B Mark and Jenny went into the travel agent's to book a holiday. These are some of the questions that were asked. Add the question tags.

1 It's a lovely place. You haven't been there before, ...*have you*.................... ?
2 It's a bit expensive. You haven't got anything cheaper, ... ?
3 You can't give us a discount, ... ?
4 You haven't had a holiday with us before, ... ?
5 That won't be too expensive, ... ?
6 We went there a couple of years ago, but we didn't like it very much, ... ?
7 Oh dear. We don't have to fly on a Saturday, ... ?
8 And we don't have to pay extra for the coach, ... ?
9 There won't be any other extras to pay for, ... ?

C Mark and Jenny were showing some family photographs to a friend. Here are some of the questions that were asked. Complete the questions by adding the question tags.

1 That's a lovely picture of Sally. She looks just like Mary, ...*doesn't she*.................. ?
2 I think you've seen this one before, ... ?
3 This one was taken in Scotland, ... ?
4 We took this one on holiday, ... ?
5 We'll be going there again next year, ... ?
6 You can see the sea in the distance, ... ?
7 That must be Jenny's mother and father, ... ?
8 The weather was lovely, ... ?
9 Yes, then it started to rain, ... ?
10 Those mountains look very high, ... ?
11 Yes. We walked right to the top, ... , Jenny?
12 Yes. We'd never done anything like that before, ... ?
13 Nearly everyone's asleep in this one, ... ?
14 There's something wrong with this one, ... ?
15 That's me. I'm looking awfully fat, ... ?

Unit 53 Question tags: uses

Main points

- You can use negative statements with positive question tags to make requests.
- You use positive statements with positive question tags to show reactions.
- You use some question tags to make imperatives more polite.

1 You can use a negative statement and a positive question tag to ask people for things, or to ask for help or information.

You wouldn't sell it to me, would you?
You won't tell anyone else this, will you?

2 When you want to show your reaction to what someone has just said, for example by expressing interest, surprise, doubt, or anger, you use a positive statement with a positive question tag.

You've been to North America before, have you?
You fell on your back, did you?
I borrowed your car last night. - Oh, you did, did you?

3 When you use an imperative, you can be more polite by adding one of the following question tags.

will you	won't you	would you

See that she gets safely back, won't you?
Look at that, would you?

When you use a negative imperative, you can only use 'will you' as a question tag.

Don't tell Howard, will you?

'Will you' and 'won't you' can also be used to emphasize anger or impatience. 'Can't you' is also used in this way.

Oh, hurry up, will you!
For goodness sake be quiet, can't you!

4 You use the question tag 'shall we' when you make a suggestion using 'let's'.

Let's forget it, shall we?

You use the question tag 'shall I' after 'I'll'.

I'll tell you, shall I?

5 You use 'they' in question tags after 'anybody', 'anyone', 'everybody', 'everyone', 'nobody', 'no one', 'somebody', or 'someone'.

Everyone will be leaving on Friday, won't they?
Nobody had bothered to plant new ones, had they?

You use 'it' in question tags after 'anything', 'everything', 'nothing', or 'something'.

Nothing matters now, does it?
Something should be done, shouldn't it?

You use 'there' in question tags after 'there is', 'there are', 'there was', or 'there were'.

There's a new course out now, isn't there?

6 When you are replying to a question tag, your answer refers to the statement, not the question tag.

If you want to confirm a positive statement, you say 'yes'. For example, if you have finished a piece of work and someone says to you 'You've finished that, haven't you?', the answer is 'yes'.

'It became stronger, didn't it?' - 'Yes, it did.'

If you want to disagree with a positive statement, you say 'no'. For example, if you have not finished your work and someone says 'You've finished that, haven't you?', the answer is 'no'.

You've just seen a performance of the play, haven't you? - No, not yet.

If you want to confirm a negative statement, you say 'no'. For example, if you have not finished your work and someone says 'You haven't finished that, have you?', the answer is 'no'.

'You didn't know that, did you?' - 'No.'

If you want to disagree with a negative statement, you say 'yes'. For example, if you have finished a piece of work and someone says 'You haven't finished that, have you?', the answer is 'yes'.

'You haven't been there, have you?' - 'Yes, I have.'

Unit 53 Practice

A Rewrite these requests using question tags.

1 Could you open the door, please? / *You couldn't open the door, could you?*

2 Do you know what time the next train leaves? / ....

3 Would you look after the children for us, please? / ....

4 Could you tell me what to do? / ....

5 Would you lend me your car, please? / ....

6 Could you come round tomorrow? / ....

7 Have you got time to help me out? / ....

8 Could you do the shopping while you're out? / ....

Now do these.

9 Please don't be late. / *You won't be late, will you?* ....

10 Please don't spend too much. / ....

11 Please don't drive too fast. / ....

12 Please don't be angry with him. / ....

B Complete these questions with the appropriate question tags.

1 I see, you've crashed the car, *have you* .... ?

2 Oh, so you just borrowed it, ... ?

3 You were going to see some friends, ... ?

4 It was only a couple of miles, ... ?

5 You were driving very carefully, ... ?

6 The other car just ran into you, ... ?

7 You forgot to write down the car's number, ... ?

8 Oh, you're very sorry, ... ?

9 And you'll pay for the damage, ... ?

10 And you'll be more careful next time, ... ?

▶ **Bank**

Unit 54 Indirect and reported questions

Main points

- You use indirect questions to ask for information or help.
- You use reported questions to talk about a question that someone else has asked.
- In indirect and reported questions, the subject of the question comes before the verb.
- You use 'if' or 'whether' in indirect and reported 'yes/no'-questions.

1 When you ask someone for information, you can use an indirect question beginning with a phrase such as 'Could you tell me..' or 'Do you know..'.

Could you tell me how far it is to the bank?
Do you know where Jane is?

2 When you want to ask someone politely to do something, you can use an indirect question after 'I wonder'.

I wonder if you can help me.

You also use 'I wonder' followed by an indirect question to indicate what you are thinking about.

I wonder what she'll look like.
I wonder which hotel it was.

3 When you are talking about a question that someone has asked, you use a reported question.

She asked me why I was so late.
He wanted to know where I was going.
I demanded to know what was going on.
I asked her if I could help her.
I asked her whether there was anything wrong.

In formal and written English, 'enquire' (also spelled 'inquire') is often used instead of 'ask'.

Wilkie had enquired if she did a lot of acting.
He inquired whether he could see her.

4 In indirect and reported questions, the subject of the question comes before the verb, just as it does in affirmative sentences.

Do you know where Jane is?
I wonder if you can help me.
She asked me why I was late.

5 You do not normally use the auxiliary 'do' in indirect or reported questions.

Can you remember when they open on Sundays?
I wonder what he feels about it.
She asked him if his parents spoke French.

The auxiliary 'do' can be used in indirect or reported questions, but only for emphasis, or to make a contrast with something that has already been said. It is not put before the subject as in direct questions.

She asked me whether I really did mean it.
I told him I didn't like classical music. He asked me what kind of music I did like.

6 You use 'if' or 'whether' to introduce indirect and reported 'yes/no'-questions.

I wonder if you'd give the children a bath?
I am writing to ask whether you would care to come and visit us.

'Whether' is used especially when there is a choice of possibilities.

I was asked whether I wanted to stay at a hotel or at his home.
They asked whether Tim was or was not in the team.

Note that you can put 'or not' immediately after 'whether', but not immediately after 'if'.

The police didn't ask whether or not they were in.

7 When you are reporting a question, the verb in the reported clause is often in a past tense. This is because you are often talking about the past when you are reporting someone else's words.

She asked me why I was so late.
Pat asked him if she had hurt him.

However, you can use a present or future tense if the question you are reporting relates to the present or future.

Mark was asking if you're enjoying your new job.
They asked if you'll be there tomorrow night.

See Units 47, 88, and 89 for more information on reporting.

Unit 54 Practice

A The questions below start with **could you tell me** and **I wonder**. Rewrite them to start with a 'wh'-word.

1 Could you tell me what time I have to start work? / *What time do I have to start work?*

2 I wonder where Tom and Mary live. / ....

3 I wonder what work Tom does. / ....

4 Could you tell me how I can get to the post-office? / ....

5 I wonder how old she is. / ....

6 Could you tell me who is in charge here? / ....

7 Could you tell me what I have to do? / ....

8 I wonder who has left his car in front of our house. / ....

9 I wonder where they've gone. / ....

10 Could you tell me when they'll be here? / ....

B Rewrite these as 'yes/no'-questions.

1 I wonder if George is at home. / *Is George at home?*

2 Could you tell me if the shop is still open? / ....

3 Do you know whether Mary will be coming? / ....

4 I want to know if I can book a room. / ....

5 Do you know if this seat is free? / ....

6 I'd like to know whether anyone has left any messages for me. / ....

7 Could you tell me if you will be staying long? / ....

8 Do you know if Bill called this evening? / ....

C Rewrite the following as polite questions using an indirect form.

1 How long will you be staying here? / Could you tell me *how long you will be staying* ....
   here .... ?

2 Where do Bill and Tessa live? / Do you know ....
   .... ?

3 Would you look after the children this evening? / I wonder ....
   ....

4 Where is the nearest post office? / Could you tell me ....
   .... ?

5 Could you give me Peter's address? / I wonder ....
   ....

6 Where will Simon be staying? / Do you know ....
   .... ?

7 Why did Jack and Jill leave so suddenly? / I wonder ....
   ....

8 Do the shops open at the weekend? / Can you tell me ....
   .... ?

9 What would he like for his birthday? / Do you know ....
   .... ?

10 Would you like to come round for a cup of coffee sometime? / I wonder ....
   ....

 Bank

109

Unit 55 Short answers

Main points

- A short answer uses an auxiliary, a modal, or the main verb 'be'.
- A short answer can be in the form of a statement or a question.

1 Short answers are very common in spoken English. For example, when someone asks you a 'yes/no'-question, you can give a short answer by using a pronoun with an auxiliary, modal, or the main verb 'be'. You usually put 'yes' or 'no' before the short answer.

'Does she still want to come?' — 'Yes, she does.'
'Can you imagine what it might feel like?' — 'No, I can't.'
'Are you married?' — 'I am.'

Note that a short answer such as 'Yes, I will' is more polite or friendly than just 'Yes', or than repeating all the words used in the question. People often repeat all the words used in the question when they feel angry or impatient.

'Will you have finished by lunchtime?' — 'Yes, I will have finished by lunchtime.'

2 You can also use short answers to agree or disagree with what someone says.

'You don't like Joan?' — 'No, I don't.'
'I'm not coming with you.' — 'Yes, you are.'

If the statement that you are commenting on does not contain an auxiliary, modal, or the main verb 'be', you use a form of 'do' in the short answer.

'He never comes on time.' — 'Oh yes he does.'

3 You often reply to what has been said by using a short question.

'He's not in Japan now.' — 'Oh, isn't he?'
'He gets free meals.' — 'Does he?'

Note that questions like these are not always asked to get information, but are often used to express your reaction to what has been said, for example to show interest or surprise.

'Dad doesn't help me at all.' — 'Doesn't he? Why not?'
'Penny has been climbing before.' — 'Oh, has she? When was that?'

4 If you want to show that you definitely agree with a positive statement that someone has just made, you can use a negative short question.

'Well, that was very nice.' — 'Yes, wasn't it?'

5 When you want to ask for more information, you can use a 'wh'-word on its own or with a noun as a short answer.

'He saw a snake.' — 'Where?'
'He knew my cousin.' — 'Which cousin?'

You can also use 'Which one' and 'Which ones'.

'Can you pass me the cup?' — 'Which one?'

6 Sometimes a statement about one person also applies to another person. When this is the case, you can use a short answer with 'so' for positive statements, and with 'neither' or 'nor' for negative statements, using the same verb that was used in the statement.
You use 'so', 'neither', or 'nor' with an auxiliary, modal, or the main verb 'be'. The verb comes before the subject.

'You were different then.' — 'So were you.'
'I don't normally drink at lunch.' — 'Neither do I.'
'I can't do it.' — 'Nor can I.'

You can use 'not either' instead of 'neither', in which case the verb comes after the subject.

'He doesn't understand.' — 'We don't either.'

7 You often use 'so' in short answers after verbs such as 'think', 'hope', 'expect', 'imagine', and 'suppose', when you think that the answer to the question is 'yes'.

'You'll be home at six?' — 'I hope so.'
'So it was worth doing?' — 'I suppose so.'

You use 'I'm afraid so' when you are sorry that the answer is 'yes'.

'Is it raining?' — 'I'm afraid so.'

With 'suppose', 'think', 'imagine', or 'expect' in short answers, you also form negatives with 'so'.

'Will I see you again?' — 'I don't suppose so.'
'Is Barry Knight a golfer?' — 'No, I don't think so.'

However, you say 'I hope not' and 'I'm afraid not'.

'It isn't empty, is it?' — 'I hope not.'

Unit 55 Practice

A Write short answers to these question tags.

1 Columbus discovered India, didn't he? / *No, he didn't.* ....

2 Milan isn't the capital of Italy, is it? / ....

3 John Kennedy was President of the USA, wasn't he? / ....

4 It'll be Wednesday tomorrow, won't it? / ....

5 You don't live in London, do you? / ....

6 You're studying English, aren't you? / ....

7 You don't enjoy learning English, do you? / ....

8 Vienna is in Germany, isn't it? / ....

9 Albert Einstein wasn't an American, was he? / ....

10 You haven't answered all these correctly, have you? / ....

B Match statements and short questions.

1 We don't live there anymore.	a Do you really?
2 I know your sister Mary very well.	b Won't they?
3 Jack and Jill will be coming.	c Haven't they?
4 I don't think your parents will like this very much.	d Wouldn't you?
5 The children have been here before.	e Don't you?
6 Most people haven't arrived yet.	f Will they?
7 I wouldn't do that if I were you.	g Have they really?
8 I'm sure they would come if they could.	h Would they?

C Match statements and short answers.

1 I always enjoy a good night out.	a So do I.
2 My husband is never on time.	b Neither did we.
3 I didn't get a holiday this year.	c So will Sue.
4 Amanda will be at University next year.	d So would I.
5 I haven't written to Jane yet.	e So am I.
6 George would be furious if he found out.	f Neither is my wife.
7 John can't stand pop music.	g Nor have I.
8 The children are tired out.	h Nor can I.

D Answer these questions in the affirmative using the words given.

1 Have you been here before? (think) / *I think so.* ....

2 Will there be any tickets left? (expect) / ....

3 Do we have to pay the full price? (suppose) / ....

4 Was he very angry? (afraid) / ....

5 Will there be lots of people there? (imagine) / ....

6 Is Jenny coming home for the holiday? (hope) / ....

E Answer these questions in the negative using the words given.

1 Do you think it'll take very long? (think) / *I don't think so.* ....

2 Do you think it's going to rain? (hope) / ....

3 Will the train be on time? (expect) / ....

4 Will Becky do as she's told? (suppose) / ....

5 Do you get an extra day off on Monday? (afraid) / ....

Unit 56 The imperative and 'let'

Main points

- The imperative is the same as the base form of a verb.
- You form a negative imperative with 'do not', 'don't', or 'never'.
- You use the imperative to ask or tell someone to do something, or to give advice, warnings, or instructions on how to do something.
- You use 'let' when you are offering to do something, making suggestions, or telling someone to do something.

1 The imperative is the same as the base form of a verb. You do not use a pronoun in front of it.

Come to my place.
Start when you hear the bell.

2 You form a negative imperative by putting 'do not', 'don't', or 'never' in front of the verb.

Do not write in this book.
Don't go so fast.
Never open the front door to strangers.

3 You use the imperative when you are:

● asking or telling someone to do something

Pass the salt.
Hurry up!

● giving someone advice or a warning

Mind your head.
Take care!

● giving someone instructions on how to do something

Put this bit over here, so it fits into that hole.
Turn right off Broadway into Caxton Street.

4 When you want to make an imperative more polite or more emphatic, you can put 'do' in front of it.

Do have a chocolate biscuit.
Do stop crying.
Do be careful.

5 The imperative is also used in written instructions on how to do something, for example on notices and packets of food, and in books.

To report faults, dial 6666.
Store in a dry place.
Fry the chopped onion and pepper in the oil.

Note that written instructions usually have to be short. This means that words such as 'the' are often omitted.

Wear rubber gloves. Turn off switch. Wipe bulb.

Written imperatives are also used to give warnings.

Reduce speed now.

6 You use 'let me' followed by the base form of a verb when you are offering to do something for someone.

Let me take your coat.
Let me give you a few details.

7 You use 'let's' followed by the base form of a verb when you are suggesting what you and someone else should do.

Let's go outside.
Let's look at our map.

Note that the form 'let us' is only used in formal or written English.

Let us consider a very simple example.

You put 'do' before 'let's' when you are very keen to do something.

Do let's get a taxi.

The negative of 'let's' is 'let's not' or 'don't let's'.

Let's not talk about that.
Don't let's actually write it in the book.

8 You use 'let' followed by a noun group and the base form of a verb when you are telling someone to do something or to allow someone else to do it.

Let me see it.
Let Philip have a look at it.

Unit 56 Practice

A Where might you find these instructions? Choose the right answer from the list below.
1 Once opened keep in fridge and eat within 3 days. ...*A jar of meat paste.*..................
2 Do not spray directly on food. Keep in a safe place away from young children. ....
3 Adults: Take 1 teaspoonful every two or three hours. ....
4 Brush regularly and thoroughly - ideally after every meal. ....
5 Dilute to taste. ....
6 Cut out this coupon and save 15p on your next packet of cornflakes. ....
7 If pouring oil back into bottle, allow it to cool first. ....
8 Shake well before opening. ....
9 Store in a cool dry place. ....

a packet of breakfast cereal	a bottle of cooking oil	a bottle of orange squash
a box of cheese biscuits	a tin of milk	a bottle of cough mixture
an insect spray	a jar of meat paste	a tube of toothpaste

B These instructions appear in public telephone boxes in Britain. Can you put them in the correct order?
1 Give the address where help is needed. ...*Dial 999 for emergency.*..................
2 Wait for the emergency service to answer. ....
3 Dial 999 for emergency. ....
4 Tell the operator which service you want. ....
5 Give any other necessary information. ....
6 Give the telephone number shown on the phone. ....

Check the answer and then complete this short paragraph.

First you ...*dial 999*.................. , ... , and ....
.... Then you give .... , ... , and ....
....

C Rewrite the suggestions and requests in bold, starting with **don't**.
1 **You shouldn't touch that.** It's very hot. / ...*Don't touch that.*..................
2 She's very tired. **I hope you won't wake her up.** / Please ....
3 He'll be in a hurry. **You mustn't keep him waiting.** / ....
4 It's a secret. **You mustn't tell anyone.** / ....
5 **You mustn't bother me now.** I'm much too busy. / ....

D Make each of the following sentences into an offer with **let me,** or a suggestion with **let's.**
1 I'll take your coat. / ...*Let me take your coat.*..................
2 I think we should go home now. / ...*Let's go home now.*..................
3 Can I carry that bag for you? / ....
4 We could telephone for help. / ....
5 I'll help you. / ....
6 I think we should start now. / ....

▶ **Bank**

Unit 57 Negative sentences with 'not'

Main points

- 'Not' is often shortened to '-n't' and added to some verbs.
- You put 'not' after the first verb in the verb group, or you use a short form.

1 In spoken and in informal written English, 'not' is often shortened to '-n't' and added to an auxiliary, a modal, or a form of the main verb 'be'.

I haven't heard from her recently.
I wasn't angry.

Here is a list of short forms.

isn't	haven't	doesn't	mightn't	won't
aren't	hasn't	didn't	mustn't	wouldn't
wasn't	hadn't	~	oughtn't	~
weren't	~	can't	shan't	daren't
~	don't	couldn't	shouldn't	needn't

If the verb is already shortened, you cannot add '-n't'.

It's not easy.
I've not had time.

You cannot add '-n't' to 'am'. You use 'I'm not'.

I'm not excited.

2 If the verb group has more than one word, you put 'not' after the first word, or you use a short form.

I was not smiling.
He hadn't attended many meetings.
They might not notice.
I haven't been playing football recently.

3 If the sentence only contains a main verb other than 'be', you use the auxiliary 'do'.
You use 'do not', 'does not', 'did not', or a short form, followed by the base form of the main verb.

They do not need to talk.
He does not speak English very well.
I didn't know that.

Note that if the main verb is 'do', you still use a form of 'do' as an auxiliary.

They didn't do anything about it.

4 If the main verb is the present or past simple of 'be', you put 'not' immediately after it, or you use a short form.

It is not difficult to understand.
It's not the same, is it?
He wasn't a bad actor actually.

5 If the main verb is 'have', you usually use a form of 'do' as an auxiliary.

They don't have any money.

You can also use a short form, or you can put 'not' after the verb but this is not very common.

He hadn't enough money.

6 You can put 'not' in front of an '-ing' form or a 'to'-infinitive.

We stood there, not knowing what to do.
Try not to worry.

7 In negative questions, you use a short form.

Why didn't she win at the Olympics?
Hasn't he put on weight?
Aren't you bored?

8 You can use a negative question:

- to express your feelings, for example to show that you are surprised or disappointed

Hasn't he done it yet?

- in exclamations

Isn't the weather awful!

- when you think you know something and you just want someone to agree with you

'Aren't you Joanne's brother?' - 'Yes, I am.'

9 Note the meaning of 'yes' and 'no' in answers to negative questions.

'Isn't Tracey going to get a bit bored in Birmingham?'
— *'Yes.'* (She is going to get bored.)
— *'No.'* (She is not going to get bored.)

Unit 57 Practice

A Make these sentences negative.

1 He works in Manchester now. / *He doesn't work in Manchester now.*
2 We have been there often. / ....
3 Mary was very happy. / ....
4 English is easy to understand. / ....
5 I've been to San Francisco. / ....
6 We might be late. / ....
7 He knows her name. / ....
8 They'll be arriving in time for lunch. / ....
9 We can go by train. / ....
10 John may be coming with his wife. / ....

B Now do the same with these.

1 Bill might have left a message. / *Bill mightn't have left a message.*
2 They will probably have telephoned. / ....
3 Mary should have told you. / ....
4 I could have arrived earlier. / ....
5 You should have asked Peter. / ....

C Rewrite these sentences using **do** as an auxiliary.

1 We hadn't any time to spare. / *We didn't have any time to spare.*
2 She hasn't any friends in London. / ....
3 He hasn't any brothers or sisters. / ....
4 I haven't any money. / ....
5 They hadn't any new clothes to wear. / ....
6 We haven't anything to eat. / ....

D Add a negative question to show surprise.

1 They'll arrive before ten. / *Won't they arrive* .... before then?
2 He earns about £100 a week. / .... more than that?
3 They gave us five pounds. / .... more than that?
4 We can stay until eleven o'clock. / .... later than that?
5 I have met Fred. / .... his brother too?

E Complete the answers to these negative questions.

1 Doesn't John live somewhere round here? / Yes, *he does.* .
2 Didn't you go to school with Peter? / No, ...
3 Haven't you finished yet? / No, I'm afraid ....
4 Won't they be back soon? / Yes, ...
5 Can't you come. / Yes, I think ....
6 Hasn't she told you? / No, ...
7 Aren't you pleased? / Yes, ...
8 Hadn't you heard? / No, ...

115

Unit 58 Negative words

Main points

- A negative sentence contains a negative word.
- You do not normally use two negative words in the same clause.

1 Negative statements contain a negative word.

not	none	no one	~
never	~	nothing	neither
no	nobody	nowhere	nor

See Unit 57 for negative statements using 'not'.

2 You use 'never' to say that something was not the case at any time, or will not be the case at any time.
If the verb group has more than one word, you put 'never' after the first word.

I've never had such a horrible meal.
He could never trust her again.

3 If the only verb in the sentence is the present simple or past simple of any main verb except 'be', you put 'never' before the verb.

She never goes abroad.
He never went to university.

If the only verb in the sentence is the present simple or past simple of the main verb 'be', you normally put 'never' after the verb.

He's never late.
There were never any people in the house.

You can also use 'never' at the beginning of an imperative sentence.

Never walk alone late at night.

4 You use 'no' before a noun to say that something does not exist or is not available.

He has given no reason for his decision.
The island has no trees at all.

Note that if there is another negative word in the clause, you use 'any', not 'no'.

It won't do any good.

5 You use 'none' or 'none of' to say that there is not even one thing or person, or not even a small amount of something.

You can't go to a college here because there are none in this area.
'Where's the coffee?' - 'There's none left.'
None of us understood the play.

See Unit 15 for more information on 'none' and 'none of'.

6 You also use 'nobody', 'no one', 'nothing', and 'nowhere' in negative statements.
You use 'nobody' or 'no one' to talk about people.

Nobody in her house knows any English.
No one knew.

'No one' can also be written 'no-one'.

There's no-one here.

You use 'nothing' to talk about things.

There's nothing you can do.

You use 'nowhere' to talk about places.

There's almost nowhere left to go.

See Unit 10 for more information about these words.

7 You do not normally use two negative words in the same clause. For example, you do not say 'Nobody could see nothing'. You say 'Nobody could see anything'.
You use 'anything', 'anyone', 'anybody', and 'anywhere' instead of 'nothing, 'no one', 'nobody', and 'nowhere' when the clause already contains a negative word.

No-one can find Howard or Barbara anywhere.
I could never discuss anything with them.

8 The only negative words that are often used together in the same clause are 'neither' and 'nor'. You use 'neither' and 'nor' together to say that two alternatives are not possible, not likely, or not true.

Neither Margaret nor John was there.
They had neither food nor money.

Unit 58 Practice

A Answer the questions below using one of the words in brackets.

1 How often have you been to Oxford?

I've ....*never*.................... been. I'd like to go one day, though. (never / none / nowhere)

2 How many books did you buy?

.... I had .... money left. (No / None / Nothing) (no / none / nothing)

3 What did you do?

.... I was too tired to do anything. (No / None / Nothing)

4 Where did you find the money?

.... We looked everywhere but we couldn't find it at all. (None / Nothing / Nowhere)

5 Who did you talk to at the party?

.... There were lots of people there but .... of them spoke English. (Nobody / None / Nothing) (no / neither / none)

6 Who won the prize, Jill or Helen?

.... of them. Mary finally won quite easily. (Neither / None / No one)

7 Have you seen John lately?

I'm afraid not. He .... comes to visit us nowadays. (never / not / no)

8 Was that the postman?

No. I answered the door but there was .... there. (no-one / nothing / none)

9 Did you both go to the show last night?

No, ... of us managed to go. We were far too busy. (neither / none / no)

10 Did you see John and Mary yesterday?

No, ... John .... Mary came to the meeting. (no / neither) (nor / not)

B Complete these sentences using one of the words in brackets.

1 I looked everywhere for Jane but I couldn't find her ...*anywhere*............... . (anywhere / somewhere / nowhere).

2 There were lots of people there but I didn't meet .... I knew. (anybody / nobody / somebody)

3 I asked lots of people but .... knew the answer. (anyone / no one / someone)

4 I asked Bill for help but he couldn't do .... (anything / nothing / something)

5 I asked Bill if he could do .... to help but he said he couldn't. (anything / nothing / something)

6 I haven't .... heard of him before. (ever / never / not)

7 I've met Frank but I've .... met his brother. (ever / never)

8 I wanted some coffee but there wasn't .... left. (any / none / some)

9 I wanted a biscuit but there were .... left. (any / none / some)

10 I knocked at the door but there was .... at home. (anybody / nobody / somebody)

Unit 59 Introduction to modals

can, could, may, might, must, ought, shall, should, will, would

Main points

- Modals are always the first word in a verb group.
- All modals except for 'ought' are followed by the base form of a verb.
- 'Ought' is followed by a 'to'-infinitive.
- Modals have only one form.

Modals can be used for various different purposes. These are explained in Units 60-71.

1 Modals are always the first word in a verb group. All modals except for 'ought' are followed by the base form of a verb.

I must leave fairly soon.
I think it will look rather nice.
Things might have been so different.
People may be watching.

2 'Ought' is always followed by a 'to'-infinitive.

She ought to go straight back to England.
Sam ought to have realized how dangerous it was.
You ought to be doing this.

3 Modals have only one form. There is no '-s' form for the third person singular of the present tense, and there are no '-ing' or '-ed' forms.

There's nothing I can do about it.
I'm sure he can do it.

4 Modals do not normally indicate the time when something happens. There are, however, a few exceptions.
'Shall' and 'will' often indicate a future event or situation.

I shall do what you suggested.
He will not return for many hours.

'Could' is used as the past form of 'can' to express ability. 'Would' is used as the past form of 'will' to express the future.

When I was young, I could run for miles.
He remembered that he would see his mother the next day.

5 In spoken English and informal written English, 'shall' and 'will' are shortened to '-'ll', and 'would' to '-'d', and added to a pronoun.

I'll see you tomorrow.
I hope you'll agree.
Posy said she'd love to stay.

'Shall', 'will', and 'would' are never shortened if they come at the end of a sentence.

Paul said he would come, and I hope he will.

In spoken English, you can also add '-'ll' and '-'d' to nouns.

My car'll be outside.
The headmaster'd be furious.

WARNING: Remember that '-d' is also the short form of the auxiliary 'had'.

I'd heard it many times.

Unit 59 Practice

A Rewrite these sentences using the modals given.

1 Perhaps he fell. (may have) (could have)
   He may have fallen.
   He could have fallen.

2 Perhaps they saw us. (could have) (might have)

3 Perhaps he said that. I don't remember. (might have) (could have)

4 We're lost. I think we've taken the wrong road. (must have)

5 I wish you had seen it. It was wonderful. (should have)

6 I ought to have known that would happen. (should have)

7 Perhaps when I am fifty I won't remember it. (will have forgotten)

8 It was possible for me to prevent that, but I didn't. (could have)

9 You should have listened to her the first time. (ought to have)

B Rewrite these sentences using **ought to have** or **should have**.

1 Why didn't you tell the truth? / *You ought to have told the truth.   You should have told the truth*

2 Why didn't they go by car? / ....

3 Why didn't you telephone? / ....

4 Why didn't you ask John to help? / ....

5 Why didn't you do the shopping? / ....

Now rewrite these with **ought not to have** or **shouldn't have**.

6 Why did you run away? / *You ought not to have run away.   You shouldn't have run away.*

7 Why did you spend so much money? / ....

8 Why did it take you so long? / ....

9 Why did they do that? / ....

10 Why did she leave so early? / ....

11 Why did he make so much noise? / ....

12 Why was he so upset? / ....

Unit 60 Modals - negatives and questions

Main points

- You use negative words with modals to make negative clauses.
- Modals go in front of the subject in questions.
- You never use two modals together.

1 To make a clause negative, you put a negative word immediately after the modal.

You must not worry.
I can never remember his name.
He ought not to have done that.

'Can not' is always written as one word, 'cannot'.

I cannot go back.

However, if 'can' is followed by 'not only', 'can' and 'not' are not joined.

We can not only book your flight for you, but also advise you about hotels.

2 In spoken English and informal written English, 'not' is often shortened to '-n't' and added to the modal. The following modals are often shortened in this way:

could not	⇨ couldn't
should not	⇨ shouldn't
must not	⇨ mustn't
would not	⇨ wouldn't

We couldn't leave the farm.
You mustn't talk about Ron like that.

Note the following irregular short forms:

shall not	⇨ shan't
will not	⇨ won't
cannot	⇨ can't

I shan't let you go.
Won't you change your mind?
We can't stop now.

'Might not' and 'ought not' are sometimes shortened to 'mightn't' and 'oughtn't'.
Note that 'may not' is very rarely shortened to 'mayn't' in modern English.

3 To make a question, you put the modal in front of the subject.

Could you give me an example?
Will you be coming in later?
Shall I shut the door?

Modals are also used in question tags. See Units 52 and 53 for more information.

4 You never use two modals together. For example, you cannot say 'He will can come'. Instead you can say 'He will be able to come'.

I shall have to go.
Your husband might have to give up work.

5 Instead of using modals, you can often use other verbs and expressions to make requests, offers, or suggestions, to express wishes or intentions, or to show that you are being polite.
For example, 'be able to' is used instead of 'can', 'be likely to' is used instead of 'might', and 'have to' is used instead of 'must'.

All members are able to claim expenses.
I think that we are likely to see more of this.

These expressions are also used after modals.

I really thought I wouldn't be able to visit you this week.

6 'Dare' and 'need' sometimes behave like modals.
See Unit 84 for information on 'dare' and Units 70 and 83 for information on 'need'.

Unit 60 Practice

A Complete these pairs of sentences appropriately using the modal given in brackets in one sentence, and its negative form in the other sentence.

1 He certainly ....*won't*.................. understand if you don't explain it. (will)

I ...*will*...................... come round later if I have time.

2 Unfortunately many elderly people .... afford telephones. (can)

You .... borrow my pen if you want to.

3 When I was young you .... buy them for under a pound. (could)

They complained that they .... sleep.

4 If you don't work harder you .... have your job much longer. (may)

This medicine .... cause sleepiness.

5 I thought I .... find you here. (might)

It's a long journey. They .... be here before midnight.

6 Schools .... teach children the difference between right and wrong. (must)

Whatever you do you .... tell anyone about it.

7 I .... get angry in a moment. (shall)

That was a moment I .... forget in a hurry.

8 We can't be certain how an unfamiliar word .... be pronounced. (should)

These birds .... be in a cage.

9 I .... be back in a few minutes. (will)

If we're lucky perhaps this time it .... rain.

10 If you can manage to help me I .... be very grateful. (would)

I invited her even though I knew she .... come.

11 You .... to wait too long. (ought)

She .... to see the doctor.

B Rewrite the following sentences to form questions beginning with the modals given.

1 I would like to help you. / Can I ...*help you?*..

2 I'd like to speak to Nicky please. / Can I ....

3 It would help if you could give me a few examples. / Could you ....

4 I'd like to have a word with you please. / May I ....

5 I wish she wouldn't be so nasty to me. / Why must she ....

6 I don't know what to give them for dinner. / What shall I ....

7 Would you like me to shut the door? / Shall I ....

8 I don't know where to meet you tonight. / Where should ....

9 I don't know who to see about my teaching programme. / Who should ....

10 Doctor, can I offer you a drink? / Will you ....

11 Please tell her that Adrian phoned. / Would you ....

Unit 61 Can, could, may, might - possibility

Main points

- You use 'can' to say that something is possible.
- You use 'could','might', and 'may' to indicate that you are not certain whether something is possible, but you think it is.

1 When you want to say that something is possible, you use 'can'.

Cooking can be a real pleasure.
In some cases this can cause difficulty.

You use 'cannot' or 'can't' to say that something is not possible.

This cannot be the answer.
You can't be serious.

2 When you want to indicate that you are not certain whether something is possible, but you think it is, you use 'could', 'might', or 'may'. There is no important difference in meaning between these modals, but 'may' is slightly more formal.

That could be one reason.
He might come.
They may help us.

You can also use 'might not' or 'may not' in this way.

He might not be in England at all.
They may not get a house with central heating.

Note that 'could not' normally refers to ability in the past. See Unit 63.

3 When there is a possibility that something happened in the past, but you are not certain if it actually happened, you use 'could have', 'may have', or 'might have', followed by a past participle.

It could have been tomato soup.
You may have noticed this advertisement.

You can also use 'might not have' or 'may not have' in this way.

He might not have seen me.
They may not have done it.

You use 'could not have' when you want to indicate that it is not possible that something happened.

He didn't have a boat, so he couldn't have rowed away.
It couldn't have been wrong.

You also use 'could have' to say that there was a possibility of something happening in the past, but it did not happen.

It could have been awful. (But it wasn't awful.)
You could have got a job last year. (But you didn't get a job.)

4 You also use 'might have' or 'could have' followed by a past participle to say that if a particular thing had happened, then there was a possibility of something else happening.

She said it might have been all right, if the weather had been good. (But the weather wasn't good, so it wasn't all right.)
If I'd been there, I could have helped you. (But I wasn't there, so I couldn't help you.)

5 'Be able to', 'not be able to', and 'be unable to' are sometimes used instead of 'can' and 'cannot', for example after another modal, or when you want to use a 'to'-infinitive, an '-ing' form, or a past participle.

When will I be able to pick them up?
He had been unable to get a ticket.

6 You use 'used to be able to' to say that something was possible in the past, but is not possible now.

Everyone used to be able to have free eye tests.
You used to be able to buy cigarettes in packs of five.

7 Note that you also use 'could' followed by a negative word and the comparative form of an adjective to emphasize a quality that someone or something has. For example, if you say 'I couldn't be happier', you mean that you are very happy indeed and cannot imagine being happier than you are now.

You couldn't be more wrong.
He could hardly have felt more ashamed of himself.

Unit 61 Practice

A Make suitable sentences from the table below using **can.**

Learning English Watching television Visiting relatives Winter sports Going to the dentist Meeting new people Travelling	can	sometimes often occasionally	be	exciting. boring. interesting. painful. hard work. dangerous. good fun.

1   *Travelling can often be boring.*
2   ....
3   ....
4   ....
5   ....
6   ....
7   ....

B Rewrite these sentences using **may** or **might.** You can use either.

1 Maybe you are right. I can't be sure. / ...*You may be right.*...............................
2 Perhaps George will help if you give him a ring. / ....
3 Possibly it's a mistake. / ....
4 Perhaps things won't be so bad after all. / ....
5 It's possible that she won't recognize you even if she sees you. / ....
6 Perhaps it's broken. / ....

Now put the sentences above into the past using **may have** or **might have.**

C You hear a strange noise at night. What do you think it **could be?** Write sentences using these ideas.

1 ...a burglar? / ...*It could be a burglar.*..
2 ...a wild animal? / ....
3 ...one of the neighbours? / ....
4 ...the wind in the trees? / ....
5 ...a car passing? / ....
6 ...someone snoring? / ....
7 ...someone at the door? / ....
8 ...a ghost? / ....

Now imagine that you heard the noise last night. Rewrite the sentences using **could have been.**

D Complete these sentences using either **may not** or **can't.**

1 There ...*may not*............ be anybody there when you arrive.
2 That .... be true! It's absolutely impossible.
3 I don't know if she will agree. She .... want to.
4 You .... be serious. You've got to be joking.
5 It may very well happen, but on the other hand it ....
6 It .... be done. It's quite out of the question.

▶ **Bank**   123

Unit 62 Cannot, can't, must, ought, should, will - probability and certainty

Main points

- You use 'must', 'ought', 'should', or 'will' to express probability or certainty.
- You use 'cannot' or 'can't' as the negative of 'must', rather than 'must not' or 'mustn't', to say that something is not probable or is not certain.

1 When you want to say that something is probably true or that it will probably happen, you use 'should' or 'ought'. 'Should' is followed by the base form of a verb. 'Ought' is followed by a 'to'-infinitive.

We should arrive by dinner time.
She ought to know.

When you want to say that you think something is probably not true or that it will probably not happen, you use 'should not' or 'ought not'.

There shouldn't be any problem.
That ought not to be too difficult.

2 When you want to say that you are fairly sure that something has happened, you use 'should have' or 'ought to have', followed by a past participle.

You should have heard by now that I'm O.K.
They ought to have arrived yesterday.

When you want to say that you do not think that something has happened, you use 'should not have' or 'ought not to have', followed by a past participle.

You shouldn't have had any difficulty in getting there.
This ought not to have been a problem.

3 You also use 'should have' or 'ought to have' to say that you expected something to happen, but that it did not happen.

Yesterday should have been the start of the soccer season.
She ought to have been home by now.

Note that you do not normally use the negative forms with this meaning.

4 When you are fairly sure that something is the case, you use 'must'.

Oh, you must be Sylvia's husband.
He must know something about it.

If you are fairly sure that something is not the case, you use 'cannot' or 'can't'.

This cannot be the whole story.
He can't be very old — he's about 25, isn't he?

WARNING: You do not use 'must not' or 'mustn't' with this meaning.

5 When you want to say that you are almost certain that something has happened, you use 'must have', followed by a past participle.

This article must have been written by a woman.
We must have taken the wrong road.

To say that you do not think that something has happened, you use 'can't have', followed by a past participle.

You can't have forgotten me.
He can't have said that.

6 You use 'will' or '-'ll' to say that something is certain to happen in the future.

People will always say the things you want to hear.
They'll manage.

You use 'will not' or 'won't' to say that something is certain not to happen.

You won't get much sympathy from them.

7 There are several ways of talking about probability and certainty without using modals. For example, you can use:

- 'bound to' followed by the base form of a verb

It was bound to happen.
You're bound to make a mistake.

- an adjective such as 'certain', 'likely', 'sure', or 'unlikely', followed by a 'to'-infinitive clause or a 'that'-clause

They were certain that you were defeated.
I am not likely to forget it.

See Unit 22 for more information on these adjectives.

Unit 62　Practice

A Use **should be** or **ought to be** with one of these phrases to comment on each of the sentences below.

> a comfortable trip　an exciting game　a nice day　　fun
> really interesting　　very profitable　　nice and quiet

1　We are going to Japan for a holiday this summer. / It *should be really interesting.*
2　Bill's asked me to his birthday party. / That *ought to be fun.*
3　There's a good match on this weekend. / Yes, it ....
4　We couldn't get standard tickets so we're travelling first class. / Well, at least it ....
5　The weather forecast for tomorrow is excellent. / Yes, it ....
6　Jan has just opened a new shop in the High Street. / I know. It ....
7　Our hotel is right out in the country. / That's good. It ....

B Write comments with **must** after the following sentences.

1　You haven't eaten for a whole day? / (you / starving) *You must be starving.*
2　They've been travelling all night? / (they / tired out) ....
3　He's passed his exam? / (he / delighted) ....
4　Your wife is in hospital? / (you / very worried) ....
5　Your son has won a scholarship? / (you / very proud of him) ....

C Rewrite the parts in bold using **must have**.

1　He drove all the way from Glasgow. **Obviously it was a long journey.**
　　It must have been a long journey.
2　He pretended to be innocent, but **I'm sure he did it.**
　　...
3　George was standing very close to you. **Of course you saw him.**
　　...
4　You look very well. **It seems you enjoyed your holiday.**
　　...
5　There's nobody in. **Probably they've gone shopping.**
　　...
6　My coat isn't there. **Perhaps someone has taken it by mistake.**
　　...

D Rewrite the sections in bold using **can't**.

1　She looks so young. **I'm sure she's not thirty yet.** *She can't be thirty yet.*
2　It's still quite early. **I'm sure it's not ten o'clock.** ....
3　She doesn't look at all like Mary. **I'm sure she isn't her sister.** ....
4　He's been very ill lately. **He's probably not very well even now.** ....
5　There's no answer. **They're probably not in.** ....
6　If you live near Coventry, **you aren't very far from Birmingham.** ....
7　He looks very ill. **I'm sure he's not feeling very well.** ....

▶ **Bank**

Unit 63 Can, could, be able to - ability

Main points

- You use 'can' to talk about ability in the present and in the future.
- You use 'could' to talk about ability in the past.
- You use 'be able to' to talk about ability in the present, future, and past.

1 You use 'can' to say that someone has the ability to do something.

You can all read and write.
Anybody can become a qualified teacher.

You use 'cannot' or 'can't' to say that they do not have the ability to do something.

He cannot dance.

2 When you want to talk about someone's ability in the past as a result of a skill they had or did not have, you use 'could', 'could not', or 'couldn't'.

He could run faster than anyone else.
A lot of them couldn't read or write.

3 You also use 'be able to', 'not be able to', and 'be unable to' to talk about someone's ability to do something, but 'can' and 'could' are more common.

She was able to tie her own shoelaces.
They are not able to run very fast.
Many people were unable to read or write.

4 You use 'was able to' and 'were able to' to say that someone managed to do something in a particular situation in the past.

After treatment he was able to return to work.
The farmers were able to pay the new wages.
We were able to find time to discuss it.

WARNING: You do not normally use 'could' to say that someone managed to do something in a particular situation. However, you can use 'could not' or 'couldn't' to say that someone did not manage to do something in a particular situation.

We couldn't stop laughing.
I just couldn't think of anything to say.

5 When you want to say that someone had the ability to do something in the past, but did not do it, you use 'could have' followed by a past participle.

You could have given it all to me.
You know, she could have done French.

You often use this form when you want to express disapproval about something that was not done.

You could have been a little bit tidier.
You could have told me!

6 You use 'could not have' or 'couldn't have' followed by a past participle to say that it is not possible that someone had the ability to do something.

I couldn't have gone with you, because I was in London at the time.
She couldn't have taken the car, because Jim was using it.

7 In most cases, you can choose to use 'can' or 'be able to'. However, you sometimes have to use 'be able to'.

You have to use 'be able to' if you are using another modal, or if you want to use an '-ing' form, a past participle, or a 'to'-infinitive.

Nobody else will be able to read it.
...the satisfaction of being able to do the job.
I don't think I'd have been able to get an answer.
You're foolish to expect to be able to do that.

8 You also use 'can' or 'could' with verbs such as 'see', 'hear', and 'smell' to say that someone is or was aware of something through one of their senses.

I can smell gas.
I can't see her.
I could see a few stars in the sky.
There was such a noise we couldn't hear.

Unit 63 Practice

A Which of these things **can** you do? Which **can't** you do? Write three true sentences like this:

I can play chess, but my sister can't.

And three like this:

My sister can't play chess, but I can.

count to twenty in Spanish	swim	ride a bike	drive a car
understand sign language	swim like a fish	ride a horse	sail a boat
use a word processor	play chess	run a marathon	ski

....

....

....

....

....

....

Now write down five questions about the things above to ask someone else.

Can you play chess really well?

....

....

....

....

....

B How many of the things above **could** you do when you were ten years old? Write down three things you **could** do and three things you **couldn't** do.

....

....

....

....

....

....

Now write down three questions to ask someone else.

When you were ten, could you ride a bike?

....

....

....

C Complete these sentences using **can, can't, could,** or **couldn't.**

1 There was a woman with a big hat right in front of me. I .....*couldn't*..................... see a thing.

2 I'm sorry, you're in my light. I .... see what I'm doing.

3 It was a huge hall and we were at the back, so we .... hear very well.

4 When she screams, you .... hear her all over the house.

5 She was phoning all the way from Singapore, but I .... hear her very clearly.

6 .... you hear me at the back?

7 Put your hands up if you .... hear me.

▶ **Bank**

Unit 64 Can, could, may - permission

Main points

- You use 'can' or 'be allowed to' to talk about whether someone has permission to do something or not.
- You usually use 'can' to give someone permission to do something.
- You usually use 'can' or 'could' to ask for permission to do something.

1 You use 'can' to say that someone is allowed to do something. You use 'cannot' or 'can't' to say that they are not allowed to do it.

Students can take a year away from university.
Children cannot bathe except in the presence of two lifesavers.

You use 'could' to say that someone was allowed to do something in the past. You use 'could not' or 'couldn't' to say that they were not allowed to do it.

We could go to any part of the island we wanted.
Both students and staff could use the swimming pool.
We couldn't go into the library after 5 pm.

2 You also use 'be allowed to' when you are talking about permission, but not when you are asking for it or giving it.

When Mr Wilt asks for a solicitor he will be allowed to see one.
It was only after several months that I was allowed to visit her.
You're not allowed to use calculators in exams.

3 In more formal situations, 'may' is used to say that someone is allowed to do something, and 'may not' is used to say that they are not allowed to do it.

They may do exactly as they like.
The retailer may not sell that book below the publisher's price.

4 When you want to give someone permission to do something, you use 'can'.

You can borrow that pen if you want to.
You can go off duty now.
She can go with you.

'May' is also used to give permission, but this is more formal.

You may speak.
You may leave as soon as you have finished.

5 When you want to refuse someone permission to do something, you use 'cannot', 'can't', 'will not', 'won't', 'shall not', or 'shan't'.

'Can I have some sweets?' - 'No, you can't!'
'I'll just go upstairs.' - 'You will not!'
You shan't leave without my permission.

6 When you are asking for permission to do something, you use 'can' or 'could'.
If you ask in a very simple and direct way, you use 'can'.

Can I ask a question?
Can we have something to wipe our hands on please?

'Could' is more polite than 'can'.

Could I just interrupt a minute?
Could we put this fire on?

'May' is also used to ask permission, but this is more formal.

May I have a cigarette?

'Might' is rather old-fashioned and is not often used in modern English in this way.

Might I inquire if you are the owner?

7 You have to use 'be allowed to' instead of a modal if you are using another modal, or if you want to use an '-ing' form, a past participle, or a 'to'-infinitive.

Teachers will be allowed to decide for themselves.
I am strongly in favour of people being allowed to put on plays.
They have not been allowed to come.
We were going to be allowed to travel on the trains.

Unit 64 Practice

A All of these sentences can be used to ask for permission. Rewrite each one using **can.**

1 Do you mind if I open this window just a little? / *Can I open this window just a little?*

2 I'd like to ask you just one more question. / ....

3 Is it all right if I give you a ring some time later? / ....

4 Is it okay if we go swimming? / ....

5 Do you mind if I sit down? / ....

6 I'd like an ice-cream please. / ....

7 Do you think I could go home now? / ....

8 I wonder if I could come back later. / ....

Make the requests more formal by changing **can** to **may.**

Now make them more polite by changing **can** to **could.**

B Rewrite these sentences asking for permission, starting with the phrases given.

1 I'd like to have a little more time. / I wonder if ... *I could have a little more time.*

2 Can I start now? / Do you think ....

3 Can I listen to the radio while you're working? / Do you mind if ....

4 May I come in now? / Is it all right if ....

5 I'd like to speak next. / Do you think ....

C Rewrite these sentences giving permission, starting with the words given.

1 You're allowed to do whatever you want. / You can ... *do whatever you want.*

2 It's all right to have visitors after three o'clock. / You're allowed to ....

3 You may all go home as soon as you've finished work. / You can all ....

4 I don't mind you coming back late as long as you don't make too much noise. / You can ....

....

5 With this banker's card you can cash a cheque for up to £250. / With this card you are allowed to ....

....

6 I'll let you use my pen until I need it myself. / You can ....

D Read this passage and complete the sentences below.

In Britain you are not allowed to leave school or to get married until you are at least sixteen years old.
You cannot drive a car until you are seventeen, and you cannot drive a taxi until you are twenty-one. You
are allowed to vote at the age of eighteen.

1 When you are sixteen you can ... *leave school* .... and you can also ...., but

you are not allowed to .... until you are eighteen.

2 You are allowed to .... when you are seventeen, but you can't ....

...... until you are twenty-one.

3 You can .... at the age of seventeen and you can .... at the

age of eighteen.

4 It seems silly that you are allowed to .... when you are only sixteen, but you're not

allowed to .... until you are seventeen.

5 I think you should be allowed to .... a year earlier, when you are seventeen.

6 If you can .... at the age of seventeen I don't see why you shouldn't be allowed to

....

Unit 65 Can, could, will, would - instructions and requests

Main points

- You use 'Could you' to tell someone politely to do something.
- Imperatives are not very polite.
- You also use 'Could you' to ask someone politely for help.
- You use 'I would like', 'Would you mind', 'Do you think you could', and 'I wonder if you could' to make requests.

1 When you want to tell someone to do something, you can use 'Could you', 'Will you', and 'Would you'. 'Could you' is very polite.

Could you make out her bill, please?
Could you just switch on the light behind you?

'Will you' and 'Would you' are normally used by people in authority. 'Would you' is more polite than 'Will you'.

Would you tell her that Adrian phoned?
Will you please leave the room?

Note that although these sentences look like questions ('Will you', not 'You will'), they are not really questions.

2 If someone in authority wants to tell someone to do something, they sometimes say 'I would like you to do this' or 'I'd like you to do this'.

Penelope, I would like you to get us the files.
I'd like you to finish this work by Thursday.

3 You can use an imperative to tell someone to do something, but this is not very polite.

Stop her.
Go away, all of you.

However, imperatives are commonly used when talking to people you know very well.

Come here, love.
Sit down and let me get you a drink.

You often use imperatives in situations of danger or urgency.

Look out! There's a car coming.
Put it away before Mum sees you.

4 When you want to ask someone to help you, you use 'Could you', 'Would you', 'Can you', or 'Will you'. 'Could you' and 'Would you' are used in formal situations, or when you want to be very polite, for example because you are asking for something that requires a lot of effort. 'Could you' is more polite than 'Would you'.

Could you show me how to do this?
Would you do me a favour?

'Will you' and 'Can you' are used in informal situations, especially when you are not asking for something that requires a lot of effort.

Will you post this for me on your way to work?
Can you make me a copy of that?

5 You also use 'I would like' or 'I'd like', followed by a 'to'-infinitive or a noun group, to make a request.

I would like to ask you one question.
I'd like steak and chips, please.

6 You can also make a request by using:

● 'Would you mind', followed by an '-ing' form

Would you mind doing the washing up?
Would you mind waiting a moment?

● 'Do you think you could', followed by the base form of a verb

Do you think you could help me?

● 'I wonder if you could', followed by the base form of a verb

I wonder if you could look after my cat for me while I'm away?

Unit 65 Practice

A Make six requests from this table, using **could I, may I,** and **could you.**

Could I May I Could you let me	have	another cup of coffee a look at your newspaper something to eat one of those biscuits a bit of advice a little more time	please?

1 *May I have something to eat, please?* ....

2 ....

3 ....

4 ....

5 ....

6 ....

Rewrite two of your requests beginning with **could you give me.**

....

....

B Make these requests more polite by starting them with **would you mind.**

1 Could you come back later, please? / ...*Would you mind coming back later please?*......

2 Will you help this lady with her bags? / ....

3 Can you pay cash, please? / ....

4 Would you tell them that I called? / ....

5 Can you close the door behind you, please? / ....

6 Do you think you could do the shopping on your way home? / ....

7 I wonder if you could help me, please? / ....

8 Will you do the cooking tonight? / ....

9 Can you come ten minutes before the meeting starts? / ....

10 Could you tell me when you're ready? / ....

C Turn these instructions into polite requests by starting with the words given.

1 I can't hear very well. Speak up. / I can't hear very well. Do you think ...*you could speak up?*...

2 Give Joan a message. / I wonder if ....

3 Give me your full name. / Would you mind ....

4 Repeat that. / Do you think ....

5 Stand up. / I wonder if ....

6 Hold this for me. / Would you mind ....

7 Open the door. / Do you think ....

8 Do it again. / Would you mind ....

9 All of you sit down quietly. / I wonder if ....

10 Give me a little more time. / Do you think ....

131

Unit 66 Could, may, might, shall - suggestions

Main points

- You use 'could', 'couldn't', or 'shall' to make a suggestion.
- You use 'Shall we' to suggest doing something with someone.
- You use 'You might like' or 'You might want' to make polite suggestions.
- You use 'may as well' or 'might as well' to suggest a sensible action.
- You use 'What about', 'Let's', 'Why don't', and 'Why not' to make suggestions.

1 You use 'could' to suggest doing something.

You could phone her.
She could go into research.
We could go on Friday.

You also use 'couldn't' in a question to suggest doing something.

Couldn't you just build some more factories?
Couldn't we do it at the weekend?

2 You use 'Shall we' to suggest doing something with somebody else.

Shall we go and see a film?
Shall we talk about something different now?

You use 'Shall I' to suggest doing something yourself.

Shall I contact the Chairman?

3 You use 'You might', followed by a verb meaning 'like' or 'want', to make a suggestion in a very polite way.

I thought perhaps you might like to come along with me.
You might want to try another shop.

You can also do this using 'It might be', followed by a noun group or an adjective, and a 'to'-infinitive.

I think it might be a good idea to stop recording now.
It might be wise to get a new car.

4 You use 'may as well' or 'might as well' to suggest doing something, but only because it seems the sensible thing to do, or because there is no reason not to do it.

You may as well open them all.
He might as well take the car.

5 You can also make a suggestion by using:

- 'What about' or 'How about' followed by an '-ing' form

What about going to Judy's?
How about using my car?

- 'Let's' followed by the base form of a verb

Let's go outside.

- 'Why don't I', 'Why don't you' or 'Why don't we' followed by the base form of a verb

Why don't I pick you up at seven?
Why don't you write to her yourself?
Why don't we just give them what they want?

- 'Why not' followed by the base form of a verb

Why not bring him along?
Why not try both?

Unit 66 Practice

A Rewrite these suggestions to make them more direct.

1 Most people try to get there a bit earlier. / Couldn't you ...*try to get there a bit earlier?*...

2 I always use a word processor. / You should ....

3 My mother borrowed the money from the bank. / Couldn't you ....

4 My father always gets the information from the local library. / You could ....

5 A lot of people take a later train. / Why not ....

B Rewrite these suggestions starting with the words given.

1 Let's go to the theatre. / How about ...*going to the theatre?*...

2 We should get started as soon as possible. / It might be a good idea ....

3 You could write and ask her yourself. / You might like to ....

4 Why don't we take a winter holiday for a change? / What about ....

5 Couldn't you just pay at the end of the month? / You could ....

6 We could take a week off in July. / Let's ....

7 You could ask Bill to help. / What ....

8 Why don't you ring and tell them you're coming? / You ....

9 We could borrow the equipment from Peter. / Couldn't ....

10 Why don't we keep quiet about that? / It might ....

C Join the parts to make sentences and then fit the suggestions to the pictures.

1 Shall we call ...   a ... something to eat.

2 Why don't you send her ...   b ... eat out tonight.

3 Perhaps you could give him ...   c ... a taxi?

4 Shall we ask her to ...   d ... before they get back?

5 Do you think we could mend it ...   e ... back to the shop.

6 I suppose we could ...   f ... a get-well card.

7 Couldn't you give him ...   g ... a bone?

8 You could always take it ...   h ... take it off?

▶ **Bank**

Unit 67 Can, could, shall, will, would - offers and invitations

Main points

- You use 'Would you like' to offer something to someone or to invite them to do something.
- You use 'Can I', 'Could I', and 'Shall I' when you offer to help someone.

1 When you are offering something to someone, or inviting them to do something, you use 'Would you like'.

Would you like a drink?
Would you like to come for a meal?

You can use 'Will you' to offer something to someone you know quite well, or to give an invitation in a fairly informal way.

Will you have another biscuit, Dave?
Will you come to my party on Saturday?

2 You use 'Can I' or 'Could I' when you are offering to do something for someone. 'Could I' is more polite.

Can I help you with the dishes?
Could I help you carry those bags?

You also use 'Shall I' when you are offering to do something, especially if you are fairly sure that your offer will be accepted.

Shall I shut the door?
Shall I spell that for you?

3 You use 'I can' or 'I could' to make an offer when you want to say that you are able to help someone.

I have a car. I can take Daisy to the station.
I could pay some of the rent.

4 You also use 'I'll' to offer to do something.

I'll give them a ring if you like.
I'll show you the hotel.

5 You use 'You must' if you want to invite someone very persuasively to do something.

You must come round for a meal some time.
You must come and visit me.

6 There are other ways of making offers and giving invitations without using modals. For example, you can use 'Let me' when offering to help someone.

Let me take you to your room.
Let me drive you to London.

You can make an offer or give an invitation in a more informal way by using an imperative sentence, when it is clear that you are not giving an order.

Have a cigar.
Come to my place.

You can add emphasis by putting 'do' in front of the verb.

Do have a chocolate biscuit.
Do help yourselves.

You can also give an invitation by using 'Why don't you' or 'How about'.

Why don't you come to lunch tomorrow?
How about coming with us to the party?

Unit 67 Practice

A Join the part sentences below to make offers to fit the situations in the pictures.

1 Would you like me to open…	a …you with the cooking?
2 Let me carry…	b …the children for you.
3 Can I help…	c …the door for you?
4 Shall I post…	d …those bags for you.
5 Could I give you…	e …these letters for you?
6 I'll look after…	f …a lift?
7 Can I telephone…	g …those parcels for you.
8 I can hold…	h …for a taxi?

B Make these invitations very welcoming by starting with **you must.**

1 Can you come to our party next week? / *You must come to our party next week.*

2 Would you like to come round for a game of chess some time? / ....

3 Why don't you bring your wife with you next time? / ....

4 I'd like you to meet my brother next time he's here. / ....

5 Do have another cup of coffee. / ....

6 Can't you stay a little longer? / ....

7 Would you like to see my holiday photographs? / ....

8 Why don't you come to the theatre with me some time next week? / ....

9 Will you stay for lunch? / ....

10 Would you like another piece of cake? / ....

C Match the sentences with the offers.

1 You look thirsty.	a I'll get lunch.
2 It's hot in here.	b I can give you a lift.
3 I've got plenty of time.	c Let me give you a bit more.
4 It's a long way to town.	d I'll turn it down.
5 The radio's a bit noisy.	e I could turn it up a bit.
6 Can't you hear the record player?	f We could go to the cinema.
7 There's plenty to eat.	g Perhaps I can get you something to drink.
8 I've got nothing to do this evening.	h Shall I open the window?

Unit 68 Would like, would rather, wouldn't mind - wants and wishes

Main points

- You use 'would like' to say what you want.
- You use 'wouldn't like' to say what you do not want.
- You use 'would rather' or 'would sooner' to say what you prefer.
- You also use 'wouldn't mind' to say what you want.

1 You can say what someone wants by using 'would like' followed by a 'to'-infinitive or a noun group.

I would like to know the date of the next meeting.
John would like his book back.

When the subject is a pronoun, you often use the short form '-'d' instead of 'would'.

I'd like more information about the work you do.
We'd like seats in the non-smoking section, please.

In spoken English, you can also use the short form '-'d' instead of 'would' when the subject is a noun.

Sally'd like to go to the circus.

2 You can say what someone does not want by using 'would not like' or 'wouldn't like'.

I would not like to see it.
They wouldn't like that.

3 You use 'would like' followed by 'to have' and a past participle to say that someone wishes now that something had happened in the past, but that it did not happen.

I would like to have felt more relaxed.
She'd like to have heard me first.

You use 'would have liked', followed by a 'to'-infinitive or a noun group, to say that someone wanted something to happen, but it did not happen.

Perhaps he would have liked to be a teacher.
I would have liked more ice cream.

Note the difference. 'Would like to have' refers to present wishes about past events. 'Would have liked' refers to past wishes about past events.

4 You can also use 'would hate', 'would love', or 'would prefer', followed by a 'to'-infinitive or a noun group.

I would hate to move to another house now.
I would prefer a cup of coffee.

Note that 'would enjoy' is followed by a noun group or an '-ing' form, not by a 'to'-infinitive.

I would enjoy a bath before we go.
I would enjoy seeing him again.

5 You can use 'would rather' or 'would sooner' followed by the base form of a verb to say that someone prefers one situation to another.

He'd rather be playing golf.
I'd sooner walk than take the bus.

6 You use 'I wouldn't mind', followed by an '-ing' form or a noun group, to say that you would like to do or have something.

I wouldn't mind being the manager of a store.
I wouldn't mind a cup of tea.

7 You can also express what you want to happen now by using 'I wish' or 'If only' followed by a past simple verb.

I wish he wasn't here.
If only she had a car.

Note that in formal English, you sometimes use 'were' instead of 'was' in sentences like these.

I often wish that I were really wealthy.

When you want to express regret about past events, you use the past perfect.

I wish I hadn't married him.

When you want to say that you wish that someone was able to do something, you use 'could'.

If only they could come with us!

When you want to say that you wish that someone was willing to do something, you use 'would'.

If only they would realise how stupid they've been.

Unit 68 Practice

A Form a question using **would you like** and the first of the phrases given below. Then form an answer using **I'd like** or **I'd rather** and the second of the phrases given below.

1 have another drink / get home early
   Would you like to have another drink? No thanks, *I'd rather get home early.*

2 go with me / go alone
   ....

3 start now / wait a few minutes
   ....

4 go shopping this morning / go this afternoon
   ....

5 pay cash / pay by cheque.
   ....

Change three sentences with **I'd rather** to **I'd sooner.**
   I'd sooner get home early. ....
   ....

B Rewrite these sentences using **would like.**

1 I wish I lived in the country. / I would like *to live in the country.* ....
2 I wish I could find a better job. / I would like ....
3 I bet she wishes she could start all over again. / I bet she'd like ....
4 I suppose you wish you saw them more often. / I suppose you'd like ....
5 They all wish they understood more about it. / They'd all like ....
6 My wife often wishes we had a bigger garden. / My wife would like ....

C Rewrite these sentences using **wouldn't mind.**

1 I'd quite like to live in London. / I wouldn't mind *living in London.* ....
2 She said she'd quite like to learn English. / She said she wouldn't mind ....
3 Bill agreed that he would quite like to be chairman. / Bill agreed he wouldn't mind ....
4 We all agreed we'd quite like to go back to work. / We all agreed we wouldn't mind ....
5 I'd quite like to go into politics. / I wouldn't mind ....
6 We'd quite like to catch an early train. / We wouldn't mind ....

D Add comments to these sentences using **I wish.**

1 I'm afraid your father can't come. / *I wish he could.* ....
2 They always come late. / *I wish they wouldn't.*
3 He always complains about everything. / ....
4 He never invites us round. / ....
5 We can't go on holiday this year. / ....
6 She won't listen to anything you say. / ....
7 They can't help out I'm afraid. / ....
8 She never comes home at weekends. / ....

▶ **Bank**

Unit 69 Have to, have got to, must, mustn't - obligation and necessity

Main points

- You use 'have to', 'must', and 'mustn't' to talk about obligation and necessity in the present and future.
- You use 'had to' to talk about obligation and necessity in the past.
- You use the auxiliary 'do' with 'have to' to make questions.
- You use 'have got to' in informal English.

1 When you want to say that someone has an obligation to do something, or that it is necessary for them to do it, you use 'must' or 'have to'.

You must come to the meeting tomorrow.
The plants must have plenty of sunshine.
I enjoy parties, unless I have to make a speech.
He has to travel to find work.

2 There is sometimes a difference between 'must' and 'have to'. When you are stating your own opinion that something is an obligation or a necessity, you normally use 'must'.

I must be very careful not to upset him.
We must eat before we go.
He must stop working so hard.

When you are giving information about what someone else considers to be an obligation or a necessity, you normally use 'have to'.

They have to pay the bill by Thursday.
She has to go now.

Note that you normally use 'have to' for things that happen repeatedly, especially with adverbs of frequency such as 'often', 'always', and 'regularly'.

I always have to do the shopping.
You often have to wait a long time for a bus.

3 You use 'must not' or 'mustn't' to say that it is important that something is not done or does not happen.

You must not talk about politics.
They mustn't find out that I came here.

Note that 'must not' does not mean the same as 'not have to'. If you 'must not' do something, it is important that you do not do it.
If you 'do not have to' do something, it is not necessary for you to do it, but you can do it if you want.

WARNING: You only use 'must' for obligation and necessity in the present and the future. When you want to talk about obligation and necessity in the past, you use 'had to' rather than 'must'.

She had to catch the six o'clock train.
I had to wear a suit.

4 You use 'do', 'does', or 'did' when you want to make a question using 'have to' and 'not have to'.

How often do you have to buy petrol for the car?
Does he have to take so long to get ready?
What did you have to do?
Don't you have to be there at one o'clock?

WARNING: You do not normally form questions like these by putting a form of 'have' before the subject. For example, you do not normally say 'How often have you to buy petrol?'

5 In informal English, you can use 'have got to' instead of 'have to'.

You've just got to make sure you tell him.
She's got to see the doctor.
Have you got to go so soon?

WARNING: You normally use 'had to', not 'had got to', for the past.

He had to know.
I had to lend him some money.

6 You can only use 'have to', not 'must', if you are using another modal, or if you want to use an '-ing' form, a past participle, or a 'to'-infinitive.

They may have to be paid by cheque.
She grumbled a lot about having to stay abroad.
I would have had to go through London.
He doesn't like to have to do the same job every day.

Unit 69 Practice

A List the things you have to do if you join the army, using **must** or **have to**.

1   *You have to keep your hair short.* ....

2   ....

3   ....

4   ....

5   ....

6   ....

7   ....

8   ....

B The doctor is giving advice. Complete these sentences with **you must** or **you mustn't**.

1   ....*You must*.......... take this before every meal.   4   .... get plenty of sleep.

2   .... take two of these every morning.   5   .... have anything to eat.

3   .... get out of bed.   6   .... drink lots of water.

C Match these clauses with the **have got to** clauses.

1   It's getting late…   a   … so I'm afraid we've got to walk.

2   You broke the window…   b   … so I've got to start all over again.

3   The car has broken down…   c   … so we've got to look after ourselves.

4   Mother is away…   d   … so you've got to pay for it.

5   I've got it all wrong…   e   … so we've got to go.

Unit 70 Need to, needn't, not have to - obligation and necessity

Main points

- You use 'need to' to talk about necessity.
- You use 'don't have to', 'don't need to', 'haven't got to', or 'needn't' to say that it is not necessary to do something.
- You use 'needn't' to give someone permission not to do something.
- You use 'need not have', 'needn't have', 'didn't need to', or 'didn't have to' to say that it was not necessary to do something in the past.

1 You can use 'need to' to talk about the necessity of doing something.

You might need to see a doctor.
A number of questions need to be asked.

2 You use 'don't have to' when there is no obligation or necessity to do something.

Many women don't have to work.
You don't have to learn any new typing skills.

You can also use 'don't need to', 'haven't got to', or 'needn't' to say that there is no obligation or necessity to do something.

You don't need to buy anything.
I haven't got to go to work today.
I can pick John up. You needn't bother.

3 You also use 'needn't' when you are giving someone permission not to do something.

You needn't say anything if you don't want to.
You needn't stay any longer tonight.

4 You use 'need not have' or 'needn't have' and a past participle to say that someone did something which was not necessary. You are often implying that the person did not know at the time that their action was not necessary.

I needn't have waited until the game began.
Nell needn't have worked.
They needn't have worried about Reagan.

5 You use 'didn't need to' to say that something was not necessary, and that it was known at the time that the action was not necessary. You do not know if the action was done, unless you are given more information.

They didn't need to talk about it.
I didn't need to worry.

6 You also use 'didn't have to' to say that it was not necessary to do something.

He didn't have to speak.
Bill and I didn't have to pay.

7 You cannot use 'must' to refer to the past, so when you want to say that it was important that something did not happen or was not done, you use other expressions.
You can say 'It was important not to', or use phrases like 'had to make sure' or 'had to make certain' in a negative sentence.

It was necessary that no one was aware of being watched.
You had to make sure that you didn't spend too much.
We had to do our best to make certain that it wasn't out of date.

It was important not to take the game too seriously.

Unit 70 Practice

A Bill has just left the army. List five things he **doesn't need to** do any more.

1 *He doesn't need to wear a uniform.*

2 ....

3 ....

4 ....

5 ....

See the pictures at Unit 69 if you need more ideas.

B Anne is better now. List four things she **doesn't have to** do now.

1 *She doesn't have to stay in bed.*

2 ....

3 ....

4 ....

C Match the sentences and comments.

1 My trousers are creased.   a I need to get it mended.

2 My computer's broken.   b I need to get it painted.

3 My torch won't work.   c I need to take a taxi.

4 The house looks awful.   d I need to get it cut.

5 My hair is too long.   e I need to get a new battery.

6 My car has broken down.   f I need to get them pressed.

D Add comments to these sentences, using **needn't have.**

1 The letter was so untidy, I wrote it out again.
    Really? You needn't have written it out again.

2 He was so worried about being late that he sent the letter by fax.
    ....

3 She was so worried about not getting a seat that she bought a first-class ticket.
    ....

4 We weren't sure about sheets and towels, so we brought our own.
    ....

5 The old people thought the room was dirty, so they cleaned it out themselves.
    ....

6 I didn't know you were coming home, so I cooked my own supper.
    ....

Now rewrite the comments using **didn't need to.**

1 *You didn't need to write it out again.*

2 ....

3 ....

4 ....

5 ....

6 ....

Unit 71 Should, ought, should have, ought to have, had better - mild obligation and advice

Main points

- You use 'should' and 'ought' to talk about mild obligation.
- You use 'should have' and 'ought to have' to say that there was a mild obligation to do something in the past, but it was not done.
- You can also use 'had better' to talk about mild obligation.

1 You can use 'should' and 'ought' to talk about a mild obligation to do something. When you use 'should' and 'ought', you are saying that the feeling of obligation is not as strong as when you use 'must'.
'Should' and 'ought' are very common in spoken English.
'Should' is followed by the base form of a verb, but 'ought' is followed by a 'to'-infinitive.
When you want to say that there is a mild obligation not to do something, you use 'should not', 'shouldn't', 'ought not', or 'oughtn't'.

2 You use 'should' and 'ought' in three main ways:

- when you are talking about what is a good thing to do, or the right thing to do.

We should send her a postcard.
We shouldn't spend all the money.
He ought to come more often.
You ought not to see him again.

- when you are trying to advise someone about what to do or what not to do.

You should claim your pension 3-4 months before you retire.
You shouldn't use a detergent.
You ought to get a new TV.
You oughtn't to marry him.

- when you are giving or asking for an opinion about a situation. You often use 'I think', 'I don't think', or 'Do you think' to start the sentence.

I think that we should be paid more.
I don't think we ought to grumble.
Do you think he ought not to go?
What do you think we should do?

3 You use 'should have' or 'ought to have' and a past participle to say that there was a mild obligation to do something in the past, but that it was not done. For example, if you say 'I should have given him the money yesterday', you mean that you had a mild obligation to give him the money yesterday, but you did not give it to him.

I should have finished my drink and gone home.
You should have realised that he was joking.
We ought to have stayed in tonight.
They ought to have taken a taxi.

You use 'should not have' or 'ought not to have' and a past participle to say that it was important not to do something in the past, but that it was done. For example, if you say 'I should not have left the door open', you mean that it was important that you did not leave the door open, but you did leave it open.

I should not have said that.
You shouldn't have given him the money.
They ought not to have told him.
She oughtn't to have sold the ring.

4 You use 'had better' followed by a base form to indicate mild obligation to do something in a particular situation. You also use 'had better' when giving advice or when giving your opinion about something. The negative is 'had better not'.

I think I had better show this to you now.
You'd better go tomorrow.

WARNING: The correct form is always 'had better' (not 'have better'). You do not use 'had better' to talk about mild obligation in the past, even though it looks like a past form.

I'd better not look at this.

Unit 71 Practice

A Complete the following sentences using **you ought to** or **you ought not to**.

1 ....*You ought to*.................... drive carefully on a busy road.
2 ....*You ought not to*............. eat between meals if you want to lose weight.
3 .... pay your bills regularly.
4 .... be selfish.
5 .... smoke too heavily.
6 .... go to the dentist's regularly.
7 .... lie in bed late every day.
8 .... clean your teeth at least twice a day.
9 .... eat a lot of sugar.
10 .... be more careful.

B Match these situations with the advice you might give in each one.

1 It's raining.
2 It's too far to walk.
3 Someone doesn't know which way to go.
4 Someone is going to live overseas.
5 Someone has to get up early in the morning.
6 Someone hasn't got any money with them.
7 It's going to be a cold day.
8 Someone is tired out.
9 Someone has seen someone breaking into a shop window.
10 Someone is feeling hot and has a headache.

a You should take a rest.
b You should ask a policeman.
c You should take an umbrella.
d You should wear an overcoat.
e You should see a doctor.
f You should learn the language before you go.
g You should pay by cheque.
h You should take a taxi.
i You should set your alarm clock.
j You should call the police.

C Rewrite these sentences using **should have** or **shouldn't have**.

1 Why didn't you phone to say you'd be late? / ...*You should have phoned to say you'd be late.*
2 I wish they hadn't made such a mess. / ...*They shouldn't have made such a mess.*
3 I wish I had got home earlier. / ....
4 We didn't read the instructions carefully. / ....
5 Why did you spend so much money? / ....
6 I wish you had told me you were coming. / ....
7 It was very bad of them to make such a noise. / ....
8 John left the restaurant without paying his bill. / ....
9 I wish Jack had explained what he was doing. / ....
10 Why didn't you send Mary a birthday card? / ....

Now rewrite the first five sentences using **ought to have** or **ought not to have**.

1 ....
2 ....
3 ....
4 ....
5 ....

▶ **Bank**

143

Unit 72 Intransitive and transitive verbs

Main points

- Intransitive verbs do not have an object.
- Transitive verbs have an object.
- Some verbs can be used with or without an object, depending on the situation or their meaning.

1 Many verbs do not normally have an object. They are called 'intransitive' verbs. They often refer to:

> **existence:** appear die disappear exist happen live occur remain vanish
> **the human body:** ache bleed blush faint shiver smile
> **human noises:** cough cry laugh scream sigh snore speak yawn
> **light, smell, vibration:** gleam glow shine sparkle stink throb vibrate
> **position, movement:** arrive come depart fall flow go jump kneel pause run sit sleep stand swim wait walk work

An awful thing has happened.
The girl screamed.
I waited.

Note that intransitive verbs cannot be used in the passive.

2 Many verbs normally have an object. These verbs are called 'transitive' verbs. They are often connected with:

> **physical objects:** build buy carry catch cover cut damage destroy fill hit own remove rent sell use waste wear
> **senses:** feel hear see smell taste touch
> **feelings:** admire dislike enjoy fear frighten hate interest like love need prefer surprise trust want
> **facts, ideas:** accept believe consider correct discuss expect express forget include know mean remember report
> **people:** address blame comfort contact convince defy kill persuade please tease thank warn

He hit the ball really hard.
Did you see the rainbow?
They both enjoyed the film.
She reported the accident to the police.
Don't blame me.

Note that transitive verbs can be used in the passive.

They were blamed for everything.

WARNING: 'Have' is a transitive verb, but cannot be used in the passive. You can say 'I have a car' but not 'A car is had by me'.

3 Often, the people you are talking to know what the object is because of the situation, or because it has already been mentioned. In this case you can omit the object, even though the verb is transitive.

accept	draw	iron	phone	study
answer	drive	know	read	type
change	eat	learn	remember	understand
choose	explain	leave	ride	wash
clean	forget	paint	sing	watch
cook	help	park	steal	write

I don't own a car. I can't drive.
You don't smoke, do you?
I asked a question and George answered.
Both dresses are beautiful. It's difficult to choose.

4 Many verbs have more than one meaning, and are transitive in one meaning and intransitive in another meaning. For example, the verb 'run' is intransitive when you use it to mean 'move quickly' but transitive when you use it to mean 'manage or operate'.

call	lose	miss	play	show
fit	manage	move	run	spread

The hare runs at enormous speed.
She runs a hotel.

She moved gracefully.
The whole incident had moved her profoundly.

5 A few verbs are normally intransitive, but can be used with an object that is closely related to the verb.

dance (a dance)	laugh (a laugh)	sigh (a sigh)
die (a death)	live (a life)	smile (a smile)
dream (a dream)		

Steve smiled his thin, cruel smile.
He appears to have lived the life of any other rich gentleman.
I once dreamed a very nice dream.

Note that you normally add more information about the object, for example by using adjectives in front of the noun.

Unit 72 Practice

A In each pair of sentences below one sentence has a transitive verb and the other an intransitive verb. Mark the sentences T (transitive) or I (intransitive). In the sentences which have a transitive verb, underline the object.

1 The postman calls at about 7 am every morning. ...*I*.............
   They are going to call <u>the new town</u> Skelmersdale. ...*T*............

2 You're not allowed to drive a car until you're seventeen. ....
   She learned to drive when she was eighteen. ....

3 I've never deliberately hurt anyone. ....
   My leg was beginning to hurt quite a lot. ....

4 You look just the same. You haven't changed a bit. ....
   You can't change human nature. ....

5 We are running a course for English teachers. ....
   I can't run as fast as I used to. ....

6 She is studying for a law degree. ....
   He had studied chemistry at university. ....

7 He turned to Joan and began to explain. ....
   He turned the handle and pushed the door open. ....

8 I don't think we've met before, have we? ....
   Dan came to the airport to meet me. ....

9 He's only young, but he's learning fast. ....
   What did you learn at school today? ....

10 Could you stop the bus, please. I want to get off. ....
   Do you think you could stop in front of the post office? ....

B Use the correct form of the verbs below to complete the sentences which follow.

accept	choose	forget	hear	know
leave	phone	remember	understand	watch

1 He offered me a drink and I ...*accepted*........................... .

2 There were so many good things to eat it was almost impossible to ....

3 He asked me for an answer but I just didn't ....

4 I hadn't time to write a letter so I decided to ....

5 No matter how I tried to .... , I just couldn't think of his name.

6 I kept thinking of the tragic accident, no matter how much I wanted to ....

7 He explained to me how to do the problem and I did my best to ....

8 We wanted to get home early so at half past two we decided it was time to ....

9 It looked as if it would be an exciting game so we stayed to ....

10 If I had .... the question, I might have been able to answer it.

Unit 73 Verbs with two objects

Main points

- Some verbs have two objects, a direct object and an indirect object.
- The indirect object can be used without a preposition, or after 'to' or 'for'.

1 Some verbs have two objects after them, a direct object and an indirect object. For example, in the sentence 'I gave John the book', 'the book' is the direct object. 'John' is the indirect object. Verbs that have two objects are sometimes called 'ditransitive' verbs or 'double-transitive' verbs.

His uncle had <u>given</u> him books on India.
She <u>sends</u> you her love.
I <u>passed</u> him the cup.

2 When the indirect object is a pronoun, or another short noun group such as a noun with 'the', you put the indirect object in front of the direct object.

Dad gave <u>me</u> a car.
You promised <u>the lad</u> a job.
He had lent <u>my cousin</u> the money.
She bought <u>Dave and me</u> an ice cream.

3 You can also use the prepositions 'to' and 'for' to introduce the indirect object. If you do this, you put the preposition and indirect object after the direct object.

He handed his room key <u>to the receptionist.</u>
Bill saved a piece of cake <u>for the children.</u>

When the indirect object consists of several words, you normally use a preposition to introduce it.

She taught physics and chemistry <u>to pupils at the local school.</u>
I made that lamp <u>for a seventy-year-old woman.</u>

You often use a preposition when you want to emphasize the indirect object.

Did you really buy that <u>for me?</u>

4 With some verbs you can only use 'for', not 'to', to introduce the indirect object.

book	cut	make	prepare
buy	find	paint	save
cook	keep	pour	win

They booked a place <u>for me.</u>
He had found some old clothes <u>for the beggar.</u>
They bought a present <u>for the teacher.</u>
She painted a picture <u>for her father.</u>

5 With some verbs you normally use 'to' to introduce the indirect object.

give	pay	read	show
lend	post	sell	teach
offer	promise	send	tell
pass			

I had lent my bicycle <u>to a friend.</u>
Ralph passed a message <u>to Jack.</u>
They say they posted the letter <u>to me</u> last week.
He sold it <u>to me.</u>

Note that you can use 'for' with these verbs, but it has a different meaning. 'For' indicates that one person does something on behalf of another person, so that the other person does not have to do it.

His mother paid the bill <u>for him.</u>
If you're going out, can you post this <u>for me</u>, please?

If you're going out, can you post this for me, please?

Unit 73 Practice

A Rewrite the sentences below putting the indirect object after the verb and using the preposition **to** or **for**.

1 He made his wife a cup of tea. / ...*He made a cup of tea for his wife.*.....................

2 John sold Mary his old car. / ....

3 Could you show your grandfather those old photographs? / ....

4 Save the rest of us something to eat. / ....

5 I'm going to book your guests a really good table. / ....

6 We've prepared you a light snack. / ....

7 We'll leave you some food in the fridge. / ....

8 I taught Peter's children French when they were younger. / ....

9 I'll try to find you those books. / ....

10 We must remember to send George and Alice a card. / ....

B Rewrite these sentences by changing the indirect object (in bold) to **him**, **her**, or **them** and putting it in front of the direct object.

1 I bought a present for **my little brother.** / ...*I bought him a present.*...................

2 She cooked a wonderful meal for **her visitors.** / ....

3 He passed the money to **the man behind the counter.** / ....

4 Cut some bread for **the children at that table.** / ....

5 Give this letter to **the lady at the desk.** / ....

6 She used to teach arithmetic to **the children at the village school.** / ....

7 I'd like to keep something for **the people who arrive late.** / ....

8 You must show these papers to **the police officers on the border.** / ....

9 He always reads a story to **his youngest daughter** before she goes to sleep. / ......

10 I'm going to write a short note to **the girl I met on holiday last year.** / ....

C Rearrange the parts of sentences given below to make sentences with two objects.

1 a long letter / her friend / wrote / she / to.
   ...*She wrote a long letter to her friend.*...

2 for / some money / left / Mrs Brown / the milkman.
   ....

3 sent a Christmas card / to / on holiday / we / the people we met.
   ....

4 her / some flowers / on her birthday / he gave.
   ....

5 Jack and Mary / the children / promised / a day at the seaside.
   ....

6 us / what to do / told / Nobody.
   ....

Unit 74 Reflexive verbs

For example: I hurt myself

Main points

- Transitive verbs are used with a reflexive pronoun to indicate that the object is the same as the subject.
- Some verbs which do not normally have a person as the object can have reflexive pronouns as the object.

1 You use a reflexive pronoun after a transitive verb to indicate that the object is the same as the subject.

He blamed <u>himself</u> for his friend's death.
I taught <u>myself</u> French.

See Unit 9 for more information on reflexive pronouns.

2 In theory, most transitive verbs can be used with a reflexive pronoun. However, you often use reflexive pronouns with the following verbs.

amuse	help	kill	restrict
blame	hurt	prepare	satisfy
cut	introduce	repeat	teach
dry			

Sam <u>amused himself</u> by throwing branches into the fire.
'Can I borrow a pencil?' - 'Yes, <u>help yourself</u>.'
<u>Prepare yourself</u> for a shock.
He <u>introduced himself</u> to me.

3 Verbs like 'dress', 'shave', and 'wash', which describe actions that people do to themselves, do not usually take reflexive pronouns in English, although they do in some other languages. With these verbs, reflexive pronouns are only used for emphasis.

I usually <u>shave</u> before breakfast.
He prefers to <u>shave himself</u>, even with that broken arm.

She <u>washed</u> very quickly and rushed downstairs.
Children were encouraged to <u>wash themselves</u>.

4 'Behave' does not normally take an object at all, but can take a reflexive pronoun as object.

If they don't <u>behave</u>, send them to bed.
He is old enough to <u>behave himself</u>.

5 Some verbs do not normally have a person as object, because they describe actions that you do not do to other people. However, these verbs can have reflexive pronouns as object, because you can do these actions to yourself.

apply	distance	excel	express
compose	enjoy	exert	strain

I really <u>enjoyed</u> the party.
Just go out there and <u>enjoy yourself</u>.

She <u>expressed</u> surprise at the news.
Professor Dale <u>expressed himself</u> very forcibly.

6 When 'busy' and 'content' are used as verbs, they always take a reflexive pronoun as their direct object. They are therefore true 'reflexive verbs'.

He had <u>busied himself</u> in the laboratory.
I had to <u>content myself</u> with watching the little moving lights.

Unit 74 Practice

A Use the verbs below with a reflexive pronoun to complete the sentences which follow.

behave   blame   describe   enjoy   excel   express
find   help   introduce kill   repeat teach

1 The children realized that they were all alone in the forest.
   The children ...*found themselves*........... all alone in the forest.

2 Have another drink.
   .... to another drink.

3 They don't know how to behave properly.
   They don't know how to ....

4 He kept on saying the same thing again and again.
   He kept ....

5 I'm afraid I didn't have a very good time.
   I'm afraid I didn't .... very much.

6 I'd like to tell you about myself.
   I'd like to ....

7 She's learning French at home, without a teacher.
   She's .... French.

8 I wouldn't really say that I'm lazy.
   I wouldn't .... as lazy.

9 You shouldn't think it's your fault.
   You shouldn't ....

10 He is difficult to understand.
   He doesn't .... very clearly.

11 They have done better than anyone expected.
   They have ....

12 She was so unhappy, she tried to commit suicide.
   She was so unhappy, she tried to ....

B Rewrite these sentences putting in a verb with a reflexive pronoun wherever you can.

1 He's still very ill but he can wash and shave.
   ..*He's still very ill, but he can wash himself and shave himself.*........................

2 You ought to behave better than that.
   ....

3 You must learn to adapt to new ideas.
   ....

4 The children tried to hide in the cupboard.
   ....

5 You can dry on that towel.
   ....

6 Billy undressed before going to bed.
   ....

149

Unit 75 Reciprocal verbs

For example: We met, I met you, We met each other

Main points

- Some verbs describe two people or two groups of people doing the same thing to each other.
- You use 'each other' or 'one another' for emphasis.
- With some verbs, you use 'each other' or 'one another' after 'with'.

1 Some verbs refer to actions that involve two people or two groups of people doing the same thing to each other. These verbs are sometimes called 'reciprocal' verbs.

We met in Delhi.
Jane and Sarah told me that they met you.
They met each other for the first time last week.

2 The two people or groups of people involved in the action are often mentioned as the plural subject of the verb, and the verb does not have an object. For example, 'John and Mary argued' means that John argued with Mary and Mary argued with John.

argue	combine	kiss	marry
clash	compete	meet	match
coincide	fight	mix	

The pair of you have argued about that for years.
We competed furiously.
Their children are always fighting.
They kissed.

3 When you want to emphasize that both people or groups of people are equally involved, you can use the pronouns 'each other' or 'one another' as the object of the verb. Verbs that refer to actions in which there is physical contact between people are often used with 'each other' or 'one another'.

cuddle	embrace	fight	hug	kiss	touch

We embraced each other.
They fought one another desperately for it.
They kissed each other in greeting.
It was the first time they had touched one another.

4 Some verbs do not take an object, so you use a preposition before 'each other' or 'one another'.

They parted from each other after only two weeks.
We talk to one another as often as possible.

5 With some verbs you have a choice of preposition before 'each other' or 'one another'. For example, you can 'fight with' one another or 'fight against' one another.

with/against: compete fight
with/from: part
with/to: correspond relate talk

Many countries are competing with each other.
Did you compete against each other in yesterday's race?

Stephen and I parted with one another on good terms.
They parted from one another quite suddenly.

6 With some verbs, you can only use 'with' before 'each other' or 'one another'. Note that most of these verbs refer to people talking or working together.

agree	clash	communicate	disagree
argue	collide	co-operate	quarrel

We do agree with each other sometimes.
Have they communicated with each other since then?
The two lorries collided with one another on the motorway.

7 If you want to focus on one of the people involved, you make them the subject of the verb and make the other person the object.

She married a young engineer.
You could meet me at the restaurant.

If the verb cannot take an object, you mention the other person after a preposition.

Youths clashed with police in Belfast.
She was always quarrelling with him.

Unit 75 Practice

A Use the correct form of the verbs below to complete the sentences which follow.

> argue attack bump communicate compete cooperate fight hurt part talk

1 Watch what you're doing with those sticks. You'll ...*hurt*........................ each other if you're not careful.

2 We have to keep these dogs separate. They .... each other on sight.

3 The children won't play peacefully together. They always .... each other.

4 I wish Jack and Jill could work together but they just refuse to .... with one another.

5 They can never agree. They .... with one another about everything.

6 Bob and I usually play together but tomorrow we are going to .... with each other for a change.

7 They've had a dreadful quarrel. Now they won't even .... to one another.

8 I met Sally yesterday. We .... into each other on the train.

9 Neither of us is on the phone so we find it difficult to .... with one another.

10 They're twins and they hate to .... from one another.

B Complete the following sentences by adding **at, into, of, on, to,** or **with.**

1 John and Helen looked ...*at*................ each other and smiled.

2 The children quarrel a lot but they're very fond .... each other.

3 They both talk at the same time. They never seem to listen .... each other.

4 They have been corresponding .... one another since they left school.

5 They were so angry they just stood and shouted .... each other.

6 They were both very sorry. They apologised .... each other.

7 The two cars just crashed .... each other.

8 We could just see one another so we waved .... each other across the park.

9 They are both very well known but they hadn't heard .... each other.

10 It was so funny. They just sat and laughed .... each other.

11 We can rely .... one another.

12 They knew that they could depend .... each other.

C Complete these sentences using **themselves** or **each other.**

1 They always send ...*each other*.................. a card at Christmas.

2 They really enjoyed ...*themselves*.................. on holiday.

3 Fred and Charles hadn't met .... before.

4 Jane and Mary went shopping together and locked .... out of the house.

5 Neither John nor Peter would take responsibility for the accident. They both blamed
....

6 John and Peter were dreadfully sorry about the accident. They blamed .... for it.

7 The two children smiled happily at ....

8 A lot of people injure .... doing jobs about the house.

Unit 76 Ergative verbs

For example: I opened the door, The door opened

Main points

- Ergative verbs are both transitive and intransitive. The object of the transitive use is the subject of the intransitive use.
- A few verbs are only ergative with particular nouns.
- A few of these verbs need an adverbial when they are used without an object.

1 Some verbs can be used as transitive verbs to focus on the person who performs an action, and as intransitive verbs to focus on the thing affected by the action.

When I opened the door, there was Laverne.
Suddenly the door opened.

Note that the object of the transitive verb, in this case 'the door', is the subject of the intransitive verb. Verbs like these are called 'ergative' verbs.

2 Ergative verbs often refer to:

- changes

begin	dry	improve	start
break	end	increase	stop
change	finish	slow	tear
crack	grow		

I broke the glass.
The glass broke all over the floor.

The driver stopped the car.
A big car stopped.

- cooking

bake	cook	fry	roast
boil	defrost	melt	simmer

I've boiled an egg.
The porridge is boiling.

I'm cooking spaghetti.
The rice is cooking.

- position or movement

balance	move	rock	stand
close	open	shake	turn
drop	rest		

She rested her head on his shoulder.
Her head rested on the table.

An explosion shook the hotel.
The whole room shook.

- vehicles

back	drive	reverse	sail
crash	fly	run	

He had crashed the car twice.
Her car crashed into a tree.

She sailed her yacht round the world.
The ship sailed on Monday.

3 Some verbs can be used in these two ways only with a small set of nouns. For example, you can say 'He fired a gun' or 'The gun fired'. You can do the same with other words referring to types of gun, 'cannon', 'pistol', or 'rifle'. However, although you can say 'He fired a bullet', you cannot say 'The bullet fired'.

catch: belt, cloth, clothing, dress, shirt, trousers
fire: cannon, gun, pistol, rifle
play: guitar, music, piano, violin
ring: alarm, bell
show: anger, disappointment, emotions, fear, joy
sound: alarm, bell, horn

I caught my dress on the fence.
My tights caught on a nail.

A car was sounding its horn.
A horn sounded in the night.

4 A few verbs can be used in both ways, but need an adverbial when they are used without an object.

clean	handle	polish	stain
freeze	mark	sell	wash

He sells books.
This book is selling well.

She had handled a machine gun.
This car handles very nicely.

Unit 76 Practice

A Complete the sentences below using the correct form of the following verbs.

begin	boil	cook	crack	handle	increase
open	ring	sell	tear	stop	wash

1 The door ..._opened_.................................and a young man came out.

2 Be careful with that paper. It'll .... easily.

3 The glass will probably .... if you pour boiling water in it.

4 Has the kettle .... yet?

5 Those jeans are very good value. They should .... really quickly.

6 The bus .... right outside the house.

7 The meat will .... quite quickly. It'll be ready in half an hour.

8 The meeting .... with a short welcome from the new chairman.

9 The doorbell .... several times before anyone answered.

10 This shirt is dreadful. It just won't .... clean.

11 Prices have .... by ten per cent since last year.

12 The plane still .... well at over twice the speed of sound.

B Complete the sentences below using the following nouns.

building	car	hand	material	pace	potatoes
ship	shirt	train	vase	water	window

1 What time does the ..._ship_............................ sail?

2 Has the .... boiled yet?

3 This .... doesn't stain. It's protected by a special chemical.

4 The .... fell off the shelf and broke.

5 The first lap was very fast but the .... slowed later.

6 He was killed when his .... ran into the back of a bus.

7 His .... caught on a nail and tore.

8 The whole .... shook in the storm.

9 Her .... rested on the arm of her chair.

10 Suddenly the .... opened and a woman poked out her head.

11 The .... stopped just outside the station.

12 The .... were cooking in a large pan.

Unit 77 Common verbs with nouns for actions

For example: have a bath, give a shout, make promises, take care

Main points

- Common verbs are often used with nouns to describe actions.
- You use 'have' with nouns referring to eating, drinking, talking, and washing.
- You use 'give' with nouns referring to noises, hitting, and talking.
- You use 'make' with nouns referring to talking, plans, and travelling.

1 When you want to talk about actions, you often use common verbs with nouns as their object. The nouns describe the action. The common verbs have very little meaning.

I had a nice rest.
She made a remark about the weather.

The nouns often have related verbs that do not take an object.

Helen went upstairs to rest.
I remarked that it would surely be better if I came.

2 Different verbs are used with different nouns. You use 'have' with nouns referring to:

> **meals:** breakfast dinner drink lunch meal taste tea
> **talking:** chat conversation discussion talk
> **washing:** bath shower wash
> **relaxation:** break holiday rest
> **disagreement:** argument fight quarrel trouble

We usually have lunch at one o'clock.
He was having his first holiday for five years.

3 You use 'give' with nouns referring to:

> **human noises:** cry gasp giggle groan laugh scream shout sigh whistle yell
> **facial expressions:** grin smile
> **hitting:** kick punch push slap
> **talking:** advice answer example information interview lecture news report speech talk warning

Mr Sutton gave a shout of triumph.
She gave a long lecture about Roosevelt.

4 You use 'make' with nouns referring to:

> **talking and sounds:** comment enquiry noise point promise remark sound speech suggestion
> **plans:** arrangement choice decision plan
> **travelling:** journey tour trip visit

He made the shortest speech I've ever heard.
In 1978 he made his first visit to Australia.

5 You use 'take' with these nouns:

> care   decision   photograph   time
> chance   interest   responsibility trouble
> charge   offence   risk   turns

He was taking no chances.
She was prepared to take great risks.

6 You use 'go' and 'come' with '-ing' nouns referring to sports and outdoor activities.

She goes climbing in her holidays.
Every morning, he goes jogging with Tommy.

Note that you can also use 'go for' and 'come for' with 'a jog', 'a run', 'a swim', 'a walk'.

They went for a run before breakfast.

7 You use 'do' with '-ing' nouns referring to jobs connected with the home, and nouns referring generally to work.

He wants to do the cooking.
He does all the shopping and I do the washing.

The man who did the job had ten years' training.
He has to get up early and do a hard day's work.

'Do' is often used instead of more specific verbs. For example, you can say 'Have you done your teeth?' instead of 'Have you brushed your teeth?'.

Do I need to do my hair?

Unit 77 Practice

A Say which of the verbs, **have, give, take, make, go,** or **do,** are used with nouns referring to:
1 Household jobs. (cleaning, tidying up) ...*do*..
2 Plans and decisions. ....
3 Nouns which involve speaking. (a speech, talk, lecture) ....
4 Facial expressions. (smile) ....
5 Something which makes you clean. (a wash) ....
6 Something to eat or drink. ....
7 Something that hurts. (a kick) ....
8 Some form of exercise. (jogging) ....

B Complete these sentences using the correct part of **do** or **go.**
1 Who ...*does*............ most of the cooking in your house?
2 I'm so busy, I have no time to .... jogging.
3 We .... most of our shopping at the weekend.
4 They often .... climbing in Wales.
5 We .... for a long walk this afternoon.
6 I .... a bit of water-skiing on my holiday.
7 She always .... the washing on Monday morning.
8 It's a lovely day. Let's .... swimming.

C Complete these sentences using the correct part of **make** or **do.**
1 Anyone can ...*make*........... a suggestion.
2 I've got an awful lot of work to ....
3 Have you .... your homework?
4 If you .... a promise, you must keep it.
5 I think there's something wrong with the car. It's .... a dreadful noise.
6 Are you using the word-processor? I need to .... some writing.
7 It wasn't a good speech, but he did .... a few good points.
8 We don't have much time to .... a decision.

D Complete the sentences below using the appropriate part of **have, give, take, make,** or **do.**
1 She looked up and ...*gave*............ me a friendly smile.
2 I always .... a bit of gardening at the weekend.
3 Skiing is dangerous enough as it is. You shouldn't .... unnecessary risks.
4 I'm awfully nervous. I have to .... a speech after dinner.
5 You must be hot. Would you like to .... a cold shower before supper?
6 It's half past twelve. Let's .... a short break before lunch.
7 Oh dear. I didn't know you were there. You .... such a dreadful scream.
8 The chairman .... a few final remarks before bringing the meeting to a close.
9 We .... some great photographs on holiday this year.
10 I'm not thirsty. I .... a drink just before I left home.
11 A horse can .... you a very nasty kick.
12 They .... arrangements to get everything ready on time.

▶ **Bank**

Unit 78 Verbs with prepositions

Main points

- Some verbs do not take an object and are normally followed by a preposition.
- Some verbs take an object followed by a particular preposition.
- Some verbs can take either an object or a preposition.

---

1 Many verbs that are used without an object are normally followed by a prepositional phrase. Some verbs take a particular preposition:

belong to	hope for	listen to	refer to
consist of	insist on	pay for	relate to
hint at	lead to	qualify for	sympathize with

The land _belongs to_ a rich family.
She then _referred to_ the Minister's report.

2 With other verbs that are used without an object, the choice of a different preposition may alter the meaning of the clause.

agree on/with	apologize for/to	result from/in
appeal for/to	conform to/with	suffer from/with

They _agreed on_ a plan of action.
You _agreed with_ me that we should buy a car.

His failure _resulted from_ lack of attention to details.
The match _resulted in_ a draw.

3 With verbs that are used without an object, different prepositions are used to introduce different types of information.

- 'about' indicates the subject matter

care	dream	hear	speak	think
complain	explain	know	talk	write

We will always _care about_ freedom.
Tonight I'm going to _talk about_ engines.

- 'at' indicates direction

glance	grin	look	smile
glare	laugh	shout	stare

I don't know why he was _laughing at_ that joke.
'Hey!' she _shouted at_ him.

- 'for' indicates purpose or reason

apologize	apply	ask	look	wait

He wanted to _apologize for_ being late.
I'm going to _wait for_ the next bus.

- 'into' indicates the object involved in a collision

bump	crash	drive	run

His car _crashed into_ the wall.
She _drove into_ the back of a lorry.

- 'of' indicates facts or information

hear	know	speak	talk	think

I've _heard of_ him but I don't know who he is.
Do you _know of_ the new plans for the sports centre?

- 'on' indicates confidence or certainty

count	depend	plan	rely

You can _count on_ me.
You can _rely on_ him to be polite.

- 'to' indicates the listener or reader

complain	listen	speak	write
explain	say	talk	

They _complained to_ me about the noise.
Mary turned her head to _speak to_ him.

- 'with' indicates someone whose opinion is the same or different

agree	argue	disagree	side

Do you _agree with_ me about this?
The daughters _sided with_ their mothers.

4 Some verbs have an object, but are also followed by a preposition.

The police _accused_ him _of_ murder.
They _borrowed_ some money _from_ the bank.

Some verbs can take either an object or a prepositional phrase with no change in meaning.

He had to fight _them_, even if it was wrong.
He was fighting _against history_.

Unit 78 Practice

A Use these verbs and prepositions in the sentences below. Use the correct form of the verbs.

| appeal to/for | belong to | depend on | hope for | insist on | pay for |
| qualify for | refer to | result in | suffer from | sympathize with | |

1 If you don't understand any of these words, you could always .....*refer to*..................... a dictionary.
2 All last winter he .... coughs and colds.
3 The accident on the A41 sadly .... the death of a child.
4 The police are .... witnesses to come forward.
5 The poor driver — I really .... him, it wasn't his fault.
6 It wasn't his car. In fact I don't know who it ....
7 The buses are often late, so you can't .... them.
8 We are still .... improvements in the bus service.
9 Nurses are very badly paid. I think they should .... higher rates of pay.
10 Do you .... a state pension when you're 65?
11 Keep enough money to .... your ticket.

B Read the sentences, then use **about** and **to** in each one, as appropriate.
1 I want to talk ....*to*.................. the group ....*about*........... their exams.
2 When will you write .... Bill .... your plans?
3 Have you heard .... what happened to those prisoners? Or don't you care
   .... them?
4 I said .... you I was thinking .... going to work in Africa, didn't I? Well, I
   actually dreamt .... Africa last night!
5 If the service is really so dreadful, you ought to complain .... it .... the
   manager.
6 She listened .... me explaining .... the bad service, and then told me
   .... the problems they were having with staffing.

C Use **at** or **into** in these sentences.
1 The brakes failed and the bus ran ...*into*.............. the wall of a house.
2 People started to shout .... the driver.
3 Who was the boy you were all laughing .... ?
4 I bumped .... an old friend the other day.
5 I saw somebody staring .... me from the other side of the road.

D Use **with** or **for** in these sentences.
1 He was always arguing ...*with*.............his brothers.
2 I agree .... you that we should wait a bit longer .... her.
3 She never apologizes .... arriving late.
4 I thought we should look .... someone else to do the job, but the boss disagreed
   .... me.
5 If you want to travel, that would be a good job to apply ....

▶ **Bank**   157

Unit 79 Phrasal verbs

Main points

- A phrasal verb is a combination of a verb and an adverb or preposition.
- The usual meaning of the verb is normally altered.
- Phrasal verbs are used in four main structures.

1 Phrasal verbs are verbs that combine with adverbs or prepositions. The adverbs and prepositions are called particles, for example 'down', 'in', 'off', 'out', and 'up'.

She turned off the radio.
Mr Knight offered to put him up.

2 Phrasal verbs extend the usual meaning of the verb or create a new meaning. For example, if you 'break' something, you damage it, but if you 'break out of' a place, you escape from it.

They broke out of prison on Thursday night.
The pain gradually wore off.

3 Phrasal verbs are normally used in one of four main structures. In the first structure, the verb is followed by a particle, and there is no object.

break out	get by	look in	stop off
catch on	give in	ring off	wait up
check up	go away	start out	watch out
come in	grow up	stay up	wear off

War broke out in September.
You'll have to stay up late tonight.

4 In the second structure, the verb is followed by a particle and an object.

fall for	grow on	part with	set about
feel for	look after	pick on	take after

She looked after her invalid mother.
Peter takes after his father but John is more like me.

5 In the third structure, the verb is followed by an object and a particle.

answer back	call back	count in	order about
ask in	catch out	invite out	tell apart

I answered him back and took my chances.
He loved to order people about.

6 Some phrasal verbs can be used in both the second structure and the third structure: verb followed by a particle and an object, or verb followed by an object and a particle.

add on	hand over	put away	take up
bring up	knock over	put up	tear up
call up	point out	rub out	throw away
fold up	pull down	sort out	try out

It took ages to clean up the mess.
It took ages to clean the mess up.
There was such a mess. It took ages to clean it up.

WARNING: If the object is a pronoun, it must go in front of the particle. You cannot say 'He cleaned up it'.

7 In the fourth structure, the verb is followed by a particle and a preposition with an object.

break out of	keep on at	put up with
catch up with	look forward to	run away with
come down with	make off with	stick up for
get on with	miss out on	talk down to
go down with	play around with	walk out on

You go on ahead. I'll catch up with you later.
Children have to learn to stick up for themselves.

8 A very few verbs are used in the structure: verb followed by an object, a particle, and a preposition with its object.

do out of	put up to	talk out of
put down to	take out on	

Kroop tried to talk her out of it.
I'll take you up on that generous invitation.

Unit 79 Practice

A Use the following phrasal verbs to complete the sentences below.

catch up	cool off	fall behind	give in	grow up
keep up	speak up	stay on	wait up	watch out

1 He still behaves like a child. I wish he'd ...*grow up*........................ .
2 Come to the party on Friday and .... for the weekend.
3 I won't be back until late. Will you .... for me?
4 He was exhausted but he still kept going. He just wouldn't ....
5 Please don't go so fast. I just can't ....
6 Could you .... a bit? I can hardly hear you.
7 .... ! Oh dear. Didn't you see that car coming?
8 You look hot and sticky. Come and sit in the shade and ....
9 You go on ahead and I'll ....
10 Wait for me. I don't want to ....

B Complete the following sentences using the phrasal verb in brackets and a personal pronoun. The pronoun must come between the verb and the particle.

1 I am in charge here. Don't ...*answer me back*.................... . (answer back)
2 We're very cold out here. Aren't you going to .... ? (ask in)
3 I'd like to speak to him again. Will you please .... ? (call back)
4 They were fighting so fiercely that it took two of us to .... (pull apart)
5 I'm afraid we're just on our way out, so I can't .... (invite in)
6 I'm afraid the money is lost. We'll never .... (get back)
7 She knows all the answers. Nobody can .... (catch out)
8 They took us to dinner last month. It's our turn to .... for a meal. (invite out)
9 It certainly is a difficult problem. I just can't .... (work out)
10 It's difficult to find your way out. Wait a minute and I'll ask someone to ....
.... (show out)

C Complete the following sentences using the phrasal verb and object given in brackets.

1 I have to ring off now. I'll ...*call you back*....................................... this evening. (you / call back)
2 It's an obvious trick. Nobody but a fool would ....*fall for that*........................... . (that / fall for)
3 I .... on my way to work yesterday. (an old friend / bumped into)
4 It's hard work having a full time job and .... as well. (the house / looking after)
5 Let's ring Tom and Molly and .... for dinner. (them / invite out)
6 Everybody tells me I .... (my mother / take after)

Unit 80 Link verbs

Main points

- Link verbs are used to join the subject with a complement.
- Link verbs can have adjectives, noun groups, or 'to'-infinitive clauses as complements.
- You can use 'it' and 'there' as impersonal subjects with link verbs.

1 A small but important group of verbs are followed by a complement rather than an object. The complement tells you more about the subject. Verbs that take complements are called 'link' verbs.

appear	feel	grow	prove	smell	taste
be	get	keep	remain	sound	turn
become	go	look	seem	stay	

I am proud of these people.
She was getting too old to play tennis.
They looked all right to me.

2 Link verbs often have adjectives as complements describing the subject.

We felt very happy.
He was the tallest in the room.

See Units 19 to 22 for more information about adjectives after link verbs.

3 You can use link verbs with noun groups as complements to give your opinion about the subject.

He's not the right man for it.
She seemed an ideal person to look after them.

You also use noun groups as complements after 'be', 'become', and 'remain' to specify the subject.

He became a geologist.
Promises by MPs remained just promises.
This one is yours.

Note that you use object pronouns after 'be'.

It's me again.

4 Some link verbs can have 'to'-infinitive clauses as complements.

appear	get	grow	look	prove	seem

He appears to have taken my keys.
She seemed to like me.

These verbs, and 'remain', can also be followed by 'to be' and a complement.

Mary seemed to be asleep.
His new job proved to be a challenge.

5 You can use 'it' and 'there' as impersonal subjects with link verbs.

It seems silly not to tell him.
There appears to have been a mistake.

See Units 96 and 97 for more information.

You can use 'be' with some abstract nouns as the subject, followed by a 'that'-clause or a 'to'-infinitive clause as the complement.

advice	answer	idea	problem
agreement	decision	plan	solution

The answer is that they are not interested in it.
The idea was to spend more money on training.

Some can only have a 'that'-clause.

conclusion	fact	reason	thought
explanation	feeling	report	understanding

The fact is that I can't go to the party.

Unit 80 Practice

A Use the link verbs below to complete the sentences which follow.

feels   gets   goes   grows   looks   smells   sounds   tastes

1 What's the matter with Chris? He ...*looks*........... very upset.
2 Why is he shouting? He .... very angry.
3 If you keep milk for too long, it .... sour.
4 Jane says she .... hungry.
5 It .... very hot in summer.
6 Are you sure this fish is all right? It certainly .... a bit funny.
7 This cake is a bit old, but it still .... pretty good.
8 Anne is getting much taller as she .... older.

B Make 8 sentences from the following table.

The picture was old and dirty, The fruit smelled awful, The problem seemed simple, It was a long programme, It was only a short walk, The animal looked quiet enough, The jacket seemed to be the right size, The food smelled all right,	but it proved to be	extremely difficult. very tasty. much too small. rather tiring. very valuable. quite vicious. uneatable. very interesting.

1 ....*The picture was old and dirty, but it proved to be very valuable.*........
2 ....
3 ....
4 ....
5 ....
6 ....
7 ....
8 ....

C Use the phrases below to complete the sentences which follow.

too cold   too dark   too expensive   too hot   too late   too old   too tired   too young

1 I'm afraid I'm getting ...*too old*............... to work such long hours.
2 We'll have to stop. It's .... for us to see what we're doing.
3 Mary looks much .... to be a grandmother.
4 We should have arrived in time but we proved to be ....
5 Turn the fire off. It's getting .... in here.
6 I'm going to bed. I feel far .... to stay up any longer.
7 You'll be .... if you don't take more warm clothes.
8 We can't afford to stay in a hotel like that. It looks much ....

▶ **Bank**

Unit 81 Verbs with '-ing' clauses

Main points

- Many verbs are followed by an '-ing' clause.
- Some verbs are followed by an object and an '-ing' clause that describes what the object is doing.

1 Many verbs are followed by an '-ing' clause. The subject of the verb is also the subject of the '-ing' clause. The '-ing' clause begins with an '-ing' form. The most common of these verbs are:

- verbs of saying and thinking

admit	deny	imagine	recall
consider	describe	mention	suggest

He denied taking drugs.
I suggested meeting her for a coffee.

Note that all of these verbs except for 'describe' can also be followed by a 'that'-clause: see Unit 88.

He denied that he was involved.

- verbs of liking and disliking

adore	dislike	enjoy	like	mind
detest	dread	fancy	love	resent

Will they enjoy using it?
I don't mind telling you.

'Like' and 'love' can also be followed by a 'to'-infinitive clause: see Unit 83.

- other common verbs

avoid	finish	miss	resist
commence	involve	postpone	risk
delay	keep	practise	stop

I've just finished reading that book.
Avoid giving any unnecessary information.

- common phrasal verbs

burst out	end up	go round	put off
carry on	give up	keep on	set about

She carried on reading.
They kept on walking for a while.

Note that some common phrases can be followed by an '-ing' clause.

can't help	can't stand	feel like

I can't help worrying.

2 After the verbs and phrases mentioned above, you can also use 'being' followed by a past participle.

They enjoy being praised.
I dislike being interrupted.

After some verbs of saying and thinking, you can use 'having' followed by a past participle.

admit	deny	mention	recall

Michael denied having seen him.

3 'Come' and 'go' are used with '-ing' clauses to describe the way that a person or thing moves.

They both came running out.
It went sliding across the road out of control.

'Go' and 'come' are also used with '-ing' nouns to talk about sports and outdoor activities: see Unit 77.

Did you say they might go camping?

4 Some verbs can be followed by an object and an '-ing' clause. The object of the verb is the subject of the '-ing' clause.

catch	imagine	prevent	watch
find	leave	stop	

It is hard to imagine him existing without it.
He left them making their calculations.

Note that 'prevent' and 'stop' are often used with 'from' in front of the '-ing' clause.

I wanted to prevent him from seeing that.

Most verbs of perception can be followed by an object and an '-ing' clause or a base form: see Unit 84.

I saw him riding a bicycle.
I saw a policeman walk over to one of them.

See also Unit 29 for '-ing' clauses after nouns.

Unit 81 Practice

A Rewrite these sentences using an '-ing' clause instead of the reported clause.

1 He denied that he had done anything illegal. / *He denied doing anything illegal.*

2 Judy remembered she had noticed him behind the building. / ....

3 When his Dad asked, did you mention that you had seen him? / ....

4 I couldn't recall that I had said anything about him at all. / ....

5 May I suggest that we give them a present of £500 each? / ....

6 Sorry, but I can't imagine I would ever agree to that! / ....

7 He then described how he escaped from prison. / ....

8 They ought to admit that they had stolen the fruit. / ....

B Rewrite the sentences using an '-ing' clause as the object of the verb, instead of the noun group.

1 The Watsons were contemplating a week's visit to Egypt. / *The Watsons were contemplating visiting Egypt for a week.*

2 Could you consider a reduction in price, for example to £6,000? / ....

3 They delayed the start of the game because of the rain. / ....

4 I want to avoid monthly payments if possible. / ....

5 They didn't finish preparations for the party till after 9pm. / ....

6 This new production process might involve an increase in staff. / ....

C Complete these dialogues using the phrases given.

dread going	fancies taking up	adore climbing	give up playing
detest getting stuck	feel like having	can't bear being told	carry on driving

1 A: They go to the mountains every week-end.
   B: Yes, they *adore climbing.*

2 A: Oh dear, only another 3 days' holidays.
   B: Yes, I .... back to school.

3 A: Oh, just look at the traffic ahead.
   B: Oh no. I .... in traffic jams.

4 A: Let's stop for something to eat. There's a restaurant in a few miles.
   B: I don't know. I think we should .... and get home as quickly as possible.

5 A: She's a very good actress, and she's only 15, you know.
   B: Yes. She really .... acting as a career.

6 A: Jack hates being in the army.
   B: Yes, he .... what to do all the time.

7 A: My grandfather's nearly eighty and he still enjoys a game of tennis.
   B: I don't think he'll ever ....

8 A: Are you taking a holiday this summer?
   B: I hope so. I certainly .... a couple of weeks off.

▶ **Bank**

Unit 82 Verbs with 'to'-infinitive clauses

Main points

- Some verbs are followed by a 'to'-infinitive clause. Others are followed by an object and a 'to'-infinitive clause.
- Some verbs are followed by a 'wh'-word and a 'to'-infinitive clause. Others are followed by an object, a 'wh'-word, and a 'to'-infinitive clause.

1 Some verbs are followed by a 'to'-infinitive clause. The subject of the verb is also the subject of the 'to'-infinitive clause. These verbs include:

- verbs of saying and thinking

agree	decide	hope	learn	offer	promise
choose	expect	intend	mean	plan	refuse

She had agreed to let us use her flat.
I decided not to go out for the evening.

- other verbs

fail	manage	pretend	tend	want

England failed to win a place in the finals.

2 Some verbs are followed by an object and a 'to'-infinitive clause. The object of the verb is the subject of the 'to'-infinitive clause.

- verbs of saying and thinking

advise	encourage	invite	persuade	teach
ask	expect	order	remind	tell

I asked her to explain.
They advised us not to wait around too long.

- other verbs

allow	force	get	help	want

I could get someone else to do it.
I didn't want him to go.

Note that 'help' can also be followed by an object and a base form.

I helped him fix it.

WARNING: You do not use 'want' with a 'that'-clause. You do not say 'I want that you do something'.

3 Some verbs are followed by 'for' and an object, then a 'to'-infinitive clause. The object of 'for' is the subject of the 'to'-infinitive clause.

appeal	arrange	ask	long	pay	wait	wish

Could you arrange for a taxi to collect us?
I waited for him to speak.

4 Some link verbs, and 'pretend', are followed by 'to be' and an '-ing' form for continuing actions, and by 'to have' and a past participle for finished actions. See also Unit 80.

We pretended to be looking inside.
I don't appear to have written down his name.

5 Some verbs are normally used in the passive when they are followed by a 'to'-infinitive clause.

believe	feel	know	say	understand
consider	find	report	think	

He is said to have died a natural death.
Is it thought to be a good thing?

6 Some verbs are followed by a 'wh'-word and a 'to'-infinitive clause. These include:

ask	explain	imagine	learn	understand
decide	forget	know	remember	wonder

I didn't know what to call him.
She had forgotten how to ride a bicycle.

Some verbs are followed by an object, then a 'wh'-word and a 'to'-infinitive clause.

ask	remind	show	teach	tell

I asked him what to do.
Who will show him how to use it?

Some verbs only take 'to'-infinitive clauses to express purpose. See Unit 93.

The captain stopped to reload the gun.
He went to get some fresh milk.

See Unit 29 for nouns with 'to'-infinitive clauses.

Unit 82 Practice

A Rewrite these sentences using a 'to'-infinitive.

1 He said that he would help if he possibly could. / He promised ....*to help*......... if he possibly could.

2 I'll go up to London tomorrow if I can. / I intend .... up to London tomorrow.

3 It wasn't easy but we drove home in two hours. / We managed .... home in two hours.

4 They said that they would sell us the house. / They agreed .... us the house.

5 He looked as if he was sleeping / He seemed .... sleeping.

6 I expect I will hear from Mary before very long. / I expect .... from Mary before very long.

7 He has a habit of being late for meetings. / He tends .... late for meetings.

8 We were not able to finish all the work in time. / We failed .... all the work in time.

B Complete these sentences using the past tense of these verbs.

| advise   allow   ask   encourage   expect   invite   remind   warn |

1 If I were you, George, I would ring the police. / He ....*advised*............... George to ring the police.

2 Mary, could you please type a letter for me? / I .... Mary to type a letter for me.

3 I am sure Bill will arrive before dark. / She .... Bill to arrive before dark.

4 I hope you will visit us in England, Maria. / We .... Maria to visit us in England.

5 Okay, children, you can go home early. / She .... the children to go home early.

6 You should take the exam. I'm sure you'd do well. / Our teacher .... us to take the exam.

7 ELECTRIC FENCE. DO NOT TOUCH. / The notice .... people not to touch the fence.

8 Don't forget to take some warm clothes with you. / My mother .... me to take some warm clothes.

C Rewrite these sentences using 'to be' and an '-ing' form or 'to have' and a past participle.

1 I think we have lost our way. / We appear ...*to have lost our way.*...........................

2 He pretended that he was working. / He pretended ...*to be working.*...........................

3 I think you've broken your leg. / You seem ....

4 It looks as if they've locked everything away. / They appear ....

5 It appears he is waiting for the doctor. / He appears ....

6 Jenny pretended she had spent the money. / She pretended ....

7 I think they are living at home now. / They seem ....

D Rewrite these sentences using 'not' in front of a 'to'-infinitive.

1 She told me I shouldn't pay so much for a ticket. / She advised me ...*not to pay*..... so much for a ticket.

2 He waved but I pretended that I didn't see him. / I pretended .... him when he waved.

3 They promised they wouldn't miss the meeting. / They promised .... the meeting.

4 I told the kids they shouldn't make so much noise. / I told the kids .... so much noise.

5 I was going to write, but John persuaded me I shouldn't. / John persuaded me ....

6 Jenny reminded Peter that he shouldn't be late. / Jenny reminded Peter .... late.

▶ **Bank**

Unit 83 Verbs with 'to'-infinitive or '-ing' clauses

Main points

- Some verbs take a 'to'-infinitive clause or an '-ing' clause with little difference in meaning. Others take a 'to'-infinitive or '-ing' clause, but the meaning is different.

1 The following verbs can be followed by a 'to'-infinitive clause or an '-ing' clause, with little difference in meaning.

begin		~ try	hate
continue	attempt	~	love
start	bother	~ fear	prefer

It started raining.
A very cold wind had started to blow.

The captain didn't bother answering.
I didn't bother to answer.

Note that if these verbs are used in a continuous tense, they are followed by a 'to'-infinitive clause.

The company is beginning to export to the West.
We are continuing to make good progress.

After 'begin', 'continue', and 'start', you use a 'to'-infinitive clause with the verbs 'understand', 'know', and 'realize'.

I began to understand her a bit better.

2 You can often use 'like' with a 'to'-infinitive or an '-ing' clause with little difference in meaning.

I like to fish.
I like fishing.

However, there is sometimes a difference. You can use 'like' followed by a 'to'-infinitive clause to say that you think something is a good idea, or the right thing to do. You cannot use an '-ing' clause with this meaning.

They like to interview you first.
I didn't like to ask him.

3 After 'remember', 'forget', and 'regret', you use an '-ing' clause if you are referring to an event after it has happened.

I remember discussing it once before.
I'll never forget going out with my old aunt.
She did not regret accepting his offer.

You use a 'to'-infinitive clause after 'remember' and 'forget' if you are referring to an event before it happens.

I must remember to send a gift for her child.
Don't forget to send in your entries.

After 'regret', in formal English, you use a 'to'-infinitive clause with these verbs to say that you are sorry about what you are saying or doing now:

announce	inform	learn	say	see	tell

I regret to say that it was all burned up.

4 If you 'try to do' something, you make an effort to do it. If you 'try doing' something, you do it as an experiment, for example to see if you like it or if it is effective.

I tried to explain.
Have you tried painting it?

5 If you 'go on doing' something, you continue to do it. If you 'go on to do' something, you do it after you have finished doing something else.

I went on writing.
He later went on to form a computer company.

6 If you 'are used to doing' something, you are accustomed to doing it. If you 'used to do' something, you did it regularly in the past, but you no longer do it now.

We are used to working together.
I used to live in this street.

7 After 'need', you use a 'to'-infinitive clause if the subject of 'need' is also the subject of the 'to'-infinitive clause. You use an '-ing' form if the subject of 'need' is the object of the '-ing' clause.

We need to ask certain questions.
It needs cutting.

Unit 83 Practice

A Complete the sentences below by using the 'to'-infinitive or '-ing' form of these verbs.

enjoy knock learn phone play rain shout stay

1 I started ...*learning*............... French when I went to secondary school.
2 It's awfully cold in winter, but the kids still love .... outside in the snow.
3 I tried .... Peter and Molly three times, but there was no answer.
4 The weather was fine when we set off, but it soon started ....
5 I'll be in my office. Don't bother .... , just come straight in.
6 Joe just lost his temper and began .... at everyone.
7 It's a pity we have to go home now. We were just beginning .... ourselves.
8 We don't go out much in the evening. We prefer .... at home.

B Look at the following pairs of sentences. Complete one sentence in each pair with the 'to'-infinitive of the verb in brackets and the other with the '-ing' form.

1 Please remember ...*to close*............... the door when you go out. (close)
   I remember ...*closing*............... the door, but I'm not sure that I locked it.
2 I paid the electricity bill, but I don't remember .... the rent. (pay)
   Oh dear! I think I forgot .... the rent this month.
3 I tried .... in a department store, but it wasn't a very good job. (work)
   You really must try .... harder.
4 She just went on .... about everything. (complain)
   She complained about everything else, and then she went on .... about the price.
5 I remember .... the money in the drawer, but it's not there now. (leave)
   I must remember .... some money to pay for the repairs.
6 I really regret .... everyone what happened. I should have kept it a secret. (tell)
   I regret .... you that there has been a serious accident.
7 I remember .... to the dentist as a child. (go)
   I must remember .... to the dentist on Wednesday.
8 I'll never forget .... Paris for the first time. (visit)
   We mustn't forget .... Monique when we're in Paris.

C Make appropriate sentences to match the pictures, using **need** and the pairs of words given.

| shoes / polish   shirt / iron   tyre / mend |
| trousers / shorten   door / paint   pencil / sharpen |

1 ...*The pencil needs sharpening.*...................
2 ....
3 ....
4 ....
5 ....
6 ....

Unit 84 Verbs with other types of clauses

Main points

- 'Make' and 'let' can be followed by an object and a base form.
- Some verbs of perception can be followed by an object and an '-ing' clause, or an object and a base form.
- 'Have' and 'get' can be followed by an object and a past participle.
- 'Dare' is followed by a 'to'-infinitive clause or a base form.

1 You can use an object and a base form after 'make' to say that one person causes another person to do something, or after 'let' to say they allow them to do something.

My father made me go for the interview.
Jenny let him talk.

2 Some verbs of perception are used with an object and an '-ing' clause if an action is unfinished or continues over a period of time, and with an object and a base form if the action is finished.

feel   hear   see   watch

He heard a distant voice shouting.
Dr Hochstadt heard her gasp.

You normally use an '-ing' clause after 'notice', 'observe', 'smell', and 'understand'.

I could smell Chinese vegetables cooking.
We can understand them wanting to go.

3 You can use an object and a past participle after 'have' or 'get', when you want to say that someone arranges for something to be done. 'Have' is slightly more formal.

We've just had the house decorated.
We must get the car repaired.

You also use 'have' and 'get' with an object and a past participle to say that something happens to someone, especially if it is unpleasant.

She had her purse stolen.
He got his car broken into at the weekend.

4 You use 'have' followed by an object and an '-ing' clause, or an object and a past participle, when you want to say that someone causes something to happen, either intentionally or unintentionally.

Alan had me looking for that book all day.
He had me utterly confused.

5 You use 'want' and 'would like' with an object and a past participle to indicate that you want something to be done.

I want the work finished by January 1st.
How would you like your hair cut, sir?

6 'Dare' can be followed by a 'to'-infinitive clause or a base form in negative or interrogative sentences:

- when there is an auxiliary or modal in front of 'dare'

He did not dare to walk to the village.
What bank would dare offer such terms?

- when you use the form 'dares' or 'dared' (but not 'dares not' or 'dared not')

No one dares disturb him.
No other manager dared to compete.

You must use a base form in:

- negative or interrogative sentences without an auxiliary or modal before 'dare'

I daren't ring Jeremy again.
Nobody dare disturb him.
Dare she go in?

- negative sentences with 'dares not' or 'dared not'

He dares not risk it.
Sonny dared not disobey.

Note that the phrase 'how dare you' is always followed by a base form.

How dare you speak to me like that?

'Dare' is rarely used in affirmative sentences.

Unit 84 Practice

A Complete the dialogues below filling the gaps with **let, make,** or **made.**

1 A: When I went to school they ....*made*.... us wear school uniform.

B: Really? At my school they ....*let*........ us wear whatever we liked.

2 A: Did you see that film at the Odeon? It was so funny. It really .... me laugh.

B: No. My parents wouldn't .... me go. They .... me stay at home and finish my homework.

3 A: Do you think they'll .... us go home early on Friday?

B: No. They always .... us work till five, even just before a holiday.

4 A: I think they should .... old people travel free on buses.

B: Yes. I certainly don't think they should .... them pay the full fare.

5 A: They wouldn't .... us go in until just before the show started.

B: No. They .... us wait out in the cold until five to eight.

6 A: Please don't make such a noise. You really .... me jump.

B: Oh please, just .... us finish this game, then we'll be quiet.

B Complete the sentences below using the following words.

burning   lying   making   playing   talking

1 There must be someone at home. I can hear people ....*talking*............ .

2 Did you turn the stove off in the kitchen? I think I can smell something ....

3 The children are outside. I can see them .... in the garden.

4 Are these your gloves? I found them .... on the table in the hall.

5 This is awful. Can't you stop those kids .... such a dreadful noise?

C Complete these sentences using a form of **have** with the words in brackets. Remember to use the correct form of the main verb.

1 It'll be a long journey. We'd better ....*have the car serviced*.... before we set out. (the car / service)

2 I'll be late back after lunch. I'm going to .... (my hair / cut)

3 Doesn't Mike look smart? He .... specially for the wedding. (that suit / make)

4 We're planning to .... while we're on holiday. (the house / redecorate)

5 This house is too small now the kids are growing up. We should ....
.... (another room / build on).

6 Poor old Bill .... while he was on holiday. (a lot of money / steal)

► **Bank**

Unit 85 The passive voice

Main points

- You use the passive voice to focus on the person or thing affected by an action.
- You form the passive by using a form of 'be' and a past participle.
- Only verbs that have an object can have a passive form. With verbs that can have two objects, either object can be the subject of the passive.

1 When you want to talk about the person or thing that performs an action, you use the active voice.

Mr Smith locks the gate at 6 o'clock every night.
The storm destroyed dozens of trees.

When you want to focus on the person or thing that is affected by an action, rather than the person or thing that performs the action, you use the passive voice.

The gate is locked at 6 o'clock every night.
Dozens of trees were destroyed.

2 The passive is formed with a form of the auxiliary 'be', followed by the past participle of a main verb.

Two new stores were opened this year.
The room had been cleaned.

Continuous passive tenses are formed with a form of the auxiliary 'be' followed by 'being' and the past participle of a main verb.

Jobs are still being lost.
It was being done without his knowledge.

3 After modals you use the base form 'be' followed by the past participle of a main verb.

What can be done?
We won't be beaten.

When you are talking about the past, you use a modal with 'have been' followed by the past participle of a main verb.

He may have been given the car.
He couldn't have been told by Jimmy.

4 You form passive infinitives by using 'to be' or 'to have been' followed by the past participle of a main verb.

He wanted to be forgiven.
The car was reported to have been stolen.

5 In informal English, 'get' is sometimes used instead of 'be' to form the passive.

Our car gets cleaned every weekend.
He got killed in a plane crash.

6 When you use the passive, you often do not mention the person or thing that performs the action at all. This may be because you do not know or do not want to say who it is, or because it does not matter.

Her boyfriend was shot in the chest.
Your application was rejected.
Such items should be carefully packed in tea chests.

7 If you are using the passive and you do want to mention the person or thing that performs the action, you use 'by'.

He had been poisoned by his girlfriend.
He was brought up by an aunt.

You use 'with' to talk about something that is used to perform the action.

A circle was drawn in the dirt with a stick.
He was killed with a knife.

8 Only verbs that usually have an object can have a passive form. You can say 'people spend money' or 'money is spent'.

An enormous amount of money is spent on beer.
The food is sold at local markets.

With verbs which can have two objects, you can form two different passive sentences. For example, you can say 'The secretary was given the key' or 'The key was given to the secretary'.

They were offered a new flat.
The books will be sent to you.

See Unit 73 for more information on verbs that can have two objects.

Unit 85 Practice

A These sentences are from a newspaper story about a stolen painting. There are twelve passive verb groups, not counting the one which has been done for you; can you underline them?

1 Two men tried to sell a painting that <u>had been stolen</u>.
2 The painting was owned by Maimi Gillies, aged 84.
3 She said it had been presented to one of her ancestors by the artist.
4 She had owned it since 1926, when it was given to her as a wedding present.
5 One of the men, Mr X, who cannot be named for legal reasons, pleaded guilty.
6 He told police he was willing to sell it cheap because it was stolen.
7 A meeting was arranged at an airfield near Retford, where the money for the painting was to be flown in and exchanged, but the airfield had been staffed by police officers in plain clothes.
8 Mr X took the painting to the airfield and was shown the money in a suitcase.
9 The buyer was then taken to see the painting in a barn.
10 Mr X was arrested but Mr Henry escaped.

B Match the parts.

1 Petrol prices ...   a ... to be won.
2 This jacket ...   b ... have been increased.
3 Competition! 5000 prizes ...   c ... has been disconnected.
4 Five people ...   d ... will be sent to candidates.
5 The telephone ...   e ... was made in Hong Kong.
6 It appears the phone bill ...   f ... were killed in the rally.
7 Further information ...   g ... is not permitted anywhere on this station.
8 Before the storm everyone ...   h ... had not been paid.
9 Smoking ...   i ... is currently being rebuilt.
10 The old town theatre ...   j ... was told to stay inside their homes.

Now look at these sentences again. Underline the past participle and note the form of the verb 'be'. How many refer to the past and how many to the future?

C These sentences are taken from job adverts. Put the verb in brackets after the modal in the sentences, using the correct passive form of the verb.

1 Application forms should .... by 12 December. (return)
2 Further particulars may .... from the Senior Tutor. (obtain)
3 Only candidates with relevant experience can .... (consider)
4 You would .... to take part in some sports. (expect)
5 This post will .... initially for three years. (fund)
6 Names of two referees should .... (give)
7 Interviews will .... in early January. (hold)
8 Applications should .... on this form only. (make)
9 Teachers might .... accommodation in college. (offer)

▶ **Bank**

Unit 86 'It' as impersonal subject

Main points

- You use impersonal 'it' as the subject of a sentence to introduce new information.
- You use 'it' to talk about the time or the date.
- You use 'it' to talk about the weather.
- You use 'it' to express opinions about places, situations, and events.
- 'It' is often used with the passive of reporting verbs to express general beliefs and opinions.

1 'It' is a pronoun. As a personal pronoun it refers back to something that has already been mentioned.

They learn to speak English before they learn to read it.
Maybe he changed his mind, but I doubt it.

You can also use 'it' as the subject of a sentence when it does not refer back to anything that has already been mentioned. This impersonal use of 'it' introduces new information, and is used particularly to talk about times, dates, the weather, and personal opinions.

2 You use impersonal 'it' with a form of 'be' to talk about the time or the date.

It is nearly one o' clock.
It's the sixth of April today.

3 You use impersonal 'it' with verbs which refer to the weather:

drizzle	pour	sleet	thunder
hail	rain	snow	

It's still raining.
It snowed steadily through the night.
It was pouring with rain.

You can describe the weather by using 'it' followed by 'be' and an adjective with or without a noun.

It's a lovely day.
It was very bright.

You can describe a change in the weather by using 'it' followed by 'get' and an adjective.

It was getting cold.
It's getting dark.

4 You use impersonal 'it', followed by a form of 'be' and an adjective or noun group, to express your opinion about a place, a situation, or an event. The adjective or noun group can be followed by an adverbial or by an '-ing' clause, a 'to'-infinitive clause, or a 'that'-clause.

It was terribly cold in the trucks.
It's fun working for him.
It was a pleasure to be there.
It's strange that it hasn't been noticed before.

5 You use 'it' followed by a verb such as 'interest', 'please', 'surprise', or 'upset' which indicates someone's reaction to a fact, situation, or event. The verb is followed by a noun group, and a 'that'-clause or a 'to'-infinitive clause.

It pleases me that he should want to talk about his work.
It surprised him to realize that he hadn't thought about them until now.

6 You can also use 'it' with the passive of a reporting verb and a 'that'-clause when you want to suggest that an opinion or belief is shared by many people. This use is particularly common in news reports, for example in newspapers, on the radio, or on television.

It was said that he could speak their language.
Nowadays it is believed that the size is unimportant.
It is thought that about a million puppies are born each year.

Note that the passive of reporting verbs can also be used without impersonal 'it' to express general opinions.

The factories were said to be much worse.
They are believed to be dangerous.

See Units 88 and 89 for more information on reporting verbs.

Unit 86 Practice

A Make ten true sentences from this table.

It	is can be	interesting difficult fun nice expensive awful boring	learning English. going abroad on holiday. meeting new people. travelling in the rush hour. going to school. buying new clothes. going shopping.

1 *It can be boring going to school.* ....
2 ....
3 ....
4 ....
5 ....
6 ....
7 ....
8 ....
9 ....
10 ....

B The word **it** has been left out of these sentences. The number in brackets tells you how many times it
should occur. Show where it should be.

1 A: What's the house like? Is *it* big or small? B: *It* Is quite big. *It* Has four bedrooms. (3)
2 We live in Hagley. Is a village near Birmingham. (1)
3 I'm learning Chinese, but is very difficult to understand. (1)
4 There's a new restaurant in the High Street. Opened about a month ago. We went there last week but
   was very expensive and we didn't like very much. (3)
5 A: Where's the tin opener? B: I think is in the kitchen. I put back in the drawer. (2)
6 She was very frightened but she tried not to show. (1)
7 A: Did you see the film about Japan on TV last night? I really enjoyed. B: Yes, I enjoyed too. I thought
   was very interesting. C: I didn't see. I went to bed before started. (5)

C Rewrite these sentences with **It** and a 'to'-infinitive clause.
1 Driving over 70 mph is illegal. / *It's illegal to drive over 70 mph.* ....
2 Missing a train is very annoying. / ....
3 Getting a letter from an old friend is nice. / ....
4 Going for a good night out is fun. / ....
5 Learning another language is interesting. / ....
6 Eating too much is unhealthy. / ....
7 Looking after young children is tiring. / ....
8 Driving too fast is very dangerous. / ....

▶ **Bank**

Unit 87 'There' as impersonal subject

Main points

- You use 'there' followed by a form of 'be' and a noun group to introduce new information.
- You use 'there' with a singular or plural verb, depending on whether the following noun is singular or plural.
- You can also use 'there' with modals.

1 'There' is often an adverb of place.

Are you comfortable there?
The book is there on the table.

You can also use 'there' as the impersonal subject of a sentence when it does not refer to a place. In this case you use 'there' to introduce new information and to focus upon it. After 'there' you use a form of 'be' and a noun group.

There is work to be done.
There will be a party tonight.
There was no damage.
There have been two telephone calls.

Note that the impersonal subject 'there' is often pronounced without stress, whereas the adverb is almost always stressed.

2 You use 'there' as the impersonal subject to talk about:
- the existence or presence of someone or something

There are two people who might know what happened.
There are many possibilities.
There is plenty of bread.

- something that happens

There was a general election that year.
There's a meeting every week.
There was a fierce battle.

- a number or amount

There are forty of us, I think.
There is a great deal of anger about his decision.
There were a lot of people camped there.

3 When the noun group after the verb is plural, you use a plural verb.

There are many reasons for this.
There were two men in the room.

You also use a plural verb before phrases such as 'a number (of)', 'a lot (of)', and 'a few (of)'.

There were a lot of people camped there.
There are only a few left.

4 When the noun group after the verb is singular or uncountable, you use a singular verb.

There is one point we must add here.
There isn't enough room in here.

You also use a singular verb when you are mentioning more than one person or thing and the first noun after the verb is singular or uncountable.

There was a man and a woman.
There was a sofa and two chairs.

5 You can also use 'there' with a modal, followed by 'be' or 'have been'.

There could be a problem.
There should be a change in government.
There can't have been anybody outside.
There must have been some mistake.

6 In spoken and informal written English, short forms of 'be' or a modal are normally used after 'there'.

There's no danger.
There'll always be a future for music.
I knew there'd be trouble.
There's been quite a lot of research into it.
I didn't even know there'd been a murder.

7 You can also use 'there' with 'appear' or 'seem', followed by 'to be' or 'to have been'.

There appears to be a vast amount of confusion on this point.
There don't seem to be many people on campus.
There seems to have been some carelessness.

Unit 87 Practice

A Use the 'to'-infinitive clauses below to complete the sentences which follow.

to ask	to drink	to do	to eat	to help
to read	to see	to sleep	to spare	to watch

1 I was thirsty, but there was nothing ....*to drink*............... .

2 I was tired out, but there was nowhere ....

3 We were all hungry, but there wasn't very much ....

4 We were late setting off, so there was no time ....

5 I couldn't do it alone, and there was no one ....

6 The children were bored. They said there was nothing ....

7 There were no books or newspapers, nothing ....

8 I couldn't find my way, and there was no one ....

9 I switched on the TV, but there wasn't really anything ....

10 We had a walk round the town, but there wasn't anything interesting ....

B Rewrite these sentences to begin with **'There'** as an impersonal subject.

1 Two general elections took place that year. / ....*There were two general elections that year.*....

2 We have a class every Friday. / ....

3 A meeting will be held at three o'clock on Tuesday. / ....

4 Lots of children will be at the concert. / ....

5 A few friends will be coming round. / ....

6 People give lots of parties at Christmas. / ....

7 An accident will happen if you're not careful. / ....

8 You must have made a mistake. / ....

C Rewrite these sentences beginning with **'There seems ...'** or **'There appears ...'**.

1 I think there is a problem here.
....*There appears to be a problem here.*...
(or) ...*There seems to be a problem here.*...

2 I think there has been a mistake.
....*There appears to have been a mistake.*...
(or) ...*There seems to have been a mistake.*...

3 I think there is something wrong with the engine. / ....

4 I think there's nothing left. / ....

5 I think there has been an accident. / ....

6 I think there was a lot of trouble. / ....

7 I think there is no one at home. / ....

8 I think there has been a fire. / ....

▶ **Bank**

Unit 88 Report structures: 'that'-clauses

Main points

- You usually use your own words to report what someone said, rather than repeating their exact words.
- Report structures contain a reporting clause first, then a reported clause.
- When you are reporting a statement, the reported clause is a 'that'-clause.
- You must mention the hearer with 'tell'. You need not mention the hearer with 'say'.

1 When you are reporting what someone said, you do not usually repeat their exact words, you use your own words in a report structure.

Jim said he wanted to go home.

Jim's actual words might have been 'It's time I went' or 'I must go'.
Report structures contain two clauses. The first clause is the reporting clause, which contains a reporting verb such as 'say', 'tell', or 'ask'.

She said that she'd been to Belgium.
The man in the shop told me how much it would cost.

You often use verbs that refer to people's thoughts and feelings to report what people say. If someone says 'I am wrong', you might report this as 'He felt that he was wrong'. See Unit 89 for more information.

2 The second clause in a report structure is the reported clause, which contains the information that you are reporting. The reported clause can be a 'that'-clause, a 'to'-infinitive clause, an 'if'-clause, or a 'wh'-word clause.

She said that she didn't know.
He told me to do it.
Mary asked if she could stay with us.
She asked where he'd gone.

3 If you want to report a statement, you use a 'that'-clause after a verb such as 'say'.

admit	argue	decide	insist	reply
agree	claim	deny	mention	say
answer	complain	explain	promise	warn

He said that he would go.
I replied that I had not read it yet.

You often omit 'that' from the 'that'-clause, but not after 'answer', 'argue', 'explain', or 'reply'.

They said I had to see a doctor first.
He answered that the price would be three pounds.

You often mention the hearer after the preposition 'to' with the following verbs.

admit	complain	mention	suggest
announce	explain	say	

He complained to me that you were rude.

4 'Tell' and some other reporting verbs are also used with a 'that'-clause, but with these verbs you have to mention the hearer as the object of the verb.

convince	notify	reassure	tell
inform	persuade	remind	

He told me that he was a farmer.
I informed her that I could not come.

The word 'that' is often omitted after 'tell'.

I told them you were at the dentist.

You can also mention the hearer as the object of the verb with 'promise' and 'warn'.

I promised her that I wouldn't be late.

5 Note the differences between 'say' and 'tell'. You cannot use 'say' with the hearer as the object of the verb. You cannot say 'I said them you had gone'. You cannot use 'tell' without the hearer as the object of the verb. You cannot say 'I told that you had gone'. You cannot use 'tell' with 'to' and the hearer. You cannot say 'I told to them you had gone'.

6 The reporting verbs that have the hearer as object, such as 'tell', can be used in the passive.

She was told that there were no tickets left.

Most reporting verbs that do not need the hearer as object, such as 'say', can be used in the passive with impersonal 'it' as subject, but not 'answer', 'complain', 'insist', 'promise', 'reply', or 'warn'.

It was said that the money had been stolen.

See also Units 89 and 47.

Unit 88 Practice

A Match the reports with the actual words used.

1 They said they had to go.
2 He said he would help if he could.
3 She promised she would visit us.
4 He suggested that we should write to the boss.
5 They insisted we should stay a bit longer.
6 They complained that they were too busy.
7 She mentioned that she had met you.
8 I explained that they should send a letter.

a 'You can't leave yet. It's only eleven o'clock.'
b 'Well, I'll do whatever I can for you.'
c 'If I were you I would get in touch with the manager.'
d 'I bumped into your brother in London yesterday.'
e 'It's no good just telephoning. Put something in writing.'
f 'I'll certainly come and see you some time.'
g 'We have far too much work at the moment.'
h 'I'm afraid it's time for us to leave.'

B Use the appropriate form of these verbs to complete the definitions and examples.

| admit   announce   argue   complain   deny   mention   explain   inform |

1 If you ....*inform*............... someone that something is the case, you tell them about it. EG I ....*informed*............ her that I was unwell and could not come to her party.

2 If you .... something, you agree, often reluctantly, that it is true. EG I must .... that I had my doubts.

3 When you .... something, you say that it is not true. EG Green .... that he had done anything illegal.

4 If you .... something, you tell people about it publicly or officially. EG It was .... that the Prime Minister would speak on television that evening.

5 If you .... , you tell someone about a situation affecting you that is wrong or unsatisfactory. EG He .... that the office was not 'businesslike'.

6 If you .... something, you say it, but do not spend long talking about it. EG I .... to Tom that I was thinking of going back to work.

7 If you .... something, you describe it so that it can be understood. EG He .... that they had to buy a return ticket.

8 If you .... that something is the case, you state your opinion about it and give reasons why you think it is true. EG Some people .... that nuclear weapons have helped to keep the peace.

C Use one of the words given in brackets to complete each of the sentences below.

1 I ....*explained*...........to him that he would have to wait. (explained / told)
2 He .... me that it was time to go. (mentioned / informed)
3 She .... to them that they should reconsider their decision. (suggested / persuaded)
4 We were .... that you would pay the bill. (told / said)
5 It was .... that there would be another meeting the following week. (informed / announced)
6 George .... to me that he might look in to see me. (promised / mentioned)

Unit 89 Other report structures

Main points

- When reporting an order, a request, or a piece of advice, the reported clause is a 'to'-infinitive clause, used after an object.
- When reporting a question, the reported clause is an 'if'-clause or a 'wh'-word clause.
- Many reporting verbs refer to people's thoughts and feelings.

1 If you want to report an order, a request, or a piece of advice, you use a 'to'-infinitive clause after a reporting verb such as 'tell', 'ask', or 'advise'. You mention the hearer as the object of the verb, before the 'to'-infinitive clause.

advise	command	invite	remind
ask	forbid	order	tell
beg	instruct	persuade	warn

Johnson _told her to wake_ him _up._
He _ordered me to fetch_ the books.
He _asked her to marry_ him.
He _advised me to buy_ it.

If the order, request, or advice is negative, you put 'not' before the 'to'-infinitive.

He had ordered his officers _not to use_ weapons.
She asked her staff _not to discuss_ it publicly.
Doctors advised him _not to play_ for three weeks.

If the subject of the 'to'-infinitive clause is the same as the subject of the main verb, you can use 'ask' or 'beg' to report a request without mentioning the hearer.

I _asked to see_ the manager.
Both men _begged not to be named._

2 If you want to report a question, you use a verb such as 'ask' followed by an 'if'-clause or a 'wh'-word clause.

I _asked if_ I could stay with them.
They _wondered whether_ the time was right.
He _asked_ me _where_ I was going.
She _inquired how_ Ibrahim was getting on.

Note that in reported questions, the subject of the question comes before the verb, just as it does in affirmative sentences. See Unit 54.

3 Many reporting verbs refer to people's thoughts and feelings but are often used to report what people say. For example, if someone says 'I must go', you might report this as 'She wanted to go' or 'She thought she should go'.
Some of these verbs are followed by:

- a 'that'-clause

accept	fear	imagine	think
believe	feel	know	understand
consider	guess	suppose	worry

We both _knew_ that the town was cut off.
I had always _believed_ that I would see him again.

- a 'to'-infinitive clause

intend	plan	want

He doesn't _want_ to get up.

- a 'that'-clause or a 'to'-infinitive clause

agree	expect	hope	regret	wish
decide	forget	prefer	remember	

She _hoped she wasn't going to cry._
They are in love and _wish to marry._

'Expect' and 'prefer' can also be followed by an object and a 'to'-infinitive.

I'm sure she _doesn't expect you to take_ the plane.
The headmaster _prefers them to act_ plays they have written themselves.

4 A speaker's exact words are more often used in stories than in ordinary conversation.

'I knew I'd seen you,' I said.
'Only one,' replied the Englishman.
'Let's go and have a look at the swimming pool,' she suggested.

In ordinary conversation, it is normal to use a report structure rather than to repeat someone's exact words.

Unit 89 Practice

A Rewrite the sentences below as orders or requests with a 'to'-infinitive clause, and the words in brackets.

1 'Do you think you could look after the children?' (David / ask / Mary)
   David asked Mary to look after the children.

2 'I think you should try to get more sleep.' (John's doctor / advise / him)

3 'You can come round and see us any time.' (We / invite / our friends)

4 'Will you take the money to the bank, please?' (Jack / tell / me)

5 'Don't forget to come half an hour early on Tuesday.' (Mr Brown / remind / the students)

6 'Please write to me every day.' (Bill / beg / Maria)

Now do these with **not** and a 'to'-infinitive clause.

7 'You shouldn't play with fire.' (I / warn / the children)

8 'I don't think you should go to England in the winter.' (My grandfather / advise / me)

9 'You really ought not to go out alone after dark.' (They / tell / the visitors)

10 'Please don't make an official complaint.' (The manager / persuade / her)

B Now do these sentences with **ask** and a 'wh'-word clause.

1 'What time does the match start please?' (I / a policeman)
   I asked a policeman what time the match started.

2 'Where are you going to spend the holiday?' (Joe / Mary)

3 'Why are the tickets so expensive?' (Everybody / us)

4 'How old are Mary's children?' (Frank / his wife)

5 'Who's going to buy your house?' (Mrs Jones / her neighbour)

6 'When are you planning to come to Darlington?' (Bill / his friend)

7 'What are you going to do next?' (I / Maria)

8 'Where can I get the bus to Liverpool?' (Peter / a policeman)

▶ **Bank**

Unit 90 Time clauses

Main points

- You use time clauses to say when something happens.
- Time clauses can refer to the past, present, or future.
- Time clauses are introduced by words such as 'after', 'when', or 'while'.
- A time clause needs a main clause to make a complete sentence. The time clause can come before or after the main clause.

1 You use time clauses to say when something happens. The verb in the time clause can be in a present or a past tense.

I look after the children while she goes to London.
I haven't given him a thing to eat since he arrived.

WARNING: You never use a future tense in a time clause. You use one of the present tenses instead.

Let me stay here till Jeannie comes to bed.
I'll do it when I've finished writing this letter.

2 When you want to say that two events happen at the same time, you use a time clause with 'as', 'when', or 'while'.

We arrived as they were leaving.

Sometimes the two events happen together for a period of time.

She wept bitterly as she told her story.

Sometimes one event interrupts another event.

He was having his dinner when the telephone rang.
John will arrive while we are watching the film.

Note that you often use a continuous tense for the interrupted action. See Unit 43.

3 When you want to say that one event happens before or after another event, you use a time clause with 'after', 'as soon as', 'before', or 'when'.

As soon as we get tickets, we'll send them to you.
Can I see you before you go, Helen?
When he had finished reading, he looked up.

Note that you use the past perfect to indicate an event that happened before another event in the past.

4 When you want to mention a situation which started in the past and continued until a later time, you use a time clause with 'since' or 'ever since'. You use a past simple or a past perfect in the time clause, and a past perfect in the main clause.

He hadn't cried since he was a boy of ten.
Janine had been busy ever since she had heard the news.
I'd wanted to come ever since I was a child.

If the situation started in the past and still continues now, you use a past simple in the time clause, and a present perfect in the main clause.

I've been in politics since I was at university.
Ever since you arrived you've been causing trouble.

Note that after impersonal 'it' and a time expression, if the main clause is in the present tense, you use 'since' with a past simple.

It is two weeks now since I wrote to you.

If the main clause is in the past tense, you use 'since' with a past perfect.

It was nearly seven years since I'd seen Toby.

For 'since' as a preposition, see Unit 33.

5 When you want to talk about when a situation ends, you use a time clause with 'till' or 'until' and a present or past tense.

We'll support them till they find work.
I stayed there talking to them until I saw Sam.
She waited until he had gone.

6 When you want to say that something happens before or at a particular time, you use a time clause with 'by the time' or 'by which time'.

By the time I went to bed, I was exhausted.
He came back later, by which time they had gone.

7 In written or formal English, if the subject of the main clause and the time clause are the same, you sometimes omit the subject in the time clause and use a participle as the verb.

I read the book before going to see the film.
The car was stolen while parked in a London street.

Unit 90 Practice

A Complete the following sentences using the past simple or past continuous of the verbs given.

1 We played chess from 6.30 to 8.30. Margaret arrived at 7.15. / We ..._were playing_.........chess when Margaret ..._arrived_................ . (play) (arrive) / Margaret .... while we .... chess. (arrive) (play)

2 Bill arrived at 7.45, so we all sat down to dinner. / We all .... down to dinner when Bill .... (sit) (arrive) / As soon as Bill .... we all .... down to dinner. (arrive) (sit)

3 I worked in the kitchen until 7.15. My mother phoned at 7.05. / I .... in the kitchen when my mother .... (work) (phone) / My mother .... while I .... in the kitchen. (phone) (work)

4 I wrote letters in my study all afternoon. I heard the explosion at about 3 pm. / When I .... the explosion I .... a letter in my study. (hear) (write) / I .... a letter in my study when I .... the explosion. (write) (hear)

5 I heard the explosion and immediately telephoned the police. / I .... the police immediately after I .... the explosion. (telephone) (hear) / As soon as I .... the explosion, I .... the police. (hear) (telephone)

B Complete these sentences using the present simple in the time clause, and either **will** or **will be** and an '-ing' form in the main clause.

1 I work from 8 am until 6 pm every Wednesday. Mary will arrive at about 4 pm. / I ..._will be working_....... when Mary ..._arrives._................ (work) (arrive)

2 Bill is going to phone me on Wednesday, so I will let you know then. / I .... you know as soon as Bill .... me. (let) (phone)

3 According to the weather forecast, it's going to rain all day tomorrow. We are going to set out at nine o'clock. / According to the weather forecast, it .... when we .... tomorrow. (rain) (set out)

4 I'll be seeing Helen next week. I'll tell her then. / I .... Helen when I .... her. (tell) (see)

5 I'm going to the supermarket soon. I always buy bread at the supermarket. / I .... some bread when I .... to the supermarket. (buy) (go)

C Complete the sentences using the **since** clauses given below.

1 George and I have been close friends ...
2 We haven't been to the cinema ...
3 He hasn't been able to play the piano ...
4 They have lived next door to us ...
5 Fred has been working at home ...
6 Mary has been looking after the children ...

a ... since they moved here in 1987.
b ... ever since he left his job at the factory.
c ... since we saw Dracula at the Odeon last year.
d ... since we were at school together.
e ... since he had his accident a month ago.
f ... ever since their mother went into hospital.

Rewrite your sentences using the past perfect.
   George and I had been close friends since we had been at school together.

▶ **Bank**

Unit 91 Conditional clauses using 'if'

Main points

- You use conditional clauses to talk about a possible situation and its results.
- Conditional clauses can begin with 'if'.
- A conditional clause needs a main clause to make a complete sentence. The conditional clause can come before or after the main clause.

1 You use conditional clauses to talk about a situation that might possibly happen and to say what its results might be.
You use 'if' to mention events and situations that happen often, that may happen in the future, that could have happened in the past but did not happen, or that are unlikely to happen at all.

If the light comes on, the battery is OK.
I'll call you if I need you.
If I had known, I'd have told you.
If she asked me, I'd help her.

2 When you are talking about something that is generally true or happens often, you use a present or present perfect tense in the main clause and the conditional clause.

If they lose weight during an illness, they soon regain it afterwards.
If an advertisement does not tell the truth, the advertiser is committing an offence.
If the baby is crying, it is probably hungry.
If they have lost any money, they report it to me.

WARNING: You do not use the present continuous in both clauses. You do not say 'If they are losing money, they are getting angry.'

3 When you use a conditional clause with a present or present perfect tense, you often use an imperative in the main clause.

Wake me up if you're worried.
If he has finished, ask him to leave quietly.
If you are very early, don't expect them to be ready.

4 When you are talking about something which may possibly happen in the future, you use a present or present perfect tense in the conditional clause, and the simple future in the main clause.

If I marry Celia, we will need the money.
If you are going to America, you will need a visa.
If he has done the windows, he will want his money.

WARNING: You do not normally use 'will' in conditional clauses. You do not say 'If I will see you tomorrow, I will give you the book'.

5 When you are talking about something that you think is unlikely to happen, you use the past simple or past continuous in the conditional clause and 'would' in the main clause.

If I had enough money, I would buy the car.
If he was coming , he would ring.

WARNING: You do not normally use 'would' in conditional clauses. You do not say 'If I would do it, I would do it like this'.

6 'Were' is sometimes used instead of 'was' in the conditional clause, especially after 'I'.

If I were as big as you, I would kill you.
If I weren't so busy, I would do it for you.

You often say 'If I were you' when you are giving someone advice.

If I were you, I would take the money.
I should keep out of Bernadette's way if I were you.

7 When you are talking about something which could have happened in the past but which did not actually happen, you use the past perfect in the conditional clause. In the main clause, you use 'would have' and a past participle.

If he had realized that, he would have run away.
I wouldn't have been so depressed if I had known how common this feeling is.

WARNING: You do not use 'would have' in the conditional clause. You do not say 'If I would have seen him, I would have told him'.

Unit 91 Practice

A Match these parts to make conditional sentences.

1 Dan might help you …	a … if they are enjoying themselves.
2 You are sure to be late …	b … if I can remember her phone number.
3 You'll enjoy the Jacques Tati film …	c … if you miss the bus.
4 They always stay out late …	d … if you don't want to.
5 They'll understand it all right …	e … if you phone while I'm out.
6 I'll give her a call …	f … if you explain it to them.
7 Bill will take a message …	g … if I have the time.
8 I'll do the shopping …	h … if you don't have a ticket.
9 You can't get in …	i … if you can understand French.
10 You needn't come to the party …	j … if you ask him.

B Complete these sentences by putting the verb in brackets in the right tense.

1 If you …*ask*…………………………………… Liz, she will tell you what to do. (ask)
2 He's going to visit some friends in Athens if he ………………………………………… time. (have)
3 You shouldn't interrupt them if they ………………………………………… . (work)
4 Maria will get you some money if she ………………………………………… to the bank. (go)
5 I'll have a word with Jack if he ………………………………………… at home. (be)

C Match these parts to make conditional sentences.

1 If I had their address …	a … it would cost over £650.
2 If you saw her now …	b … you might earn a bit more money.
3 If I took more exercise …	c … I could probably stay with Mehmet.
4 If you got a new job …	d … she must have been out at work.
5 If you asked Heather …	e … she would give you a certificate.
6 If I travelled first class …	f … she would probably give you a lift.
7 If it was a little warmer …	g … we could go for a swim.
8 If she didn't answer the phone …	h … I might lose a bit of weight.
9 If you went to the doctor …	i … I could write and ask them.
10 If I stopped off in Ankara …	j … you would hardly recognize her.

Unit 92 Conditional clauses using modals and 'unless'

Main points

- You can use a modal in a conditional clause.
- You use 'unless' to mention an exception to what you are saying.

1 You sometimes use modals in conditional clauses. In the main clause, you can still use a present tense for events that happen often, 'will' for events that are quite likely in the future, 'would' for an event that is unlikely to happen, and 'would have' for events that were possible but did not happen.

If he can't come, he usually phones me.
If they must have it today, they will have to come back at five o'clock.
If I could only find the time, I'd do it gladly.
If you could have seen him, you would have laughed too.

'Should' is sometimes used in conditional clauses to express greater uncertainty.

If any visitors should come, I'll say you aren't here.

2 You can use other modals besides 'will', 'would' and 'would have' in the main clause with their usual meanings.

She might phone me, if she has time.
You could come, if you wanted to.
If he sees you leaving, he may cry.

Note that you can have modals in both clauses: the main clause and the conditional clause.

If he can't come, he will phone.

See Units 59 to 71 for more information.

3 In formal English, if the first verb in a conditional clause is 'had', 'should', or 'were', you can put the verb at the beginning of the clause and omit 'if'. For example, instead of saying 'If he should come, I will tell him you are sick', it is possible to say 'Should he come, I will tell him you are sick'.

Should ministers decide to hold an inquiry, we would welcome it.
Were it all true, it would still not excuse their actions.
Had I known, I would not have done it.

4 When you want to mention an exception to what you are saying, you use a conditional clause beginning with 'unless'.

You will fail your exams.
You will fail your exams unless you work harder.

Note that you can often use 'if...not' instead of 'unless'.

You will fail your exams if you do not work harder.

When you use 'unless', you use the same tenses that you use with 'if'.

She spends Sundays in the garden unless the weather is awful.
We usually walk, unless we're going shopping.
He will not let you go unless he is forced to do so.
You wouldn't believe it, unless you saw it.

5 'If' and 'unless' are not the only ways of beginning conditional clauses. You can also use 'as long as', 'only if', 'provided', 'provided that', 'providing', 'providing that', or 'so long as'. These expressions are all used to indicate that one thing only happens or is true if another thing happens or is true.

I will come only if nothing is said to the press.
She was prepared to come, provided that she could bring her daughter.
Providing they remained at a safe distance, we would be all right.
Detergent cannot harm a fabric, so long as it has been properly dissolved.

We were all right as long as we kept our heads down.

Unit 92 Practice

A Rewrite these sentences as conditionals.

1 I can't write to her because I don't have her address.
   ...J could write to her, if J had her address....

2 I'd like to go abroad but I can't afford it.

3 I'm not going to buy that car because it's so expensive.

4 We can't go out because it's raining.

5 She won't come to the party because she's away on holiday.

6 The central heating isn't working so we can't turn it on.

B Rewrite these sentences as conditionals.

1 Unfortunately I didn't see him, so I couldn't give him your message.
   ...Jf J had seen him, J could have given him your message....

2 Unfortunately he didn't pass his exams or he might have gone to university.

3 He didn't realize what was happening or he would have run away.

4 Fortunately I didn't hear what she said or I would have been very angry.

5 They got in because you didn't lock the door properly.

6 It only happened because you didn't follow the instructions.

7 Luckily she didn't find out or she would have been furious.

8 It's lucky we booked a room or we would have had nowhere to stay.

9 It's a good job we weren't going any faster or someone could have been killed.

10 He was so tired that he went home at lunchtime.

C Match the two parts of these conditional sentences.

1 You can borrow the money, ...   a ... I would have invited you to lunch.

2 He'll probably get lost, ...   b ... would you ask him to call back later?

3 Had I known you were coming, ...   c ... provided he has recovered from his
                                              cold.
4 George says he will come, ...

5 You are not allowed to park in the school, ...   d ... unless you are a member of staff.

6 Should he telephone while I'm out, ... e ... as long as it was black.

7 Henry Ford said you could have any colour you   f ... provided he can stay overnight.
   wanted, ...
                                           g ... so long as you promise to pay it back.
8 Fred will be at school next week, ...
                                           h ... unless someone shows him the way.

▶ **Bank**

Unit 93 Purpose and reason clauses

Main points

- Purpose clauses are introduced by conjunctions such as 'so', 'so as to', 'so that', 'in order to' or 'in order that'.
- Reason clauses are introduced by conjunctions such as 'as', 'because', or 'in case'.
- A purpose or reason clause needs a main clause to make a complete sentence.
- A purpose clause usually comes after a main clause. A reason clause can come before or after a main clause.

1 You use a purpose clause when you are saying what someone's intention is when they do something. The most common type of purpose clause is a 'to'-infinitive clause.

The children sleep together to keep warm.
They locked the door to stop us from getting in.

Instead of using an ordinary 'to'-infinitive, you often use 'in order to' or 'so as to' with an infinitive.

He was giving up his job in order to stay at home.
I keep the window open, so as to let fresh air in.

To make a purpose clause negative, you have to use 'in order not to' or 'so as not to' with an infinitive.

I would have to give myself something to do in order not to be bored.
They went on foot, so as not to be heard.

Another way of making purpose clauses negative is by using 'to avoid' with an '-ing' form or a noun group.

I had to turn away to avoid letting him see my smile.
They drove through town to avoid the motorway.

2 Another type of purpose clause begins with 'in order that', 'so', or 'so that'. These clauses usually contain a modal.
When the main clause refers to the present, you usually use 'can', 'may', 'will', or 'shall' in the purpose clause.

Any holes should be fenced so that people can't fall down them.
I have drawn a diagram so that my explanation will be clearer.

When the main clause refers to the past you usually use 'could', 'might', 'should', or 'would' in the purpose clause.

She said she wanted tea ready at six so she could be out by eight.
Someone lifted Philip onto his shoulder so that he might see the procession.

You use 'in order that', 'so' and 'so that', when the subject of the purpose clause is different from the subject of the main clause. For example, you say 'I've underlined it so that it will be easier.' You do not say 'I've underlined it to be easier'.

3 You can also talk about the purpose of an action by using a prepositional phrase introduced by 'for'.

She went out for a run.
They said they did it for fun.
I usually check, just for safety's sake.

4 You use a reason clause when you want to explain why someone does something or why it happens. When you are simply giving the reason for something, you use 'because', 'since', or 'as'.

I couldn't see Helen's expression, because her head was turned.
Since it was Saturday, he stayed in bed.
As he had been up since 4 am, he was very tired.

You can also use 'why' and a reported question to talk about the reason for an action. See Unit 54.

I asked him why he had come.

5 When you are talking about a possible situation which explains the reason why someone does something, you use 'in case' or 'just in case' .

I've got the key in case we want to go inside.
I am here just in case anything unusual happens.

WARNING: You do not use a future tense after 'in case'. You do not say 'I'll stay behind in case she'll arrive later'.

Unit 93 Practice

A Rewrite these sentences to include a 'to'-infinitive purpose clause introduced by the words given in brackets.

1 Everyone was pushing because they wanted to get to the front of the queue. (in order to)
   Everyone was pushing in order to get to the front of the queue.

2 Try to write clearly. That way you will avoid being misunderstood. (so as to)
   ....

3 A lot of people learn English because they want to study in English. (in order to)
   ....

4 What do I need to know, if I want to be a good doctor? (in order to)
   ....

5 She turned up early because she wanted to get the room ready. (in order to)
   ....

6 If you want to have a hundred students, you will need at least three teachers. (in order to)
   ....

7 I came to live in the country because I wanted to have trees around me instead of buildings. (so as to)
   ....

8 They had to eat grass and drink melted snow if they wanted to stay alive. (in order to)
   ....

9 He wanted to keep his car out of sight so he left it in the road. (in order to)
   ....

10 I wanted to get to Madrid so I had to travel overnight from Barcelona. (to)
   ....

B Rewrite these sentences to include a negative purpose clause using **to avoid.**

1 We spoke quietly because we didn't want to disturb anyone.
   We spoke quietly to avoid disturbing anyone.

2 She moved carefully because she didn't want to wake the children.
   ....

3 He sat in the furthest corner because he didn't want to be seen.
   ....

4 I gave up sugar and butter because I didn't want to put on weight.
   ....

5 He used both hands because he didn't want to drop anything.
   ....

6 We went over everything carefully because we didn't want to make any mistakes.
   ....

7 She left quietly because she didn't want to make any trouble.
   ....

8 We covered the furniture because we didn't want to get paint all over it.
   ....

▶ **Bank**

Unit 94 Result clauses

Main points

- You use result clauses to talk about the result of an action or situation.
- Result clauses are introduced by conjunctions such as 'so', 'so...(that)', or 'such...(that)'.
- A result clause needs a main clause to make a complete sentence. The result clause always comes after the main clause.

1 You use 'so' and 'so that' to say what the result of an action or situation is.

He speaks very little English, so I talked to him through an interpreter.
My suitcase had become damaged on the journey home, so that the lid would not stay closed.

2 You also use 'so...that' or 'such...that' to talk about the result of an action or situation.

He dressed so quickly that he put his boots on the wrong feet.
She got such a shock that she dropped the bag.

'That' is often omitted.

They were so surprised they didn't try to stop him.
They got such a fright they ran away again.

3 You only use 'such' before a noun, with or without an adjective.

They obeyed him with such willingness that the strike went on for over a year.
Sometimes they say such stupid things that I don't even bother to listen.

If the noun is a singular count noun, you put 'a' or 'an' in front of it.

I was in such a panic that I didn't know it was him.

Note that you only use 'so' before an adjective or an adverb.

It all sounded so crazy that I laughed out loud.
They worked so quickly that there was no time for talking.

4 When you want to say that a situation does not happen because someone or something has an excessive amount of a quality, you use 'too' with an adjective and a 'to'-infinitive. For example, if you say 'They were too tired to walk', you mean that they did not walk because they were too tired.

He was too proud to apologise.
She was too weak to lift me.

You also use 'too' with an adverb and a 'to'-infinitive.

They had been walking too silently to be heard.
She spoke too quickly for me to understand.

5 When you want to say that a situation happens or is possible because someone or something has a sufficient amount of a quality, you use 'enough' after adjectives and adverbs, followed by a 'to'-infinitive.

He was old enough to understand.
I could see well enough to know we were losing.

You normally put 'enough' in front of a noun, not after it.

I don't think I've got enough information to speak confidently.

6 You also use 'and as a result', 'and so', or 'and therefore' to talk about the result of an action or situation.

He had been ill for six months, and as a result had lost his job.
She was having great difficulty getting her car out, and so I had to move my car to let her out.
We have a growing population and therefore we need more and more food.

You can also put 'therefore' after the subject of the clause. For example, you can say 'We have a growing population and we therefore need more food'.

'As a result' and 'therefore' can also be used at the beginning of a separate sentence.

In a group, they are not so frightened. As a result, patients reveal their problems more easily.
He lacks money to invest in improving his tools. Therefore he is poor.

You can also put 'therefore' after the subject of the separate sentence. For example, you can say 'He left us. He therefore loses his share'.

Unit 94 Practice

A Look at these pairs of sentences. Complete one sentence with **so** and the other with **such a.**

1 He was ......*such a*......... fool that no one took any notice of him.

  He was ......*so*............ silly that no one took any notice of him.

2 The room was in .... mess it took two hours to tidy.

  The room was .... untidy it took three hours to sort out.

3 We were .... tired we went straight to bed when we got home.

  We had had .... tiring day that we went straight to bed.

4 It took us .... long to get home that we missed our supper.

  It took us .... long time to get home that we missed our supper.

5 Her throat was .... sore that she could hardly speak.

  She had .... sore throat she could hardly speak.

6 He spoke in .... soft voice we could hardly hear him.

  His voice was .... soft we could hardly hear him.

7 I got .... shock when I heard the news I didn't know what to say.

  I was .... shocked when I got the news I didn't know what to say.

8 He lived .... long way off that we hardly ever saw him.

  He lived .... far away that we hardly ever saw him.

9 He was .... badly injured that they took him straight to the hospital.

  He had suffered .... serious injury that they took him straight to hospital.

10 The children made .... noise we could hardly hear ourselves speak.

  The kids were .... noisy we could hardly hear ourselves speak.

B Rewrite these sentences with **so...that.**

1 The hill was very steep. I had to get off my bike and walk.
  The hill was so steep that I had to get off my bike and walk.

2 Her writing was very small. I could hardly read it. ....

3 The winter was bitterly cold. All the streams were frozen. ....

4 His favourite shoes were very badly worn. He had to throw them away. ....

5 He looked very young. Everyone took him for a student. ....

6 Ken got very excited. He kept jumping up and down. ....

C Now rewrite these sentences with **such...that.**

1 The hill was very steep. I had to get off my bike and walk.
  It was such a steep hill that I had to get off my bike and walk.

2 He was a dreadful liar. Nobody believed anything he said. ....

3 It proved to be a very difficult problem. Nobody could solve it. ....

4 We had a very good time. We didn't want to go home. ....

5 His clothes were very old. They were falling apart. ....

6 The food was very good. We all ate far too much. ....

Unit 95 Contrast clauses

Clauses introduced by: although, in spite of, though

Main points

- You use contrast clauses when you want to make two statements, and one statement makes the other seem surprising.
- Contrast clauses are introduced by conjunctions such as 'although', 'in spite of', or 'though'.
- A contrast clause needs a main clause to make a complete sentence. The contrast clause can come before or after the main clause.

1 When you simply want to contrast two statements, you use 'although', 'though' or 'even though'.

Although he was late, he stopped to buy a sandwich.
Though he has lived for years in London, he writes in German.
I used to love listening to her, even though I could only understand about half of what she said.

Sometimes you use words like 'still', 'nevertheless', or 'just the same' in the main clause to add emphasis to the contrast.

Although I was shocked, I still couldn't blame him.
Although his company is profitable, it nevertheless needs to face up to some serious problems.
Although she hated them, she agreed to help them just the same.

When the subject of the contrast clause and the main clause are the same, you can often omit the subject and the verb 'be' in the contrast clause.

Although poor, we still have our pride. (Although we are poor...)
Though dying of cancer, he painted every day. (Though he was dying of cancer...)

2 Another way of making a contrast is to use 'despite' or 'in spite of', followed by a noun group.

Despite the difference in their ages they were close friends.
In spite of poor health, my father was always cheerful.

You say 'in spite of' but 'despite' without 'of'.

3 You can also use an '-ing' form after 'despite' or 'in spite of'.

Despite working hard, I failed my exams.
Conservative MPs are against tax rises, in spite of wanting lower inflation.

4 You can also use 'despite the fact that' or 'in spite of the fact that', followed by a clause.

Despite the fact that it sounds like science fiction, most of it is technically possible at this moment.
They ignored this order, in spite of the fact that they would probably get into trouble.

It is possible to omit 'that', especially in spoken English.

He insisted on playing, in spite of the fact he had a bad cold.

He insisted on playing, in spite of the fact he had a bad cold.

Unit 95 Practice

A The sentences below all have **though, although,** or **even though.** Use one of these phrases to complete them.

we only arrived just in time	we had no time for lunch	she kept her coat on
he was difficult to understand	you're not as tall as he was	he still wasn't tired
I used to when I was younger	the weather was awful	I really like John

1 Although we were desperately hungry, ...*we had no time for lunch*.................... .

2 We enjoyed our holiday, even though ....

3 .... , even though it was very warm.

4 I don't play the piano now, although ....

5 You look very like your grandfather, although ....

6 Though he hadn't stopped working all day, ...

7 .... , even though his English was very good.

8 .... , although he can be very annoying at times.

9 Although we set off early, ...

B The sentences below all have **in spite of** or **despite.** Use one of the noun groups given to complete them.

the unpopularity of his decision	his recent illness	her fear
the difference in their ages	all his precautions	his injury
the high cost of living	the heavy traffic	the rain

1 The air was fresh and clean in spite of ...*the heavy traffic*................................ .

2 He looked very well in spite of ....

3 Despite .... she did her best to smile bravely.

4 He refused to change his mind despite ....

5 Despite .... they were very close friends.

6 I didn't earn much in Japan in spite of ....

7 In spite of .... his money was still stolen.

8 He continued the race despite ....

9 We still had our picnic in spite of ....

Unit 96 Manner clauses

Main points

- You use manner clauses to talk about how something is done.
- Manner clauses are introduced by conjunctions such as 'as', 'as if', 'as though', or 'like'.
- A manner clause needs a main clause to make a complete sentence. The manner clause always comes after the main clause.

1 When you want to say how someone does something, or how something is done, you use 'as'.

He behaves as he does, because his father was really cruel to him.
The bricks are still made as they were in Roman times.

You often use 'just', 'exactly', or 'precisely' in front of 'as' for emphasis.

It swims on the sea floor just as its ancestors did.
I like the freedom to plan my day exactly as I want.

2 When you want to indicate that the information in the manner clause might not be true, or is definitely not true, you use 'as if' or 'as though'.

She reacted as if she didn't know about the race.
She acts as though she owns the place.

After 'as if' or 'as though', you often use a past tense even when you are talking about the present, to emphasize that the information in the manner clause is not true. In formal English, you use 'were' instead of 'was'.

Presidents can't dispose of companies as if people didn't exist.
She treats him as though he was her own son.
He looked at me as though I were mad.

3 You can also use 'as if' or 'as though' to say how someone or something feels, looks, or sounds.

She felt as if she had a fever.
He looked as if he hadn't slept very much.
Mary sounded as though she had just run all the way.

You can also use 'it looks' and 'it sounds' with 'as if' and 'as though'.

It looks to me as if he wrote down some notes.
It sounds to me as though he's just being awkward.

4 When the subject of the manner clause and the main clause are the same, you can often use a participle in the manner clause and omit the subject and the verb 'be'.

He ran off to the house as if escaping.
He shook his head as though dazzled by his own vision.

You can also use 'as if' or 'as though' with a 'to'-infinitive clause.

As if to remind him, the church clock struck eleven.

5 In informal speech, people often use 'like' instead of 'as if' or 'as' to say how a person feels, looks, or sounds. Some speakers of English think that this use of 'like' is incorrect.

He felt like he'd won the pools.
You look like you've seen a ghost.
You talk just like my father does.

You can also use 'like' in prepositional phrases to say how someone does something.

He was sleeping like a baby.
I behaved like an idiot , and I'm sorry.

6 You also use 'the way (that)', 'in a way (that)', or 'in the way (that)' to talk about how someone does something, or how something is done.

I was never allowed to sing the way I wanted to.
They did it in a way that I had never seen before.
We make it move in the way that we want it to.

7 You can use 'how' in questions and reported questions to talk about the method used to do something, and sometimes to indicate your surprise that it was possible to do it.

'How did he get in?' - 'He broke a window.'
I wondered how he could afford a new car.

Sometimes, you can use 'how' to talk about the manner in which someone does something.

I watched how he did it, then tried to copy him.
Tell me how he reacted when he saw you.

Unit 96 Practice

A Rewrite these sentences with **just as.**

1 I knew he would complain about everything, and he did. / *He complained about everything just as I knew he would.*

2 You said they would arrive late, and they did. / ....

3 Everyone believed he would run away, and he did. / ....

4 Most people thought the play would be a success, and it was. / ....

5 We hoped he would do well at school, and he did. / ....

6 We all thought Mary would win, and she did. / ....

B Rewrite these sentences with **the way.**

1 I don't like people who behave as he does. / *I don't like people who behave the way he does.*

2 They still farm as their grandfathers did. / ....

3 He accepted his punishment as everyone else did. / ....

4 She refused to dress as her colleagues did. / ....

5 He said he would work as the others did if he was paid as they were. / ....

6 They work a five day week as we do. / ....

Now rewrite the first four sentences using **like.**

1   *I don't like people who behave like he does.*

2   ....

3   ....

4   ....

C Rewrite these sentences with **as if** or **as though.**

1 The place sounds very quiet. I think it's deserted. / *The place sounds as though it's deserted.*

2 They look very happy. I think they've got some good news. / ....

3 This milk smells awful. I think it's gone sour. / ....

4 Your engine sounds very bad. I think it's worn out. / ....

5 He looks very angry. I think he's going to make trouble. / ....

6 I feel awful. I think I'm going to be sick. / ....

D Match the questions and answers.

1 I wonder how he got into the house.	a Maybe his father gave him a lift.
2 How do you think he got there so quickly?	b They were at university together.
3 Do you know how she became so wealthy?	c He must have climbed through a window.
4 I wonder how Maria heard the news.	d Perhaps she won the state lottery.
5 Do you know how they met?	e I think her husband told her about it.

Unit 97 Defining relative clauses

Main points

- You use defining relative clauses to say exactly which person or thing you are talking about.
- Defining relative clauses are usually introduced by a relative pronoun such as 'that', 'which', 'who', 'whom', or 'whose'.
- A defining relative clause comes immediately after a noun, and needs a main clause to make a complete sentence.

1 You use defining relative clauses to give information that helps to identify the person or thing you are talking about.

The man who you met yesterday was my brother.
The car which crashed into me belonged to Paul.

When you are talking about people, you use 'that' or 'who' in the relative clause.

He was the man that bought my house.
You are the only person here who knows me.

When you are talking about things, you use 'that' or 'which' in the relative clause.

There was ice cream that Mum had made herself.
I will tell you the first thing which I can remember.

2 'That', 'who', or 'which' can be:

- the subject of the verb in the relative clause

The thing that really surprised me was his attitude
The woman who lives next door is very friendly.
The car which caused the accident drove off.

- the object of the verb in the relative clause

The thing that I really liked about it was its size.
The woman who you met yesterday lives next door.
The car which I wanted to buy was not for sale.

In formal English, 'whom' is used instead of 'who' as the object of the verb in the relative clause.

She was a woman whom I greatly respected.

3 You can leave out 'that', 'who', or 'which' when they are the object of the verb in the relative clause.

The woman you met yesterday lives next door.
The car I wanted to buy was not for sale.
The thing I really liked about it was its size.

WARNING: You cannot leave out 'that', 'who', or 'which' when they are the subject of the verb in the relative clause. For example, you say 'The woman who lives next door is very friendly'. You do not say 'The woman lives next door is very friendly'.

4 A relative pronoun in a relative clause can be the object of a preposition. Usually the preposition goes at the end of the clause.

I wanted to do the job which I'd been training for.
The house that we lived in was huge.

You can often omit a relative pronoun that is the object of a preposition.

Angela was the only person I could talk to.
She's the girl I sang the song for.

The preposition always goes in front of 'whom', and in front of 'which' in formal English.

These are the people to whom Catherine was referring.
He was asking questions to which there were no answers.

5 You use 'whose' in relative clauses to indicate who something belongs to or relates to. You normally use 'whose' for people, not for things.

A child whose mother had left him was crying loudly.
We have only told the people whose work is relevant to this project.

6 You can use 'when', 'where', and 'why' in defining relative clauses after certain nouns. You use 'when' after 'time' or time words such as 'day' or 'year'. You use 'where' after 'place' or place words such as 'room' or 'street'. You use 'why' after 'reason'.

There had been a time when she hated all men.
This is the year when profits should increase.

He showed me the place where they work.
That was the room where I did my homework.

There are several reasons why we can't do that.

Unit 97 Practice

A Complete the following sentences using a relative clause with **that** as the subject.

1 The train leaves at 2.15. / You're too late to catch the train ...*that leaves at 2.15.*.......................

2 Mary has two brothers. One lives in America. / Do you know the one ....
    .... ?

3 Some things were stolen. / Have you got back the things .... ?

4 A man plays James Bond. / What's the name of the man .... ?

5 A woman answered the phone. / The woman .... asked
    me to call back later.

6 A book was left behind on the desk. / The book ....
    belongs to John.

7 Some people live in glass houses. / People .... shouldn't
    throw stones.

Now do the same with these using **that** as the object of the relative clause.

8 I read a book last week. / I really enjoyed the book ...*that I read last week.*........................

9 I met someone on the train. / Someone .... gave me
    some good advice.

10 We took some photographs on holiday. / Have you seen the photographs ....
    .... ?

11 You read things in the newspaper. / You shouldn't believe all the things ....
    ....

12 I left some money on the table. / The money .... seems to
    have disappeared.

13 The Beatles recorded this song in 1966. / This is one of the songs ....
    ....

14 You asked for some information. / We cannot provide the information ....
    ....

B Look at the sentences above. In some the relative pronoun **that** stands for a person and can be replaced by **who**. In others **that** stands for a thing and can be replaced by **which**. Write **who** or **which** in brackets after each sentence to show which word could replace **that.**

1 You're too late to catch the train ...*that leaves at 2.15* . ...*(which)*....

C Complete these sentences by adding **when, where, whose,** or **why.**

1 This is definitely the place ...*where*........... I left it.

2 Do you remember the time .... we got lost?

3 There must be a good reason .... he's late.

4 They are building a hospital on the street .... we live.

5 Peter? Is he the one .... car you borrowed?

6 Can you give me any reason .... I should help you?

7 Carl is the one .... desk is next to mine.

▶ **Bank**

Unit 98 Non-defining relative clauses

Main points

- You use non-defining relative clauses to give extra information about the person or thing you are talking about.
- Non-defining relative clauses must be introduced by a relative pronoun such as 'which', 'who', 'whom', or 'whose'.
- A non-defining relative clause comes immediately after a noun and needs a main clause to make a complete sentence.

1 You use non-defining relative clauses to give extra information about the person or thing you are talking about. The information is not needed to identify that person or thing.

Professor Marvin, who was always early, was there already.

'Who was always early' gives extra information about Professor Marvin. This is a non-defining relative clause, because it is not needed to identify the person you are talking about. We already know that you are talking about Professor Marvin.

Note that in written English, a non-defining relative clause is usually separated from the main clause by a comma, or by two commas.

I went to the cinema with Mary, who I think you met.
British Rail, which has launched an enquiry, said one coach was badly damaged.

2 You always start a non-defining relative clause with a relative pronoun. When you are talking about people, you use 'who'. 'Who' can be the subject or object of a non-defining relative clause.

Heath Robinson, who died in 1944, was a graphic artist and cartoonist.
I was in the same group as Janice, who I like a lot.

In formal English, 'whom' is sometimes used instead of 'who' as the object of a non-defining relative clause.

She was engaged to a sailor, whom she had met at Dartmouth.

3 When you are talking about things, you use 'which' as the subject or object of a non-defining relative clause.

I am teaching at the Selly Oak centre, which is just over the road.
He was a man of considerable inherited wealth, which he ultimately spent on his experiments.

WARNING: You do not normally use 'that' in non-defining relative clauses.

4 You can also use a non-defining relative clause beginning with 'which' to say something about the whole situation described in a main clause.

I never met Brando again, which was a pity.
She was a little tense, which was understandable.
Small computers need only small amounts of power, which means that they will run on small batteries.

5 When you are talking about a group of people or things and then want to say something about only some of them, you can use one of the following expressions:

many of which	none of whom	some of which
many of whom	one of which	some of whom
none of which	one of whom	

They were all friends, many of whom had known each other for years.
He talked about several very interesting people, some of whom he was still in contact with.

6 You can use 'when' and 'where' in non-defining relative clauses after expressions of time or place.

This happened in 1957, when I was still a baby.
She has just come back from a holiday in Crete, where Alex and I went last year.

Unit 98 Practice

A Join the sentences below using **who, whose,** or **which.** Make sure that the relative clause goes next to the word it gives extra information about.

1 I met Jane's father. He works at the university.
   I met Jane's father, who works at the university.

2 Peter is studying French and German. He has never been abroad.
   Peter, who is studying French and German, has never been abroad.

3 You've all met Michael Wood. He is visiting us for a couple of days.
   ....

4 Michael Wood is one of my oldest friends. He has just gone to live in Canada.
   ....

5 We are moving to Manchester. Manchester is in the north-west.
   ....

6 Manchester is in the north-west. It is one of England's fastest growing towns.
   ....

7 I'll be staying with Adrian. His brother is one of my closest friends.
   ....

8 This is Adrian. We stayed in Adrian's house for our holidays.
   ....

B Match the first clauses with the non-defining relative clauses.

1 I had to travel first class, ...   a ... which meant we had to cancel the match next day.
2 It snowed heavily all night, ...   b ... which meant we had to eat out in the evenings.
3 The car uses very little petrol, ...   c ... which really annoyed everyone.
4 He didn't get up until after eight o'clock, ...   d ... which certainly pleased her mother.
5 The food in the hotel was not very good, ...   e ... which means it is quite cheap to run.
6 He kept complaining about everything, ...   f ... which meant he was almost late for work.
7 Both the girls were late, ...   g ... which meant we had to leave without them.
8 Michelle always did very well at school, ...   h ... which was very expensive.

C Rewrite these sentences using phrases with 'of which' or 'of whom'.

1 I got four books for my birthday. I had read three of them before.
   I got four books for my birthday, three of which I had read before.

2 Only two people came to look at the house, and neither of them wanted to buy it.
   ....

3 He had a lot to say about his new computer. None of it interested me very much.
   ....

4 There were some noisy people in the audience. One of them kept interrupting the speaker.
   ....

5 She made all kinds of suggestions. I couldn't understand most of them.
   ....

197

Unit 99 Changing the focus of a sentence

Main points

- You can sometimes change the focus of a sentence by moving part of the sentence to the front.
- You can also change the focus of a sentence by using an expression such as 'The fact is', 'The thing is', or 'The problem is'.
- You can also use impersonal 'it' to change the focus of a sentence.

1 In most affirmative clauses, the subject of the verb comes first.

They went to Australia in 1956.
I've no idea who it was.

However, when you want to emphasize another part of the sentence, you can put that part first instead.

In 1956 they went to Australia.
Who it was I've no idea.

2 One common way of giving emphasis is by placing an adverbial at the beginning of the sentence.

At eight o'clock I went down for my breakfast.
For years I'd had to hide what I was thinking.

Note that after adverbials of place and negative adverbials, you normally put the subject after the verb.

She rang the bell for Sylvia. In came a girl she had not seen before.
On no account must they be let in.

After adverbials of place, you can also put the subject before the verb. You must do so, if the subject is a pronoun.

The door opened and in she came.
He'd chosen Japan, so off we went to the Japanese Embassy.

3 When you want to say that you do not know something, you can put a reported question at the beginning of the sentence.

What I'm going to do next I don't quite know.
How he managed I can't imagine.

4 Another way of focusing on information is to use a structure which introduces what you want to say by using 'the' and a noun, followed by 'is'. The nouns most commonly used in this way are:

answer	point	rule	trouble
conclusion	problem	solution	truth
fact	question	thing	

The second part of the sentence is usually a 'that'-clause or a 'wh'-clause, although it can also be a 'to'-infinitive clause or a noun group.

The problem is that she can't cook.
The thing is, how are we going to get her out?
The solution is to adopt the policy which will produce the greatest benefits.
The answer is planning, timing, and, above all, practical experience.

It is also common to use a whole sentence to introduce information in following sentences. See Unit 100 for more information.

5 You can also focus on information by using impersonal 'it', followed by 'be', a noun group, and a relative clause.
The noun group can be the subject or object of the relative clause.

It was Ted who broke the news to me.
It is usually the other vehicle that suffers most.

It's money that they want.
It was me Dookie wanted.

There are many other ways of focusing on information:

Ted was the one who broke the news to me.
Money is what we want.
What we want is money.

6 You can also focus on the information given in the other parts of a clause, or a whole clause, using impersonal 'it'. In this case, the second part of the sentence is a 'that'-clause.

It was from Francis that she first heard the news.
It was meeting Peter that really started me off on this new line of work.
Perhaps it's because he's a misfit that I get along with him.

Unit 99 Practice

A Rewrite the sentences below starting with the words given.

1 I had scarcely finished speaking when Henry jumped to his feet.

Scarcely *had J finished speaking when Henry jumped to his feet.*

2 I have never heard such a lot of nonsense before.

Never before ....

3 We got in the bus and went off to Brighton.

We got in the bus and off ....

4 She opened the box and a live mouse jumped out.

She opened the box and out ....

5 She did not tell me once that she would be coming round.

Not once ....

6 They not only spent all my money, they also wasted a good deal of my time.

Not only .... , but they also wasted a good deal of my time.

B Match these sentences.

1 I bought a beautiful pair of shoes.   a The fact is I haven't eaten for twenty-four hours.
2 I'm more than hungry, I'm starving.   b The question is can we afford one?
3 Everything's in an awful mess.   c The problem now is how to get into the house.
4 I know we need a new car.   d The only trouble is they were rather too tight.
5 I've forgotten my key.   e The only answer is to start all over again.

C Answer these questions using 'it was' or 'it is' with the words given in brackets.

1 Did Mike take this message for me? (Jenny)

No, it was Jenny who took the message.

2 Did Peter leave the message? (Ken)

No, ...

3 Does he usually come in before nine? (just after nine)

No, ...

4 Did he call in this morning? (this afternoon)

No, ...

5 Did he want to see Helen? (Becky)

No, ...

6 Is he going to call back today? (tomorrow)

No, ...

▶ **Bank**

Unit 100 Cohesion: making connections in speech and writing

Main points

- You can use pronouns and determiners to refer back to something that has already been mentioned.
- You use coordinating conjunctions to link clauses.

1 When you speak or write, you usually need to make some connection with other things that you are saying or writing. The most common way of doing this is by referring back to something that has already been mentioned.

2 One way of referring back to something is to use a personal pronoun such as 'she', 'it', or 'them', or a possessive pronoun such as 'mine' or 'hers'.

My father is fat. He weighs over fifteen stone.
Mary came in. She was a good-looking woman.
'Have you been to London?' — 'Yes, it was very crowded.'
'Have you heard of David Lodge?' — 'Yes, I've just read a novel of his.'
'Would you mind moving your car, please?' — 'It's not mine.'

3 You can also use a specific determiner such as 'the' or 'his' in front of a noun to refer back to something.

A man and a woman were walking up the hill. The man wore shorts, a T-shirt, and basketball sneakers. The woman wore a print dress.

'Thanks,' said Brody. He put the telephone down, turned out the light in his office, and walked out to his car.

4 The demonstratives 'this', 'that', 'these' and 'those' are also used to refer back to a thing or fact that has just been mentioned.

In 1973 he went on a caravan holiday. At the beginning of this holiday he began to experience pain in his chest.
There's a lot of material there. You can use some of that.

5 The following general determiners can also be used to refer back to something.

another	each	every	other
both	either	neither	

Five officials were sacked. Another four were arrested.
There are more than two hundred and fifty species of shark, and every one is different.

6 Another common way of making connections in spoken or written English is by using one of the following coordinating conjunctions:

and	but	nor	or	so	then	yet

Anna had to go into town and she wanted to go to Bride Street.
I asked if I could borrow her bicycle but she refused.
He was only a boy then, yet he was not afraid.

You can use a coordinating conjunction to link clauses that have the same subject. When you link clauses which have the same subject, you do not always need to repeat the subject in the second clause.

She was born in Budapest and raised in Manhattan.
He didn't yell or scream.
When she saw Morris she went pale, then blushed.

7 Most subordinating conjunctions can also be used to link sentences together, rather than to link a subordinate clause with a main clause in the same sentence.

'When will you do it?' — 'When I get time.'
'Can I borrow your car?' — 'So long as you drive carefully.'
We send that by airmail. Therefore it's away on Thursday and our client gets it on Monday.

8 When people are speaking or writing, they often use words that refer back to similar words, or words that refer back to a whole sentence or paragraph.

Everything was quiet. Everywhere there was the silence of the winter night.
'What are you going to do?' — 'That's a good question.'

Unit 100 Practice

A Use these words and phrases to complete the story which follows.

> her   her friend   it   the first student   the first student   the second

A student went to ...*her*............... first lecture at the university, and mentioned this to a friend, another student.

'What was .... about?' asked .... 'I don't know,' ....

.... replied. 'Why not?' asked .... 'Weren't you listening?'

'Of course I was listening,' .... replied, 'but he didn't tell us what it was about'.

Now do the same with this story.

> the customer   the curious bank manager   it   the car park   it   the car   he
> a wealthy man   his bank manager   he   the customer   it   his car

...*A wealthy man*.................. was told by .... that he owed the

bank £100 and .... would have to pay 12% interest per year. ....

.... agreed to pay, and said he would leave .... , a

Rolls Royce, as security. He then drove .... round to the bank, and left

.... in the car park.

A month later, ... returned to collect the car. ....

.... asked why .... had insisted on leaving ....

.... in ....

'Where else could I park .... for a month, for only £1?' replied ....

....

B Rearrange these clauses to tell a story.

1 the psychiatrist asked him what his problem was
2 'Well, doctor, I don't really know what's wrong with me.'
3 one day a man went to see a psychiatrist
4 and the patient explained
5 'Can you tell me how long you've had this trouble?'
6 'My main problem is, I always forget what I've said as soon as I've said it.'
7 'How long I've had what trouble?' replied the patient
8 'I see,' said the doctor

C Now rearrange these clauses to tell a story.

1 'Would you like it with or without cream?' she asked
2 The waitress asked him if he would take coffee
3 The waitress went off, but soon came back.
4 'but there's no more cream.
5 After a long wait, the waitress came back again.
6 'Without cream,' replied the customer.
7 A man was just finishing his lunch in a restaurant.
8 Would you mind having it without milk?'
9 and the customer replied that he would.
10 'I'm sorry, sir,' she said,

Appendix: Verb forms

Regular verbs have four forms: the base form, the third person singular form of the present simple, the '-ing' form or present participle, and the '-ed' form used for the past simple and for the past participle. The base form is used in the present tense, and for the imperative, and in the 'to'-infinitive. The base form is always given first in dictionaries and is the form used in the lists in this grammar.

Regular verbs

	base form	third person singular of present simple	'-ing' form or present participle	'-ed'form or past participle	EXCEPTIONS
		add '-s'	add '-ing'	add '-ed'	
	join	joins	joining	joined	
ending in '-sh' '-ch' '-ss' '-x' '-z' '-o'	finish reach pass mix buzz echo	add '-es' finishes reaches passes mixes buzzes echoes	finishing reaching passing mixing buzzing echoing	finished reached passed mixed buzzed echoed	
ending in '-e'	dance	dances	omit '-e' before adding '-ing' or '-ed' dancing	danced	age, agree, disagree, dye, free, knee, referee, singe, tiptoe
ending in '-ie'	tie	ties	change '-ie' to '-y' before adding '-ing tying	tied	
ending in consonant + '-y'	cry	change '-y' to '-ies' cries	crying	change '-y' to '-ied' cried	
one syllable ending in single vowel + consonant	dip	dips	double final consonant before adding '-ing' or '-ed' dipping	dipped	not '-w', '-x', '-y': rowing, boxing playing
two syllables ending in single vowel + '-l'	travel	travels	travelling	travelled	optional in American English: traveling, traveled
the following verbs: equip, handicap, hiccup, kidnap, program, refer, worship	equip	equips	equipping	equipped	optional in American English for: handicap, hiccup, kidnap, program, worship

Regular/irregular verbs

Irregular verbs do not add '-ed' for the past form, and some have different forms for the past simple and past participle. Some verbs have two forms for the past participle.

base form	past simple	past participle
mow	mowed	mowed, mown
prove	proved	proved, proven
swell	swelled	swelled, swollen

Some verbs have two forms for the past simple and two forms for the past participle.
If there is a regular form, it is given first, but it may not be the most common one.

base form	past simple	past participle	base form	past simple	past participle
bid	bid, bade	bid, bidden	lean	leaned, leant	leaned, leant
lie	lied, lay	lied, lain	leap	leaped, leapt	leaped, leapt
wake	waked woke	waked, woken	light	lighted, lit	lighted, lit
weave	weaved, wove	weaved, woven	smell	smelled, smelt	smelled, smelt
burn	burned, burnt	burned, burnt	speed	speeded, sped	speeded, sped
bust	busted, bust	busted, bust	spell	spelled, spelt	spelled, spelt
dream	dreamed, dreamt	dreamed, dreamt	spill	spilled, spilt	spilled, spilt
dwell	dwelled, dwelt	dwelled, dwelt	spoil	spoiled, spoilt	spoiled, spoilt
hang	hanged, hung	hanged, hung	wet	wetted, wet	wetted, wet
kneel	kneeled, knelt	kneeled, knelt			

Note that 'gotten' is sometimes used instead of 'got as the past participle of 'get' in American English. With a few verbs, different forms are used in different meanings. For example, the past form and the past participle of the verb 'hang' is normally 'hung'. However, 'hanged' is used when it means 'executed by hanging'.
Below is a list of irregular verbs which have one form for the past simple and another form for the past participle.

Irregular verbs

base form	past simple	past participle	base form	past simple	past participle	base form	past simple	past participle
arise	arose	arisen	freeze	froze	frozen	shut	shut	shut
awake	awoke	awoken	get	got	got	sing	sang	sung
bear	bore	borne	give	gave	given	sink	sank	sunk
beat	beat	beaten	go	went	gone	sit	sat	sat
become	became	become	grind	ground	ground	slay	slew	slain
begin	began	begun	grow	grew	grown	sleep	slept	slept
bend	bent	bent	hear	heard	heard	slide	slid	slid
bet	bet	bet	hide	hid	hidden	sling	slung	slung
bind	bound	bound	hit	hit	hit	slink	slink	slunk
bite	bit	bitten	hold	held	held	sow	sowed	sown
bleed	bled	bled	hurt	hurt	hurt	speak	spoke	spoken
blow	blew	blown	keep	kept	kept	spend	spend	spent
break	broke	broken	know	knew	known	spin	spun	spun
breed	bred	bred	lay	laid	laid	spread	spread	spread
bring	brought	brought	lead	led	led	spring	sprang	sprung
build	built	built	leave	left	left	stand	stood	stood
burst	burst	burst	lend	lent	lent	steal	stole	stolen
buy	bought	bought	let	let	let	stick	stuck	stuck
cast	cast	cast	lose	lost	lost	sting	stung	stung
catch	caught	caught	make	made	made	stink	stank	stunk
choose	chose	chosen	mean	meant	meant	strew	strewed	strewn
cling	clung	clung	meet	met	met	stride	strode	stridden
come	came	come	pay	paid	paid	strike	struck	struck
cost	cost	cost	put	put	put	string	strung	strung
creep	crept	crept	quit	quit	quit	strive	strove	striven
cut	cut	cut	read	read	read	swear	swore	sworn
deal	dealt	dealt	rend	rent	rent	sweep	swept	swept
dig	dug	dug	ride	rode	ridden	swim	swam	swum
drew	drew	drawn	ring	rang	rung	swing	swung	swung
drink	drank	drunk	rise	rose	risen	take	took	taken
drive	drove	driven	run	ran	run	teach	taught	taught
eat	ate	eaten	saw	sawed	sawn	tear	tore	torn
fall	fell	fallen	say	said	said	tell	told	told
feed	fed	fed	see	saw	seen	think	thought	thought
feel	felt	felt	seek	sought	sought	throw	threw	thrown
fight	fought	fought	sell	sold	sold	thrust	thrust	thrust
find	found	found	send	sent	sent	tread	trod	trodden
flee	fled	fled	set	set	set	understand	understood	understood
fling	flung	flung	sew	sewed	sewn	wear	wore	worn
fly	flew	flown	shake	shook	shaken	weep	wept	wept
forbear	forbore	forborne	shed	shed	shed	win	won	won
forbid	forbade	forbidden	shine	shone	shone	wind	wound	wound
forget	forgot	forgotten	shoe	shod	shod	wring	wrung	wrung
forgive	forgave	forgiven	shoot	shot	shot	write	wrote	written
forsake	forsook	forsaken	show	showed	shown			
forswear	forswear	forsworn	shrink	shrank	shrunk			

Bank of further exercises

The noun group

1 Plural nouns (see Unit 5 paragraph 3)

Choose the correct phrase to answer each of the questions below.

What might you use …

1	… to cut paper?	a	… a pair of binoculars.
2	… if you can't see very well?	b	… a pair of pincers.
3	… when you go to bed?	c	… a pair of pyjamas.
4	… to see something a long way off?	d	… a pair of scissors.
5	… instead of stockings?	e	… a pair of shorts.
6	… to pull nails out of a piece of wood?	f	… a pair of spectacles.
7	… if you were going jogging?	g	… a pair of sunglasses.
8	… if the sun is shining very brightly?	h	… a pair of tights.

2 Reflexive pronouns (see Unit 9 paragraph 6)

Complete these sentences using a suitable tense of the verb in brackets and a reflexive pronoun for emphasis.

1 Where did you buy those beautiful flowers?

We didn't buy them. We … *grew them ourselves.* ………… (grow)

2 It must have been pretty expensive having the house decorated.

No it was very cheap. We …………………………………… . (do)

3 Your hair looks great. Who did it for you?

Thank you. Actually I …………………………………… . (cut)

4 Do you have the newspaper delivered on Sundays?

No, I usually go and …………………………………… . (get)

5 That bag looks awfully heavy. Let me take it for you.

It's okay thanks. I can …………………………………… . (carry)

6 Are you going to send a taxi to collect your wife from the airport?

No. I always like to (meet) …………………………………… .

3 Indefinite pronouns (see Unit 10 paragraph 2)

Here is a riddle. First complete it by putting in the indefinite pronouns, then see if you can understand the story.

This is a story about four people called Everybody, Somebody, Nobody, and Anybody. There was an important job to be done and … *Everybody* ………… was asked to do it. But ……………………………… knew that ……………………could do it and thought that ……………………………… really ought to do it. As it turned out ……………………………… did it and ……………………………… was very cross because ……………………………… had done what ……………………………… could have done and ……………………………… should have done.

4 Determiners (see Units 11-18)

Complete these sentences by putting the determiner in the right place.

1 I'll lend you   *my*   new bycicle if you like. (my)
2 Children have left school now. (both)
3 Could you carry bag for me? (this)
4 I'd like to buy brown shoes please. (those)
5 I have to go to bank this afternoon. (the)
6 They live in big new house. (a)
7 I'm afraid I haven't got money left. (much)
8 I'd like to buy fruit. (some)
9 People enjoy going to the theatre. (most)
10 You can buy soap at supermarket. (any)

5 'a, an, the' (see Units 12-14)

Look at this passage. If you see a noun phrase with a singular count noun but no determiner, put in **a** or **an.**
Psychiatrist greeting new patient noticed that she was carrying live duck under her arm. He invited her to take seat and asked how he could help her. 'Oh, I don't need any help, thank you doctor,' she replied. 'My husband is the one who has problem. He thinks he's duck.'

This time put in either **a, an,** or **the.**

Young man was out for a walk in large city when he met penguin. Penguin seemed to like him and began to follow him. Young man didn't know what to do so he went up to policeman to ask for advice. 'Take it to zoo,' said policeman.

Next day policeman saw same young man again still followed by penguin. 'What are you doing with that penguin?' he asked. 'I told you to take it to zoo.' 'Yes,' said young man, 'we went to zoo yesterday. Today we are going to museum.'

6 'all of' (see Unit 15 paragraph 4)

Answer these questions using a phrase with **all of** and a pronoun.

1 How many of you saw the thief? / …*All of us.*…………………………………………………………………
2 How many students passed the exam? / ………………………………………………………………………
3 How much milk have you drunk? / …………………………………………………………………………………
4 How many of us have won a prize? / ……………………………………………………………………………
5 How many of these books have you read? / …………………………………………………………………

7 'all, none, both, neither' (see Units 15-16)

Look at the shapes. Make true sentences using **all of the, all the, none of the, both of the, both the** or **neither of the.**

1 …*None of the*………… large triangles is white.
2 ……………………… big triangles are black.
3 ……………………… big squares are white.
4 ……………………… big squares are black.
5 ……………………… large circles are black.
6 ……………………… circles are green.

8 Position of adjectives (see Unit 19 paragraph 6)

Complete these sentences using adjectives describing size or age.

1 He's tiny. He's only about four feet ....*tall*............... .

2 You can drive a car when you're seventeen years ....

3 The sea was about thirty feet .... at this point.

4 The wall was over ten feet ....

5 The lake is ten miles .... and two miles ....

What about this sentence?

6 When the baby was born it was over four kilos ....

9 Adjectives ending in '-ing' (see Unit 23 paragraphs 1,2,4)

Complete each of the following dialogues with one of the '-ing' adjectives given below.

alarming   amazing   exhausting   fascinating   terrifying   thrilling

1 A: It was surprising, wasn't it? / B: Yes, absolutely ...*amazing*........................ .

2 A: Was it interesting? / B: Yes, it was ....

3 A: Did you find it frightening? / B: Yes, it was ....

4 A: Was it tiring? / B: Tiring? It was ....

5 A: It was worrying, wasn't it? / B: Yes, very ....

6 A: Was it an exciting game? / B: Yes, it was ....

10 Comparative adjectives (see Unit 25 paragraph 4)

Read the following passage and then make six correct sentences using the table below.

John is twenty years old. He's nearly two metres tall, and weighs nearly one hundred kilos. Mary is twenty-two. She's only one metre sixty, and weighs less than fifty kilos. Peter is forty-five. He's one metre ninety-five, and weighs one hundred and eighty kilos.

John Mary Peter	is	far (very) much a lot a good deal slightly a bit a little	older taller heavier	than	John. Mary. Peter.

1 *Peter is a lot older than John.*
2 ....
3 ....
4 ....
5 ....
6 ....

11 Superlative adjectives (see Unit 25 paragraph 6)

Complete the following sentences using superlative adjectives in front of the nouns.

1 Everest is ...*the highest mountain*.......... in the world. (high mountain)

2 The Pacific is .... (big ocean)

3 China is .... in the world. (populated country)

4 Oxford is .... in Britain. (old university)

5 The Nile is .... in Africa. (long river)

6 The Amazon is .... in the world. (long river)

12 Comparative adjectives and other ways of comparing (see Units 25-26)

Look at the pictures and complete these sentences about John, Mike, and Peter.

1 ....*John*............ is taller than ....*Mike*............

and ....*Peter*.......... .

2 .... is taller than .... ,

but he isn't as tall as ....

3 .... is older than .... ,

but he isn't as old as ....

4 .... is younger than .... ,

but he isn't as young as ....

5 .... is younger than ....

and ....

6 .... is nearly as old as ....

7 .... is nearly as tall as ....

8 .... is much taller than ....

John 18   Mike 19   Peter 15

13 Possession (see Unit 27)

Rewrite these sentences using **a...of** instead of **one of.**

1 Neil is one of my friends. / ...*Neil is a friend of mine.*...........................

2 That book is one of Mary's favourites. / ....

3 Mr White is one of my father's colleagues. / ....

4 Angela is one of her classmates. / ....

5 I'm one of their employees. / ....

6 Jack is one of your neighbours. / ....

14 Nouns with prepositions (see Unit 28 paragraph 3)

Complete these sentences by changing the clause in brackets into a noun phrase with **of.** Use these nouns.

arrival behaviour death departure invasion theft

1 Trouble was prevented by ...*the sudden arrival of the police*........... . (the police suddenly

arrived)

2 The meeting was postponed following .... (the chairman

died unexpectedly)

3 British Rail apologized for .... (the train departed late)

4 She rang the police to report .... (her jewellery had

been stolen)

5 Mrs Green apologized for .... (the children behaved

dreadfully)

6 War was inevitable after .... (the island was invaded)

15 Nouns with 'to'-infinitive clauses (see Unit 29 paragraph 8)

Use the following nouns to complete the sentences below.

| decision inability need opportunity refusal willingness attempt order |

1 I was surprised that he couldn't understand.

I was surprised at his ...*inability*........................... to understand.

2 We were angry when he made up his mind to withdraw from the competition.

We were angry at his .... to withdraw from the competition.

3 John's father arranged for him to work abroad.

John's father gave him the .... to work abroad.

4 It is not necessary to send the books by air mail.

There is no .... to send the books by air mail.

5 We were disappointed when she said she wouldn't help.

We were disappointed at her .... to help.

6 We thanked the headmaster when he offered to help.

We thanked the headmaster for his .... to help.

7 He failed by two seconds when he tried to break the record.

He failed by two seconds in his .... to break the record.

8 The soldiers did not obey when they were told to advance.

The soldiers did not obey the .... to advance.

16 Review of the noun group (see Units 4-30)

Complete the passages below by choosing a determiner from the brackets, or leaving a blank if a
determiner is not needed.

1 When I was (- / a / the) .... young man (a / the / my) .... father gave me (- / an / some)
.... advice. He told me that (- / an / the) .... honesty is always (- / a / the) ....
best policy. It was (- / a / the) .... best advice I have ever had.

2 I recently bought (- / a / the) .... lot of (- / an / the) .... electronic equipment. (It was /
They were) .... very expensive.

3 He is very popular. He has (lot of / many of / a lot of) .... friends and (few / a few / some) ....
.... enemies.

4 When we were on holiday in (- / the) .... Iran we visited (- / the) .... Isfahan and
stayed in (- / a-the) .... Shah Abbas Hotel near (- / a / the) .... centre of town.

5 Because the Hodja was believed to be (- / a / the) .... wisest man in (- / a / the) ....
country, many people used to go and ask him (- / the) .... difficult questions. One day, a man
asked him which was more useful, (- / a / the) .... sun or (- / a / the) .... moon. The
Hodja thought for (a few / few / the few) .... minutes then said '(- / A / The) .... moon
is more useful because (- / a / the) .... sun only shines during (- / a / the) .... day
when it is light, but (- / a / the) .... moon shines at (- / a / the) .... night when it is
dark.'

17 Review of the noun group (see Units 4-30)

Use one of the determiners below to complete the sentences which follow.

> all   both   either   either   one   no

1 A: Have you seen Jane or Richard? They were .... here a minute ago.

   B: No, I haven't seen .... of them.

   C: No. .... of them was here when I arrived.

2 A: Six of us went to see the film, but it was dreadful. .... of us enjoyed it very much. We were .... very disappointed. B: We were planning to see it tomorrow, but we have .... free time.

18 Review of the noun group (see Units 4-30)

Choose one of the adjectives in brackets to complete each of the following sentences.

1 I was so ...._bored_........... I could hardly stay awake. (bored / boring)

2 I think it's very .... the way people keep complaining about everything. (annoyed / annoying)

3 The children did really well. I thought they were .... (amazed / amazing)

4 The children behaved very badly. I was very .... (embarrassed / embarrassing)

5 I am .... I was right. (convinced / convincing)

6 The boy .... the car looked about twelve years old. (driven / driving)

19 Review of the noun group (see Units 4-30)

Rewrite these sentences using the comparative of the adjectives in brackets.

1 I prefer my new school to the one I went to before. (good)
   My new school is better than the one I went to before. ....

2 I prefer staying in a hotel to camping. (comfortable)
   ....

3 I prefer eating out to cooking for myself. (easy)
   ....

4 I prefer living in the country to living in a town. (peaceful)
   ....

5 I prefer cycling to driving. (healthy)
   ....

Adverbials

20 Position of adverbials (see Unit 31 paragraph 3)

Rewrite these sentences with the adverbials in the normal place at the end of the clause.

1 Quickly I hid the bag under the table. / ...._I hid the bag quickly under the table._ ....

2 On Saturday morning our holiday began. / ....

3 Unhappily she shook her head. / ....

4 Slowly and sadly he walked back home. / ....

5 Before going home he locked up the office. / ....

6 In the box there was a gold ring. / ....

7 Quietly he whispered his name. / ....

8 Early in the morning she went for a jog. / ....

9 Too late I tried to stop him. / ....

10 At exactly seven o'clock the film began. / ....

21 Adverbials of time (see Unit 33 paragraphs 3-5)

Complete the following sets of sentences using **ago, for,** or **since** once each.

1 I'll be staying in Newcastle ...*for*........ about a couple of weeks.

I've been waiting here ...*since*.... five o'clock.

I got here about an hour ...*ago*........ .

2 George had already worked on the farm .... over five years.

He had started work there five years ....

He had been in charge .... summer 1988.

3 It was about ten years .... that I started learning English.

I have been learning English .... I started secondary school.

I studied English .... five years at school.

4 Judith has lived with us ever .... she was seven.

She has been with us .... nearly five years now.

She first came to live with us about five years ....

5 .... October the weather has been awful.

Fortunately we had our holiday months ....

We went to Italy .... ten days.

6 I first met Jan at a party about six months ....

I have known Jan .... just over six months.

I have known Jan .... we met at your Christmas party.

7 We will be at home .... the next hour or so.

I got home about ten minutes ....

I've been at home .... just before five.

8 Ten years .... very few people knew much about computers.

My kids have been using a home computer .... the last five years.

The youngest one has been using a computer .... the age of four.

22 Adverbials of degree (see Unit 36 paragraph 3)

Use these phrases, which consist of adverbs of degree that are modifying adjectives, to complete the sentences.

really angry   awfully good   very happy   extremely intelligent   pretty tired

1 You must be ...*pretty tired*............ . You've been working all day.

2 I'm .... I'm really enjoying myself.

3 His new book is .... I think it's one of his best.

4 The children behaved badly. Finally their father got .... with them.

5 Mary may seem a bit slow when you first meet her, but she's actually ....

23 Adverbials of degree (see Unit 36 paragraph 7)

Match the questions with the answers, which contain emphasizing adverbs.

1 Were you very frightened?   a Yes. We were absolutely furious.
2 Was it a very exciting match?   b It was really thrilling.
3 Did she get very good exam results?   c He's quite brilliant.
4 Is he a very good scientist?   d It was quite fascinating.
5 Is it very big?   e He's absolutely awful.
6 Were you very angry?   f Yes. We were completely terrified.
7 Was it a very interesting play?   g Yes. They were absolutely brilliant.
8 Were her parents very pleased?   h Yes. They were absolutely delighted.
9 Is he a very bad student?   i Yes. It's absolutely enormous.

24 Prepositions of place (see Unit 38)

Fill the gaps in these paragraphs using **at, in,** or **on.**

1 Liz lives ...*in*......... Harton. She has a flat .... the third floor of Conway House, ... Church Street. It's on the left, opposite the bank, as you drive along the road towards the traffic lights .... the end of the street.

2 There's a picture .... the wall .... the top of the stairs and Liz's flat is on the left with her name .... the door.

3 There was a good film .... the Odeon last week. The Odeon is .... the corner of the High Street. I met Judy .... the entrance to the cinema after work, but I was rather late so we didn't get very good seats. We had to sit .... the front row, right .... the end on the left.

25 Review of adverbials (see Units 31-39)

Choose the adjective or adverb from the brackets to complete these sentences.

1 Be as ....*quick*............ as you can. (quick / quickly)
2 Fortunately, he was driving very .... at the time of the accident. (slow / slowly)
3 Try to be .... with that vase. It's very valuable. (careful / carefully)
4 We lived very .... abroad for nearly five years. (happy / happily)
5 How are you? I hope you're .... (good / well)
6 Where's Henry nowadays? I haven't seen him .... (late / lately)
7 Don't worry about Francis. She always arrives .... (late / lately)
8 You'll find it if you look .... enough. (hard / hardly)

26 Review of adverbials (see Units 31-39)

Choose one of the prepositions in brackets to fill each gap in the sentence, or leave the gap empty if you think a preposition is not needed.

1 I start work (- / in / on / at) .... eight o'clock (- / in / on / at) .... the morning (- / in / on / at) .... every day, except (in / on / at / until) .... Saturday, when I don't start (in / on / at / until) .... nine thirty.

2 It's nearly two o'clock and we have had nothing to eat (at / for / since / until) .... six o'clock (- / in / on / at) .... this morning.

3 I asked him (- / in / on / at) .... yesterday, and he said the car will be ready (- / since / until / by) .... lunchtime (in / on / at) .... Friday.

4 The last time I saw Jan was (in / on / at / for) .... Christmas three years (before / since / ago / last) .... We were at a party together (- / in / on / at) .... Christmas Eve.

5 George worked in France (- / for / since / until) .... three months (- / during / for / at) .... the summer, but he's been back home (- / for / since / until) .... October.

6 I will be (- / in / at / to) .... abroad (- / in / from / until) .... October (- / at / to / since) .... Christmas.

7 Have you finished your essay (still / any more / yet / since) .... , or are you (still / yet / already / any more) .... working on it?

8 Jack hasn't phoned (still / since / until / yet) .... last month. Perhaps he (still / yet / now / already) .... isn't back from his holidays.

9 A: We have been waiting (until / since / for / already) .... more than an hour. Do you think they are coming? B: I don't know. Perhaps they have (just / already / since / now) .... left.

10 Look at the time. It's (already / until / before / yet) .... eight o'clock and we haven't even started (already / until / any more / yet) ....

27 Review of adverbials (see Units 31-39)

Use one of the following prepositions to fill each of the gaps below. You may use the same word more than once.

| above at by in off on opposite out of to |

1 Do you usuàlly go to school .... bus or .... your bike?

2 John's not .... home. He went out .... work an hour ago.

3 There was a big picture .... the wall just .... the fireplace.

4 They live .... the big house on the left .... the end of our street.

5 He was so badly injured he couldn't get .... the car by himself.

6 Meet me .... the entrance .... your way in.

7 Get .... the bus .... the end of the High Street, and you'll see my office just .... the bus stop.

8 He drove me to the hospital .... his car.

The verb group

28 Past simple and past perfect (see Unit 42 paragraphs 2,3)

Look at this narrative of a day at school.

I left home early and finished my homework at school. I had a hard morning, with tests in maths and English, then at lunchtime I got a surprise.

Now the narrative starts at lunchtime and looks back. What happens to the tenses of the verbs?

It was lunchtime and I was tired. I ....*had left*........ home early and .... my homework at school. I .... a hard morning, with tests in maths and English. Then I got a surprise.

Now complete the following narrative, using the past simple or past perfect of the verbs given.

| get | ask | choose | tell | be | be | rush | happen |

I ...*got*............ a message from the headmaster. Earlier in the week, the local TV station .... him to send a student to appear in a quiz show. After talking to several teachers, he .... me. He .... me I .... going to represent the school. I .... so excited, I .... home as fast as I could to tell my parents what ....

29 Past continuous (see Unit 43 paragraph 3)

Complete this past tense narrative, using each of the following verbs once.

| work | try | live | share |

Angela ...*was working*................ in a restaurant. She had just left school and she .... to save some money before going to university. She .... in a little village in the country where she .... a cottage with some friends.

30 Continuous tenses (see Unit 43)

Use one of the following verbs in a continuous tense to complete each of the sentences below. You may use each verb more than once.

| change | get | grow up | improve | increase |

1 Jean has been very ill but she ...*is getting*...................... better now.
2 The world's population .... by 100% every year.
3 My French isn't very good but it ....
4 Scientists believe that the world's climate .... It .... warmer every year.
5 John is a good player and he .... all the time.
6 The weather had been dreadful that year, and it .... worse.
7 My father has retired from his job now. He .... old.
8 The children .... quickly now that they have reached their teens.
9 Unemployment is still high in Britain but things .... slowly.
10 Office work .... rapidly with the introduction of computers.

31 Talking about the past (see Unit 46)

Use these verbs and verb groups to complete the paragraph below.

agreed	offered	didn't ask	used to play	had never played
asked	felt	used to go	used to go	would practise
had had	wanted	would spend	was playing	couldn't play

When I was a boy, I ...*wanted*................ to be a jazz musician. I .... the drums. I .... for hours every evening, and I .... almost every weekend practising too. I .... to my local jazz club every week to listen. One night a group called

213

The Rollers .... there. Unfortunately, their drummer .... an accident on his way to the club, so he .... They .... me to take his place, and of course I .... It was awful. I .... that I ....
.... so badly before. After that, I still .... to the club, but I never
.... to play again, and they certainly .... me.

32 Reporting the past (see Unit 47)

Here is part of a story told in the present tense.

> Late that night, as I am sitting on my bed reading, there is a knock on my door. It turns out to be the daughter of the hotel manager. He has told her I am English, and she asks if I will help her do a translation that she's been set for homework.

Imagine you are telling the author's story to someone else. Use the appropriate tense of one the following verbs to complete the story below.

sit knock tell be want

As Eric ...*sat*.......................... on his bed reading, the hotel manager's daughter ....
...... on the door. Her father .... her that Eric .... English, and she
.... him to help her with the translation she .... set for homework.

33 Reporting the past (see Unit 47)

Below there are reports of some famous sayings. Decide whether they contain advice, or things that are still true. Then complete the original sayings by putting the verbs in brackets into the right tenses.

1. Anatole France said that you should never lend books out, because no one ever returns them. He said the only books in his library were the ones that other folk had lent him.
   Never lend books, because no one ever ...*returns*............................ them. The only books I
   ...*have*.......................... in my library are books that other people ...*have lent*.....................
   me. (return) (have) (lend)

2. Someone once defined a banker as a man who lends you an umbrella when the weather's good, and takes it away when it starts to rain.
   A banker is a man who .... you an umbrella when the weather ....
   .... fine and .... it away from you when it ....
   .... (lend) (be) (take) (rain)

3. Somerset Maugham said that if you want to eat well in England, you should eat three breakfasts. That was what he always did, and he had had no cause to regret it.
   If you .... to eat well in England, eat three breakfasts. That's what I always
   .... , and I .... no cause to regret it. (want) (do)
   (have)

34 Questions (see Unit 50)

Rearrange these phrases to make questions.

1. your homework / finished / yet / have you? / ...*Have you finished your homework yet?*..........
2. French / how well / speak / do you? / ....
3. next Friday / will you / at school / be? / ....

4 who / next to you / in class / sits? / ....

5 who / next to / do you / in class / sit? / ....

35 'Wh-'words (see Unit 51)

Match the questions and answers.

1 What's the longest word in the dictionary?

2 Where does Thursday come before Wednesday?

3 Which is easier to spell, seventeen or eighteen?

4 What begins with a 't', ends with a 't', and has 't' in it?

5 Why is an island like the letter 't'?

6 Why is the letter 'e' lazy?

7 How should you dress on a cold day?

8 Why is there plenty of food in the desert?

a Because of all the sandwiches (sand which is) there.

b In a dictionary.

c A teapot.

d Because it's always in bed.

e Smiles - because it's a mile from beginning to end.

f Seventeen because it's spelt with more ease. (more 'e's)

g Because it's in the middle of water.

h As quickly as possible.

36 Question tags (see Unit 53)

Use question tags to complete these sentences.

1 Everyone was there, ...*weren't they?*......

2 Nobody was watching, ... ?

3 Everybody knew, ... ?

4 Nothing really matters, ... ?

5 Something funny happened, ... ?

6 There was nobody there, ... ?

7 There's no time to spare, ... ?

8 Nobody understands, ... ?

9 Everything is all right, ... ?

10 Everyone has arrived, ... ?

37 Indirect questions (see Unit 54)

Make these questions into indirect questions. Do each one first in the present and then in the past.

1 What time will Helen be home?

He wants to know ...*what time Helen will be home.*......................

He wanted to know ...*what time Helen would be home.*.........................

2 Does Joe still live in Liverpool?

She would like to know ....

She asked me ....

3 Have you mended the roof?

They are asking ....

They wanted to know ....

4 When will Harry be moving to Manchester?

She wants to know ....

She asked ....

5 What time does the concert finish?

They would like to know ....

They wanted to know ....

6 Will Peggy be coming too?

Everyone keeps asking ....

Everyone kept asking ....

7 Will we have to speak English all the time?

They want to know ....

They wanted to know ....

8 Who did you speak to on the phone?

She is asking me ....

She asked me ....

38 The imperative (see Unit 56)

Make these polite requests more emphatic by using **do.**

1 Would you like to come in and take a seat? / *Do come in and take a seat.*

2 Why don't you come and see us at the weekend? / ....

3 It would be nice if you could bring the children too. / ....

4 Would you like to have some more tea? / ....

5 Could you write to me when you get home? / ....

Now use **do** to make these into emphatic orders.

6 You should stop making so much noise. / *Do stop making so much noise.*

7 You ought to listen carefully. / ....

8 You should be more careful. / ....

9 Please be quiet while I'm talking. / ....

10 Sit down and behave yourself. / ....

39 Statements, questions, and commands (see Units 50-58)

Mark these sentences affirmative (A), interrogative (?) or imperative (!).

1 Don't look now. ...!............

2 What time did you have dinner. ....

3 I think it's time to go. ....

4 Ask your father to give you the answer. ....

5 Who's that knocking on the door. ....

6 Nobody knows what to do. ....

7 Please try to find out where to go. ....

8 Can you find out where to go. ....

9 You should find out where to go. ....

40 Could - possibility (see Unit 61 paragraph 2)

Complete these sentences using **could.**

1 If you don't take a map, you might easily get lost.

Without a map, *you could get lost.*

2 Even though it sounds unlikely, it may be true.

It sounds unlikely, but ....

3 If you aren't careful, you might cut yourself.

Be careful. ....

4 If they are lucky, they might easily win.

With a bit of luck, ...

5 If she gets the job, she might earn as much as £50,000 a year.

She ....

6 It's a dangerous bend. It is likely to cause a serious accident.

That bend is really dangerous. ....

7 It's possible to get there in time, if you take a taxi.

If you take a taxi, ...

8 The telephone's ringing. Perhaps it's for you.

There's the telephone. ....

9 The police said the man was armed and that he might be dangerous.

It was reported that the man was armed and ....

10 There will be rain which might turn to snow on high ground.

There is likely to be rain, ...

41 Could have, couldn't have -possibility (see Unit 61 paragraph 3)

Which of these things **could** you **have done** if you had lived a hundred years ago? Which things **couldn't** you **have done?** Write six sentences like this one.

A hundred years ago I could have ridden a horse, but I couldn't have flown in an ...
aeroplane. ....

flown in an aeroplane	gone to the cinema	learnt English
listened to Beethoven	listened to The Beatles	played chess
played computer games	read Ernest Hemingway	read Shakespeare
ridden a horse	travelled by train	watched television

42 Couldn't, couldn't have - possibility (see Unit 61 paragraph 7)

Match the sentences with the comments, which contain **couldn't** or **couldn't have** and a comparative adjective.

1 I'm absolutely delighted.   a She couldn't have felt better.

2 He was terrified.   b He couldn't have been more frightened.

3 She was as fit as a fiddle.   c I couldn't feel more tired.

4 I'm exhausted.   d I couldn't be happier.

5 She was thrilled to bits.   e He couldn't have been worse.

6 He was desperately ill.   f She couldn't have been more excited.

43 Must, must have - probability and certainty (see Unit 62 paragraphs 4,5)

Rewrite the parts of the sentence in bold, using either **must** or **must have.**

1 Our house is in Bradford Road too. **We probably live very close to you.**
    We must live very close to you. ....

2 His car's not in the garage. **I suppose he has taken it to work.**
    He must have taken it to work. ....

3 Peter has worked here for ages. **I'm sure he knows the answer.**

....

4 The children aren't at home. **They've probably left for school.**

....

5 It's a very well known book. **I'm sure you've read it.**

....

6 It's dreadfully busy. **I suppose this is the rush hour.**

....

44 Can, can't - ability (see Unit 63 paragraph 8)

Use these phrases with **can** and **can't** to complete the sentences below.

can hear   can't hear   can see   can't see   can smell   can't smell

1 I've got a really bad cold. I ...*can't smell*............... anything.
2 I .... you, but I .... you.
3 There's something good in the kitchen. You .... it from here.
4 Turn the radio up a bit. I .... it very clearly.
5 There's a lovely view. On a clear day you .... for miles.
6 Can you move over a bit? I .... anything when you're in the way.

45 Be able to - ability (see Unit 63 paragraphs 3,4,7)

Complete these sentences using the correct form of **be able to.**

1 If you sit at the back, you ...*won't be able to*................ see very well.
2 Fortunately, she .... give the police a good description of the mugger.
3 I'm sorry. We're busy on Sunday, so we .... come.
4 Experiments suggest that some dolphins .... use a complicated system of sounds for communication.
5 We got there in good time, so we .... help Janet get everything ready.

6 I hope we .... produce better results in the future.
7 The chairman sends his apologies that he .... be with us this evening.

46 Could have - ability (see Unit 63 paragraph 6)

Read the following passage.

My friend Tom had an eventful week last week. On Sunday he had a bad car accident. Tom wasn't seriously injured, but the other driver wasn't so fortunate. His leg was broken. On Monday evening, Tom played tennis. On Tuesday, he drove to the supermarket and did the shopping. On Wednesday, he went for a long walk in the country. On Thursday he mowed the lawn and weeded the garden, on Friday he cleaned the windows and tidied the garden shed, and on Saturday he cycled to the next village, where he refereed a football match. If he had broken his leg, Tom couldn't have done any of these things.

Now list six things Tom couldn't have done if he had broken his leg.

1 ...*He couldn't have driven to the supermarket.*...............
2 ....

3 ....

4 ....

5 ....

6 ....

47 Might - suggestions (see Unit 66 paragraphs 3,4)

Use the following phrases to complete the sentences below.

buy a new one	come too	come round and meet him	come with me
enjoy it	go home	go together	see a doctor

1 There's a good film on this evening. I thought perhaps you might ...*enjoy it.*...........................

2 If we're all going to London, we might as well ....

3 If your bike has been stolen, you might want to ....

4 If you're still feeling ill, it might be wise to ....

5 The party's over. We might as well ....

6 We're having a few friends round. I thought you might like to ....

7 I'm driving to Birmingham tomorrow. You might as well ....

8 George is coming tomorrow. You might like to ....

48 I wish - wants and wishes (see Unit 68 paragraph 7)

Match the comments with the wishes.

1 I feel so old.

2 The plants in the garden are dying.

3 We never hear from Angela.

4 I didn't know you were ill.

5 I can't afford to go out.

6 It takes hours to get to work.

7 She looked absolutely lovely.

8 We don't see you very often nowadays.

9 Now everyone knows the secret.

a I wish it would rain.

b I wish you had told me.

c I wish we lived nearer the office.

d I wish you could come more often.

e I wish I hadn't told anyone.

f I wish I were younger.

g I wish she would write more often.

h I wish I had more money.

i I wish I could have taken a photograph.

49 Ought to have - mild obligation (see Unit 71 paragraph 3)

Rewrite these sentences using **ought to have** or **ought not to have.**

1 I wish I had known what was going to happen. / ...*I ought to have known what was going to happen.*...

2 It was silly of John to leave home without telling us. / ...*John ought not to have left home without telling us.*...

3 Why didn't you ask for permission? / ....

4 I wish we hadn't stayed so late. / ....

5 Why didn't you go to the doctor's earlier? / ....

6 It's a pity you didn't meet Jenny while you were here. / ....

7 I'm sorry I got so angry about what happened. / ....

8 It would have been better if you had come on your own. / ....

9 It's a pity we didn't reserve seats. / ....

10 Why didn't you stop at the traffic lights? / ....

50 Had better - mild obligation and advice (see Unit 71 paragraph 4)

Rewrite these sentences using **had better** or **had better not.**

1 I think you should come back tomorrow. / *You had better come back tomorrow.*
2 He's busy. I don't think you should disturb him. / *You had better not disturb him.*
3 I think I ought to ask my father first. / ....
4 I think we should be going home now. / ....
5 I hope they won't make any trouble. / ....
6 You ought to get a return ticket. / ....
7 Don't go out alone at night. / ....
8 You're not looking well. You ought to go to bed. / ....
9 You look starving. We should get something to eat. / ....
10 It's getting late. We shouldn't waste any more time. / ....

51 Verbs with two objects (see Unit 73)

Rewrite these sentences using **for** or **to.**

1 I have reserved your friends a table.
   I have reserved a table for your friends.
....

2 He offered his next door neighbour a lot of help.
....

3 I have cooked the children a special supper.
....

4 Please send us your reply as soon as possible.
....

5 I'll try to save you a place.
....

6 Show your uncle that book you've just bought.
....

52 Common verbs with nouns for actions (see Unit 77)

Use these verbs to complete the sentences which follow. You may use each verb more than once.

| did   gave   had   made   took   went |

1 George ...*made*..... a useful suggestion.
2 It wasn't working, so I .... it a good kick.
3 You obviously .... a lot of trouble over this.
4 They .... a dreadful fight when they got home.
5 I .... the washing up before going to bed.
6 We .... for a swim every morning before breakfast.
7 John .... me some useful advice.
8 We .... a short break over the weekend.

53 Verbs with prepositions (see Unit 78)

Complete these sentences using **of** or **on.**

1 We thought ...*of*......... asking James to design it, but I'm not sure if you can count .... him to get it done.

2　I know .... two or three designers you could really depend ....

3　I'm relying .... Alphaco for the construction work. Have you heard .... them?

4　I'm depending .... you to think .... something, before the boss gets here.

5　Talking .... holidays, where were you planning .... going?

54 Verbs with prepositions (see Unit 78)

Which one of these verbs with prepositions means the same as the underlined word or phrase in the sentences below?

> apologize for   ask for   laugh at   rely on   talk   about

1　They rang the ambulance service to <u>request</u> help. / ...*ask for* ....

2　I feel silly in these clothes. Everyone will <u>make fun of</u> me. / ....

3　I would just like to say that I <u>am sorry for</u> the trouble I have caused. / ....

4　If you want help, you can always <u>depend on</u> me. / ....

5　Let's leave that for the time being. We can <u>discuss</u> it later. / ....

55 Phrasal verbs (see Unit 79)

Complete the following sentences using the phrasal verb given in brackets. You will need to use an appropriate pronoun as object.

1　Their parents were overseas so their grandparents ...*brought them up* .... (bring up)

2　I want to put these blankets away. Could you help me to .... ? (fold up)

3　I want to fold these blankets up and .... (put away)

4　When we come to Henry's house, I'll .... (point out)

5　He never read my letters, he just .... (tore up)

6　You mean he tore up your letters and .... ? (threw away)

7　These papers are in a dreadful mess. Have you got time to .... (sort out)

8　The vase was lying there broken. Someone must have .... (knock down)

9　It's my money. Please .... (hand over)

10　The garage is falling apart. The best thing is to .... and build another. (pull down)

56 Phrasal verbs (see Unit 79)

Write these sentences in two ways. First use the phrasal verb and noun group given in brackets in this structure: verb followed by noun and particle (v+n+p). Then rewrite the clause in the structure: verb followed by particle and noun (v+p+n).

1　Can I help you to (the blankets / fold up)?
　　v+n+p: ...*Can I help you to fold the blankets up?* ....
　　v+p+n: ...*Can I help you to fold up the blankets?* ....

2　We never found out who (the vase / knock over).
　　v+n+p: ....
　　v+p+n: ....

3　He refused to (the money / hand over).
　　v+n+p: ....
　　v+p+n: ....

4 Can you help me to (the papers / sort out)?

v+n+p: ....

v+p+n: ....

5 It would be useful if someone could (my mistakes / sort out).

v+n+p: ....

v+p+n: ....

6 It's very hard work (children / bringing up).

v+n+p: ....

v+p+n: ....

7 They're planning to (all the houses / pull down).

v+n+p: ....

v+p+n: ....

8 Andrew never remembers to (his books / put away).

v+n+p: ....

v+p+n: ....

57 Link verbs (see Unit 80)

Match the two clauses or sentences.

1 She looks just like her sister, ...

2 She wanted to be a pop singer, ...

3 She always seemed very quiet, ...

4 She looked exhausted, ...

5 She sounds cheerful, ...

6 She seems well qualified, ...

a ... but she became a doctor instead.

b ... but she caused a lot of trouble.

c ... but she doesn't look very happy.

d ... let's offer her the job.

e ... but she's much younger.

f ... but she soon felt better.

58 Verbs with '-ing' clauses (see Unit 81)

Use the correct forms of the verbs in brackets to complete these sentences.

1 All right, children, ...*stop*........... talking please and ...*start*........... writing. (start / stop)

2 Dan never .... talking. I hate the way he .... interrupting everyone. (stop / keep]

3 It .... raining early in the morning and .... pouring down until late afternoon. (go on / start)

4 He .... shouting and waving, until we all .... talking and .... taking notice of him. (start / keep on / stop)

5 We had .... discussing his case, but he still .... complaining about it, until the chairman told him to .... making such a fuss and .... behaving sensibly. (go on / finish / start / stop)

59 Verbs with '-ing' clauses (see Unit 81 paragraph 4)

Use these verbs to complete the sentences which follow.

| catch feel hear imagine prevent see smell stop |

1 You can't ...*stop*....................... people wasting their money, if that's what they want to do.

2 It was so quiet that I could .... people talking at the other end of the field.

3 Look over there. I think I can .... something moving.

4 If you put your hand here, you can .... the baby's heart beating.

5 You'll be in a lot of trouble, if they .... you driving without a licence.

6 They tied his hands to .... him escaping.

7 He is so serious, it's difficult to .... him playing a joke on anyone.

60 Verbs with '-ing' clauses (see Unit 81 paragraph 1)

Complete the following to make true sentences.

1 I loathe ....

2 I detest ....

3 I can't stand ....

4 I dislike ....

5 I quite enjoy ....

6 I enjoy ....

7 I really enjoy ....

Here are some ideas to help you.

being late for something	going to the dentist	learning English
going to the doctor	lying in bed in the morning	reading
listening to rock music	watching tennis on TV	playing football

61 Verbs with 'to'-infinitive clauses (see Unit 82 paragraph 5)

Rewrite these sentences, using the first verb in the passive voice.

1 At one time everybody believed that the world was flat. / At one time the world ...*was believed to be flat.*....

2 I suppose that their new house cost a million pounds. / Their new house ....

3 Our correspondent reported that the city had been hit by an earthquake early this morning. / The city ..

4 Everyone knows that he is a brilliant politician. / He ....

5 The police allege that the prisoner brought dangerous drugs into the country. / The prisoner ....

6 We understand that the man is armed and dangerous. / The man ....

62 Verbs with 'to'-infinitive clauses (see Unit 82 paragraph 6)

Rewrite these sentences using a 'wh'-word and a 'to'-infinitive clause.

1 What shall I wear? / I can't decide ...*what to wear*................................ .

2 Who shall I ask? / I don't know ....

3 Where shall we go? / Can you tell us .... ?

4 How do you open it? / Can you explain .... ?

5 When should I start? / Tell me ....

6 I want to play tennis. / Can you teach me .... ?

7 I can't swim. / I never learned ....

63 Verbs with 'to'-infinitive or '-ing' clauses (see Units 81-3)

Complete the following sentences, using the verb in brackets in a 'to'-infinitive or '-ing' clause.

1 He expects ...*to come*...... round about six this evening. (come)

2 He kept .... while we were talking. (interrupt)

3 We asked him to stop .... , but he took no notice. (shout)

4 I managed .... everything ready in time. (get)

5 The key is on the shelf. I remember .... it there. (leave)

6 Remind me .... that letter on my way to work. (post)

7 You'll have to wait for someone .... and mend it. (come)

8 Maria suggested .... Fred to help. (ask)

64 Verbs with other types of clauses (see Unit 84 paragraph 2)

Complete these sentences using the appropriate form of these verbs.

| leave   move   play   speak   steal |

1 They say Pele was the greatest footballer ever. I'm afraid I was too young to see him ...*play*........... .

2 Please stop making such a noise. We can hardly hear ourselves ....

3 I think it's still alive. I'm sure I felt it ....

4 I saw the shoplifter .... the necklace and pass it to his friend.

5 A: Is Joe still here? B: No. I saw him .... half an hour ago.

65 Verbs with other types of clauses (see Unit 84 paragraph 3)

Complete these sentences using a form of **get** with the words in brackets.

1 It's dreadful. You can hardly see out. We must ...*get the windows cleaned*........................... (the windows / clean)

2 I have to .... for a new passport. (my photograph / take)

3 The television is very bad. We really ought to .... (it / mend)

4 These trousers are too long. I think I'll .... (them / shorten)

5 John Brown .... playing football last week. (his nose / break)

66 The passive voice (see Unit 85 paragraph 8)

Some passive sentences can be expressed in two ways. Look at the example, then find another way to write the remaining five sentences.

1 I was shown their letters of appointment. / ...*Their letters of appointment were shown to me.*

2 I was sent full details of the job. / ....

3 They were all presented with signed certificates. / ....

4 A free sightseeing trip is offered to all passengers. / ....

5 Drinks and snacks have been given to everyone in our group. / ....

6 She was brought the news of their success yesterday evening. / ....

67 'It' as impersonal subject (see Unit 86 paragraph 6)

Rewrite these sentences with **it** and a 'that'-clause.

1 The earth was generally believed to be flat. / *It was generally believed that the earth was flat.*

2 He is known to be a dangerous man. / ....

3 Charlie Chaplin is said to have been a great comedian. / ....

4 She is understood to be arriving later today. / ....

5 They are rumoured to have escaped. / ....

68 'There' as impersonal subject (see Unit 87)

Match these phrases to describe the picture.

1 There's a little boy ...   a ... in the waiting room.
2 There's an old man ...   b ... reading a newspaper.
3 There's a young woman ...   c ... on the wall.
4 There's a girl ...   d ... looking round the door.
5 There are some flowers ...   e ... sitting next to the old man.
6 There's a NO SMOKING notice ...   f ... sitting on his mother's knee.
7 There's a nurse ...   g ... in a vase by the window.
8 There's a young man ...   h ... sitting on the floor.

69 Reporting (see Unit 89 paragraph 1)

Use the appropriate form of these verbs to complete the sentences below.

| advise beg command forbid instruct invite remind warn |

1 If you ...*forbid*... someone to do something, you order that it must not be done. EG I ...*forbid*... you to tell her.

2 If you .... someone to do something, you advise them to do it in order to avoid possible danger or punishment. EG I .... him not to lose his temper.

3 If you .... someone to do something, you ask them very seriously. EG She .... the doctor not to tell her husband how ill she was.

4 If someone .... you to do something or take part in something, they ask you to do it. EG I was .... by a friend to attend the committee meeting.

5 When someone .... you to do something, they say something to make you remember to do it. EG .... me to speak to you about that later.

6 If you .... someone to do something, you order them to do it. EG He .... them to lie down.

7 If you .... someone to do something, you tell them to do it in a formal or severe way. EG I've been .... to take you to London.

8 If you .... someone to do something, you say that you think they ought to do it. EG His doctor .... him to change his job.

70 Reporting (see Unit 89 paragraph 2)

Rewrite these sentences with **ask** and an 'if'-clause using the words given.

1 'Do you think you will be able to come back later?' (We / everyone)
   We asked everyone if they would be able to come back later.

2 'Are you ready to go?' (John / Jill)

3 'Can we go on the school picnic?' (The children / their parents)

4 'Is there a bus to Piccadilly?' (I / the policeman)

5 'Do you think we can afford to take a taxi?' (My wife / me)

6 'Have you anything to declare?' (The customs officer / Joe)

71 Review of tenses (see Units 40-49)

Choose the right form of the verb to complete the following sentences.

1 I *usually go* .... (usually go / am usually going / have usually gone) to work by car, but I .... (go / am going / have gone) on the bus this week while my car .... (is / is being / has been) mended.

2 A: .... (Do you know / Are you knowing / Can you know) where Brian is? B: I .... (don't see / am not seeing / haven't seen) him since lunch. I .... (think / am thinking / can think) he's in the kitchen. He .... (probably do / probably does / is probably doing) the washing up.

3 My daughter is a vegetarian. She .... (doesn't eat / isn't eating / hasn't eaten) meat. It is sometimes difficult in a restaurant when she .... (finds / is finding / will find) that they .... (don't have / aren't having / won't have) any vegetarian dishes. That's why she .... (usually telephones / is usually telephoning / will usually telephone) beforehand to find out what's on the menu.

4 A: How long .... (do you live / are you living / have you been living) in Liverpool? B: Only three weeks. We .... (stay / are staying / have been staying) in a hotel until we .... (are finding / will find / have found) a house to buy.

5 A: I .... (met / was meeting / have meeting) George while I .... (waited / was waiting / have waited) for the bus tonight. B: How is he? I .... (am not seeing / haven't seen / didn't see) him for months. A: He .... (was seeming / seemed / has seemed) to be very well. B: I .... (think / am thinking) he .... (was just getting / just got / has just got) a new job, ... (wasn't he / didn't he / hasn't he)? A: Well, he .... (is just leaving / has just left / just left) his old job about a month ago, but he .... (doesn't find / hasn't found / didn't find) anything else yet. He .... (still looks / is still looking) for something.

226

6 Everyone in the Hodja's village .... (knew / was knowing) that the Hodja was well educated and .... (went / was going / had been) to the finest schools. They .... (were often going / had often gone / would often go) to him for advice. One day a poor illiterate farmer .... (wants / was wanting / wanted) the Hodja to write a letter for him.

'Where .... (will you / do you / are you going to) send this letter?' the Hodja .... (asked / was asking / had asked). 'To Cairo,' said the farmer. 'I'm afraid I .... (can't / couldn't / don't) help you,' said the Hodja, 'I .... (don't go / am not going) to Cairo.' 'But you .... (don't need / are not needing / didn't need) to go there,' said the farmer, 'I .... (just want / am just wanting / will just want) to send the letter there.' 'Yes,' said the Hodja, 'but my writing is so bad that nobody else .... (is reading / reads / can read) it so if I .... (write / am writing / will write) the letter, I .... (have / will have / am having) to go there and read it myself.'

7 When the farmer asked the Hodja if he .... (will write / would write) the letter, the Hodja asked him where the letter .... (goes / is going / was going). The man said that it .... (is / was) to a friend in Cairo. Then the Hodja explained that he .... (cannot / could not / does not) write the letter because he .... (is not going / was not going / does not go) to Cairo. He said his writing .... (is / was) so bad that nobody else .... (can / could) read it. So if he .... (writes / wrote / is writing) the letter he .... (has / will have / would have) to go to Cairo himself to read it.

8 One day the Hodja .... (hears / heard / was hearing) some soldiers telling stories about how brave they .... (are / were / have been). 'Well,' said the Hodja, 'I .... (am remembering / remember / remembered) when I was a soldier, I .... (have once cut / once cut / was once cutting) the arm right off my enemy.' 'Really?' asked one of the soldiers. 'Why .... (haven't you cut / didn't you cut / weren't you cutting) off his head?' 'Well,' said the Hodja, 'somebody .... (was already doing / already did / had already done) that.'

72 Review of mood (see Units 50-58)

Add question tags to these statements to make them into questions asking someone to confirm what you are saying, or to agree with you.

1 You've met George, ...*haven't you?*....

2 They won't be too late, ... ?

3 Helen left a message for me, ... ?

4 There isn't time for another game, ... ?

5 Nobody saw what happened, ... ?

6 Something's wrong, ... ?

7 Somebody has made a mistake, ... ?

8 You didn't do it, ... ?

9 I'll see you tomorrow, ... ?

10 He knows where you are, ... ?

11 Don't do it again, ... ?

12 Everybody is in agreement, ... ?

73 Review of mood (see Units 50-58)

Make negative questions using the modals given.

1 You didn't stop at the traffic lights. (should) / *Shouldn't you have stopped at the traffic lights?*

2 You didn't send me a letter. (could) / ....?

3 Perhaps they went home earlier. (might) / ....?

4 We didn't pay in advance. (should) / ....?

5 Why didn't you take a bus? (could) / ....?

74 Review of mood (see Units 50-58)

Complete these short answers using the verbs in brackets.

1 A: Do you think we'll be on time. (hope) / B: Yes, *I hope so.*

2 A: Will Jacky be there? (think) / B: No, ...

3 A: Will you be going abroad this year? (suppose) / B: Yes, ...

4 A: Has the newspaper come yet? (expect) / B: Yes, ...

5 A: Did you do the shopping on your way home? (afraid) / B: No, ...

6 A: Did Jenny get my letter? (think) / B: Yes, ...

75 Review of modals (see Units 59-71)

Rewrite these sentences using the modals given.

1 Don't stay out too late. (ought) / *You ought not to stay out too late.*

2 Come home before midnight. (must) / ....

3 Don't go out in the rain. (should) / ....

4 Don't complain so much. (ought) / ....

5 Don't spend too much money. (must) / ....

76 Review of modals (see Units 59-71)

Write sentences with **I wish.**

1 It's raining very hard. / *I wish it wasn't raining so hard.*

2 We haven't time to stop. / ....

3 John didn't pass his examination. / ....

4 It's very cold in here. / ....

5 There's no time to spare. / ....

6 George won't help. / ....

7 Mary didn't come. / ....

8 I didn't see the match last week. / ....

Sentence structure

77 Time clauses (see Unit 90 paragraph 7)

Rewrite these sentences, replacing the underlined verb group with an '-ing' form on its own.

1 I was getting ready for bed, when I heard someone downstairs.
While *getting ready for bed, I heard someone downstairs.*

2 When I heard the noise, I immediately telephoned the police.
On ....

3 As soon as they <u>heard</u> my report, they promised to send two policemen round.

On ....

4 When they <u>arrived</u> at my house, one policeman found that a window had been broken.

....

5 When he <u>saw</u> this, he rang the doorbell.

....

6 When he <u>heard</u> the bell, a burglar ran out through the back door.

On ....

7 When he <u>saw</u> the burglar escaping, the second policeman chased after him.

....

8 The unlucky burglar was hit by a car as he <u>ran</u> across the road.

....

9 After they <u>had arrested</u> the man, the police called for an ambulance.

After ....

10 When they <u>arrived</u> at the hospital, they found the man had made his escape.

On ....

78 Conditional clauses (see Unit 92)

Match these parts to make conditional sentences.

1 If one of the dogs attacked, …   a … you could always go by bus.

2 If you were late for the train, …   b … I can take you by car.

3 If you moved to the country, …   c … there's sure to be an accident.

4 If the dog had attacked, …   d … you could live in our house.

5 If the train is late, …   e … you would certainly have been late.

6 If you move to London, …   f … it could have killed one of the children.

7 If you stayed in Birmingham, …   g … you could buy a bigger house.

8 If you drive too fast, …   h … you'll be closer to the office.

9 If you had missed your connection, …   i … you would get a nasty bite.

79 Purpose and reason clauses (see Unit 93 paragraph 1)

Rewrite these sentences using **in order not to.**

1 We spoke quietly, because we didn't want to disturb anyone.
We spoke quietly in order not to disturb anyone.

2 She moved carefully, because she didn't want to wake the children.

....

3 He sat in the furthest corner, because he didn't want to be seen.

....

4 I gave up sugar and butter, because I didn't want to put on weight.

....

Now rewrite these sentences using **so as not to.**

5 He used both hands, because he didn't want to drop anything.
He used both hands, so as not to drop anything.

6 We went over everything carefully, because we didn't want to make any mistakes.

....

7 She left quietly, because she didn't want to make any trouble.

....

8 We covered the furniture, because we didn't want to get paint all over it.

....

80 Purpose and reason clauses (see Unit 93 paragraph 2)

Rewrite these sentences with a purpose clause containing a modal.

1 I couldn't see what was happening, until he lifted me up.
  He lifted me up, so that I could see what was happening.

2 The houses were knocked down and replaced by car parks and office blocks.

....

3 I sat next to the window, because I wanted to see out.

....

4 He tied a knot in his handkerchief, because he didn't want to forget.

....

5 I waved my arms, because I wanted them to see me.

....

6 He wanted the report early, because he wanted to discuss it with colleagues.

....

7 We will take a telescope, because we want to see the birds without getting too close.

....

8 I'll fasten the donkey, because I don't want it to escape.

....

9 She left her address, because she wanted us to forward her letters.

....

10 He wore a disguise, because he didn't want even his friends to recognize him.

....

81 Result clauses (see Unit 94 paragraph 5)

The sentences below all have **enough** and a 'to'-infinitive. Use these nouns and adjectives to complete them.

Chinese clean food lucky money noisy old room well work

1 Most students have hardly enough ...*money*............... to live on.
2 I couldn't speak Japanese .... enough to make myself understood.
3 I hope I'll be .... enough to get a place at University when I finish school.
4 You'll soon be able to speak enough .... to get around on your own.
5 The disco is close by, and it's .... enough to be a nuisance at night.
6 There would be enough .... to feed the whole world if we ate less meat and more of other things.
7 It's a tiny place. There's hardly enough .... to swing a cat.
8 I'll be glad when the kids are .... enough to go to school.
9 I'm not sure if that water's .... enough to drink.
10 Have you got enough .... to keep you busy?

230

82 Result clauses (see Unit 94 paragraph 4)

Use **too** with one of the following adjectives or adverbs to complete each of the sentences below.

expensive far late many old quickly small tired young

1 I was .....*too tired*..................... to stay awake any longer.

2 The children are only three and four. They're .... to go to school.

3 You'd better take a bus to the city centre. It's .... to walk.

4 My French isn't very good. People always speak .... for me to understand.

5 This jacket doesn't fit properly. It's far .... for me.

6 I can't afford to go abroad this year. The air fares are much ....

7 We missed most of the party. We arrived much ....

8 There are .... students in my class. The room gets very crowded.

9 John still enjoys a game of golf, but he's getting .... to play tennis.

10 I should have gone to work today, but I felt .... to get out of bed.

83 Contrast clauses (see Unit 95 paragraph 4)

These sentences have **in spite of the fact that** or **despite the fact that.** Use one of the following phrases to complete them.

we warned them not to
I've done nothing all day
most employees were working mothers
they live in the same house
we didn't have very good seats

I've known him for years
we lived next door to a police station
they tend to live longer
it wasn't very well written
everyone else disagreed with him

1 The company refused to provide nursery facilities in spite of the fact that ...*most of the employees were working mothers.*............

2 I quite enjoyed his last book in spite of the fact that ....
....

3 Despite, or perhaps because of the fact that ....
.... , we were burgled three times.

4 I really enjoyed the play despite the fact that ....
....

5 Women retire earlier than men in spite of the fact that ....
....

6 Despite the fact that .... ,
they hardly ever speak to each other.

7 I'm exhausted in spite of the fact that ....
....

8 He insisted that he was right despite the fact that ....
....

9 They went ahead and swam in the bay despite the fact that ....
....

10 I can never remember his face in spite of the fact that ....
....

231

84 Contrast clauses (see Unit 95 paragraph 3)

Complete the rewritten sentences below using **in spite of** or **despite** and an '-ing' form.

1 He arrived on time, even though he stopped for lunch on the way. / He arrived on time ....*in spite of*... *stopping for lunch* .... on the way.

2 He died poor, although he had worked hard all his life. / He died poor ....
.... all his life.

3 She finished the race, even though she had a bad fall. / She finished the race
....
....

4 Even though I have studied French for three years, I still find it difficult to speak. / ....
.... for three years, I still find it difficult to speak.

5 Even though she's over sixty, she's still very fit. / ....
she's still very fit.

6 John is still very cheerful, even though he has lost his job. / John is still very cheerful ....
....

85 Defining relative clauses (see Unit 97 paragraph 3,4)

When the relative pronouns **that** , **who** , or **which** are the object of the relative clause, you can leave them out if you want to. Make these sentences into relative clauses with the relative pronoun left out.

1 I bought a car. / ....*the car I bought*...

2 You met a friend. / ....

3 He sent a message home. / ....

4 Jack is going to give a lecture. / ....

5 Bill had hoped to meet some friends. / ....

6 We decided to offer a prize. / ....

Now do these, in which the relative pronoun is the object of a preposition.

7 We lived in an old house. / ...*the old house we lived in*.......................................

8 You asked for some money. / ....

9 He was looking at the picture. / ....

10 They had waited for a bus. / ....

11 She is looking after some children. / ....

12 I picked up a coin. / ....

86 Changing the focus of a sentence (see Unit 99 paragraph 5)

Answer these questions using the name in brackets and **the one who.**

1 Does Sue keep the list of books? (Liz)
No, ...*Liz is the one who keeps the list of books.*..................................

2 Did Mike take the dictionary? (Jack)
No, ...

3 Was Peter waiting to borrow it? (Bill)
No, ...

4 Did Jane promise to bring it back? (Helen)
No, ...

5 Is Helen going to look after it for me? (Diana)
No, ...

Index

Note: numbers refer to Units and paragraphs, not to pages; entries in **bold** are grammar terms; entries in *italics* are actual words and forms; an arrow ⇨ tells you to look at another entry.

Key

Unit 1

A
2 The horse kicked Charlie Brown.
3 Jonah ate a big fish.
4 My father taught Mrs Jackson.
5 Jack killed the giant.

B
2 Everybody worked hard.
3 The cat caught the mouse.
4 Children love kittens.
5 Nobody knows the answer.
6 Mary bought a new dress yesterday.
7 All of us enjoyed the film last night.
8 John Black went to the supermarket.
9 Janet Black drove her car to the airport.
10 Mike drank a cup of coffee after lunch.

C
2 S + V + A
3 S + V + O + A
4 S + V + A
5 S + V + O + A
6 S + V + O + A

D
2 Didn't you see Jill last Friday?
3 Haven't they arrived yet?
4 Won't Peter help you?
5 Can't Henry speak French?
6 Doesn't he smoke any more?
7 Didn't they understand him?
8 Hasn't John met Mary yet?

Unit 2

A
2 There's a big dog.
There's a big dog running out of the shop.
There's a big dog carrying a bone running out of the shop./
There's a big dog running out of the shop carrying a bone.
3 There's a fat man.
There's a fat man with a knife in his hand.
There's a fat man with a knife in his hand running after the dog.
4 There's a young woman.
There's a young woman with long hair.
There's a young woman with long hair standing outside the shop.

B
2 to do.
3 to play.
4 to meet.
5 to post.
6 to read.
7 to wear.
8 to carry.
9 to catch.
10 to visit...to drive through.

Unit 3

A
2 come
3 heard...went
4 told...asked
5 walk...go
6 stayed...known...coming
7 said...know...coming
8 woke up...heard
9 do...tells
10 do...tells

B
2 haven't
3 were
4 are...have
5 had
6 Do...are
7 Do...haven't
8 be...are
9 has been
10 have been
Note the modal use of 'will' in 8 and 10.

C
2 'll...can
3 will...can
4 Could
5 would...could
6 should...can
7 might...might (not)
8 may...can
9 should...would
10 would...could

Unit 4

A
cows children teeth
glasses wishes lorries
stories friends buses
tomatoes parents monkeys
boxes pianos houses
mice keys ways

B
2 Lions are dangerous animals.
3 Lawyers generally earn more than teachers.
4 Computers are expensive pieces of equipment.
5 Students have to work hard.
6 Policemen only do what they are told.
7 Cats are supposed to have nine lives.
8 Buses are the best way of getting into town(s).
9 Women tend to live longer than men.
10 Good books help to pass the time.

C
2 children
3 dishes
4 tomatoes
5 box
6 man
7 people
8 tooth
9 dishes
10 boy

D
2 is
3 smells
4 have eaten
5 were
6 was hanging
7 goes
8 were
9 has
10 have

Unit 5

A
2 a rest
3 a bath / a shower...a wash
4 a bath / a shower
5 a ride
6 a jog
7 a drink
8 a fight
9 a go
10 a move

B
2 goods
3 refreshments
4 clothes
5 feelings
6 holidays
7 pictures
8 papers
9 belongings
10 sights

C
2 team
3 family
4 government
5 crew
6 staff
7 gang
8 audience
9 public
10 media

Unit 6

A
2 knowledge
3 information
4 equipment
5 money
6 advice
7 traffic
8 electricity
9 help
10 happiness

B
2 U;C
3 C;U
4 U;C
5 U;C
6 U;C

C
2 the advice you gave me
3 the strength to go on
4 the information you need
5 The traffic in London
6 the news about Bill

Unit 7

A
2 Mary
3 Tom and Jane
4 Mr and Mrs Jackson

B
2 Tom and Jane
3 Mr and Mrs Jackson
4 Mr Brown

C
The other day when I was shopping a woman stopped me and asked me the way to the post office. I gave her directions and she thanked me politely, then ran off quickly in the opposite direction. I put my hand in my pocket and found that my wallet was missing. She must have taken it while we were talking. I shouted and ran after her but it was no good. She had disappeared in the crowd.

Unit 8

A
2 He's always complaining
3 He had just got a new job
4 I've mended the radiator
5 she was tired of him
6 she doesn't like him
7 the brakes are useless
8 the children sometimes stay awake all night
9 The traffic was dreadful

10 the light goes on

B
2 ones...ones
3 one...one
4 ones...one
5 one...one

C
1 There are five books.
2 Red, green and blue.
3 Green and blue.

Unit 9

A
3 herself
4 her
5 themselves
6 himself
7 you
8 you
9 themselves
10 themselves

B
2 by herself
3 by ourselves
4 by themselves
5 by themselves
6 by yourselves
7 by myself
8 by themselves
9 by himself
10 by myself

C
2 myself
3 ourselves
4 herself
5 themselves

D
2 the Chief of Police himself who made the arrest.
3 Rembrandt himself who painted this picture.
4 was written by Shakespeare himself.
5 the captain himself who scored the winning goal.

Unit 10

A
2 Everyone...nobody
3 No one
4 somebody
5 Nobody
6 anybody
7 Anybody

B
2 arrives
3 likes
4 wants

5 lives
6 asks

C
2 them
3 they
4 They
5 them

D
2 everything
3 nothing
4 something
5 anything

E
2 anyone
3 nobody
4 anything
5 anything
6 nothing
7 anybody
8 nothing
9 Nobody

Unit 11

A
2 many...the...our...each
3 another...this...a
4 Most...this
5 Every...the...a
6 your...the
7 a...the...a...several
8 another...your...this
9 little...the...Few...any...the
10 another...the...much

B
2 Each
3 A: your
   B: that...the...my...the
4 Most...both
Note that 'either' is used as a pronoun in 4.
5 several...the
6 my
7 any...my
8 another...the...a
Note that 'some' is used as a pronoun in 8.
9 that...the
Note that 'another' is used as a pronoun in 9.
10 Most...the...the

Unit 12

A
2 Turkey
3 The three learned Christian monks
4 The Turkish sultan
5 The sultan's palace
6 The first monk
7 The centre of the earth

9 The front right foot of Hodja's donkey
10 The first monk 11 The second monk
13 The third monk
14 Hodja's donkey
15 The hairs in the third monk's beard
16 The hairs in the donkey's tail
17 The donkey's tail

8,12,18 Because there is only one.

Unit 13

A

2 The Amazon in Brazil is the longest river in South America.
3 Japan and the United States are separated by the Pacific Ocean.
4 Liverpool is in the north of England, fairly close to Wales.
5 I would love to go to Jamaica, the Bahamas or somewhere else in the Caribbean.
6 The Suez Canal flows through the north of Egypt from Port Said to Suez, joining the Mediterranean to the Gulf of Suez and the Red Sea.
7 Lake Windermere in the north-west of England is one of the largest lakes in the British Isles.
8 Iran has borders with Iraq, Turkey, the USSR, Afghanistan and West Pakistan.
9 Mount Everest is in the Himalayas on the border between Nepal and Tibet, which is part of the People's Republic of China.
10 Biarritz stands on the mouth of the Adour river which flows into the Gulf of Gascony in the Bay of Biscay.

B

2 On the first morning we went to the British Museum and had lunch at MacDonald's in Church Street.
3 In the evening we went to a pub just off Leicester Square then we went to a play at the National Theatre.
4 Next day we went to the Houses of Parliament and Westminster Abbey and had lunch at the Peking Restaurant.
5 We looked in the Evening Standard newspaper and found there was a good film at the Odeon cinema near Piccadilly Circus.

C

2 the disabled
3 the rich...the poor
4 the blind
5 the unemployed

Unit 14

A

2 A lawyer usually earns more than a policeman.
3 I love reading a good book.
4 You don't often see a good programme on TV nowadays.
5 A son is always a lot more trouble than a daughter.
6 I often have an egg for breakfast.
7 Nowadays you can buy a computer-controlled washing machine.
8 I hate to hear a baby crying or a dog barking.

B

2 We have just bought a new house with a large garden.
3 My brother is a teacher and I have a cousin who works with young children as well.
4 Would you like a biscuit or a piece of cake?
5 I spoke to an official and he gave me very good advice.

C

2 a;the
3 a;the
4 the;a
5 the;a
6 a;the
7 a;the
8 a;The
9 an;the
10 a;the

Unit 15

A

2 All cars
3 All old people
4 all alcoholic drinks
5 All banks
6 All doctors

B

2 in a library
3 in a restaurant
4 in a department store
5 at an airport
6 in a bank
7 at a railway station
8 in a hotel

C

2 Most of the children were fast asleep.
3 Most of the students passed the exam.
4 All of my friends came to the party.
5 All of the clothes were very expensive.
6 Most of the seats were booked.
7 Most of the ice cream was finished.
8 Most of the garden was full of weeds.

D

2 John had no money left.
3 He has no friends.
4 There's no milk in the fridge.
5 We got no letters today.
6 There were no girls in the class.

Unit 16

A

2 is/are
3 was
4 like...likes/like
5 come...gives/give
6 have...has/have

B

2 New York, Washington
3 London, Milan, Rome
4 London, Rome, Washington
5 Milan, Rome
6 London, Milan, Rome

C

2 Neither of them is
3 All of them are... None of them are
4 None of them are
5 All of them are... None of them are
6 Both of them are... Neither of them is

Unit 17

A

2 many...much
3 many...plenty of
4 few...little
5 a lot of...much
6 a little...a few
7 much...little
8 lots of...few

B

2 Few
3 little
4 few
5 little

C

2 a few
3 a few
4 a little
5 a few

D

2 very little
3 a few
4 very little/ a little
5 a little
6 very little
7 a few
8 very little
9 A few
10 a little

Unit 18

A
2 some...any
3 A: any
   B: some
4 some...any
5 some...any
6 A: any
   B: some
7 some...any
8 any

B
2 Some of the children understood.
3 I will be free any day next week.
4 Any bus will take you to the city centre.
5 Some people said that they would be late.
6 You can buy it at any good bookshop.
7 I'd like to give you some advice.
8 Any of the guides will show you the way.
9 Some of the children missed the bus.
10 I like any fruit except bananas.

C
2 a few...every
3 each
4 any
5 another...any
6 any...other
7 some
8 every
9 every
10 any

Unit 19

A
2 atomic power
3 a digital watch
4 the introductory paragraph
5 the maximum number
6 the northern border
7 neighbouring countries
8 an outdoor party
9 indoor plants
10 countless people

B
2 glad
3 unable
4 due
5 sorry
6 sure
7 aware
8 asleep
9 ready
10 content

C
2g 3a 4i 5d 6b 7e 8f
9c

Unit 20

A
2 large 3 round 4 wooden 8
3 nice 1 intelligent 2 young 5
4 nasty 1 ugly 2 blue 6 china 8
5 old 5 Spanish 7
6 big 3 square 4 metal 8
7 horrible 1 stinking 2
8 small 3 brown 6 paper 8
9 valuable 2 ancient 5 Egyptian 7
10 huge 3 red 6 American 7

B
2,4,5,8,10: Yes
3,6,7,9: No

C
All 'Yes', but note 5. Here, the adjective 'long' is used first, as an opinion adjective, followed by 'bitter', a descriptive adjective.

Unit 21

A
2 loyal
3 similar
4 identical
5 generous
6 good / excellent

B
2 stupid
3 used
4 different
5 surprised
6 delighted
7 responsible
8 bored
9 fond
10 senior

C
2 furious with
3 sensible of
4 suspicious of
5 jealous of
6 kind to
7 engaged to
8 responsible for

D
2 I was proud of the way she played.
3 Everyone was very critical of the way he behaved.
4 I was delighted with the way they looked.
5 We were very happy about the way they treated us.

Unit 22

A
2 a I was happy to meet George again.
   b I was pleased that George was waiting to meet me.
3 a I was sorry that Mary was ill.
   b She was unhappy to hear the news.
4 a We were surprised to see them.
   b We were delighted that everyone enjoyed the picnic.
5 a Peter was disappointed to miss the match.
   b Peter was disappointed that Anne missed the match.
6 a She was ashamed to tell the children.
   b She was ashamed that the children didn't tell her.

B
2 important
3 unlikely
4 bound
5 willing
6 due
7 impossible
8 wrong

C
2 It was brave of them to stop the thief.
3 It was very careless of you to forget to lock the door.
4 It was kind of her to look after the children.
5 It was very generous of Mary to pay the bill.
6 It was clever of you to solve the problem.
7 It was kind of Joe to send us the flowers.
8 It was mean of him to keep everything for himself.

D
2 It's very important for them to succeed.
3 It will be very difficult for me to do it.
4 It's very common for them to complain.
5 It's very easy for me to give you a lift.
6 It's unnecessary for you to come early.

Unit 23

A
2 increasing
3 existing
4 living
5 ageing
6 growing

B
2 depressed
3 astonished

4 alarmed
5 satisfied
6 bored

C
2 a interesting ; b interested
3 a depressing ; b depressed
4 a terrifying ; b terrified
5 a disappointed ; b disappointing
6 a embarrassing ; b embarrassed
7 a amazed ; b amazing
8 a exciting ; b excited

Unit 24

A
One syllable adjectives: black, great,
long, old, short, slow, small, warm
Adjectives using 'more' and 'most':
careful, certain, difficult,
expensive, fashionable,
intelligent,useful

B
more valuable - most valuable
more important - most important
funnier - funniest

C
finer - finest
bigger - biggest
fitter - fittest
better - best
hotter - hottest
whiter - whitest
slimmer - slimmest

D
simpler - simplest
angrier - angriest
more convenient - most convenient
colder - coldest
wider - widest
fatter - fattest
thinner - thinnest
more slender - most slender
more generous - most generous
more friendly - most friendly
gentler - gentlest

Unit 25

A
2 My sister is older than me.
3 Our new house is bigger than the one
   we used to live in.
4 Travelling by train is more comfortable than travelling by bus.
5 Shopping at a supermarket is
   cheaper than going to the local
   shops.

B
2 more interested...than
3 more exciting than
4 noisier than
5 older than

C
2 a younger man
3 a bigger house
4 a better idea
5 a better job

D
2 the most expensive hotel
3 the most tiring journey
4 the tastiest meal
5 the best game

Unit 26

A
2 Jean is as generous as her mother.
3 Neil is as mischievous as his brother.
4 Helen drives as fast as Mary.
5 Your home is as comfortable as ours.
6 This summer is as hot as last
   summer.
7 Becky works as hard as Jenny.
8 Jill can run as fast as Jack.

B
2 cheap
3 well
4 clever
5 cold
6 much
7 quick
8 long

C
2 They're the same height.
3 We're the same weight.
4 They're the same size.
5 They're the same length.

D
2a   3f   4b   5d   6c

Unit 27

A
2 her
3 his
4 their
5 your
6 our
8 their own
9 His own
10 my own
11 its own
12 your own

B
2 parents'
3 David and Neil's
4 James's
5 friends'
6 John and Jean's
7 Sylvia's
8 a week's
9 a couple of days'
10 two weeks'

C
2 They're mine.
3 No, I think it's yours.
4 Yes, I think it's his.
5 Yes, I'm sure it's hers.
6 Yes, it's theirs.

Unit 28

A
2 contribution
3 reply
4 invitation
5 solution
6 cure
7 room
8 sympathy
9 recipe
10 demand

B
2 comment
3 relationship
4 contact
5 increase
6 cause
7 advantage
8 difficulty
9 decision
10 difference

C
2 on
3 in
4 of
5 for
6 on
7 to
8 for
9 of
10 with

Unit 29

A
2 a attacked ; b attacking
3 a leaving ; b left
4 a carrying ; b carried
5 a faced ; b facing
6 a speaking ; b spoken

B
2 burning
3 standing
4 crying
5 drowning
6 lying
7 screaming

C
2 money
3 key
4 box
5 pen
6 room
7 meeting
8 matches

Unit 30

A
2 Yuri Gagarin
3 Marilyn Monroe
4 Canada
5 Kyoto
6 Amazon

B
Example sentence:
Life in the twentieth century is
changing very rapidly.

C
2 that
3 that
4 to
5 that
6 to
7 that

Unit 31

A
2 We enjoyed the concert last night
very much.
3 I met Mary in the supermarket
yesterday.
4 Last year we had a holiday in Greece.
5 In London most people start work
about nine o'clock.
6 This morning I got to work very late.
7 Next year they are building a new
school in our town.
8 You can buy most things cheaply in
the supermarket.
9 Andreas speaks five languages fluently.
10 Jack spoke very angrily at the meeting yesterday.
11 It rained very heavily in London last
night.
12 He wrote his name neatly at the
bottom of the page.

B
2 Quietly he opened the door.
3 Several times I have tried to call you.
4 For over an hour we waited for him.
5 By mistake he posted the wrong
letter.
6 As quickly as possible she drove to
town.
7 Carefully he folded the paper.
8 Only yesterday I spoke to him about
it.
9 In the National Gallery there are
some wonderful paintings.
10 Angrily he walked out of the room.

Unit 32

A
2 slow...slowly
3 angrily...angry
4 comfortably...comfortable
5 beautifully...beautiful
6 nervous...nervously
7 sad...sadly
8 happily...happy
9 carelessly...careless
10 unexpected...unexpectedly

B
2 well
3 carefully...fast
4 fast...late
5 slowly
6 quietly
7 hard...badly
8 anxiously
9 lately
10 quietly...suddenly

Unit 33

A
2 in...in
3 on
4 at...in...-
5 in...at...-
6 in...on
7 at...at...at
8 at...on
9 on...in...-
10 at...at...on...at

B
2 since
3 for
4 for
5 ago
6 since
7 ago
8 since
9 ago
10 since

C
1 from...until
2 in...for
3 ago...by...on
4 in...ago...since
5 from...until...By

Unit 34

C
2 My brother normally goes swimming
twice a week.
3 On Sundays Peter often went to visit
his grandparents./
Peter often went to visit his grandparents on Sundays.
4 The British are always talking about
the weather.
5 I'll probably be back in a couple of
minutes.
6 He will probably be at home at
lunchtime.
7 He should certainly have telephoned
by now./
He certainly should have telephoned
by now
8 I definitely locked the door last
night./
Last night I definitely locked the
door.
9 He usually phoned home every day.
10 Perhaps they didn't get there in time.
11 We hardly ever go to the theatre
nowadays./
Nowadays we hardly ever go to the
theatre.
12 John will probably call round tomorrow.

Unit 35

A
2 any longer
3 yet
4 yet
5 yet
6 any longer / any more

B
2 still
3 still
4 still...already
5 still
6 already

C
2 yet...still
3 A: still
  B: already
4 yet...still
5 yet...still
6 still
7 still...any more
8 already
9 any more
10 A: yet...still
  B: already

Unit 36

A

2 Wrong ; right
3 Right ; wrong
4 Right ; wrong
5 Wrong ; right
6 Right ; wrong

B

2 His success was largely the result of hard work.
3 They finally came to an agreement simply because they were tired of arguing.
4 You can often get what you want simply by asking.
5 He usually disagreed with the majority just to make things difficult.
6 I missed my flight to Cairo partly owing to a traffic hold-up.
7 He finally got what he wanted but it was mainly by good luck.
8 He used to play the fool just to annoy his father.

C

2 quite a big house.
3 quite an exciting film.
4 rather a sad childhood.
5 rather an expensive car.
6 quite a good school.
7 quite an interesting man.
8 rather a naughty child.
9 rather a difficult problem.
10 quite a rude letter.

4 She had a rather sad childhood.
5 It was a rather expensive car.
9 It was a rather difficult problem.

Unit 37

A

True sentences:
2b   3a   4a   5a   6b   7a   8b
9a   10b

B

2 round...across...down
3 opposite...round
4 at...in
5 next to...behind
6 in the middle of...close to

Unit 38

A

2 picture...corner
3 back
4 corner...phone box
5 left...front row
6 flat...Park Street...floor

7 table...bottom
8 car...bus

B

2 in...at
3 at...on...in
4 at...at
5 in...on
6 in...at...on
7 on...in
8 on...at
9 at...in
10 at...in
11 in...at

Unit 39

A

1 b on a bullet train
2 a by luxury liner
  b on a luxury liner
3 a on a jumbo jet
  b by Concorde
4 a on a double-decker bus
  b by bus
5 a by coach
  b in an air-conditioned coach
6 a by car ferry
  b on a car ferry

B

2 on...by
3 in...on
4 on...on
5 by...on
6 by...out of
7 off
8 in
9 by...on
10 in

Unit 40

A

2 do
3 Don't
4 did
5 does
6 Does

B

2 Do...have
3 don't...will
4 have been...hasn't
5 would have...had
6 was...didn't
7 had...were
8 Don't...will
9 are...haven't
10 Does...is

C

2 Have a
3 Does k

4 Has h
5 Do l
6 Have i
7 Does d
8 Do j
9 Have b
10 Has g
11 Do f
12 Does e

Unit 41

A

2 H
3 P
4 P
5 P
6 F
7 P
8 P
9 F
10 H
11 H

B

2 does the train leave
3 doesn't live
4 do you work
5 don't think...likes
6 does Ken get home
7 comes from
8 do you speak
9 does it cost
10 doesn't drink coffee...likes

C

Verbs that refer to the future:
3 B: 've heard
4 A: is coming
  B: 's coming
5 B: go
6 A: 've finished
  B: I'm meeting...'re going

Unit 42

A

3 Where did you go in England?
4 We went to London, but we didn't go to Oxford.
5 What plays did they see at Stratford?
6 They saw Hamlet but they didn't see Julius Caesar.
7 Did Angelo buy some records in London?
8 He bought some clothes but he didn't buy any records.
9 Did you enjoy your holiday?
10 I enjoyed the holiday but I didn't enjoy the food.

B

2 P ; H
3 H ; H

4 N ; N
5 H
6 N ; N
7 P ; P
8 P
9 N ; N
10 H ; H
11 P
12 N

C
2 opened...started
3 were enjoying...went
4 heard...began
5 was talking...burst
6 heard...ran

Unit 43

A
2 broke in...were sleeping
3 ran off...was swimming
4 was shopping...lost
5 was playing tennis...broke
6 met...were working

B
2 starts...are playing
3 am writing...am
4 looks...is enjoying
5 is staying...visits
6 is saving up... is spending

C
2 have been waiting
3 have been studying
4 have been playing
5 have been watching
6 has been working
7 have been walking

D
B: am working...am trying
A: Are you living
B: am living...am sharing

Unit 44

A
2 a
3 e
4 b
5 f
6 c
7 g
8 i
9 j
10 h

B
2 I had seen it before.
3 I had never met him before.
4 I had finished the washing up.
5 I had left it at home.
6 I had lived there for years.

7 I had caught a cold.
8 he had had an accident.
9 had just moved to Oxford.

C
2 will have driven
3 will have learned
4 will have used up
5 will have run

D
2 Scientists will have learned to control the weather.
3 The Third world war will have broken out.
4 Man will have destroyed the planet.
5 The world population will have grown to three billion.
6 Atomic energy will have replaced oil and coal.
7 The rhinoceros will have become extinct.
8 Scientists will have built factories in space.

Unit 45

A
2 is raining...rains
3 am going...go
4 cycles...is raining...is taking...is doing...goes
5 are playing...get...go
6 does your husband do...teaches...is teaching
7 watch...are watching

B
2 smells
3 don't understand
4 are growing up...look
5 seemed...think
6 Does this coat belong
7 is hanging
8 can hear...sounds...is trying

Unit 46

A
2 phoned...was doing
3 met...was working
4 asked...was watching
5 was driving...had
6 were doing...found

B
2 A: Have you seen
   B: saw
3 went...haven't been
4 A: have met
   B: were
5 A: have tried
   B: left

C
2 didn't come...had sent
3 was...had heard
4 had lost...didn't know
5 had finished...went

D
2 He was going to play football, but he forgot his boots.
3 We were going to go swimming, but it was too cold.
4 They were going to visit Oxford, but they didn't have time.
5 He was going to see the play, but there were no seats left.
6 I was going to do my homework, but I had forgotten my books.

Unit 47

A
Andrew was intelligent and go-ahead. He thought there was a great future for engineers in this atomic age. As a trainee, Andrew worked 44 hours in a five day week and earned about £3 per week with an allowance of £1.70. His pay rose to £8.16 at 21. Hostel accommodation was available. Books and instruments could be borrowed and there were opportunities for sport.

B
Because you are talking about the past.

C
2 hated...said...had
3 said...was...had stolen...was...would
4 said...had...looked
5 said...knew...was...wasn't

Unit 48

A
2 h
3 i
4 g
5 b
6 f
7 d
8 a
9 e

B
2 a
3 g
4 b
5 f
6 h
7 c
8 d

C

2 are going to
3 will send
4 are going to collect
5 are going
6 will go

Unit 49

A

2 We're having
3 The meeting starts
4 A few friends are coming round
5 does the last bus leave
6 The match finishes
7 I'm meeting
8 Becky finishes
9 Everybody is going
10 We change

B

2 will give...see
3 will give...see
4 will be...come
5 will have...rains
6 will be...enjoy
7 won't go...go
8 will remember...visit
9 will stay...stops

C

2 will tell...have finished
3 will go...have finished
4 will help...have done
5 will call...has got

D

2 We intend to spend our next holiday in Scotland.
3 I expect to be back at work before long.
4 We are planning to drive to Glasgow.

Unit 50

A

2 Have you read the newspaper?
3 Do you often go for a walk in the park?
4 Does Becky live near here?
5 Have your children gone back to school?
6 Will Sally and Peter be home for lunch?
7 Could you have eaten a bit more?
8 Will Sandra have arrived by noon?
9 Did you ever learn German at school?
10 Do you do most of the cooking at home?
11 Is Joe here?
12 Are Alan and Tina here?

B

2 Which team won first prize at the weekend?

3 What happened when you were late for work this morning?
4 Who told you the answer to the exam question?
5 Who lives next door to you?
6 What is the right answer to this question?
7 Whose car is that red one over there?
8 How many students come to your English class?

C

2 Which chocolates do you like best?
3 How did you come?
4 How far can Jim swim?
5 How many cards did you get?
6 What time will Mary and Bill be there?
7 When did Kathy arrive?
8 When will you have finished work by?/
What time will you have finished work by?

D

2 Who are you going to the dance with?
3 Who is your letter from?
4 Which university does your brother go to?
5 What is this afternoon's lecture about?/ What is the afternoon lecture about?

Unit 51

A

2 Who
3 Which
4 What
5 How
6 Where
7 When
8 Whose
9 how
10 How
11 Where
12 why
13 Which / What
14 Why

B

3 Who have they invited?
4 Who have you lent that book to?
5 What did they give to Peter?
6 Who answered the telephone?
7 What did the manager say?
8 Who did you ask to help?
9 What can we send?
10 Who will be at home?

C

2 How long had/has your young brother been playing outside?
3 What did he ask for?
4 What did you give him?
5 How did he hold the bread?

6 Why did he look so puzzled?
7 Why couldn't he open the door?
8 What did he do with the bread?
9 Where did he go then?

Unit 52

A

2 f
3 d
4 a/e
5 a/e
6 b
7 j
8 i
9 h
10 g

B

2 have you
3 can you
4 have you
5 will it
6 did we
7 do we
8 do we
9 will there

C

2 haven't you
3 wasn't it
4 didn't we
5 won't we
6 can't you
7 mustn't it
8 wasn't it
9 didn't it
10 don't they
11 didn't we
12 had we
13 aren't they
14 isn't there
15 aren't I

Unit 53

A

2 You don't know what time the next train leaves, do you?
3 You wouldn't look after the children, would you?
4 You couldn't tell me what to do, could you?
5 You wouldn't lend me your car, would you?
6 You couldn't come round tomorrow, could you?
7 You haven't got time to help me out, have you?
8 You couldn't do the shopping while you're out, could you?
10 You won't spend too much, will you?
11 You won't drive too fast, will you?
12 You won't be angry with him, will you?

B

2 did you
3 were you
4 was it
5 were you
6 did it
7 did you
8 are you
9 will you
10 will you

Unit 54

A

2 Where do Tom and Mary live?
3 What work does Tom do?
4 How can I get to the post office?
5 How old is she?
6 Who is in charge here?
7 What do I have to do?
8 Who has left his car in front of our house?
9 Where have they gone?
10 When will they be here?

B

2 Is the shop still open?
3 Will Mary be coming?
4 Can I book a room?
5 Is this seat free?
6 Has anyone left any messages for me?
7 Will you be staying long?
8 Did Bill call this evening?

C

2 Do you know where Bill and Tessa live?
3 I wonder if you would look after the children this evening?
4 Could you tell me where the nearest post office is?
5 I wonder if you could give me Peter's address?
6 Do you know where Simon will be staying?
7 I wonder why Jack and Jill left so suddenly?
8 Can you tell me whether the shops open at the weekend?
9 Do you know what he would like for his birthday?
10 I wonder whether you would like to come round for a cup of coffee sometime?

Unit 55

A

2 No, it isn't.
3 Yes, he was.
4 Yes, it will.
5 No, I don't.
6 Yes, I am.
7 No, I don't.

8 No, it isn't.
9 No, he wasn't.
10 Yes, I have!

B

2 a
3 f
4 b
5 g
6 c
7 d
8 h

C

2 f
3 b
4 c
5 g
6 d
7 h
8 e

D

2 I expect so.
3 I suppose so.
4 I'm afraid so.
5 I imagine so.
6 I hope so.

E

2 I hope not.
3 I don't expect so.
4 I don't suppose so.
5 I'm afraid not.

Unit 56

A

2 an insect spray
3 a bottle of cough mixture
4 a tube of toothpaste
5 a bottle of orange squash
6 a packet of breakfast cereal
7 a bottle of cooking oil
8 a tin of milk
9 a box of cheese biscuits

B

First you dial 999 for emergency, wait for the emergency service to answer, and tell the operator which service you want. Then you give the telephone number shown on the phone, give the address where help is needed, and give any other necessary information.

C

2 don't wake her up.
3 Don't keep him waiting.
4 Don't tell anyone.
5 Don't bother me now.

D

3 Let me carry that bag for you.
4 Let's telephone for help.

5 Let me help you.
6 Let's start now.

Unit 57

A

2 We haven't been there often.
3 Mary wasn't very happy.
4 English isn't easy to understand.
5 I haven't been to San Francisco.
6 We mightn't be late.
7 He doesn't know her name.
8 They won't be arriving in time for lunch.
9 We can't go by train.
10 John may not be coming with his wife.

B

2 They probably won't have telephoned.
3 Mary shouldn't have told you.
4 I couldn't have arrived earlier.
5 You shouldn't have asked Peter.
6 They might not have done the shopping.

C

2 She doesn't have any friends in London.
3 He doesn't have any brothers or sisters.
4 I don't have any money.
5 They didn't have any new clothes to wear.
6 We don't have anything to eat.

D

2 Doesn't he earn more than that?
3 Didn't they give you more than that?
4 Can't you stay later than that?
5 Haven't you met his brother too?

E

2 I didn't
3 I haven't
4 they will
5 I can
6 she hasn't
7 I am
8 I hadn't

Unit 58

A

2 None...no
3 Nothing
4 Nowhere
5 Nobody...none
6 Neither
7 never
8 no-one
9 none
10 neither...nor

B

2 anybody
3 no one

4 anything
5 something
6 ever
7 never
8 any
9 none
10 nobody

Unit 59

A

2 They could have seen us.
  They might have seen us.
3 He might have said that. I don't remember.
  He could have said that. I don't remember.
4 We're lost. I think we must have taken the wrong road.
5 You should have seen it. It was wonderful.
6 I should have known that would happen.
7 Perhaps when I am fifty I will have forgotten it.
8 I could have prevented that, but I didn't.
9 You ought to have listened to her the first time.

B

2 They ought to have gone by car./ They should have gone by car.
3 You ought to have telephoned./ You should have telephoned.
4 You ought to have asked John to help./ You should have asked John to help.
5 You ought to have done the shopping./ You should have done the shopping.
7 You ought not to have spent so much money./ You shouldn't have spent so much money.
8 It ought not to have taken you so long./ It shouldn't have taken you so long.
9 They ought not to have done that./ They shouldn't have done that.
10 She ought not to have left so early./ She shouldn't have left so early.
11 He ought not to have made so much noise./ He shouldn't have made so much noise.
12 He ought not to have been so upset./ He shouldn't have been so upset.

Unit 60

A

2 cannot...can
3 could...couldn't
4 may not...may
5 might...might not
6 must...mustn't
7 shall...shan't

8 should...shouldn't
9 will...won't
10 would...wouldn't
11 oughtn't...ought

B

2 speak to Nicky please?
3 give me a few examples?
4 have a word with you please?
5 be so nasty to me?
6 give them for dinner?
7 shut the door?
8 I meet you tonight?
9 I see about my teaching programme?
10 have a drink, Doctor?
11 please tell her that Adrian phoned?

Unit 61

A

Example sentences:
Learning English can often be hard work.
Going to the dentist can sometimes be painful.
Travelling can occasionally be boring.

B

2 George may / might help if you give him a ring.
3 It may / might be a mistake.
4 Things may not / might not be so bad after all.
5 She may not / might not recognize you even if she sees you.
6 It may / might be broken.
Past:
2 George may / might have helped if you had given him a ring.
3 It may / might have been a mistake.
4 Things may not / might not have been so bad after all.
5 She may not / might not have recognized you even if she had seen you.
6 It may / might have been broken.

C

2 It could be a wild animal.
3 It could be one of the neighbours.
4 It could be the wind in the trees.
5 It could be a car passing.
6 It could be someone snoring.
7 It could be someone at the door.
8 It could be a ghost.
Last night:
2 It could have been a wild animal.
3 It could have been one of the neighbours.
4 It could have been the wind in the trees.
5 It could have been a car passing.
6 It could have been someone snoring.
7 It could have been someone at the door.
8 It could have been a ghost.

D

2 can't
3 may not
4 can't
5 may not
6 can't

Unit 62

A

3 ought to be / should be an exciting game.
4 should be / ought to be a comfortable trip.
5 ought to be / should be a nice day.
6 should be / ought to be very profitable.
7 ought to be / should be nice and quiet.

B

2 They must be tired out.
3 He must be delighted.
4 You must be very worried.
5 You must be very proud of him.

C

2 He must have done it.
3 You must have seen him.
4 You must have enjoyed your holiday.
5 They must have gone shopping.
6 Someone must have taken it by mistake.

D

2 It can't be ten o'clock.
3 She can't be her sister.
4 He can't be very well even now.
5 They can't be in.
6 you can't be very far from Birmingham.
7 He can't be feeling very well.

Unit 63

A

Example sentences:
I can count to twenty in Spanish, but my daughter can't.
My friend John can run a marathon, but I can't.
My son can't swim, but I can.
I can't play chess, but my brother can.
Example questions:
Can you swim like a fish?
Can you understand sign language?

B

Example sentence:
When I was ten years old, I could swim, but I couldn't ride a bike.

C

2 can't
3 couldn't

4 can
5 could
6 Can
7 can't

Unit 64

A
2 Can I ask you just one more question?
3 Can I give you a ring sometime later?
4 Can we go swimming?
5 Can I sit down?
6 Can I have an ice-cream please?
7 Can I go home now?
8 Can I come back later?
Example request with 'may':
3 May I give you a ring sometime later?
Example request with 'could':
8 Could I come back later?

B
2 Do you think I could start now?
3 Do you mind if I listen to the radio while you're working?
4 Is it all right if I come in now?
5 Do you think I could speak next?

C
2 You're allowed to have visitors after three o'clock.
3 You can all go home as soon as you've finished work.
4 You can come back late as long as you don't make too much noise.
5 With this card you are allowed to cash a cheque for up to £250.
6 You can use my pen until I need it myself.

D
1 get married...vote
2 drive a car...drive a taxi
3 drive a car...vote
4 get married / leave school...drive a car
5 vote
6 drive a car...drive a taxi

Unit 65

A
Example requests:
Could I have a look at your newspaper please?
May I have one of those biscuits please?
Could you let me have a little more time please?
Could you give me another cup of coffee please?

B
2 Would you mind helping this lady with her bags.

3 Would you mind paying cash, please?.
4 Would you mind telling them that I called?
5 Would you mind closing the door behind you, please.
6 Would you mind doing the shopping on your way home?
7 Would you mind helping me, please.
8 Would you mind doing the cooking tonight?
9 Would you mind coming ten minutes before the meeting starts?
10 Would you mind telling me when you're ready?

C
2 you could give Joan a message?
3 giving me your full name?
4 you could repeat that?
5 you could stand up?
6 holding this for me?
7 you could open the door?
8 doing it again?
9 all of you could sit down quietly?
10 you could give me a little more time?

Unit 66

A
2 always use a word processor.
3 borrow the money from the bank?
4 get the information from the local library.
5 take a later train.

B
2 to get started as soon as possible.
3 write and ask her yourself.
4 taking a winter holiday for a change?
5 just pay at the end of the month.
6 take a week off in July.
7 about asking Bill to help?
8 could ring and tell them you're coming.
9 we borrow the equipment from Peter?
10 be a good idea to keep quiet about that.

C
2 f
3 g
4 h
5 d
6 b
7 a
8 e

Unit 67

A
2 d
3 a
4 e
5 f
6 b

7 h
8 g

B
2 You must come round for a game of chess some time.
3 You must bring your wife with you next time.
4 You must meet my brother next time he's here.
5 You must have another cup of coffee.
6 You must stay a little longer.
7 You must see my holiday photographs.
8 You must come to the theatre with me some time next week.
9 You must stay for lunch.
10 You must have another piece of cake.

C
2 h
3 a
4 b
5 d
6 e
7 c
8 f

Unit 68

A
2 Would you like to go with me?
No thanks, I'd like to go alone./ I'd rather go alone.
3 Would you like to start now?
No thanks, I'd like to wait a few minutes./ I'd rather wait a few minutes.
4 Would you like to go shopping this morning?
No thanks, I'd like to go this afternoon./ I'd rather go this afternoon.
5 Would you like to pay cash?
No thanks, I'd like to pay by cheque./ I'd rather pay by cheque.

B
2 to find a better job.
3 to start all over again.
4 to see them more often.
5 to understand more about it.
6 to have a bigger garden.

C
2 learning English.
3 being chairman.
4 going back to work.
5 going into politics.
6 catching an early train.

D
3 I wish he wouldn't.
4 I wish he would.
5 I wish we could.
6 I wish she should.

7 I wish they could.
8 I wish she would.

Unit 69

A
2 You must stand to attention.
3 You have to keep your boots clean.
4 You have to get up early.
5 You must keep fit. / You must do exercises.
6 You must salute your superiors.
7 You have to learn to use a rifle. / You must learn to shoot.
8 You must keep your equipment clean./ You have to clean your equipment.

B
2 You must
3 You mustn't
4 You must
5 You mustn't
6 You must

C
2 d
3 a
4 c
5 b

Unit 70

A
2 He doesn't need to keep his hair short.
3 He doesn't need to keep his boots clean.
4 He doesn't need to get up early.
5 He doesn't need to keep fit.

B
1 She doesn't need to stay in bed.
2 She doesn't need to take any more tablets.
3 She doesn't need to get plenty of sleep.
4 She doesn't need to drink lots of water.

C
2 a
3 e
4 b
5 d
6 c

D
2 What? He needn't have sent it by fax.
3 Really? She needn't have bought a first-class ticket.
4 Oh? You needn't have brought your own.
5 What? They needn't have cleaned it

out themselves.
6 Really? You needn't have cooked your own supper.
Note that in 2-6 you can use any of the exclamations given.
2 You didn't need to send it by fax.
3 She didn't need to buy a first-class ticket.
4 You didn't need to bring your own.
5 They didn't need to clean it out themselves.
6 You didn't need to cook your own supper.

Unit 71

A
3 You ought to
4 You ought not to
5 You ought not to
6 You ought to
7 You ought not to
8 You ought to
9 You ought not to
10 You ought to

B
2 h
3 b
4 f
5 i
6 g
7 d
8 a
9 j
10 e

C
3 I should have got home earlier.
4 We should have read the instructions carefully.
5 You shouldn't have spent so much money.
6 You should have told me you were coming.
7 They shouldn't have made such a noise.
8 John should have paid his bill./ John shouldn't have left the restaurant without paying his bill.
9 Jack should have explained what he was doing.
10 You should have sent Mary a birthday card.

1 You ought to have phoned.
2 They oughtn't to have made such a mess.
3 I ought to have got home earlier.
4 We ought to have read the instructions carefully.
5 You oughtn't to have spent so much money.

Unit 72

A
2 T a car ; I
3 T anyone ; I
4 I ; T human nature
5 T a course ; I
6 I ; T chemistry
7 I ; T the handle
8 I ; T me
9 I ; T What
10 T the bus ; I

B
2 choose
3 know
4 phone
5 remember
6 forget
7 understand
8 leave
9 watch
10 heard

Unit 73

A
2 John sold his old car to Mary.
3 Could you show those old photographs to your grandfather?
4 Save something to eat for the rest of us.
5 I'm going to book a really good table for your guests.
6 We've prepared a light snack for you.
7 We'll leave some food in the fridge for you.
8 I taught French to Peter's children when they were younger.
9 I'll try to find those books for you.
10 We must remember to send a card to George and Alice.

B
2 She cooked them a wonderful meal.
3 He passed him the money.
4 Cut them some bread.
5 Give her this letter.
6 She used to teach them arithmetic.
7 I'd like to keep them something.
8 You must show them these papers.
9 He always reads her a story before she goes to sleep.
10 I'm going to write her a short note.

C
2 Mrs Brown left some money for the milkman.
3 We sent a Christmas card to the people we met on holiday.
4 He gave her some flowers on her birthday.
5 Jack and Mary promised the children a day at the seaside.
6 Nobody told us what to do.

Unit 74

A

2 Help yourself / yourselves
3 behave themselves
4 repeating himself
5 enjoy myself
6 introduce myself
7 teaching herself
8 describe myself
9 blame yourself / yourselves
10 express himself
11 excelled themselves
12 kill herself

B

2 You ought to behave yourself better than that.
3 You must learn to adapt yourself / yourselves to new ideas.
4 The children tried to hide themselves in the cupboard.
5 You can dry yourself on that towel.
6 Billy undressed himself before going to bed.

Unit 75

A

2 attack
3 fight
4 cooperate
5 argue
6 compete
7 talk
8 bumped
9 communicate
10 part

B

2 of
3 to
4 with
5 at
6 to
7 into
8 at / to
9 of
10 at
11 on
12 on

C

2 themselves
3 each other
4 themselves
5 each other
6 themselves
7 each other
8 themselves

Unit 76

A

2 tear

---

3 crack
4 boiled
5 sell
6 stops
7 cook
8 began
9 rang
10 wash
11 increased
12 handles

B

2 water
3 material
4 vase
5 pace
6 car
7 shirt
8 building
9 hand
10 window
11 train
12 potatoes

Unit 77

A

2 make
3 give
4 give
5 have
6 have
7 give
8 have

B

2 go
3 do
4 go
5 are going
6 did
7 does
8 go

C

2 do
3 done
4 make
5 making
6 do
7 make
8 make

D

2 do
3 take
4 give / make
5 have
6 have
7 gave
8 made
9 took
10 had
11 give
12 made

Unit 78

A

2 suffered from
3 resulted in
4 appealing to / for
5 sympathize with
6 belonged to
7 depend on
8 hoping for
9 insist on
10 qualify for
11 pay for

B

2 to...about
3 about...about
4 to...about...about
5 about...to
6 to...about...about

C

2 at
3 at
4 into
5 at

D

2 with...for
3 for
4 for...with
5 for

Unit 79

A

2 stay on
3 wait up
4 give in
5 keep up
6 speak up
7 Watch out
8 cool off
9 catch up
10 fall behind

B

2 ask us in
3 call him back
4 pull them apart
5 invite you in
6 get it back
7 catch her out
8 invite them out
9 work it out
10 show you out

C

3 bumped into an old friend
4 looking after the house
5 invite them out
6 take after my mother

Unit 80

A
2 sounds
3 goes
4 feels
5 gets
6 smells
7 tastes
8 grows

B
2 The fruit smelled awful, but it proved to be very tasty.
3 The problem seemed simple, but it proved to be extremely difficult.
4 It was a long programme, but it proved to be very interesting.
5 It was only a short walk, but it proved to be rather tiring.
6 The animal looked quiet enough, but it proved to be quite vicious.
7 The jacket seemed to be the right size, but it proved to be much too small.
8 The food smelled all right, but it proved to be uneatable.

C
2 too dark
3 too young
4 too late
5 too hot
6 too tired
7 too cold
8 too expensive

Unit 81

A
2 Judy remembered noticing him behind the building.
3 When his Dad asked, did you mention seeing him?
4 I couldn't recall saying anything about him at all.
5 May I suggest giving them a present of £500 each?
6 Sorry, but I can't imagine ever agreeing to that!
7 He then described escaping from prison.
8 They ought to admit stealing the fruit.

B
2 Could you consider reducing the price, for example to £6,000?
3 They delayed starting the game because of the rain.
4 I want to avoid paying monthly if possible.
5 They didn't finish preparing for the party until after 9pm.
6 This new production process might involve increasing staff.

C
2 dread going
3 detest getting stuck
4 carry on driving
5 fancies taking up
6 can't bear being told
7 give up playing
8 feel like having

Unit 82

A
2 to go
3 to drive
4 to sell
5 to be
6 to hear
7 to be
8 to finish

B
2 asked
3 expected
4 invited
5 allowed
6 encouraged
7 warned
8 reminded

C
3 to have broken your leg.
4 to have locked everything away.
5 to be waiting for the doctor.
6 to have spent the money.
7 to be living at home now.

D
2 not to see
3 not to miss
4 not to make
5 not to write
6 not to be

Unit 83

A
2 playing
3 to phone
4 raining / to rain
5 knocking / to knock
6 shouting / to shout
7 to enjoy
8 staying

B
2 paying ; to pay
3 working ; to work
4 complaining ; to complain
5 leaving ; to leave
6 telling ; to tell
7 going ; to go
8 visiting ; to visit

C
The door needs painting.
The tyre needs mending.
The shirt needs ironing.
The trousers need shortening.
The shoes need polishing.

Unit 84

A
2 A: made
   B: let...made
3 A: let
   B: make
4 A: let
   B: make
5 A: let
   B: made
6 A: made
   B: let

B
2 burning
3 playing
4 lying
5 making

C
2 have my hair cut
3 had that suit made
4 have the house redecorated
5 have another room built on
6 had a lot of money stolen

Unit 85

A
2 was owned
3 had been presented
4 was given
5 cannot be named
6 was stolen
7 was arranged...was to be flown in...exchanged...had been staffed
8 was shown
9 was taken
10 was arrested

B
2 e made PAST
3 a won FUTURE
4 f killed P
5 c disconnected P
6 h paid P
7 d sent F
8 j told P
9 g permitted
10 i rebuilt

C
2 be obtained
3 be considered
4 be expected
5 be funded

6 be given
7 be held
8 be made
9 be offered

Unit 86

A

Example sentences:
It is difficult travelling in the rush hour.
It can be fun meeting new people.

B

2 It is a village near Birmingham.
3 but it is very difficult to understand.
4 It opened about a month ago. We went there last week but it was very expensive and we didn't like it very much.
5 I think it is in the kitchen. I put it back in the drawer.
6 she tried not to show it.
7 I really enjoyed it.
Yes I enjoyed it too. I thought it was very interesting.
I didn't see it. I went to bed before it started.

C

2 It's very annoying to miss a train.
3 It's nice to get a letter from an old friend.
4 It's fun to go for a good night out.
5 It's interesting to learn another language.
6 It's unhealthy to eat too much.
7 It's tiring to look after children.
8 It's very dangerous to drive too fast.

Unit 87

A

2 to sleep
3 to eat
4 to spare
5 to help
6 to do
7 to read
8 to ask
9 to watch
10 to see

B

2 There is a class every Friday.
3 There will be a meeting at three o'clock on Tuesday.
4 There will be lots of children at the concert.
5 There will be a few friends coming round.
6 There are lots of parties given by people at Christmas.
7 There will be an accident if you're not careful.
8 There must have been a mistake.

C

3 There appears to be something wrong with the engine.
4 There seems to be nothing left.
5 There seems to have been an accident.
6 There appears to have been a lot of trouble.
7 There seems to be no one at home.
8 There appears to have been a fire.
Note that in all these sentences it is possible to use either 'appears' or 'seems'.

Unit 88

A

2 b
3 f
4 c
5 a
6 g
7 d
8 e

B

2 admit...admit
3 deny...denied
4 announce...announced
5 complain...complained
6 mention...mentioned
7 explain...explained
8 argue...argue

C

2 informed
3 suggested
4 told
5 announced
6 mentioned

Unit 89

A

2 John's doctor advised him to get more sleep.
3 We invited our friends to come round and see us any time.
4 Jack told me to take the money to the bank.
5 Mr Brown reminded the students to come half an hour early on Tuesday.
6 Bill begged Maria to write to him every day.
7 I warned the children not to play with fire.
8 My grandfather advised me not to go to England in the winter.
9 They told the visitors not to go out alone after dark.
10 The manager persuaded her not to make an official complaint.

B

2 Joe asked Mary where she was going to spend the holiday.

3 Everybody asked us why the tickets were so expensive.
4 Frank asked his wife how old Mary's children were.
5 Mrs Jones asked her neighbour who was going to buy their house.
6 Bill asked his friend when he was planning to come to Darlington.
7 I asked Maria what she was going to do next.
8 Peter asked a policeman where he could get the bus to Liverpool.

Unit 90

A

1 arrived...were playing
2 sat...arrived arrived...sat
3 was working...phoned phoned...was working
4 heard...was writing was writing...heard
5 telephoned...heard heard...telephoned

B

2 will let...phones
3 will be raining...set out
4 will tell...see
5 will buy...go

C

2 c
3 e
4 a
5 b
6 f

2 We hadn't been to the cinema since we had seen Dracula at the Odeon last year.
3 He hadn't been able to play the piano since he had had his accident a month ago.
4 They had lived next door to us since they had moved here in 1987.
5 Fred had been working at home ever since he had left his job at the factory.
6 Mary had been looking after the children ever since their mother had gone into hospital.

Unit 91

A

2 c
3 i
4 a
5 f
6 b
7 e
8 g
9 h
10 d

B

2 has
3 are working
4 goes
5 is

C

2 j
3 h
4 b
5 f
6 a
7 g
8 d
9 e
10 c

Unit 92

A

2 I would go abroad if I could afford it.
3 I could buy that car if it wasn't so expensive.
4 We could go out if it wasn't raining.
5 She would come to the party if she wasn't away on holiday.
6 If the central heating was working we could turn it on.

B

2 If he had passed his exams he could have gone to university.
3 If he had realized what was happening he would have run away.
4 If I had heard what she said I would have been very angry.
5 They wouldn't have got in if you had locked the door properly.
6 It wouldn't have happened if you had followed the instructions.
7 If she had found out she would have been furious.
8 If we hadn't booked a room we would have had nowhere to stay.
9 If we had been going any faster someone could have been killed.
10 If he hadn't been so tired he wouldn't have gone home at lunchtime.

C

2 h
3 a
4 f
5 d
6 b
7 e
8 c

Unit 93

A

2 Try to write clearly so as to avoid being misunderstood.
3 A lot of people learn English in order

to study in English.
4 What do I need to know in order to be a good doctor?
5 She turned up early in order to get the room ready.
6 In order to have 100 students you will need at least three teachers.
7 I came to live in the country so as to have trees around me instead of buildings.
8 They had to eat grass and drink melted snow in order to stay alive.
9 In order to keep his car out of sight he left it in the road.
10 To get to Madrid I had to travel overnight from Barcelona.

B

2 She moved carefully to avoid waking the children.
3 He sat in the furthest corner to avoid being seen.
4 I gave up sugar and butter to avoid putting on weight.
5 He used both hands to avoid dropping anything.
6 We went over everything carefully to avoid making any mistakes.
7 She left quietly to avoid making any trouble.
8 We covered the furniture to avoid getting paint all over it.

Unit 94

A

2 such a ; so
3 so ; such a
4 so ; such a
5 so ; such a
6 such a ; so
7 such a ; so
8 such a ; so
9 so ; such a
10 such a ; so

B

2 Her writing was so small that I could hardly read it.
3 The winter was so bitterly cold that all the streams were frozen.
4 His favourite shoes were so badly worn that he had to throw them away.
5 He looked so young that everyone took him for a student.
6 Ken got so excited that he kept jumping up and down.

C

2 He was such a dreadful liar that nobody believed anything he said.
3 It proved to be such a difficult problem that nobody could solve it.
4 We had such a good time that we didn't want to go home.

5 They were such old clothes that they were falling apart.
6 It was such good food that we all ate far too much.

Unit 95

A

2 the weather was awful
3 She kept her coat on
4 I used to when I was younger
5 you're not as tall as he was
6 he still wasn't tired
7 He was difficult to understand
8 I really like John
9 we finally arrived just in time

B

2 his recent illness
3 her fear
4 the unpopularity of his decision
5 the difference in their ages
6 the high cost of living
7 all his precautions
8 his injury
9 the rain

Unit 96

A

2 They arrived late, just as you said they would.
3 He ran away, just as everyone believed he would.
4 The play was a success, just as most people thought it would be.
5 He did well at school, just as we hoped he would.
6 Mary won, just as we thought she would.

B

2 They still farm the way their grandfathers did.
3 He accepted his punishment the way everyone else did.
4 She refused to dress the way her colleagues did.
5 He said he would work the way the others did if he was paid as they were.
6 They work a five day week the way we do.
7 He trusts you the way I do.
8 She looks after him the way her mother did.
2 They still farm like their grandfathers did.
3 He accepted his punishment like everyone else did.
4 She refused to dress like her colleagues did.

C

2 They look as if they've got some good news.
3 This milk smells as though it's gone sour.
4 Your engine sounds as if it's worn out.
5 He looks as though he's going to make trouble.
6 I feel as if I'm going to be sick.
Note that it is possible to use 'as if' or 'as though' in all these sentences.

D

2 a
3 d
4 e
5 b

Unit 97

A

2 that lives in America
3 that were stolen
4 that plays James Bond
5 that answered the phone
6 that was left behind on the desk
7 that live in glass houses
9 that I met on the train
10 that we took on holiday
11 that you read in the newspaper
12 that I left on the table
13 that The Beatles recorded in 1966
14 that you asked for

B

2 who
3 which
4 who
5 who
6 which
7 who
8 which
9 who
10 which
11 which
12 which
13 which
14 which

C

2 when
3 why
4 where
5 whose
6 why
7 whose

Unit 98

A

3 You've all met Michael Wood, who is visiting us for a couple of days.
4 Michael Wood, who is one of my oldest friends, has just gone to live in Canada.

5 We are moving to Manchester, which is in the north-west.
6 Manchester, which is in the north-west, is one of England's fastest growing towns.
7 I'll be staying with Adrian, whose brother is one of my closest friends.
8 This is Adrian, whose house we stayed in for our holidays.

B

2 a
3 e
4 f
5 b
6 c
7 g
8 d

C

2 Only two people came to look at the house, neither of whom wanted to buy it.
3 He had a lot to say about his new computer, none of which interested me very much.
4 There were some noisy people in the audience, one of whom kept interrupting the speaker.
5 She made all kinds of suggestions, most of which I couldn't understand.

Unit 99

A

2 have I heard such a lot of nonsense.
3 we went to Brighton.
4 jumped a live mouse.
5 did she tell me that she would be coming round.
6 did they spend all my money

B

2 a
3 e
4 b
5 c

C

2 it was Ken who left the message.
3 it is usually just after nine when he comes in.
4 it is this afternoon that he is calling in.
5 it was Becky who he wanted to see.
6 it is tomorrow that he is going to call back.

Unit 100

A

A student went to her first lecture at the university, and mentioned this to a friend, another student. 'What was it about?' asked her friend. 'I don't know,' the first student replied. 'Why not?'

asked the second. 'Weren't you listening?' 'Of course I was listening,' the first student replied, 'but he didn't tell us what it was about.'

A wealthy man was told by his bank manager that he owed the bank £100 and that he would have to pay 12% interest per year. The customer agreed to pay, and said he would leave his car, a Rolls Royce, as security. He then drove the car round to the bank, and left it in the car park. A month later, he returned to collect the car. The curious bank manager asked why he had insisted on leaving it in the car park. 'Where else could I park it for a month, for only £1?' replied the customer.

B

3,1,4,2,6,8,5,7

C

7,2,9,3,1,6,5,10,4,8

Bank of further exercises

1
2 f
3 c
4 a
5 h
6 b
7 e
8 g

2
2 did it ourselves
3 cut it myself
4 get it myself
5 carry it myself
6 meet her myself

3
This is a story about four people called Everybody, Somebody, Nobody, and Anybody. There was an important job to be done and everybody was asked to do it. But Everybody knew that Anybody could do it and thought that Somebody really ought to do it. As it turned out Nobody did it and Everybody was very cross because Nobody had done what Anybody could have done and Somebody should have done.

4
2 Both children have left school now.
3 Could you carry this bag for me?
4 I'd like to buy those brown shoes please.
5 I have to go to the bank this afternoon.
6 They live in a big new house.
7 I'm afraid I haven't got much money left.
8 I'd like to buy some fruit.
9 Most people enjoy going to the theatre.
10 You can buy soap at any supermarket.

5
A psychiatrist greeting a new patient noticed that she was carrying a live duck under her arm. He invited her to take a seat and asked how he could help her. 'Oh, I don't need any help, thank you doctor,' she replied. 'My husband is the one who has a problem. He think's he's a duck.'

A young man was out for a walk in a large city when he met a penguin. The penguin seemed to like him and began to follow him. The young man didn't know what to do so he went up to a policeman to ask for advice. 'Take it to the zoo,' said the policeman. The next day the policeman saw the same young man again still followed by the penguin. 'What are you doing with that penguin?' he asked. 'I told you to take it to the zoo.'
'Yes,' said the young man, 'we went to the zoo yesterday. Today we are going to a / the museum.'

6
2 All of them.
3 All of it.
4 All of us.
5 All of them.

7
2 All of the / All the big triangles are black.
3 Both of the / Both the big squares are white.
4 Neither of the big squares are black.
5 Both of the / Both the large circles are black.
6 None of the circles are green.

8
2 old
3 deep
4 high / thick
5 long...wide
6 - / in weight

9
2 fascinating
3 terrifying
4 exhausting
5 alarming
6 thrilling

10
2 John is a good deal taller than Mary.
3 Mary is a little older than John.
4 Peter is far taller than Mary.
5 John is a good deal heavier than Mary.
6 Peter is far heavier than John.

11
2 the biggest ocean
3 the most populated country
4 the oldest university
5 the longest river
6 the longest river

12
2 Mike...Peter...John
3 John...Peter...Mike
4 John...Mike...Peter
5 Peter...John...Mike
6 John...Mike
7 Mike...John
8 John...Peter

13
2 That book is a favourite of Mary's.
3 Mr White is a colleague of my father's.
4 Angela is a classmate of hers.
5 I'm an employee of theirs.
6 Jack is a neighbour of yours.

14
2 the unexpected death of the chairman
3 the late departure of the train
4 the theft of her jewellery
5 the dreadful behaviour of the children
6 the invasion of the island

15
2 decision
3 opportunity
4 need
5 refusal
6 willingness
7 attempt
8 order

16
1 a...my...some...-...the...the
2 a...-...It was
3 a lot of...few
4 -...-...the...the
5 the... the...-...the... the... a few... The...the...the...the...-

17
1 A: both
B: either
C: neither
2 None...all...no

18
2 annoying
3 amazing
4 embarrassed
5 convinced
6 driving

19
2 Staying in a hotel is more comfortable than camping.
3 Eating out is easier than cooking for myself.
4 Living in the country is more peaceful than living in a town.
5 Cycling is healthier than driving.

20
2 Our holiday began on Saturday morning.
3 She shook her head unhappily.
4 He walked back home slowly and sadly.
5 He locked up the office before going home.
6 There was a gold ring in the box.
7 He whispered his name quietly.
8 She went for a jog early in the morning.
9 I tried to stop him too late.
10 The film began at exactly seven o'clock.

21
2 for ; ago ; since
3 ago ; since ; for
4 since ; for ; ago

5 Since ; ago ; for
6 ago ; for ; since
7 for ; ago ; since
8 ago ; for ; since

22
2 very happy
3 awfully good
4 really angry
5 extremely intelligent

23
2 b
3 g
4 c
5 i
6 a
7 d
8 h
9 e

24
1 on...in...at
2 on...at...on
3 at...on...at...in...at

25
2 slowly
3 careful
4 happily
5 well
6 lately
7 late
8 hard

26
1 at...in...-...-/on...until
2 since...-
3 -...by...on
4 at...ago...on
5 for...during...since
6 -...from...to
7 yet...still
8 since...still
9 for...just
10 already...yet

27
1 by...on
2 at...to
3 on...above
4 in...at
5 out of
6 in...on
7 off...at...opposite
8 in

28
had finished...had had
had asked... chose... told... was... was...
rushed ...had happened

29
was trying...was living...was sharing

30
2 is increasing
3 is improving

4 is changing...is getting
5 is improving
6 was getting
7 is getting
8 are growing up
9 are improving
10 is changing

31
I used to play the drums. I would practise for hours every evening, and I would spend almost every weekend practising too. I used to go to my local jazz club every week to listen. One night a group called The Rollers was playing there. Unfortunately, their drummer had had an accident on his way to the club, so he couldn't play. They asked me to take his place, and of course I agreed. It was awful. I felt that I had never played so badly before. After that, I still used to go to the club, but I never offered to play again, and they certainly didn't ask me.

32
As Eric sat on his bed reading, the hotel manager's daughter knocked on the door. Her father had told her that Eric was English, and she wanted him to help her with the translation she had been set for homework.

33
2 A banker is a man who lends you an umbrella when the weather is fine and takes it away from you when it rains / is raining.
3 If you want to eat well in England, eat three breakfasts. That's what I always do, and I have had no cause to regret it.

34
2 How well do you speak French?
3 Will you be at school next Friday?
4 Who sits next to you in class?
5 Who do you sit next to in class?

35
2 b
3 f
4 c
5 g
6 d
7 h
8 a

36
2 were they
3 didn't they
4 does it
5 didn't it
6 was there
7 is there
8 do they
9 isn't it
10 haven't they

37
2 if / whether Joe still lives in Liverpool.
  if / whether Joe still lived in Liverpool.
3 if / whether you have mended the roof.if / whether you had mended the roof.
4 when Harry will be moving to Manchester.
  when Harry would be moving to Manchester.
5 what time the concert finishes.
  what time the concert would finish.
6 if / whether Peggy will be coming too.
  if / whether Peggy would be coming too.
7 if / whether they will have to speak English all the time.
  if / whether they would have to speak English all the time.
8 who you spoke to on the phone.
  who you had spoken to on the phone.

38
2 Do come and see us at the weekend.
3 Do bring the children too.
4 Do have some more tea.
5 Do write to me when you get home.
7 Do listen more carefully.
8 Do be more careful.
9 Do be quiet while I'm talking.
10 Do sit down and behave yourself.

39
2 ?
3 A
4 !
5 ?
6 A
7 !
8 ?
9 A

40
2 it could be true.
3 You could cut yourself.
4 they could easily win.
5 could earn as much as £50,000 a year if she gets the job.
6 It could cause a serious accident.
7 you could get there in time.
8 It could be for you.
9 that he could be dangerous.
10 which could turn to snow on high ground.

41
Example sentence:
A hundred years ago I could have read Shakespeare, but I couldn't have read Ernest Hemingway.

42
2 b
3 a
4 c
5 f

6 e

43
3 He must know the answer.
4 They must have left for school.
5 You must have read it.
6 This must be the rush hour.

44
2 can hear...can't see
3 can smell
4 can't hear
5 can see
6 can't see

45
2 was able to
3 won't be able to
4 are able to
5 were able to
6 will be able to
7 won't be able to

46
2 He couldn't have played tennis.
3 He couldn't have done the shopping.
4 He couldn't have gone for a long walk in the country.
5 He couldn't have mown the lawn.
6 He couldn't have cycled to the next village.

47
2 go together.
3 buy a new one.
4 see a doctor.
5 go home.
6 come too.
7 come with me.
8 come round and meet him.

48
2 a
3 g
4 b
5 h
6 c
7 i
8 d
9 e

49
3 You ought to have asked for permission.
4 We ought not to have stayed so late.
5 You ought to have gone to the doctor's earlier.
6 You ought to have met Jenny while you were here.
7 I ought not to have got so angry about what happened.
8 You ought to have come on your own.
9 We ought to have reserved seats.
10 You ought to have stopped at the traffic lights.

50
3 I had better ask my father first.

4 We had better be going home now.
5 They had better not make any trouble.
6 You had better get a return ticket.
7 You had better not go out alone at night.
8 You had better go to bed.
9 We had better get something to eat.
10 We had better not waste any more time.

51
2 He offered a lot of help to his next door neighbour.
3 I have cooked a special supper for the children.
4 Please send your reply to us as soon as possible.
5 I'll try to save a place for you.
6 Show that book you've just bought to your uncle.

52
2 gave
3 took
4 had
5 did
6 went
7 gave
8 had

53
1 ...on
2 of...on
3 on...of
4 on...of
5 of...on

54
2 laugh at
3 apologize for
4 rely on
5 talk about

55
2 fold them up
3 put them away
4 point it out
5 tore them up
6 threw them away
7 sort them out
8 knocked it down
9 hand it over
10 pull it down

56
2 We never found out who knocked the vase over.
We never found out who knocked over the vase.
3 He refused to hand the money over.
He refused to hand over the money.
4 Can you help me to sort the papers out?
Can you help me to sort out the papers?
5 It would be very useful if someone could sort my mistakes out.

It would be very useful if someone could sort out my mistakes.
6 It's very hard work bringing children up.
It's very hard work bringing up children.
7 They're planning to pull all the houses down.
They're planning to pull down all the houses.
8 Andrew never remembers to put his books away.
Andrew never remembers to put away his books.

57
2 a
3 b
4 f
5 c
6 d

58
2 stops...keeps
3 started...went on
4 kept on...stopped...started
5 finished...went on...stop...start

59
2 hear
3 see
4 feel
5 stop
6 prevent
7 imagine

60
Example sentence:
1 I loathe going to the dentist.

61
2 was supposed to cost a million pounds.
3 was reported to have been hit by an earthquake early this morning.
4 is known to be a brilliant policeman.
5 is alleged to have brought dangerous drugs into the country.
6 is understood to be armed and dangerous.

62
2 who to ask.
3 where to go.
4 how to open it.
5 when to start.
6 how to play tennis.
7 how to swim.

63
2 interrupting
3 shouting
4 to get
5 leaving
6 to post
7 to come
8 asking

64

2 speak
3 move
4 steal
5 leave

65

2 get my photograph taken
3 get it mended
4 get them shortened
5 got his nose broken

66

2 Full details of the job were sent to me.
3 Signed certificates were presented to all of them.
4 All passengers are offered a free sightseeing trip.
5 Everyone in our group has been given drinks and snacks.
6 The news of their success was brought to her yesterday evening.

67

2 It is known that he is a dangerous man.
3 It is said that Charlie Chaplin was a great comedian.
4 It is understood that she will be arriving later today.
5 It is rumoured that they have escaped.

68

2 b
3 e
4 h
5 g
6 c
7 d
8 a

69

2 warn...warned
3 beg...begged
4 invites...invited
5 reminds...Remind
6 command...commanded
7 instruct...instructed
8 advise...advised

70

2 John asked Jill if she was ready to go.
3 The children asked their parents if they could go on the school picnic.
4 I asked the policeman if there was a bus to Piccadilly.
5 My wife asked me if we could afford to take a taxi.
6 The customs officer asked Joe if he had anything to declare.

71

1 usually go...am going...is being
2 A: Do you know
  B: haven't seen...think...is probably doing

3 doesn't eat...finds...don't have...usually telephones
4 A: have you been living
  B: are staying...have found
5 A: met...was waiting
  B: haven't seen
  A: seemed
  B: think...has just got...hasn't he
  A: just left...hasn't found...is still looking
6 knew...had been...would often go ...wanted...are you going to...asked ...can't...am not going...don't need...just want...can read...write ...will have
7 would write... was going... was...could not...was not going... was...could...wrote...would have
8 heard...were...remember...once cut...didn't you cut...had already done

72

2 will they
3 didn't she
4 is there
5 did they
6 isn't it
7 haven't they
8 did you
9 won't I
10 doesn't he
11 will you
12 aren't they

73

2 Couldn't you have sent me a letter?
3 Mightn't they have gone home earlier?
4 Shouldn't we have paid in advance?
5 Couldn't you have taken a bus?

74

2 I don't think so.
3 I suppose so.
4 I expect so.
5 I'm afraid not.
6 I think so.

75

2 You must come home before midnight.
3 You shouldn't go out in the rain.
4 You oughtn't to complain so much.
5 You mustn't spend too much money.

76

2 I wish we had time to stop.
3 I wish John had passed his examination.
4 I wish it wasn't so cold in here.
5 I wish there was some time to spare.
6 I wish George would help.
7 I wish Mary had come.
8 I wish I had seen the match last week.

77

2 On hearing the noise, I immediately telephoned the police.

3 On hearing my report, they promised to send two policemen round.
4 Arriving at my house, one policeman found that a window had been broken.
5 Seeing this, he rang the doorbell.
6 On hearing the bell, a burglar ran out through the back door.
7 Seeing the burglar escaping, the second policeman chased after him.
8 Running across the road, the unlucky burglar was hit by a car.
9 After having arrested the man, the police called for an ambulance.
10 On arriving at the hospital, they found the man had made his escape.

78

2 a
3 g
4 f
5 b
6 h
7 d
8 c
9 e

79

2 She moved carefully in order not to wake the children.
3 He sat in the furthest corner in order not to be seen.
4 I gave up sugar and butter in order not to put on weight.
6 We went over everything carefully, so as not to make any mistakes.
7 She left quietly, so as not to make any trouble.
8 We covered the furniture, so as not to get paint all over it.

80

2 The houses were knocked down, so that they could be replaced by car parks and office blocks.
3 I sat next to the window, so that I could see out.
4 He tied a knot in his handkerchief, so that he wouldn't forget.
5 I waved my arms, so that they would see me.
6 He wanted the report early, so that he could discuss it with colleagues.
7 We will take a telescope, so that we can see the birds without getting too close.
8 I'll fasten the donkey, so that it doesn't escape.
9 She left her address, so that we could forward her letters.
10 He wore a disguise, so that even his friends wouldn't recognize him.

81

2 well
3 lucky
4 Chinese

5 noisy
6 food
7 room
8 old
9 clean
10 work

82
2 too young
3 too far
4 too quickly
5 too small
6 too expensive
7 too late
8 too many
9 too old
10 too tired

83
2 it wasn't very well written
3 we lived next door to a police station
4 we didn't have very good seats
5 they tend to live longer
6 they live in the same house
7 I've done nothing all day
8 everyone else disagreed with him
9 we warned them not to
10 I've known him for years

84
2 despite working hard
3 in spite of having a bad fall
4 Despite learning French
5 In spite of being over sixty
6 despite having lost his job
Note that it is possible to use 'in spite
of' or 'despite' in all these sentences.

85
2 the friend you met
3 the message he sent home
4 the lecture Jack is going to give
5 some friends Bill had hoped to meet
6 the prize we decided to offer
8 the money you asked for
9 the picture he was looking at
10 the bus they had waited for
11 the children she is looking after
12 the coin I picked up
13 the party we couldn't go to
14 the office he'll be working in

86
2 Jack was the one who took the
  dictionary.
3 Bill was the one who was waiting to
  borrow it.
4 Helen was the one who promised to
  bring it back.
5 Diana is the one who is going to look
  after it for you.